Map of Dreams

M. Rickert

With a
Foreword by Christopher Barzak
and an
Afterword by
Gordon Van Gelde

Golden Gryphon Press
2006

Edited by Marty Halpern

LIBRARY OF CONGRESS CATALOGUING–IN–PUBLICATION DATA
Rickert, M. (Mary) 1959–
   Map of Dreams / by M. Rickert; with a foreword by Christopher
Barzak ; and an afterword by Gordon Van Gelder. — 1st ed.
      p.   cm.
   ISBN 1-930846-44-4 (alk. paper)
      I. Title.
PS3618.I375   M37   2006
813'.6—dc22
                          206011153

Printed in the United States of America.

First Edition

Contents

Who Is M. Rickert? — *Christopher Barzak* . . . xi

Map of Dreams . . . 3

Introduction — *Annie Merchant* . . . 97

Dreams: Dreaming of the Sun . . . 100

Leda . . . 103

Cold Fires . . . 115

Angel Face . . . 130

Night Blossoms . . . 136

Nightmares: Feeding the Beast . . . 140

Bread and Bombs . . . 142

Art Is Not a Violent Subject . . . 155

Anyway . . . 160

A Very Little Madness Goes a Long Way . . . 176

Waking: What I Saw, When I Looked . . . 192

The Girl Who Ate Butterflies . . . 194

Many Voices . . . 206

More Beautiful Than You . . . 219

Peace on Suburbia . . . 226

Rising: Flights . . . 236

Moorina of the Seals . . . 239

The Harrowing . . . 246
The Super Hero Saves the World . . . 260
The Chambered Fruit . . . 270
Afterword — *Gordon Van Gelder* . . . 301

For Bill

"Sometimes our inner light goes out, but it is blown again into flame by an encounter with another human being. Each of us owes the deepest thanks to those who have rekindled this inner light." —Albert Schweitzer

With Gratitude To:
Christopher Barzak
Thomas Canty
Dr. Richard Dunham
Charles Coleman Finlay
Gordon Van Gelder
Marty Halpern
Chris, David, and Piper Lyons
Liz Musser
My mother, Kathleen Rickert
Karen Sankewitsch
Tasha Tudor
Thomas and Patty Tunney
Gary Turner

Who Is M. Rickert?

SEVEN YEARS AGO I READ A STORY IN *THE MAGAzine of Fantasy & Science Fiction* that, upon finishing its last sentence, made me look up from the pages of the magazine and see the world around me with new eyes, full of wonder and poetry and mystery. The story was called "The Girl Who Ate Butterflies" and its author's name was as mysterious as the feelings the story evoked: M. Rickert.

There is a long tradition throughout history of authors using initials as their authorial signatures, but I rarely gave much thought to that tradition before that day. It was only after I finished this particular story that I felt a deep need to know who lay behind that individual letter. Was M. a man or a woman? Young, middle-aged, or old? Did M. live in a big city, a suburb, or in the country? Was M. even an American, as I had initially assumed, or was M. someone who lived in a far-off, exotic country? Because the story was so singular—made up of images and rhythms and narratives that are so inimitable—I couldn't assume anything about who M. Rickert, in fact, was.

Over the next few months I would occasionally ask friends, but no one knew who M. Rickert was. Nor did they know anyone who might know. And as I happened upon more and more dead ends in my search for the author's identity, it seemed that the mystery would only continue to grow. More of M. Rickert's stories appeared in *The Magazine of Fantasy & Science Fiction* eventually. Stories like "Moorina of the Seals," which has the structure and feel of an aboriginal dream, and "Angel Face," a sort of Passion play that subverts that genre of narrative while at the same time submitting to its rule to deliver inspired faith. It seemed this author could write stories set in realms that don't exist on any map, as well as those reminiscent of John Cheever's eerily familiar suburban fantasies, with characters who believe in what they can't see rather than the miracles that happen right before their eyes.

It is a strange desire that sometimes happens to us as witnesses to art, this wanting to know more about the creator of something we've read or listened to or looked at. Art has the strange ability to somehow get inside of us, into the places we guard the most; it can make us feel less alone in this world, understood when we feel most at a loss. When we're lucky enough to have that experience, we sometimes want to know more about the person who made it possible. And after reading M. Rickert's first stories, I couldn't help wanting to know more about the creator of those stories too.

One day, while I was preparing a manuscript of one of my own stories to send to *The Magazine of Fantasy & Science Fiction*, I decided at the last minute to add a note on my submission letter to Gordon Van Gelder. I wrote something to the effect of, *Dear Gordon, thank you so much for publishing M. Rickert's stories. I find them intoxicating.* I figured that, since I couldn't tell the author how much I enjoyed the stories, I should at least tell the publisher of those stories how much they affected me.

Years passed and in those years my life changed enormously. I moved from Ohio to California, back to Ohio, then to Michigan, only to move back to Ohio several years later. I completed a Master's Degree in English. I wrote a lot of short stories. My own fiction was beginning to appear in magazines and anthologies. And while I lived my life, somewhere out there, M. Rickert continued to write stories as well, which I continued to read with great pleasure.

Then, a few years ago, in the winter of 2003, I was invited to join a novel-writing workshop, called Blue Heaven, that Charles Coleman Finlay (another frequent contributor to *F&SF*) was holding later that spring. It was the first time I had heard of a workshop whose goal was to critique novels. Charlie wrote me: *I asked Maureen McHugh to come, but she can't and said I should ask you. Are you working on a novel you'd like to workshop?*

I had been thinking about writing a novel at that time, but I hadn't actually begun to work on it yet. I wasn't sure if I wanted to begin just then either. I hadn't written anything in that form before, and it seemed like a task that could crush me if I attempted to write one before I was ready. So I wrote Charlie back and asked for more details, including who else would be attending. When I received his reply, I saw the name of M. Rickert on the list of those committed to coming, and immediately I replied, saying I had a novel I had just started working on and that I would come too. Then, after I sent Charlie that message, I opened a file on my computer and began to write the novel.

Several weeks later the workshop attendees began to contact one another, and suddenly one day I received a message from M. Rickert in my email inbox. I was surprised and also a little apprehensive to open it, as M. had previously posted to the group email list and always seemed to write concise notes that were a bit reticent. I still didn't know anything more about M. Rickert at that point except that she was a woman, and that she lived in New York State. This was more than I knew before though, so I was satisfied knowing just those two general facts about her. I opened her email with much anticipation, wondering what could have made her privately contact me.

It only took me a moment to read the email. It was short and brief, like her posts to the group:

> Christopher, I was so glad to see you are going to be at Blue Heaven this year. I was already excited to come, but now I'm even more excited. A long time ago, Gordon Van Gelder sent me a copy of one of your submission letters where you mentioned how much you like my stories and I want you to know how much that means to me. Since then I've been following your stories as they appear and want to say how much I like them as well. I can't wait to finally meet you. Yours, Mary.

After all those years, finally, a name. And on top of that, I was dumbstruck to discover that as I was reading Mary's stories, she was reading mine as well. It felt perfectly right though, and so when spring arrived and us writers trooped off to Kelleys Island on Lake Erie to spend a week together, I left knowing that one of the mysteries in my life was about to be solved.

Meeting Mary was as wonderful as reading her stories. She is as delightful, full of wonder and mystery, and exuberant in surprising ways as her stories are. Her magic is a quiet sort, but it's also sharp-witted. At the workshop, she didn't like playing the games we occasionally turned to for entertainment, but she would sing at our bonfires and laugh at our jokes. Sometimes we'd see her out on the beach, alone, picking up shells. She brought a variety of teas along with her, which everyone loved her for. She did yoga on the deck of the house, beside the pool in the mornings. She was soft-spoken but what she said was always deeply felt and considered. She seemed to always have a pertinent perspective on our novels that no one else had seen and would get excited about someone else's writing as if it were her own. One of the other participants at the workshop once told me, "Mary is a bodhisattva," which in Tibetan Buddhism is someone who seeks enlightenment not only for herself but for others. And I couldn't agree more.

At one point during the week, as Mary and I and one of the other writers attending the workshop were driving to a tiny, island diner together, I told a rather personal story about myself; not the sort of story one usually tells among people you've just met. But I felt like I already had such a connection to Mary at that moment that I decided to share something private. When I had finished, and after the three of us talked about my story, Mary turned to me and said, "We won't say anything about what you told us. It's between us, unless you want to share that story with the others. You can trust us. Okay?"

I wasn't terribly worried if the others at the workshop somehow heard my private story secondhand, but I found Mary's immediate offer of loyalty to my story to be an amazing gift. That sort of quality is rare in people, and I knew at that moment that I had made a friend for life.

Since then Mary and I have gotten to know each other well. We correspond regularly, sharing our days with each other, our writing problems and successes, our ideas for stories and books to come, what we ate that morning for breakfast, whether her dog or my cats are staring at us as we type our messages back and forth. I know quite a lot about who M. Rickert is now, and could tell you many things to satisfy your curiosity. But I'm not going to tell you any more than I already have. Because the thing I've learned about Mary over the years is that you will find her in her stories. Her honesty, her compassion, her loyalty to the truth of emotions, her passion for words and her belief in the redemptive power of words—all of this and more you will find in her stories. That's where you should look. And in *Map of Dreams* you will find the map to the farthest reaches of M. Rickert's imagination.

There is one more thing I want to share. When I asked Mary once how she went about writing, she wrote me a long letter about her writing process. Throughout the letter she would occasionally interrupt her talk about process to tell me an anecdote. They were lovely, and always connected to what she was telling me about her writing in general. I think the best way to understand Mary and her stories is to share one of those anecdotes in this foreword:

> You know, it took me forever to understand what kind of writer I am. I know that more than one person (okay, I think two) said to me that they thought my writing showed talent but they had no idea who would publish it. And, I had forgotten this, but in about fourth grade, fifth grade? I don't know but I was young, and basically fairly unpopular and a skinny, cross-eyed girl with cat-eye glasses and I wrote this story that I decided to perform for the class as a monologue. So the whole thing is about how nobody likes me or plays with me and I don't know why, and how alone I am, and how I try to fit in. The last line is something like, "Then she turned and walked away dragging her tail behind her."
>
> So I'm the girl with the tail. One of the hardest parts of my life as a writer was figuring that out.

I envy the person who is about to embark on reading these stories for the first time. They are unlike any stories you've read before, and they are richly rewarding. The real gift Mary gives her readers, though, is that instant upon reading the last word of a story, when you look up from the page to see the world in its honest mystery again, knowing you aren't alone in this world, and receive a rare and precious moment of grace.

Christopher Barzak
October 2003
Ami, Japan

Map of Dreams

♦ ♦ ♦

Map of Dreams

MY SIX-YEAR-OLD DAUGHTER WAS SHOT AND KILLED by a sniper while we were visiting New York City in the summer of 1992. She bled from a head wound onto my flowered sundress; large roses of blood that hardened like scabs. Later, when I undressed in the porcelain-white hotel bathroom, as David wept across the bed, I had to peal the hardened fabric from my skin and watch, in horror, my daughter's last blood flake in the air and drift slowly to the floor like worthless dust.

Three other people died with my daughter that afternoon: an unidentified homeless man found on the rooftop, believed to be the first victim; Marie Von Feehler, the physicist (visiting the city with her husband, Max Von Feehler, the writer); and twenty-six-year-old Griffith Connor, sniper, murderer, suicide.

I didn't know of the publication of Max Von Feehler's novel until I attended a dinner party in the fall of '94 where one of the guests, ignorant of our bloody tie, mentioned that Max would be giving a lecture at the college the following Wednesday. "Seems to me he's let his wife's death ruin his clear thinking." The others, certainly aware of the disturbing nature of this topic, looked down at their plates as if suddenly fascinated by the pink slabs of fleshy salmon. "I mean, here you have a fine writer," he continued, "who's always had some literary merit, and he's turned to science fiction."

"I suppose you think he should continue as before," I said. "I suppose you think he should be over it by now."

"Well—" he raised his considerable eyebrows "—let's just say that many writers would have made better use of such powerful material."

Carol Myers leaned over and whispered to him. Though I couldn't hear her, I knew what she was saying: *You have to be gentle with Annie. She hasn't been right since it happened. Oh, you didn't know? She's the mother of the dead girl.*

Celia Fortuno betrayed her nervousness with the tone her party had developed, by asking who wanted dessert when everyone was still in the middle of the main course. My husband, David, gently patted my knee. I turned to look at him but he was smiling at Celia, complimenting her cooking, and asking her what her earliest food memory was. Deftly, my husband lifted the glum spirit of the table into a pleasant conversation of appetite. He had become expert at rescuing others from my despair.

The following Wednesday, still not having laid my hands on Von Feehler's book (it was sold out at the local bookstore and there was a long waiting list for it at the library) but curious about the man with whom I shared such a tragic tie, I attended the lecture, arriving late by a series of miscalculations the sort of which I had suffered since, what everyone had come to call (in ominous hushed tones), *that day.*

At the time of our loved ones' deaths there had been, in the flurry of newspaper and magazine articles that followed, an occasional photograph of the author. But as I observed him, I was surprised that his walrussy appearance, tousle of gray hair, long drooping mustache and slight beard, aquatic eyes behind wire-rimmed spectacles, reminded me so vividly of the days after the murder. (That blur of time from which I had previously retrieved only scattered images and reflections of a pain so deep, I could not explore it further.) He stood at the podium; stocky, aged, a man I had never met, who stirred memories of a terrible time shared.

"Well, clearly I am not a scientist," Von Feehler was saying, "but I do know something about language, and as much as I am fond of my medium, I also know its limitations. To conceive of time travel we must rid ourselves of the constructs by which we define it. For instance, what is time? There are populations who have no concept or word for time, or the passage of time, and have survived just fine without it. In fact, some would say their lives have been enhanced by a lack of the sort of restrictions we imagine time presents. Time is, after all, only a concept.

"Now, Einstein says there is a dimension defined by space-time, and certainly his was a far greater mind than mine, but what I considered, at least for the argument of fiction, is that the definition of space-time is linguistically flawed in that it breaks the cardinal rule of definition by using the word to define the word. Time, I mean. For my understanding, which I admit is pedestrian, and for the character, Steve, I decided not to concern myself with the time in time travel. Instead, I concentrated on space, getting to a certain place in space, which we, for lack of a better term, define by time. Also, I came to think of space in a sort of sixties way, not a place, but a consciousness. This space logic is like a dream logic.

"I find it fully reasonable to accept that time travel has little to do with any type of machine. We might want to use a machine, the way we use a car or an airplane to span a distance, but we do not need a machine to get there. Not really. Not physically. It's just a matter of having good directions."

A young audience member, perhaps as confused as I was, spoke up, "And having the time," which incited a scattering of giggles.

Von Feehler, however, was too impassioned by his subject to be derailed by humor. "Yes, yes. In our culture. We've built a whole system based on something that doesn't even exist but which motivates our every perception. For instance, Steve, the protagonist, suffers an extraordinary loss, which basically removes him from the mainstream. He sees things differently. He enters a different consciousness, if you will. Because of this horrible, tragic loss—" and here Von Feehler faltered, perhaps he felt the weight of speculation in the room. Even I, who had not yet read the book, began to wonder if he was talking about Steve, the character in his novel, or himself. "Because of this tragedy," he continued, "he lost his naïveté, his innocence. For a horrible period there was only the loss, but eventually, and this was a slow and painful process, those black holes, if you will, became avenues of discovery. His concept of reality changes. His mind expands. He begins this research and what he discovers, what he finds, because he recognizes it when he sees it, is basically a map. With this map he finds out how to leave the limited line of time and enter curved space.

"The picture on the cover of the book—" Von Feehler held it up "—is a curved timeline. Amateurs like me, and probably most of you in the audience, often ask how we can go back in time and not grow younger. The answer is in this curved line. When we curve space we are still encapsulated within the curve. You, the traveler, still follow local laws of physics maintained in the body of this snake. For instance, the apple that you hold does not revert to bud or seed but remains an apple. You, the traveler, do not grow younger. We are not reversing time so much as changing direction."

The young audience member interjected again, "Then could you back up, 'cause I'm getting confused." The audience laughter expressed camaraderie with this sentiment. Even Von Feehler laughed.

"If you're confused, you're probably following this fairly well, because it's confusing stuff." He chuckled as he glanced at the clock. "I'm afraid I've believed my own hype so much that I've completely lost track of time. I'll just close the way I began, with a short passage from my book." He adjusted his spectacles and opened the book to a premarked page. The audience settled into expectant silence.

"He found no solace in the well-meaning condolences of friends who presented him with everything from gold crosses, to Stars of David, to chicken casserole and banana bread. The social net enmeshed him in a world of dinners that never seemed to feed his appetite or remove the bitter taste from his mouth. Just when he thought he could not survive another such night, or endure a life of them, as if it had been marked on calendars as a prescheduled and universally agreed upon event, the calls stopped, the mail returned to its pretragedy flux of bills and coupons. He felt the effect as a welcome silence in the cacophony that had been his life since she died.

"One winter evening, as a salty snow tapped the windowpanes, he found himself paging through one of the books in her study, the room unchanged since her death. It was, he later said, as if he had been sleepwalking, finally awoken by the elixir of her notes in the margins and between the lines. When she had been alive he had barely considered the intricacies of her work; now he found himself touching the page, as if it were written in Braille. Her notes. A part of her. A way to be with her. He bent to decipher the meaning.

"It was a stormy winter. The pine trees grew supplicant with snow. In the evening the noise of the crackling fire, his pen on paper, the turning page was accompanied by the distant scrape of shovels and snow blower's hum. He read until his eyes closed against his will. He woke to read more. What he found told him not just what he'd already known, that she was a remarkable woman, but that the world was remarkable too.

"By spring people said he was over the worst of the mourning. Had he heard them, he would have agreed. He no longer saw life as an endless night filled with her absence, but as a sky of stars whose very light testified what he knew to be true, that there was more to existence than presence. She was out there, somewhere. He resolved to find her."

After the reading I joined the group that quickly surrounded Von Feehler. The questions were insistent. I was not the only one who had decided he might actually know something about finding a lost loved one in the secrets of time. I was, however, the only one who shared that moment with him. He did not stop to answer questions but walked out of the building with a stubborn gait. I panicked when I realized he might leave without us ever speaking. I called out, "Mr. Von Feehler, my daughter, Lily, died with your wife."

He peered nearsightedly into the group. I pushed past the backpacks and strong young bodies. He put one heavy hand on my shoulder and steered me quickly and wordlessly into a rental car parked in the adjoining lot. "I didn't mean to commandeer you, I just thought we should talk in private. They've put me up in a lovely suite, which has been a complete waste until now, that is, if you feel comfortable?" I nodded. His fans stood on the sidewalk, subdued, I imagined, by my connection to this man, their faces betrayed their confusion. They dared not envy me. But as Von Feehler eased the car forward, the faces scowled. He waved in the rearview mirror. "I'm afraid I've upset Mark, my host. We were supposed to go to some cheese thing."

"If this is inconvenient . . ."

"No, this is highly convenient. A wonderful excuse!" He lowered his voice, "Have you discovered that you can behave irrationally now and people accept it? You know, because of what you've been through?"

"Maybe at first. Not anymore."

"It's probably easier being a writer. People always expect a certain eccentricity. They enjoy it even."

We drove the rest of the way in silence. I didn't know what I meant to say or ask. I only knew, as I stared out the window at the familiar tree-lined streets, the profound sadness, and deep companionship I felt with this man.

In the hotel suite he offered me a sherry, which I declined. "I hope you don't mind if I . . ." He raised the glass decanter. I shook my head. He poured the amber liquid into a small glass. "Please, sit." I declined. He shrugged his shoulders and sat in the green wingchair. "I don't know what they were thinking—" he gestured at the room "—this is not the usual writer's tour sort of place. In fact, I've been feeling quite guilty about it. I'm certain some poor student, probably Mark, is in all kinds of trouble for arranging it. You know, it's the strangest thing but I think that boy has a crush on me." He took another sip of sherry, and sighed. "Not only have I lost the art of meaningless conversation but the art of the meaningful as well."

"I want to go with you." I did not realize until I blurted out these words that I had completely formulated the belief that Max had been, or was about to become, a time traveler.

He took a sip, then looked at me evenly. "Impossible."

Desperately I looked about the room as if I could find proof that would convince him. The tattered khaki knapsack with books and papers spilling out onto the carpet, the books on Australia and physics scattered throughout the room, opened face down or marked with sales receipts and napkins, the tattered notebook on the small table next to the other wingchair assured me that I was not jumping to wild conclusions. "I'm not like your other readers, I'm not asking you to take me some place you wouldn't go. I'm just asking to come with you."

Von Feehler stared. In that silence I knew he was assessing the situation. At last, he spoke: "I'm afraid we're having a misunderstanding."

"Don't do this."

"I'm taking a sabbatical. When I'm finished with this tour I'm going to visit a friend. Do some hiking, camping."

"How can you do this to me?"

Again he seemed to consider, but we were interrupted by the phone's chirpy ring. He went into the bedroom to answer it.

I walked over to the notebook on the small table and began thumbing through it. The pages were filled with formulas, numbers, and an odd penciled sketch of a curved serpent very much like that on the cover of his novel. I was certain these were Marie's notes. I closed the indecipherable book and a small travel brochure fell onto the floor. I picked it up. Australia. Bright photographs promised blue skies, koala bears chewing eucalyptus leaves, friendly tanned faces smiling beneath large, brown hats. A photograph of an Aborigine man, dressed in paint and a swatch of material, stared unsmiling from the bottom of the page. I put the brochure on the table, underneath the notebook. Another book titled *In the Serpent's Curve* lay face down on the floor behind the chair. It too was filled with notes and equations in the margins and between the lines. I didn't hear Von Feehler return to the room.

"Mrs. Merchant."

I turned, feeling both guilty and avenged. "You're going to find Marie. When you do, Lily will be there too."

"Nonsense," he spoke softly, gently.

"How can you live with yourself, if you don't help me?"

"How can I live with myself anyway?" he said with an anger that startled me. Again we shared a silence during which much was understood though not agreed upon.

"I'm begging you."

"Well, you're begging from a poor man. I don't have what you need."

I left, discouraged and depressed. In the days that followed, I considered what I had discovered by my daughter's death. How often people complained of the most mundane things, such as the weather. They suffered easy lives. When you have survived the worst, it puts rain, and snow, and traffic jams in perspective. This, I decided, was nothing but a stormy day, a snarl in traffic. If there were any way to save Lily from her death, if there were a way to travel back in time and change that day, I would get there. If Max Von Feehler would not help me, I would get there alone.

At the time of Lily's death I took a sabbatical from my job as a reporter for the Oakgrove Gazette but, in spite of David's encouragement, and the unsolicited advice of friends (Was it the great unwieldy force of my grief that motivated them?), I never did return to work. I could no longer fake an interest in gardening club luncheons and school board meetings. I did, however, retain a certain fondness for research and the collecting of data.

On a shelf in my bedroom closet were six notebooks filled with my angry scrawl, the venting of an emotion that would not be vented. Two scrapbooks bulged with clippings from newspapers and magazines, endless photographs and descriptions of Griffith Connor: the candy bar wrappings found near his body (two Hershey's and a half-eaten Snickers), his arsenal (I prefer not to list it), his childhood (a quiet boy, troubled adolescent, the anguish of his parents who tried to get him the help he insisted he did not need). Somewhere in the scrapbook I had glued a plain white envelope addressed to David and me. It contained a letter from these parents, an apology for an act beyond apology, but for which I did not blame them. Three shoeboxes were filled with letters. Most from strangers who meant to comfort us with stories of God and angels and so many descriptions of their own pain ("I know how you feel dear, it was seventeen years ago that my own little one was killed by a drunk driver and I still mourn her every day." "I prayd for you and lite a candel rite a long with the prayr and candel for my baby that was born with a face that showes her daddy kickd me in the gut and left his boot print on it . . .") that eventually I could read no more and simply stored them, unopened, in the shoeboxes.

Another small box marked *Lily* contained clippings from magazines and newspapers. Usually small portions cut from larger pieces, these clippings chronicled her short life, her teachers' descriptions, and the confusion of her young classmates. The box also contained various mementos: the birth announcement; her baby book; her first shoes; a photograph of Lily in her favorite dress-up costume, a pair of purple wings.

In spite of David's encouragement, and again, the unsolicited advice of my dwindling circle of friends (all except the most loyal grew weary of my grief), her bedroom remained just the way she left it that morning, now so long ago, when we gaily packed for our first big trip together.

Following my visit with Von Feehler I went to the library and checked out countless books on physics, supposedly written for the reader with a pedestrian intelligence of the subject, but which still made me break out in a cold sweat as I tried to follow the trajectory of meaning. Yet, even through the confusion, I found solace in these descriptions of a reality different from the one that had killed Lily.

Inexplicably—even I did not understand this at the time—I began running again. I had once been quite the jogger, a card-carrying member of FITNESS FOR U, in fact. Now I ran on the sidewalks and streets. This wasn't about vanity, the way it had been in the past. I didn't wear cute little jogging outfits. Even I, in the midst of all this, couldn't completely understand it and I didn't care. For the first time since Lily's death I found myself passionate about something other than my own pain. I didn't care that it didn't make sense. What made sense anyway? The murder of a six-year-old girl? How did that make sense?

The dreams that had plagued me since Lily's death were both better and worse, a contradiction that would have bewildered me before this all began but now seemed to define the tempers of the world which were not, as I had fooled myself for so long, defined by demarcations as blunt and clear as the black outlines in Lily's coloring book.

Yes, the dreams were less bloody, and, yes, there was much relief in that. This was a different pain, these dreams of her alive. Once, I could have sworn I still heard the glorious sound of her laughter, even as I opened my eyes to the dull, heavy darkness of a life that did not contain her. Another time, there was that smell, the lingering scent of little girl in my bed, where I dreamt she slept beside me, her bony foot pressed against my stomach, until I awoke to the bitter loneliness of David's back.

Oh yes, better to not see her shot night after night, collapsing in blood and the ugliness of her beautiful body destroyed. How terrible to feel her alive again and wake to the horrible memory, the realization as sharp and painful as it was the day she died.

In these dark hours, where once I wandered to her bedroom and watched the various stuffed animals by the streetlight glow and tinge of dawn, I now sat at the kitchen table and read until David left for work. Then I spread my books across the bed, and sat propped against pillows where often, except for a few forages to the kitchen, I remained until David returned home to find the same dishes in the sink that had been there when he left. If he didn't wash them, they were still there the next morning. In this area, I confess, I suffered delusion. You see, I thought David loved me. I'm sure he thought so too. But David loved the memory of me. I'm not blaming him. I understand what it is to love memory. When I ceased being convenient, I jarred him from his reverie. He grew irritated, until that day he came home and found me sitting in bed, still wearing my pajamas, surrounded by books.

"What are you doing home so early?"

"It isn't early." He unbuttoned his shirt cuff.

I laughed. It was a joyous thing to be so absorbed that a whole day passed as though only a couple of hours. "I want to read you something." I searched through the pile of books to find the marked passage.

"Annie, we have to talk."

"Listen to this. You're not going to believe this. Let me see if I can explain it right. A cat is put inside a box, which has a device that can release a gas; the box, I mean, has the device. Anyway, if it does release the gas it will instantly kill the cat. Now, nothing makes the box release the gas or anything, it's just a random event whether the gas is released or not. There is no way of knowing, other than looking in the box, what happens inside it. The gas has either been released or it has not been released.

"Are you following this? Now, according to classical physics, the cat is either dead or not dead. But according to quantum mechanics, the cat is in a kind of limbo, you know, limbo? And this limbo contains the possibility that the cat is dead and also the possibility that the cat is alive. The possibility isn't just an idea, see, it's an existence, in and of itself. Not just like how we usually think, in our heads, oh, that's possible and that isn't. It's like a place. That you can go to."

"I've been thinking about what's happening."

"Yes! The cat can be dead or alive!"

"This isn't about a cat."

"Well, of course it's not about a cat. It has to do with wave functions."

"I went to her grave. The flowers are all dead. Nobody's been there for a long time."

The heaviness in the room was as swift as the hypothetical gas. "What are you trying to say?"

"I want you to see somebody."

"See somebody?"

"A doctor or therapist, a grief counselor, someone."

"You think something's wrong with me?"

He pointed his cuffed hand at the book-littered bed. "Come on, Annie, time traveling cats? You need to deal with reality."

"This is real."

He exploded. "You want to bring her back to life and that's real? I'll tell you what's real—" he pointed out the bedroom door "—her grave is real. Her death is real. She's dead, Annie. She'll be dead forever. That's real."

"No, you're missing the point. That's what I'm trying to tell you. We choose. We choose which reality we want."

"Damn it, Annie! You have to stop. She isn't out there, somewhere. She's at Fieldstone Cemetery in a white casket we chose together." He leaned over me, his contorted face inches from mine. "Remember how you held her while she died?" I covered my face with my hands. He sat down. The bed creaked as he shoved books aside. "Just because I believe that, just because I know it," he said softly, "doesn't mean I didn't love her."

Then I said the sort of horrible thing that can rend a couple forever. "I'm beginning to wonder if you know what love means." I regretted it immediately but before I could take the words back he was on his feet looking down at me with a wretched expression I will always regret having inspired.

"You want to know what love means? I'll tell you what it means. It means this. It means being here, now, in the real world, fighting for what we have instead of what we want. It means not giving up on you even when, even when . . ."

"Just say it."

"I didn't mean—"

"Say it."

"We could have another child."

Again I felt the shock of how little we understood each other. "No."

"Maybe not right away but—"

"No."

"I can't do this anymore."

Sitting on the bed, with my jumble of books and ideas I didn't fully understand, I looked up at him and saw what different creatures we had become. The happier I became with my research, the more distraught he grew, his mouth, slightly open, his eyes slit and red-rimmed, the white vein on his forehead pulsed beneath his pale skin. He stood, one leg forward, arms out from his side, the unbuttoned cuffs drooping from his bony wrists.

"I can't live like this any longer but you're wrong if you think I didn't love her as much as—"

"Of course you do."

"I'm just not. We're not . . ."

"I know."

"I have to leave."

I understood completely and saw no other course. When at last his bags were packed and he had made the cursory comment about making arrangements for the rest of his things, he stood at the door as if suddenly uncertain. "I still think," he started, but I raised my hand to stop him.

The door closed softly. I wept into the darkness. So much loss. So many years of pain. How, when I finally found Lily and brought her back home, would I explain his absence to her?

*   *   *

David offered me money but I refused it. Had he believed in my mission, I could have accepted his support, but I would not take money that labeled me incompetent. My savings had long since run out and my credit cards were dangerously high. I began selling things. The antique desk inherited from Grandpa Joe, the china David and I had once lovingly chosen, the living room furniture, the dining room set. Finally, my car.

I ran into Carol Myers at the Price Chopper one day and we had a disjointed conversation during which her eyes scanned me the way we tend to look at the elderly or terminally ill. I asked her what she was looking at. She shook her head. "I'm sorry," she said, "it's just you look so different. Are you all right?"

When I got home I looked in the mirror, then at the old family portrait on the dresser. The three of us. Smiling in a world that does not include great grief. I sit with one arm around Lily, her long, brown hair clipped back with a blue bow, her face just coming out of roundness into jaw line and cheeks, her brown eyes wide above that little, freckled nose. David stands protectively over both of us, in his Father's Day tie and button-down shirt, light brown hair combed neatly back from that sharply handsome face. We were innocent then. We thought our happiness was deserved, inevitable in a way, the logical conclusion to our love. There I am, smug in my blonde curls, a soft, knowing smile on my lips. But I didn't know anything.

I leaned into the mirror. Yes, my hair had grown frizzy, I'd lost weight, I no longer had the time or the inclination for makeup. I peered so closely that I knocked over the photograph. But the real difference was my eyes. They looked darker, as though all brightness had been extinguished by my grief.

So I had changed. That was good. Because the old me would have been too afraid to do what I was about to do.

The plane to Australia is filled with old couples and college-age travelers. There's a family with a daughter in braids, around the age Lily would be now, but this doesn't pierce me with envy the way it once would have. A bright January sun crowns the passengers. The stewardess gives the tragedy instructions. I don't listen. At first, after Lily died, I was afraid of everything. Bridges, heights, the dark, strangers in the supermarket; canned food, even. (A memorable fight with David. I'm throwing all the canned food into the trash. "It's like throwing away money," he says. I hold up a can of beans, French cut. "Do you know what's breeding in here?" "You're being irrational." "What does rational have to do with anything?" I continue tossing cans into the garbage. He slams out the door.) I felt so hopeless then. So fragile.

I look down at my feet in heavy hiking boots and smile at the memory of my manicured pink toenails from a time when my happiness was defined by things like that. The stewardess is explaining how to use our seat cushions as flotation devices in case of a water "landing." I laugh. The man sitting next to me shifts in his seat. I look at his profile: soft fleshy features, dark-rimmed glasses. He stares straight ahead as if completely engrossed in the stewardess's directions, then glances at me, a quick, sideways slide of the eye. I look out the window. No one stands in the terminal waving to me. Strange, how I've become this woman alone in the world.

This had been my first Christmas without David and, in spite of that sadness, it was also the first Christmas in years where I felt some hope, and I guess you could say, if not happiness, at least the possibility of happiness. I arrived at my parents' house before my sister, Melanie, and her brood. We sat at the kitchen table and chatted almost gaily until, amidst the fake holly and snowman placemats, the savory scent and sizzling sound of roasting turkey, they told me they had looked into my options, had talked to some friends (discreetly), and had some names for me. I thought they meant lawyers but when it became clear they were talking about psychiatrists, I looked into their tired faces and said, "David."

"He's worried about you, dear." My mother wore little, gold bell earrings, which jingled as she spoke.

"I'm fine."

"Well, dear," she used her gentle talking-to-a-sick-person voice, "he seems to think you are not being reasonable." (*Jingle, jingle.*)

"Mother, we're getting a divorce. Neither of us thinks the other one is reasonable. That's why we're getting a divorce."

"Jesus Christ," my father said, "he says you think you can bring Lily back to life."

"I never said that." They both looked relieved.

"You see, Tom," (*jingle*) "I knew there had to be some misunderstanding." (*Jingle, jingle.*)

My father looked at me with narrow eyes. "What is it, exactly, you do believe?"

"It's kind of complicated."

On the radio, dogs barked a seriously weird rendition of "We Wish You a Merry Christmas." My father stared at me as if he thought I would suddenly start barking too. "We're listening."

"You have to know some basic physics. You have to believe time isn't the only reality."

"Time travel?" he asked.

I nodded.

My father's fist hit the table so hard the little Mr. and Mrs. Santa Claus salt and pepper shakers fell over. My mother covered her mouth and shook her head. The bells jingled madly.

"Jesus Christ." My father turned to my mother, "I gotta go for a walk." He left without looking at me. My mother was apparently left with the unresolved issue of my sanity. Her face had the pinched look of Lily's Cabbage Patch doll. She righted the fallen Clauses, patted her hair, rose from the table with an ancient sigh, and checked on the turkey. When she turned from the oven she smoothed down her appliquéd Christmas apron. Lily had loved that apron so much that my mother had made one for her, a miniature version with stars and bells and Christmas trees. I looked at her tired face, aged so much since Lily's death.

"Mom—"

"Where does God fit into all this?"

"What?"

"Let's just pretend any of this is possible. I'm not saying I think it is, but let's just imagine a world where the dead don't have to stay dead. Where is God?"

"Mom, you know I haven't been a Catholic for years."

"But you believe in God, don't you?" When I'm silent she turns to check on the turkey.

"Mom, you just did that."

She points the baster at me. "It's my turkey and I can baste it every five minutes if I want. Just answer the question. Where is God in all this?"

"Well, Mom," I say slowly, "I guess he's about the same place he was when Lily got shot."

Why did everything I believe suddenly make everyone so

unhappy? She stood there, in jingle earrings and Christmas apron, tears welling in her eyes.

"I'm sorry, Mom."

"My faith is what sustains me, I can't imagine living without it."

"Well, I have faith too. It's just different from yours."

"In time travel?"

"Let's just say, in a reality that's not shaped the way I once thought it was."

"Godless?"

"Maybe God's shaped differently too."

She thought about this for a moment, and then nodded, the little bells jingling. My father returned from his walk, stomping snow off his boots. He kissed my mother on the cheek, me on the top of my head. "Merry Christmas to my girls. It's nice to be together. Let's just forget about everything else and remember that."

But how could he think we were together when we were missing Lily? I nodded but knew I would never be truly happy until I had her at my side.

My sister, Melanie, arrived with her husband and their three beautiful, healthy children. It was a noisy, bright holiday. After presents and dinner, she and I prepared the coffee and servings of apple pie. "You seem good," she said, "better than you've been for a long time."

"I am good," I said, in a dreamy, after-a-big-holiday-meal state. "I keep thinking about next year."

"Oh?" She licked a finger. "What happens next year?"

"Next year Lily will be here too."

My sister's happy face quickly changed to an expression of horror.

"Never mind," I mumbled. I grabbed two plates of pie and went out to the living room where even the children seemed drowsy with joy. When I returned to the kitchen for more servings, Melanie didn't look at me but continued cutting pie as if it were a dangerous operation.

Later, she and John drove me home. (I had already sold my car.) I squeezed between them on the front seat; my nieces and nephews oddly quiet in the back. Ever since Lily died, her cousins acted strange around me, as if, somehow, I was not a safe grownup. When we got to my house, Melanie walked me to the door, kissed me on the cheek, and handed me a folded sheet of paper. "Daddy wants you to have this."

I took it reluctantly.

"Merry Christmas," she said sadly.

Inside, I flicked on the overhead light. The only furniture was a couple of large, brightly colored pillows, left over from my college days, propped against the wall. The floor was littered with books and papers; a coffee mug with a dried ring of tea and a plate with crumbs, my Christmas Eve dinner. I unfolded the paper. In my father's neat square printing was the heading SPECIALISTS IN SCHIZOPHRENIA. I glanced at the list of psychiatrists' names, balled it up, and threw it into the corner.

After the holidays I called the university where Max Von Feehler teaches. They told me he had taken a sabbatical and would not be returning for the semester after the winter break. Looking through books he'd written I found one where he thanked his agent by name. I called the agency. Luckily (I think often of luck since Lily died. How much of life is defined by it. For instance, why couldn't Griffith Connor, the sniper, have had bad luck? Why did he have any luck at all, and why didn't we, oh God, I torture myself with this thought, why didn't we have the sort of luck that put us at that corner thirty seconds earlier or later? I know somebody had that luck. Some mother stood at that crosswalk with her little girl. And the light changed. And they walked across the street. Why, why not us?) his agent wasn't in the office and the woman who answered the phone sounded young and inexperienced.

I gave her this spiel about a large shipment of Von Feehler's books I had received that were supposed to be autographed. She, in a very businesslike manner, told me that was not a matter for his agent. "Yes, yes," I said, "but I've misplaced his address, and I'm sure you have it." She politely told me that under no circumstances could she give out authors' addresses. "That's a good policy, but I'm not some fan, I'm a friend, and I am absolutely certain Max would want to be contacted about this. So, you can give me the address and this business will be concluded or I can spend the whole day hunting him down, at which point, let me assure you, I will tell him that the office of his agent does not have his best interest at heart. By the way, what did you say your name was?"

I bullied her. Me, who never even hung up on telemarketers for fear of hurting their feelings. She gave me the address, in care of Peter Herrick. I looked it up in the library atlas and, no big surprise, discovered that it was a small island off the coast of Australia. I called a travel agent. Figured expenses. Then I called David and told him I wanted to sell the house. He agreed so quickly I suspect he had been thinking along the same lines. I was surprised at the lack of sentiment I felt about it, though I did ask him to take care of Lily's bedroom, which he did, coming in one day while I was at the library and packing all her things. He wanted to donate them to Goodwill but I told him I had already made other arrangements. My only material tie to my old life now is the storage garage. I paid for six months. That should be plenty of time. There will be so many changes for Lily I think it is important that she come back to her familiar toys and favorite clothes.

"How have you been feeling?" David asked over dinner at our old favorite restaurant, where we attempted a sort of house closing, separation agreement, farewell dinner.

"You mean mentally?"

He didn't answer, which was probably the only safe response.

"How are you?" I asked. "Really."

"I'm getting married."

You'd think, after everything that had happened, I could not be shocked, but I was shocked. "Well, you seem to have made a full recovery."

"Annie."

It took some effort to look into those blue eyes.

"You didn't think we would . . ."

I was horrified to see that this idea appealed to him. I shook my head. "Anyone I know?"

"Carol Myers."

"Oh? I saw her a while ago at the grocery store. She didn't mention it."

"I think you should know we're going to have a baby."

For a moment I was confused. This was my husband speaking after all.

"I don't know what your plans are, but I'd like to move through this divorce quickly so we can . . . that is, she and I . . ."

"I believe the phrase is *get married*."

"I didn't expect you to be upset."

"We're not so different after all, are we? In our own ways we're both trying to get Lily back."

He threw the napkin onto the table. I watched his face go through strange contortions as he fought his anger. Why did I feel some jubilation for it? But of course he controlled himself. He signaled the waiter, explained that an emergency had come up and we needed to pay right away. David gave him a credit card. I continued eating. "I think you know me well enough," he said, "to understand why I won't stay here and have my family insulted."

"Oh? Which family would that be?"

"I thought we could be —"

"What David, characters out of a Woody Allen movie? Did you think I would want to throw Carol a shower? Baby-sit your child?"

The waiter returned and David signed the receipt. I asked for the dessert menu. David stood up, holding onto the edge of the table. Go ahead, I thought, say something cruel. "I hope some day you can be happy too," he said, everything in his tone suggesting he thought the possibility unlikely.

I have my moments of doubt. What am I doing? I'm going to Australia to find the man who will take me time traveling. I'm going to be reunited with my dead daughter. I know how insane this sounds. But, believing as I do, is there any other choice?

There's an old saying that Australians are so fond of festivals, they'd even have one for the drop of a leaf, and now they do, it's called the Leaf Drop Festival. I am pleasantly surprised when I arrive in Melbourne, this beautiful city teeming with happy celebrants, one who gives me friendly directions, spoken in a vernacular made popular by those Crocodile movies, a young man with a burnished face in a broad-brimmed hat. I try to hail a taxi. Another stranger stands in front of me and shouts, furiously waving both his arms. A taxi pulls over. The stranger nods me toward it and walks away before I can even properly thank him.

"Charter Field," I tell the driver.

An old Aborigine man stands at the corner. The crowd moves around him as though he is invisible, or a tree. His strange, still posture and solemn face are a sharp contrast to the happy revelers we drive past. Surely, they can't all be so carefree. Who has buried too soon? Suffered hate? Whose smile is a mask?

Wearily, I close my eyes into the darkness of Lily's funeral. The small, white coffin draped with roses (their sweet scent ever after reminds me of death), the crowded church, television cameras, reporters, gold crucifix, sun through stained-glass windows. The weight of black. The children's chorus. The priest's comfortless words: "We cannot understand God's ways, for we are only human." Stone angels and indifferent earth. The great, dark grief. Afterward, a home filled with guests and food. Their kind, useless words. ("If you need anything, let me know.") But they ate with pleasure and appetite. They spoke and thought of other things. They meant (though I didn't understand this for a long while), *we will help you, as long as you behave the way we expect you to.*

Before all this happened, I thought I was a loved person. Recently, I have felt more like a cog, a part that held a place in the workings of a structure I can no longer support.

Last week, Melanie invited me to lunch, and I went, thinking that, as my sister, she was at least biologically predisposed to understanding my plan.

"Australia?" she said when I tried to explain it to her. "And time travel? I don't see the connection. What does one have to do with the other? What does any of this have to do with reality?" But as I tried to explain, it became clear that she was just another player in the position of assault against my beliefs.

"Annie, think about what you're doing," she said. "Are you really willing to give up your marriage over this?" (I had not yet shared David's marriage-pregnancy announcement with my family.)

"My marriage was an illusion."

"No, this time travel stuff is the fantasy, can't you see that?"

"I'm not what I appear to be either. That's so clear to me now. None of us are."

"I don't know what you're talking about."

"Did you know that there are physicists who believe that energy frequencies faster than the speed of light create, no, reveal, a different reality? A reality beyond substance and form?"

"Jesus, Annie."

"I know, I know. It's amazing stuff."

"God knows, if anyone ever had a reason to lose it, you do, but would you listen to yourself? Or at least listen to the people who love you."

David's final words as I studied the dessert menu: "You really need help. I'm telling you this because I care."

My father's bon voyage card. A cartoon drawing of an ark filled with people instead of animals. Inside, the printed inscription,

"We'll Miss You," and, incongruously, above his signature, *You have to accept the fact that you're sick. There's nothing to be ashamed of.* My mother's simple note, *We love you dear.* But what is love that does not know the loved?

My ex-best friend, Sarah, came over one afternoon as I packed the odds and ends of the kitchen. We had grown distant since Lily died, not, I believed, for any lack in our friendship, but as the inevitable result of living such opposite lives. I was in mourning. She had a daughter a year younger than Lily (older now, than Lily had ever been) and a new baby boy. I didn't blame either of us for the distance the disparity of our lives had created. I thought I had, if not the friendship we once shared, at least her love, until I reached into a box of paper clips and pulled out an interlocked string of them. "I swear," I said, "sometimes I think someone follows me around and attaches all the paper clips just to annoy me."

"Do you really?" she asks.

"I'm joking."

But she doesn't look up from her sorting. "I'm saying this as a friend, I hope you don't take this the wrong way, but I think you need help."

"Oh?"

"It isn't just me, either, a lot of us, we're worried about you. We think you're suffering from depression."

During the few moments it takes to comprehend this prognosis our friendship is lost, as quickly as if it were torn by bullets. "You know, maybe you're right. I have been feeling rather blue lately. Why is that, I wonder? Do you think it could have anything to do with my daughter being murdered? But that happened a while ago, didn't it? I couldn't possibly still be upset about that."

"I'm just saying, maybe it's time to begin the healing process."

"I'm just saying, you don't know what you're talking about."

"Look. I'm sorry. Everybody's sorry about what happened. It's the worst thing anyone can imagine. Nobody blames you for losing touch with reality."

"This isn't about me losing touch with reality, this is about everyone else not facing it."

"Do you hear yourself? Do you hear how hostile you sound?"

"Oh? Am I hostile?" I lift a box from the kitchen counter, raise it to chest level, and then let go. It splits open onto the floor with a crash of silverware and broken dishes. "What makes you think I'm hostile?" I continue dropping boxes even after she leaves, until I'm exhausted and sit on the floor in the midst of all the destruction and wait for the tears that will not come.

"I can't explain it," I told Melanie. "I don't completely understand it either. But all you have to do is read some basic physics or Von Feehler's novel, he says a lot there. I don't know what Australia has to do with it, if anything, I just know he's there, so I'm going there too. I'm following him because I think he knows something but I can't explain it because I don't understand it either. But I believe it. Haven't you ever done anything based on belief? I mean, when it comes right down to it, isn't most of your life based on a series of beliefs you can't prove?"

"Not like this."

"Why can't you just accept that you don't understand, but support me anyway?"

"Because it's crazy," she said, and thereby summed up everyone's objection.

So that is how I came to be a woman alone in a strange country, alone in the world. Family, friends, husband (beside his pregnant fiancée) all stand at a distant shore and promise that they love me if only I will return to the beliefs *they* hold. They believe they stand on solid land. I finally understand that none of us do. Solid is the illusion. What is real are the waves. It's all just a matter of physics. And once you get over the shock, betrayal even, and fear, of how un-solid life is, you realize the possibilities of what it can be are infinite.

"Here you are, ma'am." I open my eyes in the bright January sun of Australian summer. I pay the driver who points to the small building at the side of the airfield where I have been told I can charter a helicopter to the island.

I'm not crazy. All anyone has to do is look. The bright sun reveals how wavy everything really is. And beyond those waves stands Lily. I can't see her yet, but I know it's true. I greet the woman behind the desk. Pay the fee. All reasonable acts. None of them, not the taxi driver, or the friendly, blue-haired lady who takes my cashier's check with a smile, or the pilot who watches me from behind dark sunglasses, none of them behave as if I am a woman who has lost her mind.

I climb into the helicopter. Clip on my seat belt. The helicopter rises, the pilot smiles at me, gives a thumbs-up. I smile back, a perfectly normal woman.

*   *   *

The pilot's name is Jack. He wears dark sunglasses, and chews gum. He has the classic features of a perfectly carved profile. I know he is attractive but I don't find myself attracted to him. That part of my body (all right, let's just admit it, this is not a matter of parts, but a matter of everything from skin, to hair, to fingertips) has been shut down for some time now. Even before Lily's death there had been a numbing which, in spite of all the reports of women's sexual peak to the contrary, I attributed to age. After she died, the shutdown became complete.

"It's a beautiful day."

Jack nods.

"You been doing this a long time?"

"Yep."

I look out the window. A vast world of creatures, starfish, whales, and seahorses live mysterious lives beneath the sparkling ocean below. Why does everyone keep insisting the world, and what we are capable of, is known? Even the ocean yields new discoveries, unnamed fish, unlearned songs.

"I'm a friend of Max Von Feehler," I say, still looking out the window. "Maybe you brought him over?"

"Ain't no one else flies to the island."

"Oh? Why's that?"

Jack glances at me, his tongue moving in his mouth as if trying to remove something from behind his teeth. "He know you're coming, ma'am?"

"Yes." But I have only recently become a liar and even I can hear the tentative ring to my reply. Jack nods but doesn't speak again until we land on the white sands of the deserted beach.

Sand whips my bare legs, my hair flies in a tangle across my face. Jack waves a goodbye salute. "Which way?" I holler over the helicopter roar. He points over my head. I turn and see a large hill behind me.

"He'll probably meet you halfway," Jack shouts, "he's seen the helicopter land and he ain't known for liking visitors."

I run, head low, shielding my face and eyes from the stinging sand. The helicopter rises until it is only a black dot flying away from me and I am, it seems, alone in the world.

The sand is bone white, the ocean, blue dotted by rainbow spots of sun. I breathe the scent of salty sea mingled with the metallic scent of wet rocks. A laugh breaks my reverie. I spin on my heels to see a flurry of wings and tail as a bird flies from one of the bristly trees on the side of the hill. A kookaburra. I've been singing about them since I was Lily's age, though I was well into my teens before I learned that the laughing creature of the song was a bird. "See," I say softly, "the world is full of all kinds of songs." Not just the wail of ambulance, my screams, the cries of strangers.

After an hour hiking, the hill remains large and imposing. I sit down on a rock and unscrew my Nalgene bottle cap. Even the water is hot. A click startles me. I look up into the barrel of a gun.

I don't know anything about guns other than the damage they do. This one is big, long, like a rifle in the old TV westerns. Sun blurs the man into a silhouette in a broad-brimmed hat.

I think of Lily. When the blast tore through the air I thought it was a car backfiring. The woman fell to the ground in front of us. Another blast and Lily's small hand opened in mine. She collapsed like a puppet cut of its strings, and I sank to the ground beside her, quickly wet with the unbelievable thing of my daughter's blood. Now this man dares to point a gun at me.

"I'm looking for Max Von Feehler."

"Don't know him." An American accent.

"It's important."

"Then you better leave 'cause he ain't here."

"You must be Peter Herrick."

He maintains the gun stance.

"My name is Annie Merchant. I have business with Mr. Feehler."

"Who?"

"I know he's here." I screw the cap on the bottle, tuck it into the backpack. Stand. "I know who's lying in this conversation."

He laughs, lowers the gun, and takes half a step forward. Now that he is not shadowed, his features display a confusing lack of symmetry. His eyes are wide apart and slightly protruding, which gives him an eager, friendly look in spite of the gun and this unfriendly exchange. His eyebrows are dark, one, a perfectly formed curious arch and the other interrupted by a jagged line that runs down the side of his face. His lips are full but his smile stopped on that same side by this jagged line, where on the other, it is dimpled. It is as though a handsome face was torn apart and pasted together from the pieces. Even as I study it, his countenance changes. The amused expression becomes angry. "There's a mail drop in two days. You can go back then." He turns and begins walking up the hill. I struggle into my backpack. He takes broad, easy strides while I feel the weight of each step.

I hate this creep, but I'm not afraid of him and all his macho gun-waving. Which is what I tell him. "Believe me, if I didn't have to follow you, I wouldn't. But you know where Max Von Feehler is and what you don't seem to comprehend is that's more important to me than anything else. I'm not afraid of your stupid gun, okay? I'm not afraid of you. And I'm not afraid to die. The only thing I'm afraid of is not doing what I came here to do. You probably think I'm crazy. Well, here's the scary part. You wouldn't be the first with that opinion."

He turns and looks at me with dark eyes, cold, as though reflective of an inner vacuum. "No," he says, "the scary part is this. Now there's two of us."

When we crest the hill, I see, in a clearing surrounded on three sides by forest, a cabin and a much larger building, like a barn with large windows. I follow him into this shadowed valley, suddenly aware of the stupidity of my situation. I hate those movies where the woman hears a loud crash and walks into the dark room, when every person I know would walk in the opposite direction, but now I've done just that, followed this uncivil stranger whose only personal revelation has been that people say he's crazy, deep into this deserted island.

How can I explain myself? When Lily was shot everything changed. People think they understand this, people whose children weren't murdered. But they can't. Sympathy, empathy, compassion do not make the experience your own, and I wouldn't wish this on anyone, but when I say, everything changed, I mean, *everything*. It was an explosion that never stopped reverberating. I follow a stranger into this valley. It might be the stupidest thing I've done since that stupid day when I told Lily to hurry, and brought her to that corner, where Griffith Connor aimed his gun. But Max is here, and somehow there is a door, a passageway, something he knows that will take me back to my little girl. No risk is too great.

Herrick walks into the large building and returns without the gun. He hangs his hat from the pump and washes his face and hands. When I join him, he speaks without looking up. "You can wash here or there's a shower out back by the outhouse. It's fueled by wood—" he nods toward a large woodpile at the side of the house "—I'd appreciate it if you took only one shower during your stay." He dries his face and hands on a towel hanging from a rope on the pump, and then, without ever looking at me, goes into the cabin.

Does he really expect me to share his dirty water? I dump it, pump fresh, wash my face and hands, reach under my T-shirt to wash my armpits. I decide to air dry rather than share the dingy towel hanging from the rope. I'm so tired I half drag, half carry my backpack to the small cabin. At the door I turn, and for a moment indulge myself, imagine Lily running in the clearing, playing butterfly in her purple wings. Then, once again, I see the pump, the towel, the large building, the dark forest, the emptiness. There's no escaping the emptiness. I turn to the door and knock.

"It's open."

A savory spiciness fills the room. My stomach responds with a low growl. It takes a few moments to adjust to the dim light. The space is simply furnished. There is a square table, two straight-back chairs, a small, blue vase filled with lavender. A twin bed covered with a cotton material (reminiscent of my college days) in shades of blue, green, black, and red appears to serve day-use as a couch. Colorful pillows line the back. A kerosene lamp rests on a small wooden table beside a tightly packed bookshelf.

Herrick stands at the small counter between the sink and stove. In this light I see that the uneven quality of his face is composed of many jagged lines, some small and faint as spider webs, others deep and large like the one that jags down the left side of his face. "Plates in the cupboard." He uses the knife to point.

It takes only a minute to set the table with the ceramic dishes: a blue plate, a green one, a purple mug, and a red. I offer to help with the cooking but when he shakes his head I'm happy to just sit in a wooden chair at the table. In spite of the small windows and dim light and, especially, in spite of the dark humor of the man who lives here, there is a warm, bright feeling about the place. As I look around I see something I missed on my first appraisal. On the bookshelf, next to a marked copy of *Dead Souls* by Gogol, rests a folded pair of spectacles. "When did he leave?"

He turns to me, his full face a confusion of angles in opposition, his large eyes dark as underwater stones. "I thought you under-stood."

"Look, I know about it."

He stands at the stove, pans simmering behind him, and looks at me with the sort of expression I think I sometimes wore when Lily offered her explanations for the extraordinary and ordinary ways of the world. ("I know how God sees us all the time," she said, not long before she died. "He closes his eyes.") "What do you know?"

"I know Max is here and why he came. I know it's about time travel and Max knows how to do it. That's why I'm here. It's no use trying to hide it."

"I'm afraid you're not speaking rationally."

"Those are his glasses."

I don't know his face well enough to be certain, but I think I see something alter in its stony set as he turns to where I point. He picks up the glasses, looks at them, and then places them gently on the shelf. "Maybe these are his glasses," he says slowly, "but it doesn't mean he's here now. It doesn't even mean I know where he is."

"It means you keep missing the point."

"I know. People say you're crazy."

"That's not what I mean."

He reaches over to the table. I jump slightly. His hand rests for a moment on my plate. I can feel him study my face. He picks up the plate, turns back to the stove, and returns it filled with what appears to be rice and some sort of fish. He fills the other plate, sits down across from me, and begins to eat. I stare at the food and consider refusing it, but he is intent on eating. He probably doesn't care whether I do or not. I pick up the fork, stab the fish and rice, shove it into my mouth. It's delicious. We eat in silence until, with a scrape of his chair, he rises suddenly, walks across the room, and returns with two bottles which he sets next to the mugs. I pour myself a mug full and drink greedily.

"You might want to take it easy with that."

"What? This lemonade?"

His smile changes his face though it cannot heal the broken quality, the misaligned angles. "Two dogs lemonade, Aussie beer."

I frown at the mug and set it down on the table.

"You're either very hungry, or you thought that was very good."

"Both, I guess." He drinks, watching me. "What?"

"I was just thinking where I should begin my apologies. I'm

sorry if I frightened you. This is beautiful land but it's lonely, and it's strange." His hand brushes his face in a quick, slight gesture. "There are real dangers here. I like it this way but, obviously, I don't get too many drop-in visitors."

"I can see why, with a greeting like that."

He shrugs. "I meant what I said out there, about people thinking I'm crazy but if you meant what you said, about people thinking you are too, I think we can both feel safe." He pauses, looks at me. I nod. "As to Max. You're right. I lied to you." He opens his arms and shows me his palms, an ancient gesture meant to prove no hidden weapons. "He's a friend of mine who asked for shelter and privacy. He's gone. I don't know where he is." He rises from his chair, picks up the plates and mugs, and starts to do the dishes at the pump by the sink. I offer to help but he refuses. "There's a mail drop day after tomorrow. You can go back then. I'll sleep in the studio tonight. You can sleep here." He picks up the kerosene lamp and sets it on the table in front of me.

"Do you know how to use this?"

"Of course."

"You should be all right then." He puts on his broad-brimmed hat and walks to the door.

"You're going to bed now?"

"Actually, I have an appointment."

"You're going to Max."

"I promise you I'm not."

"Why should I believe you?"

"Because it's the truth."

"I'm coming too."

"You're not invited."

"Then I'll follow you."

"I advise you not to. There are dangers here you don't understand."

"I told you—"

"I know, I know." He holds up his hand. "You're not afraid to die. But have you ever been attacked by wild dogs? Not being afraid to die is one thing, wishing you would, another. Get some rest. You look like you haven't slept for a long time." He shuts the door softly behind him.

How I want to take his advice. I want to sleep and wake to find this all a dream. I rub my tired eyes. I can almost imagine Lily breathing in her sleep, her cold foot against my leg when she crawled into bed with David and me. I open my eyes. How can I rest when I'm certain Herrick is going to Max? I rise, open the door, quietly shut it behind me.

Herrick is entering the forest on the other side of his studio. When I get there, I find a small path, which we follow in a circuit I can't keep track of. The forest is filled with strange noises, the dark shape of bats, the blink of red eyes. Why have I kept insisting I'm not afraid? What's true is that I no longer let my fear rule me. I follow him; tired, afraid, certain he will lead me to Max who will lead me to Lily. Finally he leaves the woods and walks through a small clearing to a cabin. He stands on the porch and looks out to the darkness where I hide. I survey my surroundings, the small cabin, the other building, the pump and bucket, the dingy towel hanging on a rope. "Shit."

"You better come in now. I wasn't lying about the dogs."

I step into the clearing. He stands at the porch watching me. He opens the door. I don't speak or look at him as I pass. I slam the door shut. The tears come quickly. I cry loudly and with abandon; the first time I've allowed myself to do this since they drugged my noisy grief before Lily's funeral. Maybe I'm already asleep when I hear a noise. As though someone who had been standing outside, listening, now walks away.

Strange noises and an odd light. I walk to the window above the sink. A small fire burns in the darkness. I go to the door. Open it. The fire is surrounded by men dressed in feathers and bones; strange markings on their faces and skin. They circle the fire, chanting. Herrick stands in the center, bare-chested. I should hide. Drumming. I think I hear drumming or is that my heart? One of the men holds up a knife. He brings it to Herrick's chest and with a quick swipe draws a streak of bright red blood. I scream. All eyes turn to me. The chanting stops and changes to a low murmur. Herrick looks at me and shakes his head. The strange men walk toward me. "No. Don't," Herrick says. He walks faster than any of them. He stands across from me, so close I can see that his eyes are filled with kindness. "She's looking for her daughter," he says. "She's yudirini. Yudirini." The strange men stop. I touch Herrick's wound. "This is my sorrow mark," he says.

Squint through rays of bright sun at blue vase, lavender-laced stems, tightly packed bookshelf, the spectacles, the small window over the sink. My whole body aches, bones and skin, even my eyes ache, heavy with the dull feeling of too many tears. Walk to the window. In that dream I walked to the window and saw . . . see Herrick in shorts and shoes, no shirt, his back a rhythm of muscles as he raises ax, brings it down. He turns. Step away from the window. His bare chest. The blood. A dream. That was a dream. Rub forehead but it doesn't help. A shower. Rummage through backpack for shower kit, clean clothes, the hotel towel. Did I pack this? This towel. Oh, Lily. I press my face into it. No. I cannot spend the day weeping. Walk to the door. The morning sun hot. He turns. Ax at his side. His chest tan and strong. Hairless. No cut. No cut or scar. No sorrow . . . the surprise of that face. That perfect torso, a Michelangelo thing. That face, a contortion. A mask.

"I'm going to take that shower now," the words, thick as a hangover.

He nods slowly. Those dark eyes. Can he see my fear? Walk away. To the shower.

Undress. Hang towel from hook. That towel. The hotel room. Lily's dried blood flaking off my dress like worthless dust. The shower. I took the towel and the sheets. "Why are you doing this?" David asked. *She slept here. This was her last bed.* "But these are clean sheets. That's a fresh towel." *I don't care. I'm taking it.* Reach to turn on the shower. Blood.

Blood on my fingertips. But it was a dream. Or is this a dream? Close eyes. Open them. Blood on my fingertips where I touched his . . . sorrow mark. Turn on the water. Step into hot steam. Wash hands. See. There's no blood. Of course not. Just washed it off. I'm losing my—

Look for cut or scratch. That's it. A scratch. Nothing. Only clean skin. Just like him. A dream then. Why am I so upset? Oh. The blood.

I'm losing my . . . Scrub clean. Clean, clean. Maybe I ate some-thing bad. Yes. He poisoned me. I shut off the water. Stand in hot steam. Pull back the curtain. Step into the little dressing area. Towel dry. The death towel. How appropriate. Dress. Step out of the hot, little booth into the hot sun. Silence.

I will say, *I know you poisoned me.* Another evil stranger. Walk to where he was. Only stacks of wood. Maybe this is a fairy tale. He is turned to wood. I am invisible. Oh, Lily, what is happening? I think I'm losing my . . .

Walk to the large building. Open the closed door. Heavy. Dark. The oily heavy smell of paint. Can't smell colors. Smell purple, blue, heavy green, and black. Lots of black. Feel the strokes. Thick. Angry. Sharp. Swirls. Slashes. A mask. Heavy and dark hangs a bleeding face of agony. Another one smiles, an eternal happy coun-tenance, a lie. A painting of a jungle scene but the leaves change, as I watch them, into man, woman. A red painting. Weeping lady. A twist of limbs and skin, a stream of black. Another, broken glass in the center. On one side a man and woman in grinning masks, a baby, its face turned away; on the other side, severed limbs, blood.

Lily's blood, red and wet. The dried scab of it on my dress, flak-ing like worthless dust. The blood on my fingertips. But it was a dream. No. The blood. A long table cluttered with paints and rags. A pegboard on the wall. The gun. A penciled sketch. A woman's hand, long fingers, delicate wrist.

"What are you doing here?" His face contorted.

"I'm looking for my daughter."

He shakes his head, whispers, "She's not here."

"No, I mean Max Von Feehler."

"He's not here either."

"Yes he is."

"Come on, I made tea." He turns to walk away. I take the gun. Point it.

"Stop. I have a gun."

"Don't be so dramatic."

"Don't tell me about dramatic." I use the gun to point at the room.

"This is private." He steps toward me.

"I'll shoot."

"We both know you never would."

"Keep walking and we'll find out." He doesn't move. "Tell me where he is."

"I don't know."

"In that case, I guess you're about as much good to me dead as you are alive."

He laughs.

"Damn it, I have a gun."

"I still don't know. I wouldn't know, even if it was loaded."

I step out of my Wild West pose. He lunges, twists the gun easily from me. Steps back. Raises the gun to his shoulder. Shifts his stance and shoots. Glass shatters on the table behind me. He lowers the gun. Unloads it. Pockets the bullets. Hangs the gun from its rack on the wall. Walks to me, so close I can feel his breath on my cheek. I glance at the jagged face. "What are you feeling now?" he whispers. I feel his breath against my cheek. He turns and walks away.

My God, whatever you may be, what am I? Was everyone right all along? My reasoning, only foggy fear and despair? What reason did Griffith Connor have? How I'd like to believe we were not from the same species. Has all my fear, paranoia even, been rooted, not as I thought, in the mean outside world, but rather, in some meanness in me?

In the corner, a painting of a woman's slender back, and long, dark hair draped around a perfect arch of neck. Another painting, a woman's legs in a swirl of autumn leaves. The penciled sketch of a woman's hand. What does all this mean? Never before would I have believed I could point a gun at someone. How to take it back? It's become a lengthy list, the things I would undo.

He sits on the cabin step drinking from a mug. Another mug steams beside him. I have just threatened to kill the first man who ever fixed me a cup of tea. I sit close so that I don't have to speak loudly. "My six-year-old daughter was shot and killed by a sniper while we were visiting New York City." The familiar words have become almost a mantra. "It was her first big trip to the city. I was taking her to see Cats. She always loved cats. She begged us to get her one but I kept saying, wait until you're eight. I thought she'd be old enough then to really take care of one. I never imagined . . .

"She was shot by Griffith Connor; the same guy who killed Max Von Feehler's wife. When I found out what he was writing about, Max, I mean, I asked him to help me, but he wouldn't.

"My husband and I, who knows what we would have been if this had never happened? We were happy. I think. But at our core we were so different. We dealt with Lily's death so differently. So he got our marriage too. Connor, I mean.

"When I found out about Max, and started reading about physics, I came to believe, I still believe, we didn't have to let her go. He, David, and, actually, almost everyone I know, thinks I'm losing my mind, and until this morning I was certain it all just made so much sense to me. For the first time since that unreasonable, senseless thing, something made sense to me. So I followed him. Here.

"Maybe I'm wrong about a lot. Maybe I'm more afraid than I thought I was, and maybe I do care if I live or die and maybe even . . .

"Last night I had this dream. You were in it. You said I was *yud* . . . *yudi* something and you were cut, on your chest, over your heart, and you said, 'This is my sorrow mark.' But this morning, there's no cut on your chest, no fire circle."

"Fire?"

"Out here, you were out here with these men. Aborigines, I guess, and there was a fire."

He nods.

"So this morning I have blood on my fingertips right where I touched you in my dream. It doesn't make sense. Maybe everybody's been right all along. I don't even know what's real anymore.

"All I know is that I had a daughter that I love more than life and I won't let anything keep me from her. As long as any part of me believes I can find her, nothing, not even the parts of me that believe I can't, will stop me."

Herrick sips his tea. In the bright sun, his face looks almost shattered, like the broken glass in his painting. "I want to tell you what I know, about what's happening to you. The Aborigines believe that dreaming is another equally real consciousness. Not state. Consciousness. The blood you say you found on your fingertips means you're further along on your journey than you realize."

"I don't understand what you mean."

"The Aborigines develop the ability to bring messages from the dream world to the waking one. The blood on your fingertips was telling you something."

"It was your blood, Herrick."

"You're not losing your sanity, you're just losing your mind. Let it go."

"What are you talking about?"

" 'Are you willing to be sponged out, erased, canceled, made nothing? Dipped into oblivion? If not, you will never really change.' "

"D. H. Lawrence."

"Yes."

"I read it, but never understood it, not really. Until now."

"You never lived it."

"Okay. I never thought I'd be saying something like this, but thanks for talking to me after I threatened to kill you, and thanks for helping me not feel so crazy, I really mean it, but are you ever going to tell me where Max is?"

"Here he is now."

Max Von Feehler stands at the edge of the clearing, a strange and exhausted traveler dressed in hiking gear. His face, hands, legs, and arms painted with swirls of color and lines, similar to the markings on my dream Aborigines. Herrick walks quickly to Max's side and puts his arms around him as he sinks to the ground.

I rush to the pump. What strange reason, except the strangest one I had suspected all along, can there be for his odd appearance? When I return with the water, Herrick sits beside Max, supporting him with his arm. I dump out the tea and dip the mug into the water.

Max drinks three cups before he looks at either of us. I've never seen him without his glasses. Maybe that's what creates the startling effect of his eyes. They are wide, his stare, unblinking. "I saw her," he says.

"Are you sure you want to say anything?"

Max looks at me, then at Herrick. "Do you know what she's been through?" He turns to me. "Your daughter is lovely."

I cover my mouth as if this gesture will contain the joy forever. My daughter is lovely. My daughter *is*.

"I saw you too. You've changed quite a bit. I almost didn't recognize you." Then, as though a cloud blocks the sun, his expression darkens. He is there, not in the time traveling way, but in the horrible moments when memory burns through the barriers of time and we are there and not there, helpless, in a way that is the worst of horrors. "She wouldn't come," he weeps, "she wouldn't come."

For a moment I think he means Lily, then I realize he's talking about his wife.

"I saw it happen." He turns to me, his face twisted with grief. "How could you survive that?" I shake my head. It is too terrible to remember so soon after hearing Lily spoken of as alive. He weeps into the palms of his hands. His whole body shakes with grief. Herrick lifts him under the arms. We walk slowly to the cabin. In the midst of Max's despair, I hold in myself, like a sharp but precious stone, the realization of what he's done. Somewhere, Lily is.

"I'll make some tea," I say, an excuse to turn my face away. Just as, all those years ago, my tea makers tried to feed me against my grief, even as they embraced their blessings, and turned away, and walked away because (I understand the awkwardness of it now) my sorrow filled them with their joy.

Max sits at the edge of the couch, staring. I bring him his tea with shaking hands. He takes it, then frowns as if he doesn't know how it came to be there or what to do with it. Herrick takes the mug from him and places it on the floor at his feet. The dark cabin, the heavy silence, and especially Max's face, the expression of a man who has suffered the worst and then suffered it again, all increase the weight of sorrow in this room but even so I cannot contain my joy. I look to Herrick's face and find him scowling at me. I turn away; pretend to be busy at the sink. Oh, but Lily is. She is!

A heavy gasp breaks the silence. Max sobs into his hands. Herrick sits beside him, his arm around his shoulders. After a while the sobbing subsides. Max looks first at Herrick, then at me. "She wouldn't come." He shakes his head against the horrible memory. "She wouldn't come and I let her make that choice."

"You don't have to talk about this," says Herrick. I open my mouth to object but Max continues.

"You understand that back in time is Lily and you—you how you were then—and Marie, and me. There's me here, but there's also me, who I was then."

I nod.

"I could not know what effect I would have on myself so I avoided, at all costs, running into the *me* I was then, my doppel-gänger, my double." He stops suddenly and looks about him, as if he's lost something. "I'd forgotten how much time Marie and I spent together in the days before she died. It was like a second honeymoon. She'd set aside her work, for the most part, and I'd set aside mine, although it was the work that brought us there. We did everything together. Shopping. Plays. Movies. We were so happy.

"Then, that day, she had a meeting with Dr. Kestler and I had a meeting with Kieran, my agent. So I waited outside the hotel until I saw *me* leave the building. I wasn't sure how to explain all of it but I knew by her research that she would believe me.

"I knocked on the door. 'Oh Max,' she said when she opened it, 'how can such a brilliant mind always forget the key?' But her expression changed. 'What happened to you? You look like human graffiti.'

"What does one say at such a moment? She was beautiful. Alive. We embraced. We kissed. 'I've come from the future,' I said.

"All I wanted to do was make love to her. To keep her in that room, to stay with her. But of course I was quite a shock. She believed me. But to her we had just parted, really, for the first time in weeks. Her mood was far more analytical.

" 'The future has not been kind to you,' she said.

"I did not really know how to approach the subject delicately. How to spare her the grief of what no one should ever hear. 'I've been miserable since you died.'

"She took it well. She bit her lip. She sat down on the hotel couch and signaled the chair for me. We were silent for a long time. She looked out the window. I looked at her. Finally, she spoke. 'If you love me—and Max, I know you do—you will do this one thing. Promise.'

" 'Oh anything, anything.' How these years I've only dreamed to make her promises. 'Yes, yes,' I said.

" 'Don't tell me how it happens, or when.'

"Of course I immediately began to object.

" 'Max, for our love, I beg you.'

"What could I do? I had to agree. This seemed to relax her. She leaned back, crossed her legs, shook her head, and smiled. 'So you've done it. You've done what I've only dreamed. Max, you've time traveled.'

"She was jubilant. She raised her arms in the air and let out a little scream, then leaned forward and asked, 'So what is it, Max? A CTL? Einstein's river? Alternate planes?'

"I shook my head. 'I don't know, Marie, I don't know. It all seems the same. I can't tell until this—'

"She raised a warning eyebrow at me.

" 'I can't tell until later. You must come with me.'

"She agreed. She was talking about physics, equations, things I still don't understand. Laughing. She walked over and kissed me on the cheek. Then suddenly she stopped. 'But Max,' she said, 'can you promise you'll bring me back to *here*, to this place, at this moment?'

"She saw me hesitate. I was trying to understand the significance of the question. But the hesitation was all the answer she needed. For a moment I saw something of fear shadow her face. It was as though a light dimmed. 'I can't,' she said.

" 'Marie, you don't understand.' Though of course I knew she must. Hers was a mind that understood everything.

"She shook her head. She covered her mouth with her hand.

" 'You'll die if you don't come with me.'

"She just stood there, shaking her head. 'Max, oh Maxie,' she clucked her tongue at me. 'You have not thought through this.'

"She reached over and touched my shoulder, my cheek. She knelt on the floor and rested her head on my lap. I brushed her hair with my fingers. It was just beginning to turn gray. When she looked up at me there were tears in her eyes. 'Don't you realize, Maxie, don't you realize how much I love you?

" 'If I were to leave with you today, disappear without a trace, what would the Max of today, the one who kissed me goodbye this morning, the one who is now meeting with his agent, what would he think?'

" 'He would understand.'

" 'Max,' she shook her head, 'he would think I deserted him. There would be a police investigation. He would insist I was a victim of foul play but somebody would say, "No officer, I saw her leave with a man. He looked a bit like her husband, but older." The police would finally tell him, there is no sign of a struggle. There are reports she was seen with another man.'

" 'We'll leave a note. Explain everything. I would understand.'

" 'No, Max, you understand now.' She shook her head and laughed. 'Obviously you've been doing some studying since I've been gone. But remember who you are, here, in 1992. You'd think I made a fool out of you. And because of it, you'd fall out of love with me. You would want nothing to do with my world, physics. You'd never study it, and you would never understand it, and you would never believe it.'

" 'I'm willing to suffer that.'

" 'No, Max, it would kill you. This . . .' For a moment she seemed unable to say the word. '. . . death of mine will break your heart, but if you thought I left you for another man it would break your soul as well. I could never do that to you.'

"Just then the clock clicked to three. She noticed me looking at it. 'Remember what you promised, Max,' she said, and then cruelly bargained, 'remember I asked you to keep that promise out of love for me.'

"She turned from me. I think she did not want to see my expression. 'I have an appointment I must keep,' she said.

" 'Marie.' For a moment she would not look at me. When she did there were tears in her eyes. There were tears in mine. She leaned over and kissed me, the way she used to, one kiss on my forehead, then one for each cheek, and one on my lips.

" 'Maxie, remember this,' she said, 'I love you.'

" 'Marie, I'm not sure you're being reasonable.'

" 'Oh, Max,' she said, 'for love we do so many things we would not do for reason.' She picked up her purse. Looked in the mirror and fixed her hair. I walked with her to the door. We kissed but did not speak. Then, just as startling as finding myself in her arms again, she was gone.

"I guess you could say I was stunned. In some kind of shock. I should have locked her in the room, held her captive, if that's what it took. Be damned her desires. Be damned our love if she must die to preserve it. Be damned me. Most of all, me. I ran from the room. I didn't even shut the door. I remember, that day, returning to the hotel, this was before I knew what had happened, and finding the door wide open. I thought the maids had left it like that and I was just reaching for the phone to complain when I got the call. Anyway, I ran to catch her. That's when I saw you and your daughter. I tried to stop you but you just pulled her closer and kept walking."

Vaguely I remember the strange man approaching from the side, ranting about time and space. "I thought you were . . ."

"You couldn't have known," Herrick says.

"I saw it all." Max closes his eyes and leans back against the couch. "This new memory is the worst. I would not wish it on anyone."

A perfect day at the cusp of summer and autumn. A cloudless sky. A faint breeze. Lily's small hand in mine, her voice a babble of excitement. The crazy man coming from the side. I pull her closer and walk faster, as if I know where danger is. She's talking about cats. We hurry to the corner. We wait for the light. The crack of noise. The confusion of screams. The woman (Marie) who falls to the ground beside us. The noise again and Lily's hand opens in mine like a sudden flower. The horrible sinking to ground. The blood in her hair. The scream.

"All this has done," Herrick says softly, "is bring more grief."

"No," says Max. "I thought you, of all people, would understand."

Herrick glances at me and shakes his head.

A brief smile passes across Max's face. "You, with your true face, still full of secrets."

"A man has a right to his privacy."

"A man has a right to his privacy," Max mimics, shaking his head.

"Tell me what I need to do. When can we go?"

Both men turn to me. Max shakes his head, as if I've said something unbelievable. "No. I'll never go back there."

"What do you mean? You can't just quit now."

Herrick walks across the room and stands in front of me, the lines and jags on his face deep with anger. "Leave him alone," he whispers, "for God's sake think what he's been through."

"Fuck what he's been through. I've been through it too and let me tell you, it's nothing compared to what Lily went through."

"He's finally letting her go. Let him."

"You would say that. You, with your whole little world right here where you can control everything. What do you know about love anyway? Besides letting go."

His eyes widen and then close, as if against an unbearable sight. He turns and leaves the cabin, quietly shutting the door behind.

"Mrs. Merchant, you seem like an intelligent woman —" Max lies down on the couch, rolls to his side, his back to me "— can you really think you're the only one who has suffered?"

"You have to tell me how to get there."

"I'm sorry. I'm just so tired. I feel like Dorothy in the poppy field."

"But you have to tell me." His breathing is already changed to the heavy rhythm of sleep. I leave the dark cabin and stand on the porch beneath a bright, cheerful sun. What have I become? A woman who used to cry over coffee commercials, now expertly mean. I sit on the porch step, look at the blue sky. This same sky. I close my eyes. She was talking about cats. Something about cats. Oh Lily, if only I could hear your voice. I put my face in my hands and cry.

The studio door opens and Herrick emerges. He stands there, wearing an old shirt streaked with paint, his hair a mess of Einstein proportions. He rubs a hand through the wild hair, looks at me, frowns, and turns back to the studio but I call to him to wait. When I'm close enough, I can see that his eyes hold a special hurt just for me.

"Listen Herrick, I'm sorry. I know I'm . . ." I shrug; there isn't the language to describe my current state. "I shouldn't have said that in there. I know *I* got plenty tired of people analyzing me."

He nods, glances back into the studio. "You were right. I have sheltered myself here. I thought I'd return eventually, but I never will. Not to that world. I don't think of it as just giving up, it's been more a process of conversion. Do you know the second law of thermodynamics?"

"Energy cannot be created or destroyed—"

"It can only be converted from one form into another."

"Your paintings?"

He nods.

"And that's enough for you?"

"Enough? I don't know about that. But it's something. It's creation. Haven't you ever had that feeling of creating something, losing yourself as this small thing, and becoming part of the infinite?"

"Herrick, you're a poet."

He shakes his head and laughs.

"I have had that feeling." He smiles. I'm over tired, over emotional, but even with the jags and lines I find myself thinking his is a beautiful face. "I felt that way when Lily was born." He nods, rubs his fingers through his hair, glances back into the studio. "You have reminded me of something else though. Do you have some paper and a pen I could use?"

He nods, goes into the studio, and returns with a sketchpad and pen. "You write?"

"A little."

He grins. There it is again, a fleeting moment when his face seems like a perfect thing. I find myself smiling at him. Abruptly, he turns back into the studio. I sit on the porch step. The stress has confused my emotions. I think of Dr. Bruhlia, my college creative writing teacher, standing in front of class, her red hair vibrant above a purple dress, her wrinkled face glowing as she read Dylan Thomas to us. " 'Rage, rage against the dying of the light.' Do you feel that? What makes you rage? What makes you burn? Hmm?" She waved a loose-skinned, bangled arm as if conducting us. "Do you know yet? Find it. Burn."

Most of us took this to be an exhortation to party and drink. We were so young. I had no idea what she was talking about. Later, in those months between David's first kiss and our first sex, I thought I understood it in the warmth and bodyaching heat of desire. I discovered the writing of Anaïs Nin, and imitated her with my virginal pen, until, at last, I acquiesced to David and the heat dissipated. Now I think maybe I confused my passions. I never felt that way again, writing fervently in the school library, underneath the elm tree, in the dark dorm room by the light of a candle. When did I decide all that passion was David's? Why did I let it go?

I doodle a flower, a tree, a little house. Before Lily died I wrote articles on gardening and school board meetings but I also wrote poems that I hadn't shown to anyone since Dr. Bruhlia, who said my writing showed promise. Only now does it seem strange that I never showed them to David. Not one in all those years. What was that all about? I doodle a spiral, a star. How I treasured those mornings when I woke up while it was still dark, made a pot of tea (Earl Grey with warm milk and sugar), lit a candle, and sat writing at the kitchen table until I heard David in the shower. But burn? Lily, my light, the burning, pulling pain of your birth. Your little mouth against my breast, and I promised you life, love, happiness. Burn? The sear of that promise.

I turn the page. I write. I don't stop until the sun has already begun its afternoon arc. I close the pad and rub my tired hand. What I've been writing is a sad story but I don't feel heavy with grief, rather, lightened, as if unburdened of its weight.

The studio door opens. Herrick stands in the doorway. For a moment I feel his bright gaze and all the peace it carries. He shakes his head, rubs his fingers through his wild hair, walks over to join me, his face returned to its usual mask. "Still writing?"

"I don't know how to finish it."

He nods. "Sometimes that happens in my paintings. I'll start with an idea that usually gets lost and turns into a question, and then something happens, or someone says something, or I just see it differently, and I can finish it."

"You mean life gives you the answer?"

He laughs. "No. It's more like they aren't separate, the painting and life. When I let go of my ideas, then I can finish it and I usually know something I didn't know when I started. When you're finished, I'd like to read it. He still asleep?"

"As far as I know."

"He's probably going to sleep for hours."

I think I slept for two months after Lily died before the dreams began. First there were the nightmares, the horrible visions of her death, then the sweeter dreams, when she came to me alive and laughing. Waking became the nightmare. I look up and find Herrick studying me closely. "You know, there are those who believe a trip like that can have only one end. If it happened, it will happen again and again."

"And there are those who believe there are alternate realities, that each moment is a splitting of infinite possibility," I respond.

He turns away. "You're really going to try it then? Time traveling?"

"Don't say it like that, as if I'm being ridiculous. You heard him. He was there."

He nods, turns to me with that severed smile. "I would like to introduce you to someone, a friend."

"You have a friend? I mean, here?"

"Yes, even I—"

"I didn't mean it like that. I just thought we were alone here." I remember the dream and all the kindness I saw in his eyes. For a moment, I think I see it again. What was that strange dream word he used to describe me? "It would be nice to meet your friend."

He extends his hand. I reach up and place my hand in his. For a moment he hesitates, looking at me as if I have surprised him. His hand is warm and strong. He pulls gently. I stand. He lets go, nods at the notebook that I clutch against my chest. "I can put that in the studio for you."

I hand it to him. What is this schoolgirl blush? He meant to take the notebook, not hold my hand. He closes the studio door, walks to the path we had taken the night before. "Not again." He laughs but keeps walking and I follow.

It's all the fresh air. Or maybe it's just been a matter of time, and

like those fairy tale love potions, he's just the first man I've seen
since my body awoke from its long slumber. I think of the clumsy
attempts at lovemaking after Lily's death, which David and I finally
abandoned. "It isn't you," I would say, "don't you see how everything I feel is connected? I can't feel right now, without feeling
sorrow. I don't want to feel anything." David, helpless against my
grief, and against an invisible barrier I am beginning to believe
always existed but which first became insurmountable with her
death. Why didn't he, even once, ask to see what I wrote? In my
closet (and now in storage), shoeboxes, scrapbooks, and those notebooks filled with pain and sorrow, and the ones from before filled
with my poems, observations, stories. He called it my scribbling so I
did too.

Herrick looks over his shoulder. "Doing okay?"

I nod. This body awakening is just biology. Herrick, only a coincidence. It had to happen eventually. I can shut it down again. After
everything I've tackled to get here, my own body seems an easy con-
quest.

The vegetation changes, the trees are closer together, and then,
it seems suddenly, they tower one hundred feet into the sky, which
is a green canopy that lets in little sun, the tall tree trunks covered
with vines and ferns. Herrick grins. "What do you think?"

"It's like walking into a dream."

He brushes my arm with his finger then points above and I see
the most beautiful bird, small as a parakeet, brightly colored green,
red, yellow, and blue with a red beak.

"The Aborigines believe that this world is the dreaming of our
ancestors," he says.

"If this is the dream what is it when we sleep?"

"The life of the Gods."

The trees thin out. The air is warm, the day bright. We stand at
the top of a hill and look into a valley below. For just a moment I
think he has done it again. The scene is that familiar. A pump. A
woodpile. A small cabin. But there is no larger building. Smoke
curls into the blue sky. "Good, she's home."

Does he have a girlfriend out here? How ridiculous that I find
this thought unnerving. When I get close enough to see the woman
standing on the porch I realize the possibility is unlikely. Her gray
hair in a bun, her face a study of wrinkles, she is old enough to
be his mother. She smiles up at him and he bends to kiss her
cheek. He says something. She nods. Herrick introduces us. "Annie
Merchant, this is Loma." I offer my hand but she looks at me as

though I am a bad purchase. She nods, grunts, and turns. We follow her into the cabin.

The walls are covered with paintings. She nods us to the table. Herrick sits while she goes to the stove but I walk about the room, inspecting the beautiful landscapes. Lavender fields, dark rocks in gray water, a forest at night by the light of the moon. "These are beautiful." I look at Loma's back. She appears to be making tea and doesn't acknowledge the compliment.

"You think so?" Herrick says.

"Yes, of course. You're very talented," I say to Loma who still ignores me.

"Thank you," says Herrick.

"You?"

"Yep."

"Why don't you do more of this kind of work?"

"Because this isn't the only landscape I know."

Loma sets a blue teapot on the table. She places a delicate, flow-ered cup and saucer before me, a blue willow cup and saucer before Herrick, and a butterfly cup for herself. Herrick passes the tea, a strange smoky blend that reminds me of wood stoves and fire. She looks at Herrick.

"Max is back," he says. "Things didn't go as he had hoped."

She sighs, looks down at the tea, and then from me to Herrick.

"Now Annie wants to try it. Her daughter is there."

Once again Loma looks at me. I squirm under her silent appraisal. Who is this woman and what does she know about all this? "If there's anything you know . . ."

She shakes her head vehemently.

"No. She doesn't do that anymore." He smiles at Loma. She smiles back. He sips his tea and she sips hers. I look at the beau-tiful art that surrounds us. Loma taps the table. "She wants to show you something." Herrick sips from his cup and seems to be making a point of not looking at me. Loma watches me with those bright blue eyes. She stands. "She would like you to come with her."

She leads me across the room to a corner where a small paint-ing hangs. This one is more like what I've seen of Herrick's work. At first it appears to be almost a red flower, but slowly the shapes take form and it is a scene of a woman's legs, a head crowning. A birth. I turn to Loma. She squints at me and points back to the painting. I look where she points at the corner, to the small lettering. "Yudirini," I say. I look at Loma and she nods. I turn to Herrick. He drinks his tea and does not look at us. "That's what you said in my dream. You said I was yudirini. What does it mean?"

Herrick takes another sip of tea. Loma watches him closely. Finally, he looks at her. She nods. He shakes his head, no. She nods, yes. He sighs. "It means, being born and returning." I watch him drink his tea, waiting for more explanation, but he doesn't give any. I turn back to Loma for clues of this strange exchange, and find her pointing at me.

I point to myself.

She nods.

"Yudirini? Being born and returning?"

She points to Herrick.

"Both of us?"

She nods again, but does not look happy with my success at this odd game of charades. She returns to the table. Sits across from Herrick. Places a gentle hand over his. He looks at her and then down, as if bent by a heavy weight. She pats his hand, then reaches for her cup. They drink together. I turn back to the painting. Yudirini. Being born and returning.

Both of us.

When we leave, Loma hands me a small, leather-bound book. "Max wrote it," says Herrick. "He used to do one every year for his friends. This was the last, from the year before Marie died." I brush my hand over the soft cover, and gently flip through the gold-edged pages. "It's mostly stories about Aborigines."

"I didn't know he wrote anything like that."

Loma taps the cover with one thick finger. I look up into her unwavering blue eyes. "Do you want me to read it?"

She nods.

Herrick kisses her goodbye. I'm surprised when she gives me a gentle hug; she smells like a combination of wood smoke and cinnamon.

As we walk back to his place I ask Herrick why she can't speak.

"She can. She just chooses not to."

"Why?"

"That isn't for me to say."

I don't pursue it. I'm weary of mysteries and portents, and in too good of a mood to give into these heavy distractions. After all, Max has returned from a place where he saw my daughter, alive. Who knows how long before I'll be with her?

When we return to the cabin, though the sky is tinged with the lavender haze of evening, Max still sleeps, snoring loudly. Herrick offers to sleep on the floor and lend me the studio space but thinking of the bloody art there, I insist on sleeping on the porch. "After all, you might want to work on a painting." Herrick shrugs, as if it doesn't really matter, but looks relieved. He lends me a sleeping bag, which I lay out on the porch. I watch the stars flicker out of the darkness until my eyes grow heavy beneath their gentle light.

The world is on fire. I stand beneath blazing buildings, shouting Lily's name. An Aborigine man points at me, then at a door. I open the door.

A Bach violin sonata. A cool, white room. "What do you think?" Herrick stands beside me frowning at a large canvas, a painting of me standing on a burning horizon. Flames engulf my feet.

Suddenly a woman stands before us. She has long, black hair and an alabaster complexion. Dark eyebrows arch over blue eyes. Herrick gasps. She smiles, and says, "You didn't think the door opened only one way, did you?" He reaches to touch her but she steps back. "Not this time," she says, "I came for her."

Everything else disappears. It is just the beautiful woman and me. She rests her hand on my arm. "All these paintings about death," she says, "don't let them fool you. He is alive." She looks at me with unblinking eyes. I look down at her graceful hand but it has been replaced by a skeleton's.

I wake with a start. It takes a few moments to adjust to the dark of this wilderness night. Max and Herrick stand in the clearing facing a small group of Aborigines and a petite woman, dressed like a Victorian in lace collar, long skirt, buttonhook shoes, white gloves.

Max turns to Herrick, "It doesn't make any sense, her being here."

The little woman laughs. "What does it matter to reality if you can reason it or not?" She looks up at me with cold, gray eyes. Max and Herrick follow her gaze. Over his shoulder, Herrick meets my questioning expression with a shrug and shake of his head. The little woman squints at me and frowns. "Go away. I see death all around you."

"We won't hurt anyone."

"What? You think the door opens only one way?" She laughs, wide-mouthed and loud, then turns to Max and Herrick. "You bleed, we bleed."

"What do you want from us?" Herrick asks.

"You people, always think it's about desire."

Max raises his face to the sky, as if questioning the stars, instead of this odd woman. "Why are you here?"

"Why are you here?" She repeats, and laughs, waves one pretty white-gloved hand in front of her. "This is our song." She lifts her white skirt above the ground and continues through the clearing. All but one of the Aborigines follow her.

He is a tall fellow, his gray hair shaved at the forehead, naked except for the markings on his skin: slashes and spirals of ochre paint and clay. Elsewhere he is scarred with raised markings I assume are sorrow marks, like the one Herrick received in that dream. He turns and looks at me. I feel, what? . . . struck, no, that's too harsh a word, touched. It's as if no one else has ever seen me, known me, in the way his dark gaze has accomplished both. In that moment, I think I see something in his eyes, I mean, really *see* something, like looking at a movie screen, right there in his pupils: buildings collapse, a city burns. He turns his back to me and speaks in his language. He stops for a moment and bows his head. Herrick translates. In this way, with the Aborigine talking, then waiting while Herrick speaks, we are given this story.

There is a sunny plain where no one dies. There is no darkness. Women live there making weapons. One day Ooglan chances upon this bright tribe. They are excited by the animal skins he carries. They have never seen animals before. He gives them kangaroo pelts. They give him weapons.

When Ooglan returns to his people he tells them of the death-less land.

His people murmur, "Ooglan, where have you been?"

"I've traveled far. I went to a sunny plain. I met some women."

"Ooglan, what happened then?"

"I gave them kangaroo skins. They gave me weapons."

"Ooglan, think, were there any animals on this sunny plain?"

Ooglan remembers the white heat, the lack of shadows, the smiling women. "No. Only the dead I carried."

"Ooglan, be careful. This deathless place, these spirit women, who knows what danger they carry?"

That night Ooglan makes a plan. He unlaces the leather pouch, shakes the magic into his open palm. When he looks up, he looks into his brothers' eyes. The brothers do not run or hide. They feel the change happening, the skin reformed, the face reshaped. It hurts at first, the orange beak, the splaying of feet into webbed, the shrinking of body, the arching of neck, the itch of feathers, the eyes contracting. Two white swans stand where Ooglan's brothers stood. They flap their wings. They cry.

"Follow me," Ooglan says, and the swans and all the men follow. The men walk and walk until finally Ooglan points ahead. The sun shines down on a shadowless plain. There is a breeze but no sound or shape of animal. They can hear the women singing.

The white swans fly into the land. The women stop their singing and point to the sky. They run after the white birds while Ooglan and the men raid their camp. They leave a stack of animal pelts but take all the weapons. The women realize what is happening and with a great scream give chase. They have strong legs and they chase the tired men all the way to their land where it is just getting dark. The women will not follow them into darkness. They stand at the edge and argue about whose fault it is that the weapons were stolen. They argue and argue and then they fight. Blood flows and fills the western sky.

The brothers are not used to flying. They grow tired during the chase and rest in a lagoon. Two spirit birds see these strangers there. Spirit world knows how the men raided the women's camp. The spirit birds attack the brothers. They grab them with sharp claws and drop them against the rocks. They pick them up again and carry them across the land, stopping on trees and craggy cliffs to pull at their feathers. White feathers drop to the ground, splattered with blood.

Spirit birds land in a large lagoon where they drop the brothers again and again against the rocks. They swoop down, pluck out more feathers. Suddenly they remember what they were doing when they found these two intruders: delivering a message for spirit women who will be angry at them for forgetting. They fly away, leaving the brothers plucked and bloody. The rocks drip with their blood. The water turns red with it.

The sky goes black. The brothers think it is death. Black feathers spill over them. Hundreds and hundreds of mountain crows shed their feathers onto the brothers' wounded bodies. They no longer shiver in cold pain. They are not dying. Saved by the crows they always thought were their enemies. The white feathers that had been plucked from them take root where they fell, and flower.

Recovered, the black swans fly back to their brother who at first does not recognize them. They have thought often, since being birds, of the lives of men. Ooglan's face is filled with sorrow. He tells them there is nothing he can do for them. Ever since they raided the women's camp his leather pouch holds only stones. The black swans bow their graceful heads. Ooglan tries to comfort them. But he uses the words of men and before he is finished speaking they fly away.

They learn to live as swans. They learn to recognize spirit birds and spirit lagoons. They stay away from both. One day they are gliding in a peaceful lagoon and talking about what happened to them. They are wondering about death. A mountain crow hears their conversation. "I know why there is death," the mountain crow says.

"Spider and Caterpillar sat and had a talk. What should happen when people get so sick that they die? Spider wove a web. Caterpillar ate a leaf. When they each had come to some conclusion they met to share their ideas.

" 'What I think,' said Caterpillar, 'is that when a person dies his body should stay in the cave and rot, only his spirit should rise.'

" 'No, no,' said Spider. 'When a person dies her body should be wrapped in a web with a trap door, and the door closed and left for three days. During this time the person can heal and at the end of three days she would come out, just like a butterfly from a cocoon.'

"They argued and argued about it until, in the end, Caterpillar won.

"So, when people become so very sick that they die, their bodies should stay in the grave and rot, and only their spirits rise."

Without turning to speak further or look at us again, the old Aborigine quietly leaves, following the path the others took. Herrick and Max join me on the porch. "What kind of story was that?" I ask. Max sighs, rubs his eyes, and sits on the step. "We have a problem here."

I look at Herrick who seems to be making a point of not looking at me. "What is that story supposed to mean?"

"Shh." He lifts a hand. We listen to the crash of leaves and twigs. A large gray kangaroo hops into the clearing, quickly followed and encircled by three men pointing guns at it.

"We got him now, mates."

"It'll be kangaroo meat for this night. Good God, will you look at the size of him."

As if any of this could get any stranger, the kangaroo shouts, "Wait! Don't shoot!" The kangaroo skin falls away, costume-like, but releases an un-costumey stench. Out steps a bedraggled man, clothed in rags. "It's jus' me, jus' poor ol' Michael Leary tryin' to get off this devil's land and go to China."

"You'll have China, will you?" The hunters level their guns at this shorter human target. "We should shoot you just the same and roast you tonight for getting us all in appetite for kangaroo meat."

The second hunter spits but maintains his aim. "Ah, but the meat is bad and we would all get the runs."

The third grins as he speaks. "Let's just find out what seven years on the chain does for all your hopping about." With a sweep of the gun he strikes the man in the face. I step forward but Herrick grabs my arm and shakes his head, no. Michael Leary looks at me with sorrowful eyes. The hunters tie his hands, pull him roughly up, and lead him out of the clearing. He moves with downcast head, blood streaming down his face.

"What's happening? Who are all these people?"

Max rubs a trembling hand through his hair. "Did you hear what he called this place, 'devil's land'?"

Herrick paces the porch. "Something's gone wrong."

"That woman."

"Daisy Bates. But she can't be."

"Right. Because Daisy Bates is dead." Max sits, elbows on his knees, rests his forehead in his hands. "I've done something terrible."

"Are you saying they're ghosts?"

"Not ghosts," Herrick says, "more like travelers, lost in time. What did she say about the door?"

"She said, 'You think the door opens only one way?' "

Herrick looks at me, frowns, as if trying to remember something, then shakes his head and turns to Max. "Maybe it has something to do with the way you've been feeling. She also said, 'You bleed, we bleed.' It's almost as though their sorrow got attached to yours."

"Are you saying that these people have come back through time with Max like a burr on his sock?"

"Something like that."

Max rubs his eyes. "I seem to have made a mess of everything."

"You had to do it," I say, "because of Marie."

He shakes his head. "No. I did it for myself. It was a colossal act of selfishness."

Suddenly, I feel a constriction in my chest and throat. The frightening implication is becoming clear. Herrick watches me with a kind, pitying expression. Max does not look at me at all. "You weren't serious, about not going back?"

"I'll never go back there."

"What about Lily?"

He looks at me with watery eyes. "She's dead."

"No!" I want to shake him, but Herrick holds me so I hit him instead, punching his arms until he lets go. "You can't let him do this."

"Annie, I know you're disappointed."

"Disappointed? Disappointed? My daughter is back there, some-where, and she's alive and you think I'm disappointed? Because he's willing to let her die?"

"That's not his choice. Look at him. Think about what hap-pened with Marie. Think about what's happening here; we have an obligation."

"Fuck you and your obligation. My daughter's in danger and he—" I point at Max who remains in his dejected posture on the porch step as if what is happening between Herrick and me has nothing to do with him "—is choosing not to help. Why should she have to die just because he fucked up with Marie?"

"Stop it, Annie."

"What's so goddamn bad about wanting to save my daughter? What's so bad about wanting to save her?"

As if I am an embarrassment, neither of them looks at me. I turn on my heels, scoop up the sleeping bag and book from the porch, and let the door slam behind me as I enter the cabin. I shove clothes and the book into my backpack, checking for the Australian travel guide in the side pocket. It's still there though I am certain it does not have the information I most need. I take a few apples, a brown bag of nuts, fill my Nalgene bottle.

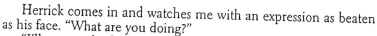

Herrick comes in and watches me with an expression as beaten as his face. "What are you doing?"

"I'll pay you back."

"I don't care about that. Where do you think you're going?"

I screw the cap on the bottle, thrust it into the side pocket, and cinch the pack shut. "I came here for Lily. If you two aren't going to help me find her, I'll do it alone."

"You don't know what you're doing."

"I know. The wild dogs, the snakes."

"The convicts. Do you know what's happening here? This island once was a penal colony and it's a penal colony again. You don't understand what you're getting into."

I stand, adjust the weight of the pack on my shoulders, strap it at the hips and chest. When Lily was little I used to carry her in something like this. I stare into Herrick's brown eyes, the earnest expression of his confused face. "You can just quit acting like you're above all this human drama because I know you aren't." There is no mistaking the effect. His mouth drops open. He steps back. "You just stay right here, in this world you've created, where there's no risk you'll ever get hurt by the messy implications of people, but I'm leaving."

His eyes narrow. "Right. You're right. But just remember, you're not leaving to go immerse yourself in human life, you're chasing the dead."

I think I hate him. He steps back as I pass. I slam out the door. Max still sits like a statue of a weeping man. I can think of nothing to say to him as I walk past. I hear the door open and Herrick step out onto the porch behind me. Dawn lights the sky and trees with gold. I go to the path I've taken twice before, not certain where it will lead me now. The path is overgrown, the smells strange, less floral, more loamy. An animal growls. A bird cries. I hear Max say, "Where does she think she's going?"

"She says she's doing it alone."

"Have you told her yet?"

Though I strain to hear his reply, either Herrick doesn't answer or I've walked out of earshot. I readjust the pack and look for signs of those who have passed before me. It's true, I don't know what I'm doing, but I've lived my life with plans, only to find out I didn't know what I was doing then either. Now I follow the curve of mountain as if the land can tell me what the mind will not. Like the brothers who turn into swans, that's how I feel. As if some magic has made me a different creature. As if I have sprouted wings or at least let go of my self and become a part of everything else.

At each crack of noise I think of the large-pawed tracks I came across early this morning. I can't escape the feeling of being stalked. I follow a patch of sun through a thinning of the green until the frightening forest is behind me, though the feeling of being watched remains.

Is there such a thing as fear of paranoia? In all the excitement of Max's return I haven't enjoyed the freedom from the burden I'd been carrying (more heavily than I realized) of doubting my own sanity. Even now I can't enjoy it for fear that this feeling of being watched is symptomatic. Why am I worried about this? After all, Max did see Lily alive.

At the sound of voices, I back into the brush and crouch behind a large boulder. A sort of rickshaw cart of people pulled by four bedraggled men slows to a stop in the clearing. The passengers, two women dressed in Victorian fashion with large hats and raised parasols and two men in full suits, talk about the heat. The men who pulled the cart do not speak as sweat drips down their tired faces. The male passengers excuse themselves and head in my direction.

"Did you hear that?"

There is a moment's silence punctuated by a kookaburra's laugh.

"Are you trying to scare me?"

"I thought I heard something, one of those damn savages."

"Nobody hears them. That's why they're so hard to catch. They're like ghosts."

"Not here, they can see us." They are so close I'm afraid even my breathing is too loud. I hold my breath and close my eyes to the streaming sound and dank smell of urine.

"What do you think of this railroad system?"

"It doesn't sit right with me and that's a fact, using men like this, even if they are convicts."

"Mrs. Vallory says it's unchristian."

"I don't know about that. There's nothing in the Bible about it. But I don't like it. If there was any other way—"

"If there was any other way, we would both take it. In the meantime we best get back. I don't like leaving the women too long with them."

"It's going to be a real scorcher, don't you think?"

The women greet the men as the rickshaw creaks to adjust to their weight. Then, slowly continues on its way.

It's easily the hottest day since I've arrived. By noon (I'm guessing, using my old Girl Scout knowledge of the sun) I'm sweating and exhausted. I feel like a grown woman suffering the consequences of a temper tantrum. Herrick was right. I don't know what I'm doing here, or exactly what I'm looking for. None of this seems to be bringing me any closer to Lily. Yet this confusion of past and present is something, isn't it?

"I canna figga yeh out."

The voice startles me so much, I jump. Standing behind me is a short man dressed in raggedy patched clothes. His burnished face grins a smile of missing and poor teeth, a bulbous, red nose, and small, dark eyes. He looks up at me, then rakes a look across my body, tips his tattered hat, "Ma'm."

"Who are you?"

"Ah, in't that intrestin' I was jus' about ter ask the same question. What I figga is yeh in't a convict. None of them dress like yeh. No, yeh're more like one of them 'brigines. 'Cept yeh in't a darkie. Some kinna forrner, s'what I'm guessin'."

"You're a convict?"

"I'm goin' ter take a risk here since I've been followin' yeh now fer while an' I see yeh don' wan no one to catch yeh neither. Lawrence P. O'Toole, recently 'scaped."

"Mister O'Toole."

"Jus' call me Larry. Feel most like I knows yeh."

"Well, while you've been spending the day following me, I didn't even know you existed until now and I—"

"Must be quite a place, where yeh come from. Gets a man to wondrin'. Are yeh all mixed up underneath them clothes? Me cousin saw one like that once and he nevah got it outta his head. He use ter have these dreams—"

I pivot on my heels and walk away. Incredibly, the annoying little man follows.

"My 'pologies. I jus' got ter ramblin' back there, ma'm, don' pay it no mind."

I turn and plow into him. He's just a little guy, barely up to my chest. For a moment his small, dirty hands brace against the backpack then fumble at my waist. I push him back. "Go away," I say, as though he's a pesty fly, "I don't want to go anywhere with you."

"As yeh say," he tips his hat and smiles gap-toothed amiably. "Jus' thought yeh is one of them time travelers in need of some 'sistance."

"Wait."

"I won' botha yeh no more, ma'm, I'll jus' be on me way."

"Please stop." He turns, looks at me, one gray, wild eyebrow cocked. "What do you know about time traveling?"

"I know how ter gets yeh where yeh wanna go."

"What do you want?"

"I wanna go with yeh."

"If you know all about this, what do you need me for?"

"Now that *is* confusin', in't it?" He takes off his cap and wipes his bald head. "Best I can figga, s'got summat ter do with me commin' from me time, an' yeh in yeh'rs, an' us bein' togetha."

"You mean, because you're basically a ghost?"

For a moment I see what Lawrence P. O'Toole's face looks like unmasked of his usual countenance, maybe even a touch of the expression he wore as a child. Shock, fear, and a sort of incredulous innocence are quickly replaced by the cocky grin. "Well, there's those who'd say yeh was the spook."

I don't like this man, this little troll, but he knows something about all of this. "Okay. What do we do?"

He licks his lip. "This kinna travel can wear a fellow or—" he looks me over with a frown "—whatever, out."

I definitely don't like him but he is hungry and I have food. We share the water and nuts. I give him an apple which he eats whole, right through the core. As he wipes his dripping chin with the back of his hand I once again ask him how we begin. He scrunches up his face like a moldering jack-o'-lantern. "Well now, I gotta allow as how I got me concerns 'bout this mission."

"Oh?"

"Yes, ma'm." He scratches his stubbly chin with small, dirty fingers. "I do." He nods. "Most certainly do." He leans back against a tree, every bit the picture of a man about to take a long, afternoon nap.

"Actually," I cinch my pack shut, "I'm having my doubts too. Maybe we should just part here."

He sits up so quickly he almost falls over. "Now, that in't a wise decision a'tall. Yeh shouldna be movin' about these parts alone. Yeh needs me protection."

I look down at him and laugh.

"Yeh don' know what's out there, ma'm. Yeh don' know what this place is like. I been here fifteen years, if they catches us now, this will be our grave an' I hate ter think of your spirit trappt in such a evil place."

"Fifteen years? A murderer?" I cannot be talking to him. I cannot take his help. I cannot be indebted to a murderer.

"No ma'm, I in't that kin' a'tall. I'm a pickpocket," he says proudly. "S'might more respectable." He reaches into his pocket and pulls out my wallet, tosses it to me.

"How did you . . . ?" Lawrence P. O'Toole grins up at me proudly, shrugs his shoulders and blushes. "Fifteen years for pickpocketing?"

"Well, first I got sev'n and then sev'n on the chain once I tried ter 'scape and then 'nother ten 'cause I was blig'rent though I tries ter 'splain that I don' mean no disrispect, it's jus' me nature."

"How bad is this place?"

He leans close. I bend to hear his hushed voice. His breath has the sour odor of sickness. "Ma'm, this is the devil's land." He speaks with a hiss. A speck of saliva lands next to my mouth. I wipe it away as I stand to full height. "The devil lives here sure as me name is Lawrence P. O'Toole. I seen him."

"You've seen him?"

"Yes, ma'm. I seen him in the ahys of men who whip a man fer stealin' bread when he is hungry. I seen him ridin' the railroad they gots here. I seen his shadow on the women's faces that in't got no heart left an' I seen his babes who cry fer hunger an' love and don' get 'nough of neither.

"Trust me, ma'm, yeh don' wanna be walkin' these hills alone an' allum askin' ter do yeh this favor, is that yeh behave honrable ter me and when we gets ter the place where we make our 'scape, yeh don' forget who got yeh there."

"Listen, I'm trying to go to a time in my past, but it would be years into the future for you. You'll be lost there."

He scrunches up his lips, nods. "Well, I 'bout set meself ter the idea of a new life. This one ain't worked fer me so well."

"Okay, O'Toole, it's a deal."

He shrugs as if, oh well, what choice does he really have and begins walking. Of course I hesitate. But my options are thin and my chance for success without any help seems bleak, so I follow him. When we pass a distant farmhouse he tells me to stay low. "They all convict run, but they turn yeh in jus' like yeh was a wanderin' cow. They even turn their own brothers in. S'a dismal thin' how men will treat each other in their mis'ry."

The day seems endless. The sun beats us with relentless heat. O'Toole points to a dark spot in the distance. "There's the penal colony, I don' nevah wanna see it from this distance, I don' nevah wanna see it agin."

You can't fake pain like this. Whatever else he is or has been I recognize the suffering. Not the typical suburban suffering of wanting a new car, a more beautiful face, but the truly deep suffering, that loss of faith in the basic decency of human life.

It is evening, the sky a sandy shade, when he points to a clearing. Even though we have taken all day to arrive here, it reminds me so much of Loma's place that I expect to see her house. Instead there is the pitched shape of a tent. "There it is," he says, "yeh're ticket home, an' me ticket ter freedom."

The simple tent forms a solitary space against the vast horizon. I glance at O'Toole. He kneels down, signals for me to do the same. He stares ahead, with an expression I cannot define other than by my own feelings. Freedom? Home? Once, I thought I knew what those words meant.

A small figure emerges from the tent. It's that odd woman, Bates. Was it only last night she spoke to us? She stands beside the tent in her Victorian outfit, facing the setting sun. "Her?" I ask O'Toole. He nods.

"Daisy Bates. Some say she's a witch. I don' know nothin' 'bout that but she in't one of us, that's fer sure."

Daisy Bates, a small figure against the evening sky, raises her arm. For a moment I think she is waving to the setting sun but then I see the dark figures cresting the horizon, as though they have come out of the earth, walking toward her.

"The Aborigines."

"Yeh, she in't scared of them and they in't scared of her."

"O'Toole, I've met her. I don't know if she'll help us. I don't think she likes me."

"What's that got ter do with it? Yeh don't like me. I in't sure I like yeh. S'bout need, that's what."

"I don't know how she needs us."

"Well that's what we gotta fin' out." He jabs the air between us with an instructive, dirty finger. "Like I always say, firsts yeh got ter fin' the pocket. Then yeh dicide how ter gets inside."

The small group of Aborigines approaches Daisy Bates. It appears to be a happy greeting. Children run and play while the adults begin building a fire. It has all the feeling of a party.

Two little girls run down the hill holding hands and laughing, and then, like the sudden spark of fire that lights the evening dark, my heart ignites. Lily runs behind them in her fairy dress-up dress, the gauzy wings bouncing on her back. "Wait," she calls, "wait for me." I stand, my arms open.

"Trucannini!" Immediately she is gone. The two little Aborigine girls stop and turn to the woman who stands at the top of the hill, calling. The girls walk hand in hand up the hill.

O'Toole stares at me, his mouth hung open. "O'Toole, did you just see something strange?"

He grins his lopsided, yellow smile, wipes his eyes. "I must be more tired than I realized. I guess I dozed fer a minute there." He shakes his head. "I dreamt I was lookin' right at yeh and yeh dis'peared."

"I disappeared?"

"I'm over tired, that's what it is." Then, as if to prove his point, he lies down, pulls his hat over his face, and rolls over onto his side.

Lily was here. Alive. But now there is only the little Aborigine girls, the woman at the top of the hill. I turn around, lean against my backpack.

Thousands of stars dot the vast sky. O'Toole lays flat on the ground, snoring lightly. On the hill I see the fire, the tent, and by the light of the fire, dancers. I hear drums and a strange humming noise. In the silhouettes I once again think I see a little girl with wings.

When I wake, the sun is bright and I face the spear of an angry-looking Aborigine man who taps the point lightly against my shoulder, as if to convince me that it is sharp.

"What the—"

He speaks, short quick words that I don't understand.

"O'Toole?" I'm careful to keep my voice soft. If all I have by way of communication with this spear-carrying man is the timbre of my voice I want to sound unthreatening. He jabs O'Toole who wakes with a flurry of arms and legs. The Aborigine steps back. O'Toole whistles between his teeth.

"What should we do?" I ask.

"Might be time ter make amends with yeh're maker."

The Aborigine thrusts the spear toward O'Toole's chest, which causes him to jump so high, he almost impales himself.

"We're friends," I say, desperately borrowing from every western movie I can remember from my childhood. His black eyes stare from under lowered brow. "Daisy Bates?" I say.

He lowers the spear and lifts his chin as he maintains that hunter's stare.

"Daisy Bates," I say again, encouraged.

"Kabbarli."

"What's that mean?"

"He could be tellin' us we're gonna die," O'Toole offers.

The Aborigine turns and begins to walk up the hill. He stops, looks at me, then continues.

"I think we should follow him." I scramble to my feet.

"Well, ma'm, I think I should stay right here," says O'Toole, " 'case you need rescuin'."

"O'Toole," I say as I shoulder my pack, "if I needed rescuing you would run so fast—"

"Ma'm, yeh misjudge me summat terr'ble."

I don't bother to look back. The Aborigine does not look back either.

Daisy Bates comes out of her tent wearing a long, black skirt, her feet laced in little buttonhook shoes. She wears a white blouse with a black tie and a white hat with a black ribbon. She greets the Aborigine. They speak softly.

"Miss Bates," I say, offering my hand.

She looks at it as if it were a fish. "What are you doing here? Do you know what will happen to my work if white people are here?"

"I'm sorry. I'm looking for my daughter."

"You think she's with the Aborigines?"

"No. Yes. Maybe. She's from a different time. Last night I saw her. But I don't know, that might have been a dream. I'm not sure. I think the Aborigines know how to get there."

"To this dream?"

"To this different time."

"Where are you from?"

"The United States. The future."

"Tell me," she says earnestly, "what will happen to my people?"

"Are you English?"

"No, no. My Aborigines. Tell me what happens to them."

I shift, remembering the sad account in the travel book. "Maybe it's better not to know."

She bows her head. When she looks up her eyes are bright with held tears. "I know it anyway. I feel it. I tell them to stay away from the white people. But they have no language for it. They do not yet know how poorly people can treat each other. Tell me what happens so I do not waver from my purpose."

We stand in front of her tent, the sky wide behind us, a group of Aborigines laughing and talking, children running, the two of us, she, strangely Victorian, and me, in what must appear an odd costume, facing each other across time, as though there is no time, only two women in some odd way united by our separate quests for the people we love.

"The Aborigines lose more and more of their hunting grounds to farms. The Europeans won't share the land so the Aborigines fight for it. They kill shepherds and sheep. Then the farmers abduct the Aborigine children, rape and torture the women, and give poisoned flour to tribes. Eventually, the governor gives soldiers the right to shoot on sight any aboriginal person found in a European settlement. The Aborigines are resettled on Flinders Island to be civilized and taught Christianity. They die of despair, homesickness, poor food, and disease."

She stands, staring into the distance, her face almost as white as her dress.

"Maybe I shouldn't have told you."

"You must be eager to freshen up."

I bring my pack into the tent. The small, hot space is furnished simply with a cot, a large metal box that I guess is where she stores her food, a table covered with papers weighted by stones, a typewriter, a blue willow cup and saucer, a mirror. Cloth pockets are fitted around the sides of the table. One pocket bulges with the heavy shape of a gun. Underneath the table is an open suitcase filled with white gloves, black ties, skirts. Next to it stands a small table on which rests a porcelain bowl, a pitcher of water.

I undress in the musty heat, using my bandanna as a washcloth. How can she tolerate all that clothing? I put on clean underpants, shorts, a T-shirt. My feet are sore and filthy. I wash them last, immediately sliding into the pleasure of clean socks, and regretfully, the heavy hiking boots. Then I dump the dirty water, return the bowl, and get two apples from my pack, one which I give to Daisy. She holds it like it's a thing of wonder, gently brushing it with her thumb, looks at me, then places it carefully on the flat rock by the side of the fire.

The Aborigines are nowhere to be seen.

"Mrs. Bates."

"No. My name is Kabbarli."

"Kabbarli, I need your help."

"Yes. I can see that. We will make a trade. I will help you and you will help me." I nod. If she'll help me, I'll do anything. "You must stop the carnage."

"But it's already happened."

"I understand. I do not know how to help you either."

"Please. She was only six years old." Daisy Kabbarli nods. I know she understands, in the way I understood her earlier, how much pain there is, though I don't weep. "I can't stop it but I can help. Something has happened to you. You are lost. You and your Aborigines. You're all trapped in this sorrow. Like an endless dream."

She chuckles softly.

"You have to try and understand."

"Oh, I understand." She tries to stifle her laugh with a delicate hand. "We are in a dream?"

"Yes."

"And you will wake us?"

I nod.

"When you wake us from the dream," she says, "where will you be?"

I open my mouth, shut it.

The sound of her laugh is bright and clear in the vast silence that surrounds us.

There's no way to approach this tent during the day without being seen. I wave at the small figure trudging up the hill. "Who is this?" Daisy Kabbarli asks.

"Lawrence P. O'Toole."

He nods as he approaches, grinning his yellow smile.

"A convict," she says.

"Top o' the mornin'," he says brightly, tipping his hat, eyeing the pan of rice. His chin is dark with stubble, his wrinkles lined with dust. The tip of his thick tongue runs along the edge of his lips.

"Would you like a drink?"

"Don' mind if I do." He sits down beside me. I hand him my cup. He drinks the precious water noisily, like a thirsty dog. "Well now," he looks longingly at the pot of rice cooling on a rock. "If yeh don' mind I'll jus' help yeh finish this off as well." He reaches into the pot and scoops up a handful of rice with his dirty fingers. With a scowl Daisy Kabbarli rises and goes to her tent.

O'Toole watches her leave. "Not the friendliest sort, yeh're probela glad fer me company. Summat troublin' yeh, ma'm?"

"I have to talk to her."

"Oh yeah, sure." He continues scooping rice with his fingers while his pliable face scrunches up like a wet rag.

"I have to make arrangements to leave. Do you still want to come along?"

He stops scooping rice and stares straight ahead. "Oh yeah, I gotta go."

"You sound sad."

He nods, shrugs, scoops up another handful of rice.

"But this place has caused you so much pain."

"Oh sure, summat terr'ble pain. But I don't s'pect ter get way from that by leavin'."

"I thought that's why you want to leave."

He stops in midscoop. "Yeh mus' be jokin', I guess. I know no matta where I go there's gonna be sufferin'. It's the human condition. What I figga is all I get ter choose is what kinna sufferin' it is, and, ma'm, I'm jus' so weary of this partic'lar load." He continues scooping rice into his mouth, his cheeks bulging like an autumn squirrel until he realizes I'm watching him. He looks up at me, eyes wide, eyebrows raised. I nod. He's right, of course. He grins and rice falls from his mouth and lands on his chest. He picks it up and puts it back into his mouth. I turn to the tent, "Kabbarli."

"Who is it?" she says, as if she receives a dozen callers a day.

"It's me, can I come in?"

"Yes, I think you should."

She sits in the middle of her simple bed in a silk camisole and slip, her long hair hanging down her back. She holds open in her lap, my copy of Max's book. My backpack, beside her bed, with clothes tumbling out of the various pockets, has obviously been rifled through. I open my mouth to protest but she looks up at me with teary eyes. "I know this girl. She was just here last night." She points at the title: *Trucannini, Queen of the Aborigines.* I remember the two little girls running down the hill, that odd moment when I thought I saw Lily, the women's voice breaking the spell, calling, *Trucannini.*

"A queen?"

"Read it," she thrusts the book at me.

I sit across from her on the bed and begin to read.

"No. Out loud."

"You don't have to know this."

"These are my people, my family."

"It might only bring you sadness."

"That is why you must read it to me, so I may weep."

Trucannini, Queen of the Aborigines

Her first memory is of stars. Her father holds her over his head into the great black sky. It is a memory of floating, held by the night like a star, and it is a memory of love. She comes to it often because the next one is so horrible. A different night filled with screams. She runs and crouches behind a large boulder. It is cold and creviced like the sky, not with stars, but with small holes. In the dark she sees the terrifying white faces of the dead and the frightened black faces of her family. She hears her mother call, "Trucannini." She stands. She is so small she is hidden by the rock. Her mother sees her and opens her arms but the white faces and white hands slash the night sky with silver blades, and red blood. Her mother falls. Trucannini crouches behind the rock, places her small hand against the cold granite, and presses until it hurts. She looks at the stars. Now her mother is one of them. A sharp point of light she cannot reach.

Her family is much smaller after the death raid. They walk days and sleep nights, being careful to stay away from the place where the land holds so much sorrow. One day Soonyan sits before Trucannini's father. He hands her the small wooden cup. She holds it close to the dried grass. He spins the rod inside the cup until the grass bursts into flames. Soonyan and her father look into each other's eyes. Trucannini now has a new mother.

Trucannini remembers playing with her sisters by the river, finding a nest of honey ants, the delicious taste popping in her mouth. She remembers lily roots and long yams. She remembers the fear slithering away from her like a lizard. It does not go far. It crouches nearby and watches.

John Baker comes with his boat of white men. Her family prepares a feast for them. Food for the lost dead to journey home. They eat, then pull the women by the hair into the dust and carry them to their boats. When it is all over Trucannini has lost three sisters and her new mother.

They walk and walk and do not return to their places of sorrow. They are careful never to speak the names of the dead. They scream, and cry, and weep to try to leave the sadness which can hold the dead to them, like stinking corpses. Even so, her father cannot seem to walk away from the sadness and Trucannini accepts the return of the lizard fear, a permanent clawing in her chest.

Trucannini is small for her age but she is not really so young anymore. Woolary begins to walk beside her. Woolary is from a different tribe. He has not known all this sorrow. He draws pictures in the sand and tells her stories.

Trucannini likes Woolary's stories and his sand drawings. She agrees to marry him. One day she must cross to Bruny Island with Woolary and his two brothers. They must ride in a boat with the white dead that seem everywhere now, so many that the land seems made of bones. When they are far out on the water the white men throw Woolary and his brothers overboard. Woolary and Silva hang on to the side of the boat. The white men chop off their hands and they sink in a swirl of red from which Woolary rises, raising his bloody stumps, and calling out her name, "Trucannini, Trucannini." Until at last he sinks into the red and does not rise again.

The white men row to shore where they push her to the sand and enter her body with their violence. It is then she notices. Even the sky is almost white. The white men leave. Other white men come. She learns to recognize the sealers' boats. They learn to recognize her small figure on the shore. Death enters her and becomes so much a part of her that they call her a new name. Whore.

She has been among them long enough to understand what he is saying when the white man called Robinson asks her to come with him. They will go to other tribes. Her people. He brings the healing stick of a shaman named Jesus. She will help them understand. It is no use to fight the white laws. Death is everywhere and Jesus loves them. He gives her tea and sugar but does not touch her. He calls her Trucannini. She goes with him.

The journey is long. She grows tired in the heavy drape of clothes he insists she wear. When she sees her first tribes after so many years she notices how naked they are, how useless the spears, how unprotected the women. They exchange gifts and share a feast.

Robinson carries a book so thin it can be torn in the wind and a strange stick that seems filled with endless paint. Writing, he tells her, taking notes. She looks at what he draws but it is ugly and she cannot understand his fascination with it. She remembers Woolary's sand drawings. She looks at Robinson again. He takes notes and takes notes and takes notes. This dead one, she thinks, is not like the rest. He is not dangerous. Only stupid.

They are taken to Flinders Island, given clothes, new names. Robinson hands each of them something he calls the Bible. It is filled with pages as ugly as the ones he makes but he tells them it is an important totem. Over and over he says to Trucannini the words, "Jesus. God. Property." She does not understand and only translates, "He says to take this."

Trucannini watches the tribal people die in ways she has never seen before.

"Disease," says Robinson.

One night she is awoken by the sound of her name. "Trucannini," the voice shouts. For a moment she is confused. She remembers her mother's voice and Woolary's voice. This is an old man's voice. "Trucannini." The voice calls across the darkness. It is Grandfather Billy. He has the disease. She sits up. "Trucannini," he says loudly, "you have brought us great harm. You said we would be safe. But we are dying. We thought you were one of us." He coughs. Trucannini feels heat rise through her skin. She remembers this old way, complaining into the dark. "Trucannini, you led us here," Grandfather Billy shouts, "and made us wear new names and heavy cloth and death. Trucannini, your brothers and sisters cry when they say your name. I am happy to die and go to them. I am happy to leave you, Trucannini."

Trucannini lies very still, as if any movement will stir him to speak again. But he does not speak. In the morning he is dead.

None of them say anything about the night before but the hot feeling will not leave her body. She wonders if this is the beginning of disease. "What was all that shouting about?" Robinson asks.

"Old man dying," she says.

She tries to explain to Robinson that they must leave. He looks up from taking notes and smiles. "This is your home now," he says, "you don't have to keep running." The sorrow fills them with more disease. They are dying. No one repeats what Grandfather Billy said but with each death she hears it. "I am happy to leave you, Trucannini."

One day Robinson leaves too. "I want to go home," he says. "I miss my people." He does not take Trucannini. She is not his people. When he leaves, other men come. They call the remaining tribes prisoners and they change the island name to jail. They do not take notes. The people are dying so fast now Trucannini knows they are all happy to leave her. When there are only so many left as will fill a single boat they are taken away from the jail. Trucannini thinks they finally understand. Who could live on land filled with so much sorrow? But the new land is no better. They are given huts and told to call them home. They are given straw hats. If they stand for the flashing bulbs called photographs they are given meat, sugar, and rum. Trucannini is the last of the island women. William Lane, the last island man. They are married. All the others are from some place else. The young Aborigines do not even know how to dig lily roots or catch honey ants. They do nothing but sit in front of their huts and talk nonsense all day.

William's death is fast and silent. He dies with his eyes closed. Trucannini thinks this is because he cannot look at her face. Grandfather Billy was right. She kneels next to William and weeps. All her people are gone now. They have left her here, alone, with the walking dead. The white men called doctors take his body. She understands they think it is valuable somehow. "No, no," she cries, "his people wait for him."

"What's she talking about?" one of the doctors asks.

"Too much rum," says the other. They laugh.

They all want the body of the last island Aborigine man. They take him to a cold building. Trucannini follows but they ignore her. She is the last island Aborigine woman but she is still alive so what use is she to them? They put William's body in the cold building. Trucannini can see them through a window. They wave their arms; their faces stretched like masks. When they finally leave, they each walk in separate directions.

Trucannini squats on the little hill behind the building. No one notices her. She has not forgotten how to sit still and empty her mind so that no one sees her. The afternoon drifts to gray evening. The night sky deepens around her. One of the doctors returns. He creeps and looks over his shoulder in such an obvious manner she almost laughs. He rattles keys in his hands and mutters as he opens the door.

She sees a small light in the window. She walks on quiet feet so she can better observe. Trucannini is an old woman now. She has seen much horror in her life. But this is the worst. The doctor has a large knife. He saws like a man with wood. He cuts off William's head. Trucannini feels her body heave as though her insides do not want to be inside of her anymore. She heaves and clutches her stomach. Her body gives up its food in a splash of greens and browns. The stench rises and she lifts her face to the sky. The stars shine there the same as they always have, the ancestors, watching.

In the morning the other doctors are furious. They chop off William's hands and feet. Now, no one will ever have the entire corpse of the last island Aborigine man. He is buried in the pieces that remain.

The first doctor wraps the stolen skull in sealskin. He takes it on the ship for the long journey home. But it is a secret so it is not identified. When the stink begins to fill the whole ship with nausea, one of the sailors throws the skull overboard. The doctor is disappointed. The whole trip has been a waste of time and money. He can't wait to get back to civilization.

White people come to look at Trucannini. Some take notes, just like Robinson. She is afraid to die and be cut up, her spirit trapped here. She is afraid to die and go to her people. Afraid of their anger. Afraid they will not take her. When she falls into fever the old lizard fear rests on her chest. "Don't let them cut me," she says to the priest as he waves his Jesus stick. The lizard grows until it is as big as her chest and its weight presses against her breath. "She is dead," says the priest.

Huge crowds line the pavement to see the funeral of the last island Aborigine. The small coffin rolls by and is lowered to the grave. The crowds do not know that it is empty. The officials have to consider her value. Trucannini's body is placed in a vault in the chapel at the cemetery.

Years later, students slough the flesh off her bones, and boil them. Trucannini's bones are strung together like a marionette or an odd wind chime. They hang where the winds never touch them, behind glass; the constant light highlights them for the tourists.

At last this is against fashion and she is buried in the black earth. A simple marker is placed at her grave, inscribed, *Trucannini, Queen of the Aborigines*. It is an important tourist attraction, proving the white man's point, that what is precious must be preserved.

"Oh the lady she is, oh the lady she'll be, oh the lady, my lady, come lay down with me." O'Toole sings loud and off key. Daisy Kabbarli looks at me as if I am to blame for everything.

"I'm sorry."

"Oh lady, oh lady ooh lady love me," his voice rises to an unexplored pitch.

Daisy Kabbarli wipes her eyes, sniffs. "You have to make him leave."

He stops singing.

"No. I can't. They'll beat him, lock him up in chains."

She looks up at me with cold, gray eyes. "I have a son I haven't seen for years. Once, I thought I saw him, but that didn't make sense because he would have waved. I'll help you find your daughter, but you must help me."

"Oooh me and me mates are drinkin' one night."

She acknowledges O'Toole's song with the expression of someone who has just tasted something sour. "I find that you are a woman of loyalty."

I nod.

"I ask for your promise that you will make sure this story of the Aborigines is told, that your people will know the future."

"But in the time I come from, this has already happened."

"Here's your first lesson," she says as she pins up her long hair. "Throw a stone in water and watch all the circles that form. Time is like that."

"Still, there's an order to that, a beginning."

She slips into a white blouse. "Oh? What's the beginning?"

"The moment the stone hits the water."

"What is the stone? What is the pond? What are you? If the stone hitting the water is the beginning, what is everything else?"

"But we're talking about how to measure time. I thought it was all contained in the pond."

"Why do you think that?" she rises, picks up a black skirt and, raising her arms, glides into it then cinches a belt around her tiny waist.

"Oooh, three thousand miles from me bonny lass, three thousand miles from the shape of her—"

"Why don't you take these buckets—" she points to several stacked neatly near the tent door flap "—and go fill them at the stream."

Like a dutiful school child I pick up the buckets.

"Think about it," she says, "why didn't you include yourself?"

"Because I wasn't standing in the pond."

"Now you are starting to understand."

"What do you mean?"

"You placed yourself outside time. That's your first lesson." She nods toward O'Toole's bad singing. "Take him with you."

I pull back the tent flap, bucket handles hooked in my fingers, and clatter over to O'Toole who lies beside the fire embers, his hat low on his face, singing loudly. I lightly tap the sole of his shoe with my boot. He stops singing, lifts his hat off his face. "Come on, bring that pan and those plates. We've got dishes to do." He grins a yellow-gapped smile. "I think you might want to be more quiet; remember, you're still a wanted man."

"Yeh're right," he says. "I've been awful careless this mornin'. Happy I am, I gots me freedom back. I 'spect yeh're right though, I near lost me head over it."

As we walk to the stream, O'Toole continues grinning at me. "What?" I finally ask.

"I heard what yeh said."

"About?"

He grins and shakes his head, then, suddenly, removes his hat and clutches it against his chest. "Yeh're a true friend, that's fer fact. Yeh kept yeh're word an' I want yeh ter know that yeh got me friendship fer life." He puts his hat back on and continues walking, my new and loyal friend, singing softly.

She is burying the dead. Red sand. Red sun. She digs graves in her Victorian dress, the yellowed white of bones. Aborigines rise from the earth the color of mud and dirt, as if formed in the earth's center. They rise and fall into her frail arms. She shares her tea and flour. She nurses their burning skin. They look at her with red-rimmed eyes and speak in the language she is beginning to understand. *You are one of us. Returned.*

The stars spin. The night sky is filled with the dead. Her nails are black with dirt. There is a gentle breeze. She dances with Breaker Morant, that old criminal, oh, but he could say a poem! He holds her so close she must pull away.

She is feverish in her tent. Restless in her sleep. She thinks she sees her son, but no. She is standing before an audience of men, telling them the Aborigines need land, freedom. They stare at her as if she is incomprehensible. But no. She is burying dead Aborigines. The sky is bloody with setting sun. The earth is filled with sorrow song. The blade digs in. The mourners keen. The sun bleeds. She is as thin as a skeleton. She is dying. Alone. In a hospital room. The sharp-cornered walls pierce her.

"Who are you reading about now?"

I shut the book. Daisy Kabbarli looks down at me and I try to make my face innocent but I think she knows. She glances at the book then says it's time to go. O'Toole is not invited.

"I don' know if this is such a good idea," he says, "don' get me wrong, I trust yeh, it's her that's got me worried. I gotta get off this island an' I don' wanna be left agin like me mate who I 'scaped with did to me."

"You escaped with someone?"

"Michael Leary. Said he had a perfect plan, summat 'bout a kang'roo skin and I in't seen him sincet."

"Oh, I'm sorry, I saw him. He was caught." O'Toole turns away. "Are you going to be all right?"

He shrugs, shakes his head. When he turns to face me he has tears in his eyes. "I don' know as we can trust her, ma'm, an' let me tell yeh, I in't goin' back there, shovlin' coal fer the devil. An' I don' know if I feel so safe sittin' here like this."

"Like a bird in its nest!" Daisy calls from the tent.

O'Toole leans over to whisper, "She don' like me. How do we know she in't settin' me up ter be captured?"

"Listen, O'Toole, you were right, she needs us. She'll keep us safe."

"Uh-uh, she needs yeh. She don' need me."

Daisy Kabbarli comes out of her tent, her outfit accented with a bright flowered hat.

" 'Scuse me, ma'm," says O'Toole, "but what'm I spose ter do if any of them 'brigines shows up?"

"That won't happen."

He nods. "And how can yeh be so certin', ma'm, if yeh don' min' me askin'?"

"Because I won't be here."

"Listen, O'Toole," I say quickly because she is already walking away, "I know she's not polite but that doesn't mean she's cruel."

"I don' trust her."

"Sometimes you just have to risk it, you know like how you risked it with me. We can't do this alone."

"Don' ferget me, ma'm."

"I won't forget you. I wouldn't be here if it weren't for you."

He nods and then I surprise us both by lifting his hat and kissing the top of his bald head. He looks up at me in amazement. "Nobody done nothin' like that to me, sincet me own motha."

I run to catch up with Daisy Kabbarli who does not turn to look at me but says, "You should be careful about giving him the wrong impression."

"He's been a good friend to me."

"Don't be naïve. That kind doesn't know friendship. Remember Breaker Morant? He was so charming but he was still a criminal, all lies, twisted to sound like poetry."

Her first husband, according to the story I just read. I decide to veer away from this uncertain subject. "Think of him like your son. Imagine your son in some foreign land; wouldn't you want someone to be kind to him?"

"I don't know what you're talking about. I don't have a son."

"But you said—" I stop in midsentence; cut cold by the look she gives me, an icy expression that actually makes me shiver. Maybe

O'Toole is right. Who is this woman? Can she be trusted? I steal a glance at her hard profile. There was a time when I felt I knew who I could trust, who I couldn't, when I knew what was true, real, right. I squint through the bright sunlight at my surroundings. Though I walk on land and see land all around me I feel as uncertain as if even the ground is no longer solid.

What if Lily's death did put me over the edge? What if, even as I think I walk these unsteady hills beside an Emily-Dickinson-in-Australia character, I'm really in some white room, sitting in some straight chair, staring blankly through reality to here. What if—

"You should be emptying your mind. Put your thought in the rocks and trees."

Oh, wouldn't that be nice? That rock over there holds all my fears. That tree is everything I know and wonder about Daisy Kabbarli. That stone is David and all the pain of our marriage. That green grass is Lily. No. I glance at Kabbarli.

"You must let everything go."

"It's all I have of her."

"It's all you will ever have if you don't empty your mind."

That grass is Lily. But it isn't. Not really. It is impossible to put her there. To make her anything other than alive is unacceptable.

We walk and walk. This small island seems endless. Kabbarli walks beside me, almost ghostly in her white, apparently not touched by dust or exhaustion, or thirst. I lick my lips. I had no idea we would walk so far.

Kabbarli stops and raises her arms to the endless blaze of sun. She tilts her head back and sings a wordless song. I watch her, hot, thirsty, and irritated. She stops singing and turns to me.

"If two Aborigines from different tribes meet, and one sings, the other can join in the song, even if they've never met before, even if they don't know each other's language. The song belongs to everyone. But you must understand, no one owns it and no one has the whole song.

"All the earth is covered in this song. From desert, to valley, to mountains, to cities. The song lines cover the land. It is one song, but many voices.

"The song is a map. When you hear it, you can hear the creation, the past, the future, the timeless, the dreaming."

Kabbarli watches me closely. "What do you hear?" Her voice, a distant echo beneath the sound. I turn, and turn, trying to find her until I am so dizzy I stop. "What do you see?" Again that voice, insistent.

I squint through all the colors, the waves of light and shadow. "I'm underwater."

"You're in a cave."

Immediately a heavy darkness surrounds me. The air is cool and dank. "Where are you?" I'm surprised to hear the tenor of fear in my voice. "Mrs. Bates? Kabbarli?"

A small flame ignites on the ground and flickers a golden light. Standing beside it is the old Aborigine, his black eyes locked, like a man asleep with his eyes open. Dressed in bones and shells, his face and body painted with swirls and stripes. He holds, upright at his side, a long spear. He does not blink or turn his head or acknowledge me in any way, even when I say hello to him.

The cave walls are covered with paintings. Dots of color and light, nothing outlined, framed, or shaped, and yet, it all reminds me of something. The more I look, the more the dots spin and drone that deep humming noise. Where is Kabbarli? The thought rises and is gone. These paintings. I'm sucked into them. Color, light, shadow, song. I'm color. Light. Shadow. Song.

With a scream the cave explodes with activity. A dance of masked men and women surrounds me. Dark naked bodies move snakelike in the flickering light. A hand reaches up and tears at my shirt. Hands brush my skin with painted feathers. I dance around the fire. The masked men. The lean lined bodies. Feathers lift my arms and brush my face. The light flickers. The song deepens. The dance swirls through the paintings of color. Light. Shadow.

Pain. Pierces my heart. I gasp and see only the old Aborigine man, his spear red with blood. Blood trickles down my breast. I sink to the ground with sudden exhaustion. Alone. The flame goes out.

Kneeling beside me, playing in the dirt, in her favorite purple dress-up dress with wings of a fairy, angel, or butterfly. "Lily."

"I can't talk to strangers."

"I'm your mother."

"You're not my mother."

"Oh, honey, I've changed, but I've been looking for you a long, long time."

She cries. She is sitting in her bed wailing, pointing at me. The bedroom door opens and I see how it is. My pretty blonde curls, my naïve face. "Honey, what is it, what's wrong? Did you have a bad dream?"

She cries and points at me in the shadows. "Monster," she says. I close my eyes. When I open them, I am alone on the cold cave floor. A dim light reveals the entrance. There are no Aborigines, no paintings. I'm naked. Marked in swirls of paint. A swell of scabbed skin over my chest where I was cut.

I rise slowly. The world tilts. My head aches. I find my clothes. I tie the shirt to cover my breasts. The shorts are not as badly torn. I walk out of the cave, shield my eyes. Everything is brighter, surrounded by light and song like the paintings. How had I ever seen the world as sharp planes of mute color when it's formed by dots of light, shadow, and song?

I don't know where Kabbarli is or how to return to the tent. But I hear O'Toole singing. I follow the sound. When I finally see the tent, O'Toole sitting beside it singing softly, I know that his voice did not carry all that distance. Yet, somehow I heard him. Next to him sits Herrick, and it looks like his arms are tied behind his back. The tent flap opens. Kabbarli comes out in her white dress and buttonhook shoes. Shading her eyes, she looks in my direction and raises her arm in greeting, just the way she raised it to the Aborigines.

O'Toole stops singing and squints but I know he doesn't see me yet. Herrick looks at Kabbarli, then at O'Toole. I must hurry. If I mean to keep my word to O'Toole I must get to him soon. I run.

I've forgotten about my appearance until I see the strange expressions of my friends as I approach. O'Toole's jaw drops open and remains there. Herrick displays a similar countenance. Only Kabbarli, in her long, white dress, seems unshaken. She watches me with wise, gray eyes, a faint smile on her lips.

"My God," Herrick says, "you look like some B-movie character."

I look down at my skin, swirled with paint, lined with colors, my breasts covered, bralike, by the ripped T-shirt.

O'Toole turns away. Kabbarli looks at me directly, tilts her chin up slightly. I do the same.

"I'm glad you're here," Herrick says, "tell them I'm your friend."

I turn slowly to look at him. It's as if I move against ether. In the periphery of my vision darkness creeps in, tunnel-like. He looks up at me with a crooked smile as he twists in the ropes. I hear myself speak as though from a distance. "O'Toole, untie him, we're leaving." O'Toole stares at me with bulging eyes. "Hurry." He unties Herrick who rubs his wrists and stands up slowly.

"If it's all the same, m'am, I'll jus' stay behind," O'Toole says.

The tunnel creeps closer, the noise increases. "What are you talking about?" I shout. They all step back with surprised expressions. "You begged me to take you."

"All the same, m'am," O'Toole says, wide-eyed and spinning his cap in his hands, "I think yeh've gone crazy or yeh may be a ghost."

The darkness folds in with a rush of noise so deafening I scream. I grab O'Toole's wrist. He yells as he tries to twist it free. Just before it all turns to black he grabs Herrick. Dark. Cold. Noise. Silence.

Light. Shadow. Light. The metallic screech. The press of bodies. "Nice getup, sista."

"Jesus, Mother Mary," O'Toole's says, "is it always this fast?"

Herrick turns to me. "I never wanted to come back here."

"Whoa, check this out." A group of teenage boys pushes through our little group. Someone whistles.

"Excuse me," I say to a seated woman who looks at me with raised eyebrows, her mouth agape, "what time is it?"

She looks at her watch, then quickly up. "Eleven forty-eight."

"Morning or night?"

She pulls her face in as though trying to get as far away from me as possible in this tight space. "Morning."

"The date, what's the date?"

Her large eyes look from Herrick to O'Toole and then past them, darting back and forth. "August fifteenth."

"What year?" She presses her lips in a firm line, stands, and hurriedly walks past, holding her shoulders in so she doesn't touch any of us. "Just tell me the year," I shout, "that's all I want! I just want to know the year!"

Strange eyes, all downcast. At last, a woman's voice from somewhere in the back. "Nineteen ninety-two."

"Thank you." How ridiculous is this? Griffith Connor walks unhindered with his dangerous packages and I can't even get anyone to tell me the date. I turn to Herrick. "This is the day."

"Nineteen ninety-two," he says, his face pale.

"Jesus, Mary, Joseph." O'Toole shakes his head. "Nineteen ninety-two."

"Come on. We get off here."

"I never heard no one so excited about the year as that group." A smattering of laughter. O'Toole almost gets left behind because he stands in the doorway, wide-eyed. Herrick pulls him at the last minute and the train speeds away.

"Holy Jesus," says O'Toole, "are all time travel machines so fast?"

"It's not a time travel machine," says Herrick, "it's the subway, just regular transportation in 1992."

"Jesus, Jesus, Jesus." O'Toole makes the sign of the cross.

"Hey, babe, like the look."

I remember myself in the cave, naked, painted, unembarrassed. Here, men stare or make noise about my clothes, my body.

"What time does it happen?"

"Three twenty-six. But it won't happen *today*." I point to a women's bathroom and walk toward it.

"What's she talkin' 'bout?" O'Toole asks.

Herrick looks at me. I shrug my shoulders. Nod. It's a story living its last hours. As I walk into the bathroom I hear him say, "Her six-year-old daughter was shot and killed by a sniper, a man with a gun. . . ."

No, I think as I turn on the water, it's August 15, 1992. It's a little before noon. I have a daughter, and she is alive. I wash my arms, my legs, my stomach, my face. The paint swirls ochre down the drain. It's 1992 and there are still paper towels in the world. I dry myself with the rough paper, retie my shirt. I can't still the beating of my heart, the trembling in my hands. She is alive. I throw the paper towels toward the trashcan and hurry out. I walk right past Herrick and O'Toole who take little running steps to catch up to me.

"Awful sorry ter hear 'bout yeh're little girl, ma'm."

I spin on my heels. "There's nothing to be sorry about."

"Annie, you need to calm down."

I keep walking. They can follow or stay behind. I don't care.

"I don' mean no insult, ma'm, I hope yeh knows."

"Don't worry," says Herrick, "she's just going through a lot of emotions right now."

"Oh, yeah, I undastan'. Yeh know I in't never gonna see no one I know agin."

"Are you sorry?"

"Yeah. Yeah, I am. I'm feelin' powaful sadness, but that don' mean it wan't the right thin' ter do."

"It's a lot to lose."

" 'S a lot ter lose and a lot ter gain."

We emerge into the bright sunshine of a summer day. Herrick is trying to explain the city, and the century, to O'Toole who is amazed that we just came out of the "center of the earth" as he calls it. He's frightened of the cars and tall buildings. I've only been thinking of our destination, The Blue Diner. When I see the corner ahead, I gasp.

"What is it?"

"She's gonna faint, get the salts!"

The light changes. All around me people cross the street, hurrying past with the blank expression of watching a not particularly good TV show. I cannot move. I look up at the tall building across the street. "That's where he stood."

The newspaper accounts that pieced together Griffith Connor's last day could not account for his movements after he left home at around 11:00 in the morning until he entered the Wise Building at approximately 3:15 P.M. dressed in a UPS uniform (never returned after he quit his job there, or was fired, depending on which "unidentifiable" source was quoted). The receptionist (memorable from her brief stint on the now-canceled soap opera, a role I always believed was created for her by the fame she garnered from my daughter's death) saw him and waved him past (another stroke of criminal luck) because she and the security guard were distracted by a strange woman who, in spite of countless tips and rumors, was never accounted for. The receptionist noted the time because she had a date that night and was hoping that the dress she'd ordered would arrive that day, but the man she assumed was from UPS (He was dressed like one, right? And he carried packages. Later, she felt horrible of course, especially about the little girl, though it was all so horrible, the worst thing that ever happened to her.) walked past to one of the elevators and she glanced at her watch and it was exactly 3:15. She decided she would leave early, so she'd have time to check out some of the shops, but then, of course, at 3:26 everyone's plans changed.

Except for Griffith Connor, a man with a plan that worked. Police found several candy bar wrappers and one half-eaten Snickers bar on the ground beside him. They believed the homeless man had surprised Connor on the roof and was his first victim; Marie, his second; Lily, his third.

"Let's just cross over there," Herrick says.

The light changes. I tremble as we cross the street. Herrick gently guides my elbow. O'Toole's dirty face is lined with pity. "Stop it, both of you. This is a happy day."

"Did yeh ever think of the poss'bility, ma'm, that yeh little girl in't goin' ter wanna leave with yeh?"

"What are you still doing here? I kept my bargain, didn't I? You're free now. Go away."

O'Toole's face turns into the shocked and hurt expression of a wrongly scolded child.

"O'Toole." I reach to touch him but he steps back.

"Jus' wanted ter be sure yeh is okay, ma'm, before I go off. Seein' as how yeh've been so good ter me. Fact is I'm quite—" his wide eyes dart back and forth "—'cited ter get to know me new life."

"Please, don't go."

"Now, ma'm, yeh got yeh're suitor here—" he nods to Herrick "—and yeh're daughter is watin' fer yeh. Me, I gotta start 'splorin' me new life. Don' be sad now, ma'm, we knew this time would come."

"O'Toole—"

He tips his hat and walks into the crowd, a short, ragged-looking man. Herrick follows and stops him. I vacillate between thinking this is the right thing to do and being irritated by the delay. O'Toole maintains that stuck-out chin, stubborn expression. He looks up at Herrick, listens, then speaks shortly, and continues on his way.

Herrick comes back, shaking his head. "He says he's more thankful than he can ever show you."

"Is he going to be all right?"

"I don't know. He might be fine. He's a survivor."

"I wasn't always like this, Herrick. I just want her back."

"Come on," he says, "don't lose courage now."

We walk in silence the rest of the way to The Blue Diner. I press my hands against the large, front window and try to peer inside but all I see is my own reflection. "Have you thought about what happens next?" Herrick asks.

"I'm going to save her."

"You realize you can't just go in there and take her."

"She's my daughter."

"Annie, you have to think about this. You probably get one chance here. What do you think will happen if you just go in there and grab her?"

"I don't care. I don't care if I go to jail forever. I just want her alive."

"Yeah, but if you do try to take her, you won't get out the door,

and then the police will come and if they arrest you, Lily and her
mom could still leave on time, they could still end up on that
corner."

"I have to see her. I have to do something."

"Okay, then. Let's just go in, sit at the counter, okay? Then we'll
figure out the next step."

We enter the diner, which is decorated with an eclectic assortment of blue. Prints from Picasso's blue period hang next to photographs of blues singers and blue suede shoes. Lush spider plants
hang from the ceiling. Waitresses hurry past carrying large, blue
trays. We walk to the counter and sit facing a large mirror that
reflects the restaurant behind us. I immediately search the crowd,
confused by memory, or the mirror, where exactly to look. Someone puts two menus down on the counter. Herrick speaks and there
is a woman's voice, our waitress I guess, but I don't listen to either
of them. I study the mirror hungrily. Then, just as the Louis Arm-
strong song comes on, I see her.

Her dark braids bounce slightly as she speaks. She lifts her arms
and gestures widely. I swivel on my seat and for a moment panic
rises in the confusion before I find her again. There. Sitting in her
purple, sleeveless dress and talking. Alive, alive, alive! I strain to
hear her words but they are trapped in the din of voices, dishes
clanking, and Louis singing what is absolutely true, what a wonderful, wonderful world.

"Where?" Herrick says.

I point. He follows the line and then, gently, presses my hand
down. "Remember, you don't want to call attention to yourself."

I nod.

"She's lovely."

"Oh, yes."

"Is that you?"

I am reluctant to move my eyes from Lily. There I am, in my
neat curly hairdo, my carefully applied makeup.

"You look really different."

I feel an odd jealousy for that woman sitting there with Lily who
eats her hamburger with great determination.

"Can I take your order?"

"I'm sorry," says Herrick, "we're having some trouble deciding."

The waitress says she'll check with us in a little while. I stand
up. Herrick grabs my arm. Lily laughs. "Let go," I hiss.

"Do you want to come all this way just to blow it now?" he whispers.

"I'm not going to make it any worse, Herrick. Give me a break. I came here to save her."

Herrick releases his grasp. They are standing now, walking away from the table. I follow them to the back of the restaurant, into the women's bathroom.

From beneath one of the stall doors I see the shoes I remember wearing that day, and in the next stall, the dangling feet in dirty white sandals, the chipped pink toenails. How could I have forgotten that detail? Lily and me sitting side by side, cotton between our toes. Her toilet flushes. The door opens.

"Honey, stay in here until I come out," calls the voice of a woman who thinks she can prevent danger.

Lily stands so close, I could touch her. She looks up at me, smiles politely, and walks to the sink. She strains over the sink toward the faucet. I could grab her now.

"Lily, wait for me, all right, honey?"

"Okay, Mommy."

I turn the faucet on for her. She smiles at me, rubs her hands under the water, reaches to turn it off. I turn the knob. Herrick's right. If I grab her I won't get anywhere but trouble and they could still be at that corner at 3:26, my chance to save her, lost.

Would it be lost? I wish I understood this time thing better. I wish I knew how to control it. Strange, that while time's potential has increased, I remain uncertain of life's important outcomes.

She walks over to the paper towels, looks up at the too-high lever and then at me with almost adult amusement. I crank the lever, tear off a sheet, and hand it to her, brushing my hand across her fingers. I smile, a soft smile, meant to reassure her. She studies my face seriously and does not smile back.

The toilet flushes. I step into the empty stall, close the door behind me.

"Wash your hands, Lily."

"I already did. That lady helped me."

I hear the bathroom door open, shut. Silence. I cannot contain the tears. They roll down my face and cheeks, taste salty on my lips. I want to collapse in a heap on the bathroom floor. I want to tear my hair out. I want to pierce myself with spears and make my whole body a sorrow mark. But she still needs me.

I walk out of the stall. Splash my face with cold water. Look at my reflection in the mirror. What stares back at me is a woman who has discovered just how much she can lose.

When I come out of the bathroom, their table is being cleared and they are gone. Herrick stands up. He sees everything in my face. He opens his arms and I lean into him, comforted by the warm embrace. His shirt holds the smell of the island. He touches my hair. I step back. We stand for a moment looking at each other before I turn away.

"What do you want to do now?"

"I want to stop the shooting."

"Do you know what that means, if you succeed?"

"It means I'll never be here. David and I will stay married, at least for a while. His new baby won't be born, I guess. He'll make pleasant conversation with the woman who in a different reality would be his wife. I'll never fly to Australia, meet Daisy Bates, Lawrence P. O'Toole, or you." For just the briefest moment there is that tunnel feeling. I see me sitting at a desk, writing. In the distance a man's voice, a child's laugh. The tunnel evaporates. "It means today won't be the last day of her life."

Herrick puts a hand on my elbow. "Let's go then."

The afternoon heat is sudden and bright after the air-conditioned diner; the blare of concrete and traffic, the noise of hurried people, disorienting. I think of the quiet island, the green.

"Where now? The rooftop?"

"No, not yet. We have time, I think. I don't completely understand time anymore. It seems like it exists and it doesn't. What about you? Isn't there someone you want to see?"

"I don't know what good it'll do."

"You might never get another chance."

He nods and begins walking. We walk the few blocks in silence until he stops in front of an art gallery. I follow the direction of his gaze to where she sits at a desk, doing paperwork, her long, dark hair hiding her face. A man walks to the desk. She looks up and smiles. Herrick gasps.

I turn to him but the expression on his face is so private I turn away. Is that an Aborigine man, here in New York? "Herrick." The Aborigine seems to be walking in our direction but not getting any closer. "Herrick."

Suddenly there's the rushing noise, the dark tunneling feeling. I grab Herrick by the wrist. "Make it stop," I scream. He looks at me, helplessly, and we are sucked into the tunnel again.

From darkness, a sense of loss and wandering, I come to awareness in what appears to be someone's apartment. Dark wood, oriental carpets, a table set in silver and lace, white candles. This isn't possible. I haven't come all this way to end up in some strange apartment. Where is Lily?

Herrick stands beside me, his face, wrenched in agony.

"Herrick—"

"Shh," he whispers, "we can't let them hear us."

The place smells of thyme, sage, the savory scent of Thanksgiving. The walls are covered with paintings and sketches. I recognize Herrick's work, though these are more like the gentle landscapes I had seen at Loma's house. There are also photographs. The beautiful woman from the art gallery, in a sweater and jeans, her hair blowing, ocean waves behind her. In some of the photographs there's a man who looks a lot like Herrick. A brother? A handsome, perfect face. A beautiful couple.

We stand at the edge of a brightly lit hall, which I guess, from sound and smell, leads to the kitchen. Where are we? Where is Lily? How can we get back to her? There is the sound of a woman's voice, the low murmuring of a man's reply, laughter. Herrick looks at me with tears in his eyes.

"What?" I whisper. What is happening to us? What are we doing here? What is causing you such pain? What can I do to help? What does any of this mean? What is happening to Lily?

Herrick takes me by the elbow. With a glance at the large glass doors that frame a cold, gray sky, he opens a closet, reaches in for two heavy coats. The doorbell rings. He hesitates. Turns to the glass doors, takes my hand, leads me out onto the porch where we crouch behind the skeleton of a couch, the pillows removed for this snowy season. He hands me the coat, which I eagerly slip into. It's a beautiful blue cashmere wraparound, a little tight in the shoulders, sleeves way too long. He puts on the other one; a gray-specked black wool coat that fits him perfectly.

From this position we can see into the pretty room, softly lit by candles and golden light. The man enters, carrying a silver nut bowl, which he places on the coffee table in front of the couch, and salt and pepper shakers, which he places hurriedly on the dining table. He moves out of the picture, I assume to the front door. We stare into the perfect room, shivering against the cold.

"Herrick, I have to find Lily. I can't be here right now."

Herrick continues to stare at the scene before us. "Don't you get it?" he says. "Lily is still there. She's always there."

"But how can I find her?"

"You're not going to start believing we're stuck in time now, are you?" he says.

The woman comes into the room, smiling. The man returns, carrying a winter coat. He goes to the closet. I turn to Herrick.

"Don't worry," he says, "nobody notices these missing."

"How do you . . ." but I don't finish the question. I gasp when she enters the room, smiling, years younger, in neat curls and a flowing dress, big jewelry. "Loma. What is she doing here?"

She hands the man a bottle of wine, says something. He smiles, kisses her on the cheek. She goes to the younger woman. They hug.

"Herrick?"

He turns to me reluctantly. Tears glisten in his eyes. "Her mother." The man leaves the room and returns with a young couple, another bottle of wine, and flowers. Coats are removed, hugs and kisses exchanged. "Bill and Mary," Herrick murmurs.

"Are you coming to this?" I say.

Slowly he turns to me. "I thought you understood." He points at the handsome man who stands with his arm around the beautiful woman. "That's me," he says.

"But—"

"Before the accident."

He is serving drinks. She leaves the room. The others chat happily. She returns, goes to the stereo. Through the glass I hear strains of Bach. They sit at the far side of the room. She drinks from a wine-

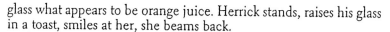

glass what appears to be orange juice. Herrick stands, raises his glass in a toast, smiles at her, she beams back.

"To eternal happiness," says Herrick at my side, providing sound for our silent picture, "as it is increased and multiplied." He lowers the glass. Bill and Mary sip from theirs but Loma stands and looks at her daughter. She speaks.

"You're pregnant?" says Herrick.

She nods.

Bill and Mary put down their glasses. They stand too. Bill pats Herrick on the back. Mary hugs her, but her eyes remain on her mother who stands staring, her mouth open. Finally, she closes her mouth in a firm and resolute line that more closely resembles the woman I know. She bends and kisses her daughter on the cheek.

"I think I'm going to get a little air," Herrick says as Loma's lips move.

"Herrick, what are we. . . ?" But I don't even finish the sentence because really, what can we do?

She comes out, walks to the balcony, so close I can smell her perfume. "Who's out here?"

"This is going to be a shock. You should know there was an accident. I don't look the same."

She continues looking over the balcony. A pigeon lands on the porch and pecks the barren ground, then flies off. "So," she says, "it's you. I always knew this strange day would come." Still, when she looks down at the two of us, huddled in the dark, she gasps. She touches Herrick's face. "And Nora?" she says.

"Before the accident."

She closes her eyes. "I've always known. This curse." She wraps her arms around herself.

"Here," says Herrick, and starts to take off his coat.

"Stop. Do you want to be seen by everyone?"

"But you see—"

"I've always had the sight, though I must say this particular mode is new. What are you doing here?"

"We've come from the future."

"And her?" she points at me.

"I'm looking for my daughter. Can you help?"

"Nora is going to come out," says Herrick, "you should probably move." She walks to the other side of the porch. The beautiful woman comes out, carrying the older women's coat.

"Mom, please be happy."

"Oh, sweetie, I am."

Nora smiles. "I was afraid you knew something."

Loma hugs her daughter; her bracelets jingle. "Oh, my dear, it's just a mother's worrying."

"Everything's going to be all right," says Nora, "it's the first time I really understood how it is when you get the feeling." She places her hand on her belly. "A boy, strong and healthy."

"When?"

"Spring."

Loma nods.

"I have to make the gravy."

"You go ahead, I'll be just a minute."

She gives her mother a kiss. "I can't believe how lucky I am."

Loma smiles. But when Nora shuts the door she turns and stares over the balcony at the darkening sky. "All my life I've worked on knowing how it ends, and not letting that ruin the joy. But this is the hardest. I would never deny her this joy. I've learned to live like this and I finally realized it's not really so different from everyone else. People don't give themselves enough credit for this, that in spite of the inevitable death, we continue to believe in life."

The door opens. "Mrs. Mensford," says Mary, "we're sitting down now."

"I'm coming."

Mary, obviously confused by the fact that she is not coming, nods and shuts the door.

"I have to be quick now. Apparently you've discovered the time thing, or it's discovered you. I don't completely understand it and judging by the two of you, huddled on the porch, you obviously have your own confusion about the subject too.

"It has something to do with perception. You've broken through; it shouldn't be so hard to do it again. Just don't try. That can get in the way. I think."

The door opens. "Mom?"

"Here I come. You know, I do so love silence. Sometimes I think I'm a reincarnated monk."

"Either that or a Sherpa. Jeez, Mom, it's cold out here."

The door clicks shut. We watch them sit for Thanksgiving dinner, the turkey decorated with a string of cranberries, dishes of steaming food. They hold hands and bow their heads for grace

"Do you still love her?"

"Oh, yes, of course"

I close my eyes.

"I've finally learned," says Herrick, "that I can love her completely and still have room to love someone else completely too."

I open my eyes to see him watching me. He smiles that crooked, half-stopped smile.

"Tell me what you want," he says.

"I want this. I want happiness."

"And Lily?"

"I have to try. Even though I don't know what all the ramifications are, I have to try to save her. She's the reason I'm here. I realize how much I've changed, how frightened she would be of me. I don't know how this all works; just when I think I understand it I realize I don't. Sort of like my whole life actually.

"You know, when I started all this I just wanted her back. But now I think I have to accept that I'll never have her. I mean, what happens to me if I save her? If she doesn't die that day, then I . . . the way I am now, never happens. In a way I think that's too bad because the other me, the mother she knew, was sleepwalking through life. But I have to try. For her, and really for the world. I really think the world lost something very special when it lost her. Don't you feel the same way, about your life, about Nora?"

"I do; I want, well, not this." He points at the room. "That's not me anymore. But I want my own version of it."

"I mean, why don't you feel like you have to save her?"

"My story is different from yours."

The door opens. Loma walks over to us, quickly places two plates of food at our feet. "Here," she hands us forks and knives. From her purse she removes two small bottles of water. "It's the best I could do and I had a dickens of a time with even this. I'm afraid I'm only increasing my strange reputation tonight."

"You said you were feeding the birds," says Herrick.

"So you can chirp. The look *you* gave me when you saw me take the silverware."

Herrick laughs, "Oh God, that's right."

She bends over, looks closely at him. "Really, you are so much more handsome like this. Less pretty. More interesting." She looks at me. "As you know."

"What if we're stuck here?" I ask.

"I doubt it, but if that happens, wait until they're in bed, then you can come to my place. But I don't think that's the way it goes." She turns to Herrick. "I will be changed too, won't I, by all this?"

He nods.

She stands. "Hmm. I guess I was foolish to think this was the final product." She turns her back to us. At the door she stops.

"There will be a baby," she says, "my daughter is right about that." Then she leaves. I turn to Herrick. He shakes his head, no.

Herrick hands me a bottle of water. "It was our first pregnancy. It was very hard on her. She had planned to work almost until the birth but she quit her job in January and that seemed to help for a while. Then, in February she really started to feel terrible. She made an appointment with her doctor. She called me at work.

"I used to be a set designer, you know. I had a studio and I always complained that it wasn't real art but actually I was scared stiff of 'real' art. I had seen what that life had done to some of my friends. Really talented people but not one of them as successful as I was. Back then that was my standard, the measure of my material possessions against theirs.

"Anyway, she called me at the studio. Said she felt terrible and she was afraid she might need to go to the hospital. Later, I realized that I didn't even lock the studio door. In New York City, if you can imagine, thousands of dollars of equipment and nobody discovered it, although after everything, I went in there one day and tore the place apart.

"By the time I got home she had collapsed on the kitchen floor. Unconscious. I called 9-1-1. I held her. I did not know these would be our last moments together and, in all their horror, more peaceful than anything I would experience for a long time.

"The paramedics arrived, bearing a sense of controlled urgency. White uniforms. A stretcher. Strangers asking questions, raising her body, carrying her out the door. I follow them. Neighbors peek from open doors. Someone says something. But it is all a roar. This can't be happening. Yet it is. I get into the ambulance. They make me sit in the front. I don't want to get in their way. I suppose if I could change anything it would be that. I should have been with her, not those strangers.

"The siren wails. It screams. We pull into the parking lot. I rush behind them, and watch helplessly as the doctors and nurses communicate in language I cannot follow. 'You the husband,' someone says, 'sign here.' I sign. They wheel her away from me. 'Let's save the baby,' I hear someone say and my mind reels.

"Someone guides me into a hall. I sit. I don't call anyone.

"When the doctor comes I study her face but I cannot read it. 'Mr. Herrick?' she says, 'your wife suffered a cerebral aneurysm. We could not save her. I'm sorry. Or the baby.'

"I look at her with madness. This is madness. Not in this day and age. Anyone can be saved.

"You know, even to this day, I'm not certain how I got home. Sometimes I think it was a cab. Sometimes I think I walked the whole way. I just can't remember.

"I called no one. There were a few knocks at the door. Neighbors I guess. I didn't answer. The phone rang. I listened to her mother's voice on the answering machine. Ever since she found out about the pregnancy she called every day. Later, Bill called and left a message about some weekend plans. I sat there, pretending. For the rest of that day I pretended that she had only gone out shopping, for a walk, to a movie with friends, that any minute she would come through the door. It was as if I thought I could reverse it all if I only just believed. I didn't go to bed. I don't know if I slept but toward morning, there was this feeling, as though she was in the apartment, in another room.

"I shouted her name, and in the silence that followed, the feeling left. I was alone. I went to the phone. Called Loma. It was only after I hung up that I wept, and then, once I started, I couldn't stop.

"The funeral was . . . I think it was probably beautiful. Loma handled all of it. I used to wonder where she got the strength but now I understand that she knew about all this. She had it planned. The music, everything. Perfect. Horrible."

He takes a sip of water. "Well, you know what I mean.

"For a while everyone was patient with my attitude problem. I was in mourning after all. People expected me to act strange. But there was a point, and I'd have to think hard to remember the timing, when people grew tired of it. Of me. Yes, it was horrible, that was understood, but I had to go on. That's what they said. Bill suggested therapy. But I didn't want that. He accused me of loving the pain. It wasn't true. I just understood that it was mine, and not a community event.

"The only one who really seemed to understand was Loma. You think we could have been a comfort to each other, but there are some things that must be done alone. I don't think anyone could have helped me.

"At night I would lie on the couch—I couldn't sleep in our bed—and imagine creative ways to die. In May a package arrived from an old friend of Nora's who had been out of the country. Through some sort of freak breach in the line of communication she had found out about the pregnancy and not their deaths. It was a little sleeper outfit, a rattle, a blanket. I threw it across the room. Walked out of the apartment, downstairs to the garage. Got into the car. It was a beautiful spring day. I drove to the bridge, pulled over, got out, and stood there.

"I don't know what happened. I think I stood there for a long time. Eventually I understood that I was not going to jump. As great as this grief was, as much as I felt close to death, I wanted to live.

"I wish I could report that it was a joyful feeling but it wasn't. The change was miniscule, but it made all the difference. I got back in the car. Headed home. Not a happier man. Not more at peace. Just more aware of what my choices were, and what I had chosen. I didn't see the other driver veer across the road. I don't remember feeling pain.

"The other driver, he had a heart attack. They say he was dead before our cars crashed.

"I once again suffered a flurry of well-meaning intentions. Doctors, nurses, friends. They could not understand it, when they got my face to this point and I said it was enough.

"The doctors, especially, were insulted. They promised they could make me look better. But I had enough. Besides, this face seemed right.

"It's not, as they said, that I wanted the pity. It's just that my life, well, this is what it is. This is who I am. The incredible thing is everyone was convinced that this was about hating life but really, it's about loving it. For the way it really is. I wouldn't pretend none of this has happened. The other face, the one they kept promising me, was a mask. This is the one that is real."

I don't know what to say. He holds me in his arms, and I guess I fall asleep for a while. When I wake up, the guests inside are putting on coats and hats. Hugging. They leave the room. Herrick returns with Nora and turns off most of the lights. They sit on the couch, she leans against him.

"Talking about the baby," he says. "She is certain she can see our future happiness. The thing is, it's her own body that kills her so how can I change that?"

He caresses her hair. She smiles softly and talks.

"She's picking out names. All boys because she believes we will have a son. She tells me she has seen him in her dreams, a three-year-old playing dress up with purple angel wings."

The didjeridoo's droning noise seeps through the closed room. It is suddenly dark, as though the stars and the lights have all been snuffed out. I reach for Herrick but can't find him. It's so cold. Then I realize. I am traveling.

Why did I ever think that a life where time was no longer con-
strained would be any less random, any less impacted by chance
than the life I'd been living when Lily was shot? Why did I think
I could control this new reality any better than I had controlled
the old one? Had I really thought that the acquisition of timeless
space would be the acquisition of a life without chaos? Had I really
been so naïve?

I am standing on a city street listening to the sidewalk staccato
of clicking shoes and murmured voices, a man walks by carrying a
large boombox pounding out rap lyrics, cars rush past, their windows open, adding to the noise with classical, rock, the loud voices
of disc jockeys, and commercials.

Before me is the building where he stood, raining bullets down
on all of us.

There is a newsstand on the corner and I walk over to it to
check the date, and ask the time. In only minutes, this sunny street
of strangers will be filled with screams and dripped with blood. I am
here again.

I must make a choice. Do I stand and wait for Lily and the
woman I once was? I could stop them long enough. Keep them
from the corner until the shooting starts, at which point they would
be safe, and I could just disappear from my own life, a crazy woman
I would forget about and never recognize. But if I do only that, the
rest will die, maybe even someone else's little girl. If I let that
happen, am I a murderer too?

Sweating in the heavy coat Herrick gave me, I walk toward the
building, that giant tombstone.

Oh, Herrick, where are you now? What is happening? Am I
exchanging one loss for another? Can there really be such a system of balance in the universe? All right then, I'll suffer, but not my
little girl.

I take off the coat and hand it to a homeless woman. She asks me what she's supposed to do with it. I don't stop to answer. I don't have time for conversation.

I open a heavy glass door, then another. The large, air-conditioned foyer is decorated in gray and white with accents of potted palms and a trickling fountain. A young, about to be temporarily famous woman sits at a large desk. She smiles, a pressing of lips and display of teeth. I go to the elevator. She calls me back. I press the button. Who has time to talk to her? "Ma'am, you must sign in!" The security guard, a tall, doughy-looking man in a wrinkled uniform, walks over to me, a bemused smirk on his basset hound face.

Together, we walk to the desk. Should I tell them? If I tell them, will they listen, will they spring to action and save my little girl, and all the rest, or instead keep me here or send me away, call me crazy, or, after the shooting has stopped, arrest me as an accomplice? I'm struck with the realization. Why didn't I realize it sooner? *I'm* the woman. The one who distracts them while he passes by. I grab the edge of the desk. She looks past me, smiles, waves. I turn against the weight of knowledge. He stands at the elevator. Smiles, lifts his long and evil package in salute.

Tell them. Tell them, I think. But this new realization only paralyzes me further. What's the right thing to do? "I'm here to see Winkle, Irin, and Stein." How many times did I read the names of the lawyers who rushed up the stairs first and found him? I should tell them. Will they believe me? It would be a delay at least, long enough for me, Lily, and Marie to walk past, unharmed, unaware of the avoided death. But what if he opens fire here, on us? I glance at the innocent receptionist, the security guard with the sleepy face. Will I get them killed? Am I willing to do that?

"Sign here," one long, red nail points.

I lift the pen with shaking hand. I sign a scrawl of letters. I'll never get away with this. Lily will die again. No.

They have already lost interest. The security guard walks back to the door. I walk to the elevator. Press the button. Hit the button. I must be calm. Where is Herrick? How can there be this amazing thing, a world unlimited by time, and still be death? Why did I ever think it would be otherwise? The door dings open. I walk in. Press the top-floor button. The door closes slowly.

The elevator rises. I should have a plan. I don't have a plan. What will I do? Delay him. Somehow. But what, oh what if this delay happened then, what if it is my own interference that brings us to that corner, at that moment when he shoots?

I would die for her. Yes. I would give up my life for her. That is an easy choice. But what if it is not enough? What if it was not enough then and it is not enough now? What's changed, really? I am here again. She is walking down the sidewalk, holding her mother's hand, talking about cats. She is going to die. No.

The door opens and I run down the carpeted hall toward the red EXIT sign. Will I make it or be swept away before I have done what I came here to do? I push open the door to the stairwell and run up the spiraling steps to the door at the top. It will not open. It doesn't open. On the other side I hear voices. This can't be happening. A shot. With a scream, I push against the panic bar and the door opens into bright sunlight.

He stands at the roof edge in his UPS uniform, candy bar wrappings at his feet. He turns to look at me, his face surprisingly boyish, wide eyes above a small, freckled nose, his sandy-brown hair cowlicked.

"Don't!"

He grins. Raises the gun to his shoulder. Aims at me.

Yes. Me. Not Lily. I close my eyes and open my arms wide, feeling the sun on my face and skin. Yes. Me. The blast of noise, the small moment when I think I am dying, happy to save Lily, and then the horrible realization that I am still standing in the sun, unharmed, alive. I open my eyes. His back to me, he aims over the wall. First shot, the homeless man. There he is, face down, bloody. The second, Marie. The third, "No!" I scream. Third shot. Lily. I scream and scream. Slowly Griffith Connor turns. Still grinning, he lowers the gun. I cover my eyes. The fourth shot. Him.

Screams. From the street below I hear the screams and one of them is mine. I could not save her. I stand here, helpless as I've always been, thinking, *She is dead for all time. She is dead everywhere.*

The homeless man, face down in a bloody pool, groans, and I walk to him, gently roll him over.

"O'Toole."

His breath heaving, he opens his eyes with a flutter, and a labored grin. "Oh, ma'm, I wanted ter do jus' one thin' right in this life."

"Shh. Don't talk."

He coughs. Licks his lips. "I wanted to save her fer yeh."

"Shh. Don't."

He breathes the broken breath of the dying but his eyes open wider and he smiles. "Oh, ma'm, there's yeh're little girl now, in't she a angel?" And then he is gone, and I recoil from the sudden stench, which accompanies the release of body.

Sirens. Blood on my hands and sirens again. Screams and sirens. Pounding on the door. What am I to do? Shouts, the sound of the door opening, and shouting voices, the sound of Herrick, calling me, Lily's voice, talking about cats, Max Von Feehler, reading from his book, and the distant, mournful, droning sound. The tunnel closes, cavelike, around me. It is black, cold. I am traveling.

Black. Cold. Herrick, in his studio, painting violently. Slash. Red. Slash. Blue. I touch his face. He drops the brush.

Lily's white casket, horribly small, draped in roses. Everywhere I look, roses. A children's choir. The young voices raised in angelic song.

A scream. David's earnest face. "Push." Legs spread. The head. The groans. "You're doing great." She bares her teeth. Presses at his command. The baby born in blood and love. David kisses her. She reaches for their son.

Daisy Kabbarli thrashing in a fever, her hair in a sweat, her skin pale and wet. She looks up at me. "What are you doing back here? You promised. You have to tell what you know. You have to. Go away."

Max inside the cabin, writing. Herrick and Loma on the porch. She turns to him. Her mouth opens and shuts. He doesn't notice. She works her jaw like a tired hinge. Swallows. Licks her lips. Makes a noise, a grunt. Herrick turns. She swallows again. Slowly she forms the words. "She's. Coming. Back."

Blue sky. Blue and blue and blue. The heat of sun. The taste of dirt and grass. A fly crawls across my cheek. I brush it away. Alive. I'm alive.

I rise slowly against the aches and pains, uncertain where to go. When I walk I still don't know. The sun blazes hot and I walk and walk until, I see him. I think he's an illusion. He's walking with his head bent. I would call his name but what if it breaks the spell? He looks up. His mouth opens. He is running toward me. I try to run but my legs are confused. When I stumble, he catches me. I hold him tight, my face pressed against his shirt, which smells of paint, the heat of his skin, the island, home. We stay like this for a long time breathing as though our breath is joined, and then we turn. We walk arm in arm. Our pasts walk with us.

Some nights I dream a strange map, its terrain marked by blue meridian lines and green circles measuring the height of sorrow, the rivered depths of despair. Sometimes I dream this map all night long and wake to a sunny morning, confused by where I am, but relieved to have found the way. Other times the endless map tracing is disturbed by the sound of shoveling that buries the dead. I fold the map, rise from the bed, and go to the porch where I listen to the forest sounds; my face turned to the consoling stars.

Sometimes I try to understand it, how time opened up the way it did, how the dead and living were joined in a place I had only been to in my dreams. Max says it was all of us, Peter, Loma, me, and him, having suffered a tragedy that left us, untethered, on this island with the Aborigines who have always known the dreaming.

I used to hope Lily would come to us, the way Daisy did, and Lawrence P. O'Toole, but then I thought of Daisy, forever burying the dead, and O'Toole in eternal fear. I finally accepted that if I held Lily to this world, I held her to eternal suffering. I let her go instead.

Sometimes I think it was a dream, a long nightmare after her death. I wake and go to the porch. I find solace in the night sky. Sometimes Herrick joins me. We stand together, arm in arm, holding hands, or not touching at all. When we go inside we watch her sleeping, our little Daisy, her dark curls matted against her forehead, her pink cheeks and lips, the delicate fabric of her eyelids.

Finally, I let Lily go. I released her to timeless space, no longer confined by the beautiful, but limited, and inevitable aspects of body.

Sometimes, when I stand on the porch and look at the starry sky, I think I hear the island's song; the whales moaning in the ocean, Daisy Kabbarli digging graves, O'Toole's bawdy carols, the Aborigines dreaming, the song of love making, children playing, birth cries, death gasps, the song that both connects, and disconnects us, shared, but never owned, life.

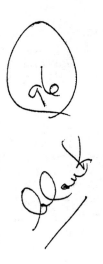

Introduction

I DON'T KNOW HOW THEY COME HERE; AT FIRST I was frightened of them. Some are bleeding. Many are quite young. *What can I do for you?* I'd ask. *Write this down,* they'd say. Or they simply wouldn't respond and stared glumly past me, as if they couldn't see me at all. Sometimes there was no one. I would sit at my desk and stare out the window, or at the blank paper, the sprig of dried lavender in the vase, the whorl-like lines in the wood, the crack of light under the door. I would whisper, *Did I do something wrong?*

Is it possible I missed these wounded spirits, these odd ghosts, these lost travelers? The next day, or the day after that, they would return, clamoring like bells, laughing, bringing butterflies, trailing puddles, laying giant eggs, singing, weeping, fluttering wings, they came from the future, the past, and places I have never been.

I spend each morning with these dark creatures, in the writing cabin Herrick and I built together. Then, after five or six hours, I blow out the candle, straighten my papers, pick up the empty teapot, and close the door behind me. I walk down the path to my family. I am greeted with grins and hugs, or distracted grunts and murmurs; I am welcomed as though joyously returned from a long voyage, or ignored by those absorbed in their own tasks.

I still don't completely understand it, but I know that somewhere in there, between the dark and the light, there is something like a shadow that walks beside me. What I still don't know, what I have finally accepted I may never know, is what casts it. Is it good or bad? Human? Or beast? And what's the difference between these aspects I once considered opposites? The shadow sulks at the edge of the woods. *Don't forget us,* it whispers, in its strange muffled voice, like bees or a broken vacuum cleaner, but soft.

I won't, I say, *I can't. But tell me, who are you? What do you want from me?*

Words, it says.

So I bring them.

Annie Merchant
August 2005

Dreams

◆ ◆ ◆

Dreaming of the Sun

BEFORE WORDS AND BEFORE SUN, THERE WAS darkness. The sky was dark. The world was dark. Everything was dark. One small boy collected bird eggs. He tossed one of those eggs to the ground and it broke open. The bright yellow yolk splattered up to the dark sky. Two spirits were up there. They used the yolk to start a fire. They saw how the people enjoyed the light. They said, "We must really see what we can do to keep giving these people this light. Look how happy they are." They worked hard to keep that fire going. But, after a while, it burned out and once again the world was dark. "What should we do?" they said. "Should we ask the boy to break another egg?" They couldn't think what else to do so they went to the boy to ask him to break another egg. Like everyone else, except bandits and criminals, the boy was sleeping in the dark. They woke him up and said, "Would you go to that tree again and steal the egg and break it so the people can have light?" The boy grumbled and complained and rolled back to sleep but finally he woke up. The boy went back to the tree, stole another egg, and broke it against the ground. The two spirits used the yellow to start another fire. This went on for a long time until there were no more eggs in the bird's nest.

"Well, what did you expect?" the bird said.

They looked everywhere for more eggs to throw against the ground but they could find none.

"You killed all of them," the bird said, and flew away.

The boy was too tired to keep looking for eggs. "I have to go to sleep," he said. "I can't keep looking into empty nests."

The boy went to sleep. The two spirits stood nearby. After a while they saw a dream floating around him. "I know!" one of the spirits said. "We can take a little of his dream and use that to start the fire instead." So that is what they did. They took a little bit of the boy's dream and brought it up to the sky where they started a fire with it. After a while, the spirits learned that they could keep the fire going with anyone's dreams. So that is what they do. Sometimes, if you look into the night sky, you can see the spirits' shadows on the moon as they walk about the earth, collecting dreams for the sun.

◆ ◆ ◆

Leda

I CANNOT CRACK AN EGG WITHOUT THINKING OF her. How could she do this to me, beautiful Leda, how could you do this to me? I begin each day with a three-egg omelet. I hold each fragile orb and think of the swell of her vulva. Then I hit it against the bowl. It breaks. A few shell pieces fall in with the sticky egg white and I chase them around with the tines of a fork and they always seem out of grasp and I think, just like her. But not really. Not ever-graspable Leda.

How do you love a beautiful woman? I thought I knew. I thought my love was enough. My devotion. I remember, when she went through that dragonfly stage and wore dragonfly earrings and we had dragonfly sheets and dragonfly lampshades and dragonfly pajamas, and I was just about sick of dragonflies, did I tell her? Did I say, Leda, I am just about sick of these goddamn dragonflies. No. I said nothing. In fact, I sent away for dragonfly eggs. Eggs, imagine how that mocks me now! I followed the directions carefully and kept them a secret from her, oh it pains my heart to think of what she learned from my gift, I was like a dragonfly mother for Christ's sake. I kept them in pond water. I kept them warm. At last they hatched, or uncocooned, however you'd call it, and still I tended them, secretly, until almost a thousand were born and these I pre-sented to her in a box and when she opened it (quickly or the results might have changed) they flew out, blue and silver, yellow green purple. A thousand dragonflies for her and she looked at me with those violet eyes, and she looked at them as they flitted about and then she said, and I'll never forget this, she said, "They look different from the ones on our pajamas."

Oh Leda! My Leda in the garden bent over the summer roses, in her silk kimono with the dragonflies on it, and nothing underneath, and I come upon her like that, a vision, my wife, and she looks up just then and sees me watching and knows what she is doing when she unties the robe and lets it fall to the ground and then turns, and bends over, to prune the roses! Ha! In the dirt, in the sun, in the night. Always Leda. Always. Except for this.

She comes into the kitchen. Her eyes, black-ringed, her feet bare and swollen, her belly juts out before her. She stands for a moment, just watching me crack eggs, and then she coughs and shuffles over to the coffee maker and pours herself a cup into which she starts spooning heaps of sugar and I try to resist the impulse but I cannot stop myself, after all, didn't I once love her, and I say, "S'not decaf."

I can tell she looks at me with those tired, violet eyes but I refuse to return the courtesy, and with proper wrist action (Oh, what Leda knew about proper wrist action!) whisk the eggs to a froth.

"How many times do I gotta tell you," she says, "it ain't that kinda birth."

I shrug. Well, what would I know about it? A swan, she says. An egg.

*   *   *

Yeah, he did that thing with the dragonflies and I ain't never heard the end of it. "Don't you know how I love you?" he goes. "Don't you remember all them dragonflies?"

Yeah, I remember. I remember dragonflies in the sugar bowl, dragonflies in the honey. I remember dragonflies trapped in the window screens and dragonflies in my hair and on my bare skin with their tiny, sticky legs creeping me out.

What I remember most about the dragonflies is how he didn't get it. He always thinks he has to, you know, improve on me. That's how he loves me. I know that and I've known it for a long time and it didn't matter because he was good in bed, and in the dirt, and on the kitchen table, and I thought we was friends, so what if he didn't really understand? A nice pair of dragonfly earrings, a necklace, that would have been enough. If I wanted bugs I wouldn't of been wearing them. Anyway, that's how I always felt and I didn't care that he's kinda stupid but now I do.

He cracks those eggs like it means something. I'm too tired to try to understand. I pour myself a coffee and he makes a big point of not looking at me and mumbling about how it ain't decaf and I wanta pour the coffee right over his head but I resist the impulse and go sit in the living room in the green recliner that I got cozied up with piles of blankets like a nest and I drink my coffee and watch the birds. My whole body aches. I should leave him. He's failed me so completely. I sip the coffee. I try not to remember. Wings, oh impossible wings. The smell of feathers. The sharp beak. The cry. The pulsing beat. I press my hands against my belly. I should call someone but, after that first night, and that first phone call, I don't have the energy. I've entered a different life. I am no longer beautiful and loved. I am strange and lonely.

Rape hotline.
I . . . I . . .
Okay, take a deep breath.
He . . . he . . .
Yes?
He . . .
Yes?
Raped.
Okay. Okay. I am so sorry. It's good you called. We're here
    to help you. Is he gone?
Yes.
Are you safe?
What?
Is anyone with you?
My husband but . . .
Your husband is with you now?
Yes, but . . .
If you give me your address I can send someone over.
I . . .
Okay, are you crying?
He . . .
Yes?
Raped me.
Your husband?
No, no. He don't believe . . .

I'm sorry, I'm really sorry.
It happened.
I know. I know. Okay, can you give me your address?
A swan.
What?
Horrible.
Did you say swan?
I always thought they was so beautiful.
Swans?
Yes.
What do swans, I mean—
I was just taking a walk in our yard, you know, the moon
    was so pretty tonight and then he flew at me.
The swan?
Oh . . . god . . . yes. It was horrible.
Ma'am, are you saying you were raped by a swan?
Yes. I think I could recognize him in a line up.
Could, could you put your husband on the phone?
He don't believe me.
I would really like to speak to him.
I showed him the feathers, the claw marks. I got red welts
    all over my skin, and bites, and he, do you know what
    he thinks?
Ma'am—
He thinks I cheated on him. He thinks I just made this up.
Ma'am, I think you've called the wrong number. There are
    other help lines.
You don't believe me either.
I believe you've suffered some kind of trauma.
You don't believe a swan raped me, do you?
Ma'am, there are people who can help you.
No, I don't think so. I think everyone loves birds too much.
    Maybe not crows or blue jays 'cause everyone knows
    they steal eggs and peck out the brains of little birds,
    but swans, everyone loves swans, right?
Please, let me give you a different number to call.
No. I don't think so.

Yes, I remember that particular phone call. It's always bothered me.
What really happened to her? Or was it a joke? We do get prank
calls, you know, though I can't imagine how confused someone
must be to think calling a rape hotline could be entertaining. I

mean, after all, if I'm talking to someone who isn't even serious, I'm not available for somebody who might really need my help.

What? Well, no, it wasn't a busy night at all. This isn't New York, for God's sake, we average, maybe, two, three rapes a year.

Well, she said she was raped by a swan. How believable is that? Not very, I can tell you. But I don't know . . . ever since then I've thought I could have handled that call better, you know? I'm a psych major and so I wonder, what really happened? What did the swan symbolize? I mean it's a classically beautiful bird, associated with fairy tales and innocence. Sometimes I wonder, was she really raped?

What? No. Of course I don't mean by a bird. I said a psych major, not a fairy tale believer. I mean, I know what's real and imagined. That's my area of expertise. Women are not raped by birds. But they are raped. Sometimes I wonder if that's what happened, you know, she was raped and it was all so horrible that she lost her mind and grasped this winged symbol of innocence, a swan. I mean let's not be too graphic here, but after all, how big is a swan's penis?

Excuse me? Well, no, of course I don't mean to suggest that the horror of rape is measured by the size of the instrument used. What newspaper did you say you're from again? I think I've answered enough questions anyway. What can you tell me about this girl, I mean, woman?

WOMAN LAYS EGG!

Emergency room physicians were shocked and surprised at the delivery of a twenty-pound egg laid by a woman brought to the hospital by her husband Thursday night.

"She just look pregnant," said H. O. Mckille, an orderly at the hospital. "She didn't look no different from any other pregnant lady except maybe a little more hysterical 'cause she was shouting about the egg coming but nobody paid no attention really. Ladies, when they is in labor say all sorts a things. But then I heard Dr. Stephens saying, call Dr. Hogan, and he says, he's a veterinarian in town and that's when I walked over and got a good look and sure enough, ain't no baby coming out of that lady. It's a egg, for sure. But then Nurse Hiet pulls the curtain shut and I'm just standing there next to the husband and so I says, 'You can go in there, that Nurse Hiet just trying to keep me out. You're the husband, right?' He looked kind of in shock, poor guy, I mean who can blame him, it ain't every day your wife lays a twenty-pound egg."

Hospital officials refuse to comment on rumors that the woman is still a patient in a private room in the hospital, where she sits on her egg except for small periods of time when her husband relieves her.

An anonymous source reports, "None of us are supposed to be talking about it. I could lose my job. But, yeah, she's in there, trying to hatch the thing, and let me tell you something else, she's not too happy of a lady and she wants to go home to do this there but she's getting a lot of attention from the doctors and I'm not sure it's because they care about her. You know what I mean? I mean, remember that sheep that got cloned? Well, this is way more exciting than that, a woman who lays eggs. You ask me, there'll be some pressure for her to do it again. It ain't right really. She's a woman. She's gonna be a mama. She ain't some pet in the zoo. Don't use my name, okay, I need this job."

Sometimes she falls asleep on the egg. My Leda, who used to be so beautiful. Why did this happen to her? Why did it happen to us? I lift her up. She's light again since she's laid that thing. I lay her down on the bed. Her violet eyes flutter open. "My egg," she says, and struggles against me, "my baby."

"Shh," I say, "go to sleep. I'll sit on it," and I do. I sit on this egg, which is still warm from Leda's upside-down heart-shaped ass that I used to cup in my hands and call my favorite valentine, and I think how life seems so strange to me now, all the things I used to know are confused.

Leda sleeps, gently snoring. I readjust my weight. It's rather uncomfortable on the egg. Even in sleep she looks exhausted. I can see the blue of her veins, new lines in her face. I never believed she was raped. By a swan. And now there's this, this impossible thing. Does it mean the whole story was true? If so, I have really failed her. How will I ever make it up to her? If not, if she cuckolded me, an old-fashioned word that seems so appropriate here, then she is making me into a laughingstock. You should hear the guys at work. The women just look at me and don't say anything at all.

I dream of a gun I do not own. I point it in different directions. Sometimes I am a hunter in red and black, stalking swans. Sometimes, I bring the gun to work and spray the office with bullets. Sometimes I point it at a mirror. Sometimes it is Leda's violet eyes I see. She doesn't scream. She doesn't really care about anything now. Except this egg.

*   *   *

He lifts me off the egg and carries me to the bed. "My egg. My baby." I'll sit on it, he says, and he does. I sink into sleep. I dream of feathers falling like snow. The sweep of wings across the sky. The pale white moon. My garden roses closed in the night. The sound of wings. A great white bird. White. I dream white. Silence and emptiness. The inside of an egg. A perfect world.

When I wake up he is still sitting on the egg. "Are you crying?" I say.

"Yes," he says, like it's something noble.

"Get off," I go, "I'll sit on it now."

"Don't you want to know why I'm crying?" he says.

"Get off. I don't want you making the baby sad with all your sad energy, it's had a hard enough beginning already."

"Leda, I'm sorry," he goes.

"Get off!" I shout. "Get off! Get off!"

He stands up.

A bunch of hospital people run into the room.

"Leave us alone!" I shout.

He turns to the hospital people, those tears still on his face but drying up some, and he goes, "We need to be alone."

"No!" I shout. "You go too. Leave me and my baby alone." Then I pick up the egg.

They all gasp.

The egg is very heavy. I hold it close to my chest. "Forget it. I'll leave," I say.

That Nurse Hiet steps toward me but Dr. Hogan, the veterinarian, puts up his hand like a school crossing guard and she stops. "We don't want her to hurt the egg," he says.

Which shows how they don't understand. Hurt the egg? Why would I hurt the egg? My baby. It's not my baby's fault what the father did.

They all take a step back. Even my husband—which just proves, whatever he was loving, ain't about me. It was someone he imagined. Someone mean enough to crush my baby just to make a point.

I hold the egg real close. I am leaving the hospital. I was not prepared for the photographers.

CHICKEN WOMAN ESCAPES HOSPITAL WITH EGG!
EXCLUSIVE PHOTOS!

Well, I thought they were artists or something like that. I was very surprised to learn that he is an insurance salesman. There's not much I can really tell you for certain. Their house is set back,

off the road a bit, and for most of the year it's well hidden by the
foliage. During the winter months I've seen it, from a distance. It
looks cute, bungalowish. I have a friend who knows somebody who
once went to a party there, before they owned it, and she said it was
very charming. The only personal experience I have had with
either of them was a couple of springs ago when I was at Flormine's
Garden Shop and she was there looking at rosebushes. I remember
this so vividly because she was one of the most beautiful women I
have ever seen. She had purple eyes, quite striking really, pale skin,
blonde hair, a stunning figure. Everyone noticed her. When I look
at these photographs, I have a hard time believing this is the same
person. What happened to her? She looks quite frightened, doesn't
she? I can't comment on the egg. I mean it's pretty obvious, isn't it?
I don't know how she fooled the doctors but of course she didn't lay
that egg. She's an ordinary woman. And by all appearances she
needs help. I wish everyone would forget this nonsense and just get
her the help she needs.

When he came home I had to let him in because sometimes I
would get so tired I'd fall asleep and then when I woke up, I was
kind of only half on the egg and half off and so I let him in if he
promised to sit on it and he goes, "Leda, I love you," but I've heard
that before and it don't mean nothing anymore from him. "Leda,
please forgive me," he goes. I say, sit on the egg. I ain't got the
strength to begin forgiving and I don't know if I ever will. I go
upstairs and stare out the window at the garden which is all over-
growed now and I think how sorry just ain't enough.

We just made love, me and him and he fell asleep like he does,
and I thought it would be nice to walk near my roses underneath
that pale, full moon and I put on my dragonfly kimono, it's silk and
it feels so nice against my skin, and it was a beautiful night just a
little bit smelling of roses and I thought I was happy and then that
swan comes swooping down and for just a moment I thought it was
a sign, like of a good thing happening to me 'cause I ain't never
seen a swan in my garden and I ain't never seen one flying and then
it was on top of me. It was much heavier than I ever thought and
when it flew into me I fell to the ground and I couldn't imagine, it
was all feathers and wings and claws and beak and I was hitting it
and trying to get away and also, at the same time feeling like why
would a bird attack me and I didn't wanta hurt it I just wanted out
and then, my god, I felt it, you know, and my mind could not, I
couldn't . . . a swan doing this to me. I hit at it and clawed at it and
it bit me and scratched me and the whole time those wings was

flapping and . . . So now people are making jokes about it, about me. I ain't stupid. I know that. Don't tell me about some lady I never met who feels sorry for me because she don't really believe it happened. I don't give a shit. And when my husband keeps saying, sorry, sorry, what am I supposed to do with that? This happened to me and it was horrible and when I needed him most he was making three-egg omelets and trying to figure out who I cheated on him with. So, he's sorry? Well, what's he gonna do about that? I can't take care of him. It's all I can do to take care of myself and my baby.

Also, one more thing. Since it's truth time. It did occur to me once or twice to break the egg, I mean in the beginning. What will I do if I hatch a swan? Thanksgiving, I guess. Yeah, sometimes I think like that and don't gasp and look away from me. I ain't evil. I'm just a regular woman that something really bad happened to and when it did I learned some things about the world and myself that maybe I'd rather not know. But that don't change it. I stand at the bedroom window and watch my garden dying. What do I believe in now? I don't know.

*   *   *

I don't know what to do for her. I sit on the egg and remember the good times. Leda laughing. Leda in the garden. Leda dancing. Leda naked. Beautiful, beautiful Leda. Beneath me I feel a movement, hear a sound. I sit very still, listen very carefully. There it is again. "Leda!" I shout. "Leda!" She comes running down the stairs. Where'd she get that robe? I didn't even know she owned such a thing. Blue terry cloth, stained with coffee. She stares at me with those dark-rimmed eyes, wide with fright. "What?" she says.

"Baby's coming," I whisper, and slide off the egg.

*   *   *

We stand side by side watching the egg shake. I can hardly breathe. A chip of eggshell falls on the quilt. I find myself praying. Just a general sort of plea. Please.

Please let my baby not be a swan.

He takes my hand. I let him. It is the first human touch other than the doctors and I don't feel like they count, since the night when it happened. It feels strange to be touched. I can feel his pulse, his heat. It feels good and strange. Not bad. I just ain't sure how long I will let it continue.

We watch the egg tremble and crack and I feel like I am standing at the edge of something big, like the white in my dreams.

Everything is here now. All my life. All my love. What comes out of that egg will make me either drown in the white or fly out of it. I wanta fly out of it but I ain't got the strength to do anything about it.

That's when I see a tiny fist.

I pull my hand away from him and cover my mouth. No wings, I pray, please.

A violet eye!

I am standing so still in case if I move we fall into a different reality.

No beak, I think, and just then, like the world was made of what we want, I see the mouth and I start to laugh but I stop because some more eggshell falls off and a second mouth appears right beside the first one and I don't know what that's all about.

Please, I think, please.

*   *   *

I didn't know what to think. I've been pretty ambivalent about the whole egg thing to be honest. I mean, I only sat on it for her. But as soon as it started hatching I felt excited and then kind of nervous. Like, what's happening here? Are we going to have a baby bird? How do I feel about that? I didn't even think about it when I reached over and took her hand. I just did it like we hadn't been having all this trouble and then I realized we were holding hands and I was so happy about that, it distracted me from the egg for a minute.

I think we were both relieved to see the little fist. Of course, I knew we weren't in the clear yet. I mean it was very possible that we were hatching some kind of feathered human, or some such combination.

Could I love the baby? Yes, this thought occurred to me. Could I love this baby from this horrible act? To be honest, I didn't know if I could.

She pulled her hand away. I ached for her immediately. We saw an eye, violet, just like hers, and I thought I could definitely love the baby if it looked like her and then we saw the mouth, and after a moment, another mouth and I thought FREAK. I know I shouldn't have thought it, but I did. I thought, we are going to have this freak for a child.

All these images flashed through my mind of me carrying around this two-mouthed baby, of it growing feathers during puberty, long talks about inner beauty. I had it all figured out. That's when I knew. Even if it had two mouths and feathers, I could love this kid.

I looked at Leda. It was like something momentous had happened to me and she didn't even realize it. She stood there in that old, blue terry cloth robe, with the coffee stains down the front, her hair all a tangle, her violet eyes circled in fright, her face creased with lines, her hands in fists near her mouth and I wanted to tell her, "Shh, don't worry. Everything's going to be all right. It doesn't matter how it looks." But I didn't say anything because I also finally realized I wasn't going to teach her anything about love. Not Leda, who carried this thing, and laid it, and took it away from all those cold and curious doctors and brought it home and sat on it and let her own beauty go untended so she could tend to it. I have nothing to teach her. I have much to learn.

*   *   *

Then I knowed what was happening. When the egg really started to fall apart. Two mouths. Four fists. Four legs. Two heads. And, thank god, two separate, beautiful perfect little girl bodies. Two babies, exhausted and crying. I walked over to them and kneeled down beside them and then I just brushed the eggshell off and that gooey stuff and one of them had violet eyes, and the other looks like my husband I realized that on that night I got pregnant twice. Once by my husband and once by that swan and both babies are beautiful in their own way though I gotta admit the one that looks kinda like me, from before this all happened, will probably grow to be the greater beauty, and for this reason I hold her a little tighter, 'cause I know how hard it can be to be beautiful.

My husband bends over and helps brush the eggshell and gooey stuff off and we carry the babies to the couch and I lay down with them and untie my robe and I can hear my husband gasp, whether for pleasure or sorrow I don't know. My body has changed so much. I lay there, one baby at each breast sucking.

*   *   *

Oh Leda, will you ever forgive me? Will you trust me with our girls? Will I fail them too? Is this what love means? The horrible burden of the damage we do to each other? If only I could have loved you perfectly. Like a god, instead of a human. Forgive me. Let me love you and the children. Please.

She smiles for the first time in months, yawns and closes those beautiful eyes, then opens them wide, a frightened expression on her face. She looks at me, but I'm not sure she sees me, and she says, "swan" or was it "swine"? I can't be sure. I am only certain that I love her, that I will always love her. Leda. Always, always Leda.

In your terry cloth robe with coffee stains, while the girls nap and you do too, the sun bright on the lines of your face; as you walk to the garden, careful and unsure; as you weed around the roses, Leda, I will always love you, Leda in the dirt, Leda in the sun, Leda shading her eyes and looking up at the horrible memory of what was done to you, always Leda, always.

◆ ◆ ◆

Cold Fires

IT WAS SO COLD THAT DAGGERED ICE HUNG from the eaves with dangerous points that broke off and speared the snow in the afternoon sun, only to be formed again the next morning. Snowmobile shops and ski rental stores, filled with brightly polished snowmobiles and helmets and skis and poles and wool knitted caps and mittens with stars stitched on them and down jackets and bright-colored boots, stood frozen at the point of expectation when that first great snow fell on Christmas night and everyone thought that all that was needed for a good winter season was a good winter snow, until the cold reality set in and the employees munched popcorn or played cards in the back room because it was so cold that no one even wanted to go shopping, much less ride a snowmobile. Cars didn't start but heaved and ticked and remained solidly immobile, stalagmites of ice holding them firm. Motorists called Triple A and Triple A's phone lines became so congested that calls were routed to a trucking company in Pennsylvania, where a woman with a very stressed voice answered the calls with the curt suggestion that the caller hang up and dial again.

It was so cold dogs barked to go outside, and immediately barked to come back in, and then barked to go back out again; frustrated dog owners leashed their pets and stood shivering in the snow as shivering dogs lifted icy paws, walking in a kind of Irish dance, spinning in that dog circle thing, trying to find the perfect spot to relieve themselves while dancing high paws to keep from freezing to the ground.

It was so cold birds fell from the sky like tossed rocks, frozen except for their tiny eyes, which focused on the sun as if trying to understand its betrayal.

That night the ice hung so heavy from the power lines that they could no longer maintain the electric arc and the whole state went black, followed within the hour by the breakdown of the phone lines. Many people would have a miserable night but the couple had a wood-burning stove. It crackled with flame that bit the dry and brittle birch and consumed the chill air where even in the house they had been wearing coats and scarves that they removed as the hot aura expanded. It was a good night for soup, heated on the cast-iron stove and scenting the whole house with rosemary and onion; a good night for wine, the bottle of red they bought on their honeymoon and had been saving for a special occasion; and it was a good night to sit by the stove on the floor, their backs resting against the couch pillows, watching the candles flicker in the waves of heat while the house cracked and heaved beneath its thick-iced roof. They decided to tell stories, the sort of stories that only the cold and the fire, the wind and the silent dark combined could make them tell.

"I grew up on an island," she said, "well, you know that. I've already told you about the smell of salt and how it still brings the sea to my breath, how the sound of bathwater can make me weep, how before the birds fell from the sky like thrown rocks, the dark arc of their wings, in certain light, turned white, and how certain tones of metal, a chain being dragged by a car, a heavy pan that clangs against its lid become the sound of ships and boats leaving the harbor. I've already told you all that, but I think you should know that my family is descended from pirates, we are not decent people, everything we own has been stolen, even who we are, my hair for instance, these blonde curls can be traced not to any relatives for they are all dark and swarthy but to the young woman my great-great-grandfather brought home to his wife, intended as a sort of help-mate but apparently quite worthless in the kitchen, though she displayed a certain fondness for anything to do with strawberries, you understand the same fruit I embrace for its short season, oh how they taste of summer, and my youth!

"Now that I have told you this, I may as well tell you the rest. This blonde maid of my great-great-grandfather's house, who could

not sew, or cook, or even garden well but who loved strawberries as
if they gave her life, became quite adept at rejecting any slightly
imperfect fruit. She picked through the bowls that great-great-
Grandmother brought in from the garden and tossed those not
perfectly swollen or those with seeds too coarse to the dogs who ate
them greedily then panted at her feet and became worthless
hunters, so enamored were they with the sweet. Only perfect
berries remained in the white bowl and these she ate with such a
manner of tongue and lips that great-great-Grandfather who came
upon her like that, once by chance and ever after by intention, sitting in the sun at the wooden kitchen table, the dogs slathering at
her feet, sucking strawberries, ordered all the pirates to steal more of
the red fruit, which he traded unreasonably for until he became
quite the laughingstock and the whole family was in ruin.

"But even this was not enough to bring great-great-Grandfather
to his senses and he did what just was not done in those days and
certainly not by a pirate who could take whatever woman he
desired—he divorced great-great-Grandmother and married the
strawberry girl who, it is said, came to her wedding in a wreath of
strawberry ivy, and carried a bouquet of strawberries from which she
plucked, even in the midst of the sacred ceremony, red bulbs of
fruit which she ate so greedily that when it came time to offer her
assent she could only nod and smile bright red lips the color of sin.

"The strawberry season is short and it is said she grew pale and
weak in its waning. Great-great-Grandfather took to the high seas
and had many adventures, raiding boats where he passed the gold
and coffers of jewels, glanced at the most beautiful woman and
glanced away (so that later, after the excitement had passed, these
same women looked into mirrors to see what beauty had been lost),
and went instead, quite eagerly, to the kitchen where he raided the
fruit. He became known as a bit of a kook.

"In the meantime, the villagers began to suspect that the strawberry girl was a witch. She did not appreciate the gravity of her
situation but continued to visit great-great-Grandmother's house as
if the other woman was her own mother and not the woman whose
husband she had stolen. It is said that great-great-Grandmother
sicced the dogs on her but they saw the blonde curls and smelled
her strawberry scent and licked her fingers and toes and came back
to the house with her, tongues hanging out and grinning doggedly
at great-great-Grandmother who, it is said, then turned her back on
the girl who was either so naïve or so cunning that she spoke in a
rush about her husband's long departures, the lonely house on the

hill, the dread of coming winter, a perfect babble of noise and non-sense that was not affected by great-great-Grandmother's cold back until, the villagers said, the enchantment became perfect and she and great-great-Grandmother were seen walking the cragged hills to market days as happy as if they were mother and daughter or two old friends, and perhaps this is where it would have all ended, a confusion of rumor and memory, were it not for the strange appear-ance of the rounded bellies of both women and the shocking news that they both carried great-great-Grandfather's child, which some said was a strange coincidence and others said was some kind of trick.

"Great-great-Grandfather's ship did not return when the others did and the other pirate wives did not offer this strawberry one any condolences. He was a famous seaman, and it was generally agreed that he had not drowned, or crashed his ship at the lure of sirens, but had simply abandoned his witchy wife.

"All that winter great-great-Grandfather's first and second wives grew suspiciously similar bellies, as if size were measured against size to keep an even girth. At long last the strawberry wife took some minor interest in hearth and home and learned to bake bread that great-great-Grandfather's first wife said would be more successfully called crackers, and soup that smelled a bit too ripe but which the dogs seemed to enjoy. During this time great-great-Grandmother grew curls, and her lips, which had always seemed a mastless ship anchored to the plane of her face, became strawberry shaped. By spring when the two were seen together, stomachs returned to corset size, and carrying between them a bald, blue-eyed baby, they were often mistaken for sisters. The villagers even became confused about which was the witch and which, the bewitched.

"About this time, in the midst of a hushed ongoing debate amongst the villagers regarding when to best proceed with the witch burning (after the baby, whose lineage was uncertain, had been weaned seemed the general consensus) great-great-Grandfather returned and brought with him a shipload of strawberries. The heavy scent drove the dogs wild. Great-great-Grandfather drove the villagers mad with strawberries and then, when the absolute height of their passion had been aroused, stopped giving them away and charged gold for them, a plan that was whispered in his ears by the two wives while he held his baby who sucked on strawberries the way other babies sucked on tits.

"In this way, great-great-Grandfather grew quite rich and built a castle shaped like a ship covered in strawberry vines and with a room at the back, away from the sea, which was made entirely of glass and housed strawberries all year. He lived there with the two wives and the baby daughter and nobody is certain who is whose mother in our family line.

"Of course the strawberry wife did not stay but left one night, too cruel and heartless to even offer an explanation. Great-great-Grandfather shouted her name for hours as if she was simply lost until, at last, he collapsed in the strawberry room, crushing the fruit with his large body and rolling in the juice until he was quite red with it and as frightening as a wounded animal. His first wife found him there and steered him to a hot bath. They learned to live together again without the strawberry maid. Strangers who didn't know their story often commented on the love between them. The villagers insisted they were both bewitched, the lit candles in the window to guide her return given as evidence. Of course she never did come back."

Outside in the cold night, even the moon was frozen. It shed a white light of ice over their pale yard and cast a ghost glow into the living room that haunted her face. He studied her as if she were someone new in his life and not the woman he'd known for seven years. Something about that moonglow combined with the firelight made her look strange, like a statue at a revolt.

She smiled down at him and cocked her head. "I tell you this story," she said, "to explain if ever you should wake and find me gone, it is not an expression of lack of affection for you, but rather, her witchy blood that is to be blamed."

"What became of her?"

"Oh, no one knows. Some say she had a lover, a pirate from a nearby cove, and they left together, sailing the seas for strawberries. Some say she was an enchanted mermaid and returned to the sea. Some say she came to America and was burned at the stake."

"Which do you think is true?"

She leaned back and sighed, closing her eyes. "I think she's still alive," she whispered, "breaking men's hearts, because she is insatiable."

He studied her in repose, a toppled statue while everything burned.

"Now it's your turn," she said, not opening her eyes, and sounding strangely distant. Was that a tear at the corner of her eye? He turned away from her. He cleared his throat.

"All right then. For a while I had a job in Castor, near Rhome, in a small art museum there. I was not the most qualified for the work but apparently I was the most qualified who was willing to live in Castor, population 954, I kid you not. The museum had a nice little collection, actually. Most of the population of Castor had come through to view the paintings at least once but it was my experience they seemed just as interested in the carpeting, the light fixtures, and the quantity of fish in the river, as they were in the work of the old masters. Certainly the museum never saw the kind of popular attention the baseball field hosted, or the bowling lanes just outside of town.

"What had happened was this. In the 1930s Emile Castor, who had made his fortune on sweet cough drops, had decided to build a fishing lodge. He purchased a beautiful piece of forested property at the edge of what was then a small community, and built his 'cabin,' a six-bedroom, three-bath house with four stone-hearth fireplaces, and large windows that overlooked the river in the backyard. Even though Castor had blossomed to a population of nearly a thousand by the time I arrived, deer still came to drink from that river.

"When Emile Castor died in 1989, he stated in his will that the house be converted into a museum to display his private collection. He bequeathed all his estate to the support of this project. Of course, his relatives, a sister, a few old cousins, and several nieces and nephews, contested this for years, but Mr. Castor was a thorough man and the legalities were tight as a rock. What his family couldn't understand, other than, of course, what they believed was the sheer cruelty of his act, was where this love of art had come from. Mr. Castor, who fished and hunted and was known as something of a ladies' man (though he never married), smoked cigars (chased by lemon cough drops), and built his small fortune on his 'masculine attitude,' as his sister referred to it in an archived letter.

"The kitchen was subdivided. A wall was put up which cut an ugly line right down the middle of what had once been a large picture window that overlooked the river. Whoever made this decision and executed it so poorly was certainly no appreciator of architecture. It was ugly and distorted and an insult to the integrity of the place. What remained of the original room became the employee kitchen: a refrigerator, a stove, a large sink, marble countertops, and a tiled mosaic floor. A small, stained-glass window by Chagall was set beside the remaining slice of larger window. It remained, in spite of the assault it suffered, a beautiful room, and an elaborate employee kitchen for our small staff.

"The other half of the kitchen was now completely blocked off and inaccessible other than by walking through the employee kitchen. That, combined with the large window which shed too much light to expose any works of art to, had caused this room to develop into a sort of oversized storage room. It was a real mess when I got there.

"The first thing I did was sort through all that junk, unearthing boxes of outdated pamphlets and old stationery, a box of old toilet paper, and several boxes of old Castor photographs which I carried to my office to be cataloged and preserved. After a week or so of this I found the paintings, box after box of canvasses painted by an amateur hand, quite bad, almost at the level of a school child, but without a child's whimsy, and all of the same woman. I asked Darlene, who acted as bookkeeper, ticket taker, and town gossip what she thought of them.

" 'That must be Mr. Castor's work,' she said.

" 'I didn't know he painted.'

" 'Well, he did, you can see for yourself. Folks said he was nuts about painting out here. Are they all like these?'

" 'More or less.'

" 'Should have stuck to cough drops,' she pronounced. (This from a woman who once confided in me her absolute glee at seeing a famous jigsaw puzzle, glued and framed, hanging in some restaurant in a nearby town.)

"When all was said and done we had fifteen boxes of those paintings and I decided to hang them in the room that was half of what had once been a magnificent kitchen. Few people would see them there, and that seemed right; they really were quite horrid. The sunlight could cause no more damage than their very presence already exuded.

"When they were at last all hung, I counted a thousand various shapes and sizes of the same dark-haired, gray-eyed lady painted in various styles, the deep velvet colors of Renaissance, the soft pastel hues of Baroque, some frightening bright green reminiscent of Matisse, and strokes that swirled wildly from imitation of van Gogh to the thick direct lines of a grade schooler. I stood in the waning evening light staring at this grotesquerie, this man's art, his poor art, and I must admit I was moved by it. Was his love any less than that of the artist who painted well? Some people have talent. Some don't. Some people have a love that can move them like this. One thousand faces, all imperfectly rendered, but attempted nonetheless. Some of us can only imagine such devotion.

"I had a lot of free time in Castor. I don't like to bowl. I don't care for greasy hamburgers. I have never been interested in stock car racing or farming. Let's just say I didn't really fit in. I spent my evenings cataloging Emile Castor's photographs. Who doesn't like a mystery? I thought the photographic history of this man's life would yield some clues about the object of his affection. I was quite excited about it actually, until I became quite weary with it. You can't imagine what it's like to look through one man's life like that, family, friends, trips, beautiful women (though none were her). The more I looked at them, the more depressed I grew. It was clear Emile Castor had really lived his life and I, I felt, was wasting mine. Well, I am given to fits of melancholy, as you well know, and such a fit rooted inside me at this point. I could not forgive myself for being so ordinary. Night after night I stood in that room of the worst art ever assembled in one place and knew it was more than I had ever attempted, the ugliness of it all somehow more beautiful than anything I had ever done.

"I decided to take a break. I asked Darlene to come in, even though she usually took weekends off, to oversee our current high school girl, Eileen something or other, who seemed to be working through some kind of teenage hormonal thing because every time I saw her she appeared to have just finished a good cry. She was a good kid, I think, but at the time she depressed the hell out of me. 'She can't get over what happened between her and Randy,' Darlene told me. 'The abortion really shook her up. But don't say anything to her parents. They don't know.'

" 'Darlene, I don't want to know.'

"Eventually it was settled. I was getting away from Castor and all things Castor related. I'd booked a room in a B&B in Sundale, on the shore. My duffel bag was packed with two novels, plenty of sunscreen, shorts and swimwear and flip-flops. I would sit in the sun. Walk along the shore. Swim. Read. Eat. I would not think about Emile Castor or the gray-eyed woman. Maybe I would meet somebody. Somebody real. Hey, anything was possible now that I was getting away from Castor.

"Of course it rained. It started almost as soon as I left town and at times the rain became so heavy that I had to pull over on the side of the road. When I finally got to the small town on the shore I was pretty wiped out. I drove in circles looking for the ironically named 'Sunshine Bed and Breakfast' until in frustration at the eccentricity of small towns, I decided that the pleasant-looking house with the simple sign 'B&B' must be it. I sat in the car for a moment hoping the rain would give me a break, and craned my neck at the distant looming steeple of a small chapel on the cliff above the roiling waters.

"It was clear the rain would continue its steady torrent, so I grabbed my duffel bag and slopped through the puddles in a sort of half trot, and entered a pleasant foyer of classical music, overstuffed chairs, a calico asleep in a basket on a table, and a large painting of, you probably already guessed, Emile Castor's gray-eyed beauty. Only in this rendition she really was. Beautiful. This artist had captured what Emile had not. It wasn't just a portrait, a photograph with paint if you will, no, this painting went beyond its subject's beauty into the realm of what is beautiful in art. I heard footsteps, deep breathing, a cough. I turned with reluctance and beheld the oldest man I'd ever seen. He was a lace of wrinkles and skin that sagged from his bones like an ill-fitting suit. He leaned on a walking stick and appraised me with gray eyes almost lost in the fold of wrinkles.

" 'A beautiful piece of work,' I said.

"He nodded.

"I introduced myself and after a few confused minutes discovered that I was neither in Sundale nor at the Sunshine B&B. But I could not have been more pleased on any sunny day, in any location, than I was there, especially when I found out I could stay the night. When I asked about the painting and its subject, Ed, as he told me to call him, invited me to join him in the parlor for tea after I had 'settled in.'

"My room was pleasant, cozy, and clean without the creepy assortment of teddy bears too often assembled in B&Bs. From the window I had a view of the roiling sea, gray waves, the mournful swoop of seagulls, and the cliff with the white chapel, its tall steeple tipped, not with a cross, but a ship, its great sails unfurled.

"When I found him in the parlor, Ed had a tray of tea and cookies set out on a low table before the fireplace which was nicely ablaze. The room was pleasant and inviting. The cold rain pounded the windows but inside it was warm and dry, the faint scent of lavender in the air.

" 'Come, come join us,' Ed waved his hand, as arthritic as any I've ever seen, gnarled to almost a paw. I sat in the green wingchair across from him. An overstuffed rocking chair made a triangle of our seating arrangement but it was empty; not even the cat sat there.

" 'Theresa!' he shouted, and he shouted again in a loud voice that reminded me of the young Marlon Brando calling for Stella.

"It occurred to me he might not be completely sane. But at the same moment I thought this I heard a woman's voice and the sound of footsteps approaching from the other end of the house. I confess that for a moment I entertained the notion that it would be the gray-eyed woman, as if I had fallen into a Brigadoon of sorts, a magical place time could not reach, all time-ravaged evidence on Ed's face to the contrary.

"Just then that old face temporarily lost its wrinkled look and took on a divine expression. I followed the course of his gaze and saw the oldest woman in the world entering the room. I rose from my seat.

" 'Theresa,' Ed said, 'Mr. Delano of Castor.'

"I strode across the room and offered my hand. She slid into it a small, soft glove of a hand and smiled at me with green eyes. She walked smoothly and with grace but her steps were excruciatingly small and slow. To walk beside her was a lesson in patience, as we traversed the distance to Ed who had taken to pouring the tea with hands that quivered so badly the china sounded like wind chimes. How had these two survived so long? In the distance, a cuckoo sang and I almost expected I would hear it again before we reached our destination.

" 'Goodness,' she said, when I finally stood beside the rocking chair, 'I've never known a young man to walk so slowly.' She sat in the chair swiftly, and without any assistance on my part. I realized she'd been keeping her pace to mine as I thought I was keeping mine to hers. I turned to take my own seat and Ed grinned up at me, offering in his quivering hand a chiming teacup and saucer, which I quickly took.

" 'Mr. Delano is interested in Elizabeth,' Ed said as he extended another jangling cup and saucer to her. She reached across and took it, leaning out of the chair in a manner I thought unwise.

" 'What do you know about her?' she asked.

" 'Mr. Emile Castor has made several, many, at least a thousand paintings of the same woman but nothing near to the quality of this one. That's all I know. I don't know what she was to him. I don't know anything.'

"Ed and Theresa both sipped their tea. A look passed between them. Theresa sighed. 'You tell him, Ed.'

" 'It begins with Emile Castor arriving in town, a city man clear enough, with a mustache, and in his red roadster.'

" 'But pleasant.'

" 'He knew his manners.'

" 'He was a sincerely pleasant man.'

" 'He drove up to the chapel and like the idiot he mostly was, turns his back on it and sets up his easel and tries to paint the water down below.'

" 'He wasn't an idiot. He was a decent man, and a good businessman. He just wasn't an artist.'

" 'He couldn't paint water either.'

" 'Well, water's difficult.'

" 'Then it started to rain.'

" 'You seem to get a lot.'

" 'So finally he realizes there's a church right behind him and he packs up his puddle of paints and goes inside.'

" 'That's when he sees her.'

" 'Elizabeth?'

" 'No. Our Lady. Oh, Mr. Delano, you really must see it.'

" 'Maybe he shouldn't.'

" 'Oh, Edward, why shouldn't he?'

"Edward shrugs. 'He was a rich man so he couldn't simply admire her without deciding that he must possess her as well. That's how the rich are.'

" 'Edward, we don't know Mr. Delano's circumstances.'

" 'He ain't rich.'

" 'Well, we don't really—'

" 'All you gotta do is look at his shoes. You ain't, are you?'

" 'No.'

" 'Can you imagine being so foolish you don't think nothing of trying to buy a miracle?'

" 'A miracle? No.'

" 'Well, that's how rich he was.'

" 'He stayed on while he tried to convince the church to sell it to him.'

" 'Idiot.'

" 'They fell in love.'

"Ed grunted.

" 'They did. They both did.'

" 'He offered a couple a barrels full of money.'

" 'For the painting.'

" 'I gotta say I do believe some on the church board wavered a bit but the women wouldn't hear of it.'

" 'She is a miracle.'

" 'Yep, that's what all the women folk said.'

" 'Edward, you know it's true. More tea, Mr. Delano?'

" 'Yes. Thank you. I'm not sure I'm following . . .'

" 'You haven't seen it yet, have you?'

" 'Theresa, he just arrived.'

" 'We saw some of those other paintings he did of Elizabeth.'

"Ed snorts.

" 'Well, he wasn't a quitter, you have to give him that.'

"Ed bites into a cookie and glares at the teapot.

" 'What inspired him, well, what inspired him was Elizabeth but what kept him at it was Our Lady.'

" 'So are you saying, do you mean to imply that this painting, this Our Lady is magical?'

" 'Not magic, a miracle.'

" 'I'm not sure I understand.'

" 'It's an icon, Mr. Delano, surely you've heard of them?'

" 'Well, supposedly an icon is not just a painting, it is the holy manifested in the painting, basically.'

" 'You must see it. Tomorrow. After the rain stops.'

" 'Maybe he shouldn't.'

" 'Why do you keep saying that, Edward? Of course he should see it.'

"Ed just shrugged.

" 'Of course we didn't sell it to him and over time he stopped asking. They fell in love.'

" 'He wanted her instead.'

" 'Don't make it sound like that. He made her happy during what none of us knew were the last days of her life.'

" 'After she died, he started the paintings.'

" 'He wanted to keep her alive.'

" 'He wanted to paint an icon.'

" 'He never gave up until he succeeded. Finally, he painted our Elizabeth.'

" 'Are you saying Emile Castor painted that, in the foyer?'

" 'It took years.'

" 'He wanted to keep her alive somehow.'

" 'But that painting, it's quite spectacular and his other work is so—'

" 'Lousy.'

" 'Anyone who enters this house wants to know about her.'

" 'I don't mean to be rude but how did she, I'm sorry, please excuse me.'

" 'Die?'

" 'It doesn't matter.'

" 'Of course it does. She fell from the church cliff. She'd gone up there to light a candle for Our Lady, a flame of gratitude. Emile had proposed and she had accepted. She went up there and it started raining while she was inside. She slipped and fell on her way home.'

"'How terrible.'

"'Oh yes, but there are really so few pleasant ways to die.'

"Our own rain still lashed the windows. The fat calico came into the room and stopped to lick her paws. We just sat there, listening to the rain and the clink of china cup set neatly in saucer. The tea was good and hot. The fire smelled strangely of chocolate. I looked at their two old faces in profile, wrinkled as poorly folded maps. Then I proceeded to make a fool of myself by explaining to them my position as curator of the Castor museum. I described the collection, the beautiful house and location by a stream visited by deer (but I did not describe the dismal town), and ended with a description of Emile's horrible work, the room filled with poor paintings of their daughter, surely, I told them, Elizabeth belonged there, redeemed against the vast assortment of clowns, for the angel she was. When I was finished the silence was sharp. Neither spoke nor looked at me, but even so, as though possessed by some horrible tic, I continued. 'Of course we'd pay you handsomely.' Theresa bowed her head and I thought that perhaps this was the posture she took for important decisions until I realized she was crying.

"Ed turned slowly, his old head like a marionette's on an uncertain string. He fixed me with a look that told me what a fool I was and will always be.

"'Please accept my apology for being so . . .' I said, finding myself speaking and rising as though driven by the same puppeteer's hand. 'I can't tell you how . . . Thank you.' I turned abruptly and walked out of the room, angry at my clumsy social skills, in despair actually, that I had made a mess of such a pleasant afternoon. I intended to hurry to my room and read my book until dinner when I would skulk down the stairs and try to find a decent place to eat. That I could insult and hurt two such kind people was unforgivable. I was actually almost blind with self-loathing until I entered the foyer and saw her out of the corner of my eye.

"It is really quite impossible to describe that other thing that brings a painting beyond competent, even beyond beauty into the realm of great art. Of course she was a beautiful woman; of course the lighting, colors, composition, brushstroke, all of these elements could be separated and described but this still did not account for that ethereal feeling, the sense one gets standing next to a masterpiece, the need to take a deep breath as if suddenly the air consumed by one is needed for two.

"Instead of going upstairs I went out the front door. If this other painting was anything like the one of Elizabeth then I must see it.

"It was dark, the rain only a drizzle now, the town a slick black oil, maybe something by Dali with disappearing ink. I had, out of habit, pocketed my car keys. I had to circle the town a few times, make a few false starts, once finding myself in someone's driveway, before I selected the road that arched above the town to the white chapel, which even in the rain glowed as though lit from within. The road was winding but not treacherous. When I got to the top and stood on that cliff the wind whipped me, the town below was lost in a haze of fog that only a few yellow lights shone through. I had the sensation of looking down on the heavens from above. The waves crashed and I felt the salt on my face, tasted it on my lips. Up close the chapel was much larger than it looked from below, the steeple that narrowed to a needle point on which its ship balanced into the dark sky, quite imposing. As I walked up those stone steps I thought again of Edward saying he wasn't sure I should see it. I reached for the hammered iron handle and pulled. For a moment I thought it was locked, but it was just incredibly heavy. I pulled the door open and entered the darkness of the church. Behind me, the door heaved shut. I smelled a flowery smoky scent, the oily odor of wood, and heard from somewhere a faint drip of water as though there was a leak. I was in the church foyer, there was another door before me, marked in the darkness by the thin line of light that shone beneath it. I walked gingerly, uncertain in the dark. It too was extremely heavy. I pulled it open."

He coughed and cleared his throat as though suddenly suffering a cold. She opened her eyes just a slit. The heat from the wood stove must have been the reason for the red in his cheeks; how strange he looked, as though in pain or fever! She let her eyes droop shut and it seemed a long time before he continued, his voice raspy.

"All I can say is, I never should have looked. I wish I'd never seen either of those paintings. It was there that I made myself the promise I would never settle for a love any less than spectacular, a love so great that it would take me past my limitations, the way Emile's love for Elizabeth had taken him past his, that somehow such a love would leave an imprint on the world, the way great art does, that all who saw it would be changed by it, as I was.

"So you see, when you find me sad and ask what's on my mind, or when I am quiet and cannot explain to you the reason, there it is. If I had never seen the paintings, maybe I would be a happy man. But always, now, I wonder."

She waited but he said no more. After a long time, she whispered his name. But he did not answer and when she peeked at him from the squint of her eyes, he appeared to be asleep. Eventually, she fell asleep too.

All that night, as they told their stories, the flames burned heat onto that icy roof, which melted down the sides of the house and over the windows so that in the cold morning when they woke up, the fire gone to ash and cinder, the house was encased in a sort of skin of ice which they tried to alleviate by burning another fire, not realizing they were only sealing themselves in more firmly. They spent the rest of that whole winter in their ice house. By burning all the wood and most of the furniture and eating canned food even if it was out of date, they survived, thinner and less certain of fate, into a spring morning thaw, though they never could forget those winter stories, not all that spring or summer and especially not that autumn, when the winds began to carry that chill in the leaves, that odd combination of sun and decay, about which they did not speak, but which they knew would exist between them forever.

♦ ♦ ♦

Angel Face

THIS USED TO BE JUST A REGULAR BARN AND now it's a holy place. Have you ever seen so much Godly art? That painting of the crucifix was specially made by Michael Roma who's only nineteen, if you can imagine. God directed his hands, what other explanation is there for such skill? Look at the sufferen on Jesus' face, the blood at his side. Oftentimes people comment on how real it all is. Michael Roma didn't do it. Not really. How could a kid barely out of high school know about such sufferen? God used Michael's hands, that's what's generally said. What's become of him since is the devil's ways. Everyone agrees. We pray for him since what happened with that girl. Folks are divided about her. Some think she's the devil's maid and others think she works for the CIA because the government don't want us to have our faith. If we have our faith, what do we need them for?

Some of the other paintings are done by locals too. That black velvet one over there was done by Anna Marie Tina Louise. How's that for a beautiful name? Would you guess she's never painted before? See how Jesus rolls his eyes up to heaven like that. Some say they've seen those eyes move but others say that's just hysterics. These other paintings, people just leave behind when they come. Here's an interesting one in the corner. There's Jesus, look at all that blood dripping from him, and by the blood I would judge he's just stepped down from the cross, and standen beside him, well I don't know 'cause he's dressed like a apostle but there's those who say it's Elvis. I'm not sure what that's all about but one thing I've learned, it takes all kinds to serve the Lord.

Did you see that one over there? Now what it is, is one of those styrofoam heads like they have in stores to show off wigs and hats but what someone's done here is made it into Jesus' face and this is a real crown of thorns pressed into his head, just like it was. What people started doing, and no one knows how it began, is they prick their fingers right here on this thorned crown and let their blood drip down his face. So this is the blood of the pilgrims.

I see you noticing the plastic flowers. They brighten up the place, don't they? I don't know when that all started either. You know, it's just what moves in people's hearts. They come here with bouquets of flowers and they drop them around the room and eventually there's a whole room filled with them and they still keep coming. They're plastic so they last forever and we didn't know what to do with them all so finally we started hanging them from the ceiling. There are those that say this is what inspired that girl, or devil, or spy for the CIA to talk the way she did, the one who got Michael Roma turned.

You should see this place when all the candles are lit and it's filled with pilgrims. How much holiness can you imagine? The Hail Mary starts getting said and the roof shakes with it.

Over here is where she comes. Bow your head. Don't get too close. This is a holy place. She appeared right here to Mrs. Vandewhitter when she was milking the cow and she appears here every month, the first Saturday in the month at 4:00 P.M., since. You should come back then. It's so different. The parking lot is full and there's music and dancers, and families and folks come in wheelchairs and crutches because she cures them. Well, not all of them. Who knows the reason? Why did she choose to appear to Mrs. Vandewhitter, on this crummy rundown farm and not to Father Christen who has devoted his whole life to the Holy Lord? Why did she appear to Mrs. Vandewhitter and not to Harry Miller's son who lays around shriveled up like a tadpole ever since that horse kicked him, and when Harry went through all that trouble, with the ambulance and everything, to bring little Harry here, why did he leave the same way he come, drooling and asleep? Who can understand about these things?

She wears a white robe with a blue sash, is what Mrs. Vandewhitter says, and she is T.O.'d. That's just how Mrs. Vandewhitter says it. "Our Blessed Virgin Mother is T.O.'d with you all," she says. Every time. Though really, the pilgrims pray and pray. You can see it by the way they clutch those rosaries so tight and squeeze their eyes shut or look to heaven, or the ceiling of the barn depending if they get to be inside or not. "She's T.O.'d at you all, and she says her son" (that would be Jesus) "is really pissed."

Oh, you should see the photographs. Here, let me see if I can find you one. People leave these pictures of their family, dogs, cats. I don't know what that's about. Here's one, this is what I was looking for. See that cloud, now this has happened many times but most people, they take the photographs with them, see, right there in the sky? That's the door to heaven, you know. It appears when she comes and you can get a picture of it too, when you come back, but it only occurs with a instamatic camera. Who knows the reason?

Faith and God's hands. That's the best explanation for what can't be understood by any other route. Thousands know that. They come here because of it. They spend their savings to get here. Quit their jobs. Leave families. Right there. She stands in her white robe with the blue sash and she says, "Pray." And they pray. "Because the Blessed Virgin is T.O.'d and Jesus is pissed." And who can blame them? Look at the mess we have in this world. Thousands come here and that little girl, all she got is Michael Roma. What does that tell you? Flower angel, my foot.

There have been false claims before. People ain't so naïve as maybe they once were. There was the lady from Albany who said the virgin appeared to her in the shape of a potato but she never could find that particular potato again and folks had a hard time believing that if what she said was true she would just up and forget and make potato salad out of the virgin's miracle. There was also the fellow who said he was Jesus but he didn't know most of the Bible, couldn't recite a whole Hail Mary, and was seen singing rap songs with some kids in Felder's pasture. Then there's her. Sure, she was pretty, nobody will deny you that. Some say she had a glow about her, which, it is also reasoned, is no difficulty for the devil to conjure such a thing and if the CIA can make the whole world believe that Russia is no longer a threat, then certainly it is no problem for them to make a girl glow.

So the first disruptive thing she does is she says, right while Mrs. Vandewhitter is repeating what the virgin has just told her (the part about being T.O.'d), she says, in a clear voice, not necessarily that loud, but how loud do you have to be to disrupt the entire proceedings in a place so quiet as a church? She says, "But there's nothing there at all." This is what's been quoted generally. "But there's nothing there at all." People shifted some, hushed her up. They came to listen to Mrs. Vandewhitter. Well, not even Mrs. Vandewhitter, they came to listen to the Blessed Virgin speaking to Mrs. Vandewhitter who then relays the message.

Maybe you noticed there ain't no pews or benches. More people can fill the space that way. But don't let that throw you. It's holy in here when she comes. They always say the rosary for a few hours before she appears so there's just this feeling in the air. The general excitement. It's golden with all the candles. And Michael Roma's painting is right up there. It used to be right there near to where Mrs. Vandewhitter speaks but it got moved since the controversy. Michael Roma used to stand right next to the painting and it would be fair to say he's a handsome lad. Dark hair. Blue eyes. Good teeth.

So when she says this thing, "But there's nothing there," folks just hushed her up and leaned away from her just enough so that Michael could see who spoke and I heard at least one account that suggests she wasn't the devil, or a CIA spy, and it was all just a matter of love at first sight, what with him so dark and intense by that painting of his, and her, so pale and blonde, and somehow sort of glowing. "What did you say?" he said as if Mrs. Vandewhitter was not just then speaking the Virgin's words, as if the miracle that was occurring was not that, but this pretty girl's face.

"I said, nothing's there."

Mrs. Vandewhitter frowned and raised her voice.

"She's gone now," Michael said, just as though he was having a private conversation and not standing in a full-to-capacity room, interrupting a miracle.

"But she was never there," said the girl. "I can see perfectly well, and there was nothing there at all."

The crowd was restless and murmuring. They did not come here to listen to teenagers prattling. They came to hear the message of Mary, the Holy Virgin, and this little blonde person was ruining everything.

Michael sensed this. He stood at the helm, so to speak, and could see the crowd's impatience. "Not everyone can see her," he said.

Even Mrs. Vandewhitter nodded, though she seemed to be bravely trying to ignore the whole thing. Later, I heard her say one word to Emmet Grady who cleans up around here after the miracles. "Hormones," she said.

"Well, I don't know why that would be the case," said this girl, "because she makes it rain roses in my backyard every morning, why wouldn't she let me see her here?"

It is said that you could see the change come over Michael, like his whole posture changed and people even murmured, no, no. Even Mrs. Vandewhitter had lost her place and was up there shaking her head at him.

He goes, "Roses?"

"Yes," she says, "every morning it rains roses in my backyard. Hundreds and hundreds of them."

"With thorns or without?"

"Without," she said. "Shorn, so I can pick them up and never prick my skin."

Michael stood there, considering. There are those who say you could see the way he was fighting inside but the devil was just so strong and that girl was just too pretty. He just stands there so Mrs. Vandewhitter, confused where she left off, starts at the beginning again which is always the same. "The Blessed Virgin Mother is T.O.'d at you all, she said, and Jesus is—"

"What kind of roses?"

"Oh there's Topaz, Jewel, Windrush, Pearl Drift, Lavender Dream, Angel Face, Sweet Juliet, China Doll, French Lace, Maiden's Blush, Sea Foam, Fairy. Should I continue?"

"What do you do with them?"

"Potpourri, dream pillows, perfume, shampoo, candles, rose jam, rose chicken, rose butter, rose bread. I give them away to children, to the old, to the sick."

"Because you are not praying enough," Mrs. Vandewhitter says to the distracted pilgrims.

"Where do you live?" Michael asks.

"In the hills outside of town."

"Why haven't I seen you before?"

"My mother home-schooled me, and after she died last winter, that's when the roses started to fall."

"They fall in winter?"

It was a miracle and a pickup all occurring at the same time. Mrs. Vandewhitter, having raised five teenagers of her own, just ignored them as did most of the pilgrims. Some of their conversation has been lost in the confusion but this is about the gist of it. And, I'm sorry to say, he left with her. Even before Mrs. Vandewhitter was done saying the holy words.

Who can understand the ways of the Lord? That's what Mrs.

Vandewhitter says. The need is so great. People just keep coming and coming and they are, generally, wanting. Whatever you give them, they want more. More than the Blessed Virgin's words, or pictures of the door to heaven even. It's like they can't be satisfied. So the Blessed Virgin told Mrs. Vandewhitter to build a gift shop and—Oh, the boy?

Well, there are rumors that he comes into town with bouquets of roses for the hospital and nursing home. Those that seen him say he's grown his dark hair long and curly and wears a little gold earring shaped like a rose and paints pictures of that girl, naked pictures that he sells in the city, and also, that he sort of glows. But of course that don't mean a thing. Roses can be bought or grown. And it don't take much to guess what's got a boy his age, in his situation, glowing.

◆ ◆ ◆

Night Blossoms

*A*FAMILY OF BREASTS. BRAS ON CHAIR BACKS, towel rods, floor. Defeated. Lace. Flowers. Cotton. Snaps and straps. A history of fingers doing and undoing. Pale, slender, and sure fingers. Bored fingers. Fumbling, thick, and hot fingers. Long fingers. Faintly scented of Old Spice fingers. Fingers slick with the oily scent of released peepers that chirp in the pond at the foot of the driveway those dark nights of early spring, car windows rolled down slightly to relieve the steam. Yawning Sunday morning in with stretch of limbs and breasts, a house of daughters. All of them wild and uncertain as black butterflies.

He sits at the kitchen table and drinks coffee flavored with chicory. Who can sleep in a house of girls? Their dreams find him in bed or couch or recliner. Wherever his head rests in sleep, the dreams find him, with their scent of orchids, crushed in back seats of leather coat dates, breath of cinnamon and cigarettes and Schnapp's. He rubs his temple. Well, this is what his own mother foretold when he brought home Elspeth in her lace and painted boots, feather earrings and wild hair a flame of red that lit her face. "She's a witch," his mother said. "Only trouble will come of her."

He married her beneath a full moon in a garden planted with night-blooming jasmine and chocolate mint, so sweet he was dizzy throughout the ceremony and can only remember parts of it: the scent, the weight of moon, the honey he licked from her fingertips, the sound of laughter, the blink of fireflies, the yellow in her eyes.

Seven daughters, and his mother was right. He had everything to lose and the losing had already begun.

Soon the kitchen will be full of them. Their hair a tangle of curls and smoke, barefoot with pink-painted toenails, or in white socks scrunched around ankles, in cotton pants and skinny-strapped T-shirts, in pale yellow robe, in shorts, long shirts, long legs, long arms, yawning and stretching, fighting over coffee mugs, laughing wildly at whispered words, kissing him on cheek, chin, or forehead, rubbing his hair with a quick swipe of hand, leaning into him with many shapes of breasts. Their night scent. "You should get some sleep," they'll say with milk breath, peach breath, dark and hot breath. "You look wiped out."

He tries to sleep in the crook of his hand. The chicory cools in the mug. And he does sleep. For a few minutes. His daughters' dreams, used and discarded, find him. The pull of zipper. The scent of leather. Heat. Wet. He wakes with a start. Through the kitchen window he sees the dreams float over the quiet yard of pecking robins, shoots of daffodils, tulip stems unflowered. He picks up his mug. Turns.

Elspeth. The flame of her hair, gone. She stares at him with yellow eyes. He walks past her to dump the coffee down the drain, brushing her shoulder when he does. She smells like old wood, the autumn forest behind the house. But this is spring! The coffee leaves a brown circle on the porcelain. He turns to fill his mug with fresh. She moves to the stove. Lifts the teakettle to check its weight for water. Sets it on the burner. Turns the switch to high. Opens the cupboard for a jar of tea, dried from garden herbs. She looks at jars of cat's claw, dandelion, rosehips, burdock root, chamomile, peppermint. She stares and stares until the teakettle whistles. She takes it off the burner. Reaches up. Opens another cupboard. Takes out a bottle of red wine.

"What are you doing?" he says.

She finds the corkscrew shaped like a man with a tremendous and strange cock. She pierces the cork. Screws it. Ha!

"You shouldn't," he says.

She brushes past him to reach for a wineglass.

She smells of dirt and sun, heat of a large animal. She pours red wine. The kitchen smells of chicory, the sweet wine, and her. He will go mad. He will go crazy holding all of it in. Soon the girls will wake and fill the kitchen with their young breasts and sleeping voices and laughter and he is drowning, a dry drowning, unexpected so far from water.

"You are still having their dreams," she says. It is not a question. She gulps the wine, staring at him.

He sits at the kitchen table again. Defeated. "I can't stop them."

The ceiling creaks with the weight of footsteps. A door opens and shuts. They are waking up. They will fill the kitchen with their own brand of innocence, the scent of exploration on fingertips and skin, so soft, bra straps and T-shirts always seem to be sliding off.

"You wouldn't believe the things they're dreaming," he says.

She grunts. Takes another gulp. "You've got that wrong."

The ceiling creaks and pounds. Those little feet sound like sons up there! Doors open and close. A radio is turned on.

He covers his face with his hands and sobs.

She sets the glass on the counter and walks over to him. He wraps his arm around her hips, buries his face into the smoked-fish scent of her. Reaches up.

"They're coming," she says.

He parts her robe and reaches to touch the breast with blue lines webbing to aureole. His hand moves across to the flattened space, the bone they left her with, the smooth planed skin as if she is both, girl and woman.

Footsteps pound down the stairs. She steps back. Shuts her robe.

They are everywhere. The kitchen fills with them. Wisps of discarded dreams cling to them like smoke. They do not notice the wineglass or the way their parents look at them, as if they are ghosts they've learned to live with. They make toast. Leave crumbs on the counter. Put feet up on chairs. Insult each other.

Then, for a moment, as if the whole family is enchanted, the kitchen quiets. There is only the sound of juice glass set on table, clank of butter knife. A sigh. They stare out the window at the spring grass, thatched with unblossomed flowers, and try to remember the dreams, the perfect dreams they had.

(139)

Blank

Nightmares

Feeding the Beast

IT MOVES THROUGH THE HOUSE ON BEASTY legs, slithering, putrid, waving flags of flesh and skin while pillow feathers float overhead. It turns screaming children into whorls of blood, wipes the ash-red stains, and says, "It isn't vengeance, it's dessert."

The monster eats the children who try to defend themselves with toy guns and playing dead. The littlest child hides in my closet, clutching her doll. The monster shits torn limbs onto the rug. Dreams hang in the air like mosquitoes, which dive uselessly at his thick skin. The wide-eyed child whispers to me in the dark. "I'm coming," I say. But I am paralyzed, in the monster's caw.

♦ ♦ ♦

Bread and Bombs

THE STRANGE CHILDREN OF THE MANMENS-
vitzender family did not go to school so we only knew they
had moved into the old house on the hill because Bobby had
watched them move in with their strange assortment of rocking
chairs and goats. We couldn't imagine how anyone would live
there, where the windows were all broken and the yard was thorny
with brambles. For a while we expected to see the children, two
sisters who, Bobby said, had hair like smoke and eyes like black
olives, at school. But they never came.

We were in the fourth grade, that age that seems like waking
from a long slumber into the world the adults imposed, streets we
weren't allowed to cross, things we weren't allowed to say, and crossing them, and saying them. The mysterious Manmensvitzender
children were just another in a series of revelations that year,
including the much more exciting (and sometimes disturbing) evo-
lution of our bodies. Our parents, without exception, had raised us
with this subject so thoroughly explored that Lisa Bitten knew how
to say vagina before she knew her address and Ralph Linster delivered his little brother, Petey, when his mother went into labor one
night when it suddenly started snowing before his father could get
home. But the real significance of this information didn't start to

sink in until that year. We were waking to the wonders of the world and the body; the strange realizations that a friend was cute, or stinky, or picked her nose, or was fat, or wore dirty underpants, or had eyes that didn't blink when he looked at you real close and all of a sudden you felt like blushing.

When the crab apple tree blossomed a brilliant pink, buzzing with honey bees, and our teacher, Mrs. Graymoore, looked out the window and sighed, we passed notes across the rows and made wild plans for the school picnic, how we would ambush her with water balloons and throw pies at the principal. Of course none of this happened. Only Trina Needles was disappointed because she really believed it would but she still wore bows in her hair and secretly sucked her thumb and was nothing but a big baby.

Released into summer we ran home or biked home shouting for joy and escape and then began doing everything we could think of, all those things we'd imagined doing while Mrs. Graymoore sighed at the crab apple tree which had already lost its brilliance and once again looked ordinary. We threw balls, rode bikes, rolled skateboards down the driveway, picked flowers, fought, made up, and it was still hours before dinner. We watched TV, and didn't think about being bored, but after a while we hung upside down and watched it that way, or switched the channels back and forth or found reasons to fight with anyone in the house. (I was alone, however, and could not indulge in this.) That's when we heard the strange noise of goats and bells. In the mothy gray of TV rooms, we pulled back the drapes, and peered out windows into a yellowed sunlight.

The two Manmensvitzender girls in bright clothes the color of a circus, and gauzy scarves, one purple, the other red, glittering with sequins, came riding down the street in a wooden wagon pulled by two goats with bells around their necks. That is how the trouble began. The news accounts never mention any of this; the flame of crab apple blossoms, our innocence, the sound of bells. Instead they focus on the unhappy results. They say we were wild. Uncared for. Strange. They say we were dangerous. As if life were amber and we were molded and suspended in that form, not evolved into that ungainly shape of horror, and evolved out of it, as we are, into a teacher, a dancer, a welder, a lawyer, several soldiers, two doctors, and me, a writer.

Everybody promises during times like those days immediately following the tragedy that lives have been ruined, futures shattered but only Trina Needles fell for that and eventually committed suicide. The rest of us suffered various forms of censure and then went on with our lives. Yes, it is true, with a dark past but, you may be surprised to learn, that can be lived with. The hand that holds the pen (or chalk, or stethoscope, or gun, or lover's skin) is so different from the hand that lit the match, and so incapable of such an act that it is not even a matter of forgiveness, or healing. It's strange to look back and believe that any of that was me or us. Are you who you were then? Eleven years old and watching the dust motes spin lazily down a beam of sunlight that ruins the picture on the TV and there is a sound of bells and goats and a laugh so pure we all come running to watch the girls in their bright-colored scarves, sitting in the goat cart which stops in a stutter of goat-hoofed steps and clatter of wooden wheels when we surround it to observe those dark eyes and pretty faces. The younger girl, if size is any indication, smiling, and the other, younger than us, but at least eight or nine, with huge tears rolling down her brown cheeks.

We stand there for a while, staring, and then Bobby says, "What's a matter with her?"

The younger girl looks at her sister who seems to be trying to smile in spite of the tears. "She just cries all the time."

Bobby nods and squints at the girl who continues to cry though she manages to ask, "Where have you kids come from?"

He looks around the group with an are-you-kidding kind of look but anyone can tell he likes the weeping girl, whose dark eyes and lashes glisten with tears that glitter in the sun. "It's summer vacation."

Trina, who has been furtively sucking her thumb, says, "Can I have a ride?" The girls say sure. She pushes her way through the little crowd and climbs into the cart. The younger girl smiles at her. The other seems to try but cries especially loud. Trina looks like she might start crying too until the younger one says, "Don't worry. It's just how she is." The crying girl shakes the reins and the little bells ring and the goats and cart go clattering down the hill. We listen to Trina's shrill scream but we know she's all right. When they come back we take turns until our parents call us home with whistles and shouts and screen doors slam. We go home for dinner, and the girls head home themselves, the one still crying, the other singing to the accompaniment of bells.

"I see you were playing with the refugees," my mother says. "You be careful around those girls. I don't want you going to their house."

"I didn't go to their house. We just played with the goats and the wagon."

"Well, all right then, but stay away from there. What are they like?"

"One laughs a lot. The other cries all the time."

"Don't eat anything they offer you."

"Why not?"

"Just don't."

"Can't you just explain to me why not?"

"I don't have to explain to you, young lady, I'm your mother."

We didn't see the girls the next day or the day after that. On the third day Bobby, who had begun to carry a comb in his back pocket and part his hair on the side, said, "Well hell, let's just go there." He started up the hill but none of us followed.

When he came back that evening we rushed him for information about his visit, shouting questions at him like reporters. "Did you eat anything?" I asked. "My mother says not to eat anything there."

He turned and fixed me with such a look that for a moment I forgot he was my age, just a kid like me, in spite of the new way he was combing his hair and the steady gaze of his blue eyes. "Your mother is prejudiced," he said. He turned his back to me and reached into his pocket, pulling out a fist that he opened to reveal a handful of small, brightly wrapped candies. Trina reached her pudgy fingers into Bobby's palm and plucked out one bright orange one. This was followed by a flurry of hands until there was only Bobby's empty palm.

Parents started calling kids home. My mother stood in the doorway but she was too far away to see what we were doing. Candy wrappers floated down the sidewalk in swirls of blue, green, red, yellow, and orange.

My mother and I usually ate separately. When I was at my dad's we ate together in front of the TV, which she said was barbaric.

"Was he drinking?" she'd ask. Mother was convinced my father was an alcoholic and thought I didn't remember those years when he had to leave work early because I'd called and told him how she was asleep on the couch, still in her pajamas, the coffee table littered with cans and bottles, which he threw in the trash with a grim expression and few words.

My mother stands, leaning against the counter, and watches me. "Did you play with those girls today?"

"No. Bobby did though."

"Well, that figures, nobody really watches out for that boy. I remember when his daddy was in high school with me. Did I ever tell you that?"

"Uh-huh."

"He was a handsome man. Bobby's a nice looking boy too but you stay away from him. I think you play with him too much."

"I hardly play with him at all. He plays with those girls all day."

"Did he say anything about them?"

"He said some people are prejudiced."

"Oh, he did, did he? Where'd he get such an idea anyway? Must be his grandpa. You listen to me, there's nobody even talks that way anymore except for a few rabble rousers, and there's a reason for that. People are dead because of that family. You just remember that. Many, many people died because of them."

"You mean Bobby's, or the girls?"

"Well, both actually. But most especially those girls. He didn't eat anything, did he?"

I looked out the window, pretending a new interest in our backyard, then, at her, with a little start, as though suddenly awoken. "What? Uh, no."

She stared at me with squinted eyes. I pretended to be unconcerned. She tapped her red fingernails against the kitchen counter. "You listen to me," she said in a sharp voice, "there's a war going on."

I rolled my eyes.

"You don't even remember, do you? Well, how could you, you were just a toddler. But there was a time when this country didn't know war. Why, people used to fly in airplanes all the time."

I stopped my fork halfway to my mouth. "Well, how stupid was that?"

"You don't understand. Everybody did it. It was a way to get from one place to another. Your grandparents did it a lot, and your father and I did too."

"You were on an airplane?"

"Even you." She smiled. "See, you don't know so much, missy. The world used to be safe, and then, one day, it wasn't. And those people —" she pointed at the kitchen window, straight at the Miller's house, but I knew that wasn't who she meant "— started it."

"They're just a couple of kids."

"Well, not them exactly, but I mean the country they come from. That's why I want you to be careful. There's no telling what they're doing here. So little Bobby and his radical grandpa can say we're all prejudiced but who even talks that way anymore?" She walked over to the table, pulled out a chair, and sat down in front of

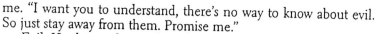

me. "I want you to understand, there's no way to know about evil. So just stay away from them. Promise me."

Evil. Hard to understand. I nodded.

"Well, all right." She pushed back the chair, stood up, grabbed her pack of cigarettes from the windowsill. "Make sure not to leave any crumbs. This is the time of year for ants."

From the kitchen window I could see my mother sitting on the picnic table, a gray plume of smoke spiraling away from her. I rinsed my dishes, loaded the dishwasher, wiped the table, and went outside to sit on the front steps and think about the world I never knew. The house on top of the hill blazed in the full sun. The broken windows had been covered by some sort of plastic that swallowed the light.

That night one flew over Oakgrove. I woke up and put my helmet on. My mother was screaming in her room, too frightened to help. My hands didn't shake the way hers did, and I didn't lie in my bed screaming. I put the helmet on and listened to it fly past. Not us. Not our town. Not tonight. I fell asleep with the helmet on and in the morning woke up with the marks of it dented on my cheeks.

Now, when summer approaches, I count the weeks when the apple trees and lilacs are in blossom, the tulips and daffodils in bloom before they droop with summer's heat, and I think how it is so much like that period of our innocence, that waking into the world with all its incandescence, before being subdued by its shadows into what we have become.

"You should have known the world then," my father says, when I visit him at the nursing home.

We've heard it so much it doesn't mean anything. The cakes, the money, the endless assortment of everything.

"We used to have six different kinds of cereal at one time—" he raises his finger instructively "—coated in sugar, can you imagine? It used to go stale. We threw it out. And the planes. The sky used to be filled with them. Really. People traveled that way, whole families did. It didn't matter if someone moved away. Hell, you just got on a plane to go see them."

Whenever he speaks like this, whenever any of them do, they sound bewildered, amazed. He shakes his head, he sighs. "We were so happy."

I cannot hear about those times without thinking of spring flowers, children's laughter, the sound of bells and clatter of goats. Smoke.

Bobby sits in the cart, holding the reins, a pretty, dark-skinned girl on either side of him. They ride up and down the street all morning, laughing and crying, their gauzy scarves blowing behind them like rainbows.

The flags droop listlessly from flagpoles and porches. Butterflies flit in and out of gardens. The Whitehall twins play in their back-yard and the squeaky sound of their unoiled swings echoes through the neighborhood. Mrs. Renquat has taken the day off to take several kids to the park. I am not invited, probably because I hate Becky Renquat and told her so several times during the school year, pulling her hair, which was a stream of white gold so bright I could not resist it. It is Ralph Paterson's birthday and most of the little kids are spending the day with him and his dad at The Snowman's Cave Amusement Park where they get to do all the things kids used to do when snow was still safe, like sledding, and building snowmen. Lina Breedsore and Carol Minstreet went to the mall with their baby sitter who has a boyfriend who works at the movie theater and can sneak them in to watch movies all day long. The town is empty except for the baby Whitehall twins, Trina Needles who is sucking her thumb and reading a book on her porch swing, and Bobby, going up and down the street with the Manmensvitzender girls and their goats. I sit on my porch picking at the scabs on my knees but Bobby speaks only to them, in a voice so low I can't hear what he says. Finally I stand up and block their way. The goats and cart stutter to a stop, the bells still jingling as Bobby says, "What's up, Weyers?"

He has eyes so blue, I recently discovered, I cannot look into them for more than thirty seconds, as though they burn me. Instead I look at the girls who are both smiling, even the one who is crying.

"What's your problem?" I say.

Her dark eyes widen, increasing the pool of milky white around them. She looks at Bobby. The sequins of her scarf catch the sun.

"Jesus Christ, Weyers, what are you talking about?"

"I just wanta know," I say still looking at her, "what it is with all this crying all the time, I mean like is it a disease, or what?"

"Oh for Christ's sake." The goats' heads rear, and the bells jingle. Bobby pulls on the reins. The goats step back with clomps and the rattle of wheels but I continue to block their path. "What's your problem?"

"It's a perfectly reasonable question," I shout at his shadow against the bright sun. "I just wanta know what her problem is."

"It's none of your business," he shouts and at the same time the smaller girl speaks.

"What?" I say to her.

"It's the war, and all the suffering."

Bobby holds the goats steady. The other girl holds onto his arm. She smiles at me but continues to weep.

"Well, so? Did something happen to her?"

"It's just how she is. She always cries."

"That's stupid."

"Oh for Christ's sake, Weyers!"

"You can't cry all the time, that's no way to live."

Bobby steers the goats and cart around me. The younger girl turns and stares at me until, at some distance, she waves but I turn away without waving back.

Before it was abandoned and then occupied by the Manmensvitzenders the big house on the hill had been owned by the Richters. "Oh, sure they were rich," my father says when I tell him I am researching a book. "But you know, we all were. You should have seen the cakes! And the catalogs. We used to get these catalogs in the mail and you could buy anything that way, they'd mail it to you, even cake. We used to get this catalog, what was it called, Henry and Danny? Something like that. Two guys' names. Anyhow, when we were young it was just fruit but then, when the whole country was rich you could order spongecake with buttercream, or they had these towers of packages they'd send you, filled with candy and nuts and cookies, and chocolate, and oh my God, right in the mail."

"You were telling me about the Richters."

"Terrible thing what happened to them, the whole family."

"It was the snow, right?"

"Your brother, Jaime, that's when we lost him."

"We don't have to talk about that."

"Everything changed after that, you know. That's what got your mother started. Most folks just lost one, some not even, but you know those Richters. That big house on the hill and when it snowed they all went sledding. The world was different then."

"I can't imagine."

"Well, neither could we. Nobody could of guessed it. And believe me, we were guessing. Everyone tried to figure what they would do next. But snow? I mean how evil is that anyway?"

"How many?"

"Oh, thousands. Thousands."

"No, I mean how many Richters?"

"All six of them. First the children and then the parents."

"Wasn't it unusual for adults to get infected?"

"Well, not that many of us played in the snow the way they did."

"So you must have sensed it, or something."

"What? No. We were just so busy then. Very busy. I wish I could remember. But I can't. What we were so busy with." He rubs his eyes and stares out the window. "It wasn't your fault. I want you to know I understand that."

"Pop."

"I mean you kids, that's just the world we gave you, so full of evil you didn't even know the difference."

"We knew, Pop."

"You still don't know. What do you think of when you think of snow?"

"I think of death."

"Well, there you have it. Before that happened it meant joy. Peace and joy."

"I can't imagine."

"Well, that's my point."

"Are you feeling all right?" She dishes out the macaroni, puts the bowl in front of me, and stands, leaning against the counter, to watch me eat.

I shrug.

She places a cold palm on my forehead. Steps back and frowns. "You didn't eat anything, from those girls, did you?"

I shake my head. She is just about to speak when I say, "But the other kids did."

"Who? When?" She leans so close that I can see the lines of makeup sharp against her skin.

"Bobby. Some of the other kids. They ate candy."

Her hand comes palm down, hard, against the table. The macaroni bowl jumps, and the silverware. Some milk spills. "Didn't I tell you?" she shouts.

"Bobby plays with them all the time now."

She squints at me, shakes her head, then snaps her jaw with grim resolve. "When? When did they eat this candy?"

"I don't know. Days ago. Nothing happened. They said it was good."

Her mouth opens and closes like a fish. She turns on her heels and grabs the phone as she leaves the kitchen. The door slams. I can see her through the window, pacing the backyard, her arms gesturing wildly.

My mother organized the town meeting and everybody came, dressed up like it was church. The only people who weren't there were the Manmensvitzenders, for obvious reasons. Most people brought their kids, even the babies who sucked thumbs or blanket corners. I was there and so was Bobby with his grandpa who chewed the stem of a cold pipe and kept leaning over and whispering to his grandson during the proceedings, which quickly became heated, though there wasn't much argument, the heat being fueled by just the general excitement of it, my mother especially in her roses dress, her lips painted a bright red so that even I came to some understanding that she had a certain beauty though I was too young to understand what about that beauty wasn't entirely pleasing. "We have to remember that we are all soldiers in this war," she said to much applause.

Mr. Smyths suggested a sort of house arrest but my mother pointed out that would entail someone from town bringing groceries to them. "Everybody knows these people are starving. Who's going to pay for all this bread anyway?" she said. "Why should we have to pay for it?"

Mrs. Mathers said something about justice.

Mr. Hallensway said, "No one is innocent anymore."

My mother, who stood at the front of the room, leaning slightly against the village board table, said, "Then it's decided."

Mrs. Foley, who had just moved to town from the recently destroyed Chesterville, stood up, in that way she had of sort of crouching into her shoulders, with those eyes that looked around nervously so that some of us had secretly taken to calling her Bird Woman, and with a shaky voice, so soft everyone had to lean forward to hear, said, "Are any of the children actually sick?"

The adults looked at each other and each other's children. I could tell that my mother was disappointed that no one reported any symptoms. The discussion turned to the bright-colored candies when Bobby, without standing or raising his hand, said in a loud voice, "Is that what this is about? Do you mean these?" He leaned back in his chair to wiggle his hand into his pocket and pulled out a handful of them.

There was a general murmur. My mother grabbed the edge of the table. Bobby's grandfather, grinning around his dry pipe, plucked one of the candies from Bobby's palm, unwrapped it, and popped it into his mouth.

Mr. Galvin Wright had to use his gavel to hush the noise. My mother stood up straight and said, "Fine thing, risking your own life like that, just to make a point."

"Well, you're right about making a point, Maylene," he said, looking right at my mother and shaking his head as if they were having a private discussion, "but this is candy I keep around the house to get me out of the habit of smoking. I order it through the Government Issue catalogue. It's perfectly safe."

"I never said it was from them," said Bobby, who looked first at my mother and then searched the room until he found my face, but I pretend not to notice.

When we left, my mother took me by the hand, her red fingernails digging into my wrist. "Don't talk," she said, "just don't say another word." She sent me to my room and I fell asleep with my clothes on still formulating my apology.

The next morning when I hear the bells, I grab a loaf of bread and wait on the porch until they come back up the hill. Then I stand in their path.

"Now what d'you want?" Bobby says.

I offer the loaf, like a tiny baby being held up to God in church. The weeping girl cries louder, her sister clutches Bobby's arm. "What d'you think you're doing?" he shouts.

"It's a present."

"What kind of stupid present is that? Put it away! Jesus Christ, would you put it down?"

My arms drop to my sides, the loaf dangles in its bag from my hand. Both girls are crying. "I just was trying to be nice," I say, my voice wavering like the Bird Woman's.

"God, don't you know anything?" Bobby says. "They're afraid of our food, don't you even know that?"

"Why?"

" 'Cause of the bombs, you idiot. Why don't you think once in a while?"

"I don't know what you're talking about."

The goats rattle their bells and the cart shifts back and forth. "The bombs! Don't you even read your history books? In the beginning of the war we sent them food packages all wrapped up the same color as these bombs that would go off when someone touched them."

"We did that?"

"Well, our parents did." He shakes his head and pulls the reins. The cart rattles past, both girls pressed against him as if I am dangerous.

"Oh, we were so happy!" my father says, rocking into the memory. "We were like children, you know, so innocent, we didn't even know."

"Know what, Pop?"

"That we had enough."

"Enough what?"

"Oh, everything. We had enough everything. Is that a plane?" he looks at me with watery blue eyes.

"Here, let me help you put your helmet on."

He slaps at it, bruising his fragile hands.

"Quit it, Dad. Stop!"

He fumbles with arthritic fingers to unbuckle the strap but finds he cannot. He weeps into his spotted hands. It drones past.

Now that I look back on how we were that summer, before the tragedy, I get a glimmer of what my father's been trying to say all along. It isn't really about the cakes, and the mail-order catalogs, or the air travel they used to take. Even though he uses stuff to describe it that's not what he means. Once there was a different emotion. People used to have a way of feeling and being in the world that is gone, destroyed so thoroughly we inherited only its absence.

"Sometimes," I tell my husband, "I wonder if my happiness is really happiness."

"Of course it's really happiness," he says, "what else would it be?"

We were under attack is how it felt. The Manmensvitzenders with their tears and fear of bread, their strange clothes, and stinky goats were children like us and we could not get the town meeting out of our heads, what the adults had considered doing. We climbed trees, chased balls, came home when called, brushed our teeth when told, finished our milk, but we had lost that feeling we'd had before. It is true we didn't understand what had been taken from us, but we knew what we had been given and who had done the giving.

We didn't call a meeting the way they did. Ours just happened on a day so hot we sat in Trina Needles's playhouse fanning ourselves with our hands and complaining about the weather like the grownups. We mentioned house arrest but that seemed impossible to enforce. We discussed things like water balloons, T.P.ing. Someone mentioned dog shit in brown paper bags set on fire. I think that's when the discussion turned the way it did.

You may ask, who locked the door? Who made the stick piles? Who lit the matches? We all did. And if I am to find solace, twenty-five years after I destroyed all ability to feel that my happiness, or anyone's, really exists, I find it in this. It was all of us.

Maybe there will be no more town meetings. Maybe this plan is like the ones we've made before. But a town meeting is called. The grownups assemble to discuss how we will not be ruled by evil, and also, the possibility of widening Main Street. Nobody notices when we children sneak out. We had to leave behind the babies, sucking thumbs or blanket corners and not really part of our plan for redemption. We were children. It wasn't well thought out.

When the police came we were not "careening in some wild imitation of barbaric dance" or having seizures as has been reported. I can still see Bobby, his hair damp against his forehead, the bright red of his cheeks as he danced beneath the white flakes that fell from a sky we never trusted; Trina spinning in circles, her arms stretched wide, and the Manmensvitzender girls with their goats and cart piled high with rocking chairs, riding away from us, the jingle bells ringing, just like in the old song. Once again the world was safe and beautiful. Except by the town hall where the large white flakes rose like ghosts and the flames ate the sky like a hungry monster who could never get enough.

◆ ◆ ◆

Art Is Not a Violent Subject

"I would rather be whole than good."
—Carl Jung

THE IMPORTANT THING TO REMEMBER IS THAT initially she did not bleed. Had she bled with that first cut-thin sliver of wood I would have stopped immediately. I am not a beast, after all, the heathen dark angel they are making me to be. I am an artist. I create, you see, not destroy. If first cut had brought blood or tears, revealed chips of bone, as happened later, there would have been no further. I could not have handled a knife red and wet. It was only later, when I had to continue, you see, as she revealed herself to me that I realized the horrible duality. To release her from the block of wood, grained with whorls and dead as the rootless, growthless thing it was, I had to confront the blood and bone. But what to do then? I ask you, what would any man do? Was I to ignore her imprisonment or release her? A Solomon's choice I tell you. The damned mess of creation.

I found her in a National Park. There. That is probably the first and really, only confession. Law is that nothing can be removed from the National Parks but it seems a much ignored decree. The day I was there I saw a woman stealing a huge bag of pinecones. I also saw a whole family feeding squirrels (against the law) and all I did was find this beautiful temple, yes, this beautiful temple of wood, grained golden and brown, smoothed by rain and wind, lying there, all that time in a tangle of moss.

Like a stone in my pocket. Really, such a little stealing. And this park, vast and continuous, yielded it so easily. I reasoned it was not a crime. Creation a crime? Man's laws and God's laws are not the same. Artists and saints know the difference. I was not making the world smaller by this simple little theft. I was increasing it.

I took her back to my car. It was so easy. I did pass a family on the path but the mother was carrying a bouquet of pilfered flowers and the children were dragging stolen sticks and I dared the father with my eyes, in the silent language of men, to challenge my possession, and he looked at me for only a moment until he conceded I was the stronger one and then he looked away and I could hear him rushing his family along after they passed. But I am meandering here and must get back to the carving. (My sweet.)

I named her Olivia even before that first slivered cut. It was a name that came to me as I put the wood in the trunk of the car, gently caressed by a blanket to soften against any blows. As I lowered the hood, something in the angle of light, the dimness of shadows played through the trees, the sun-spotted movement across the grain made me know. I let the trunk slam shut with firm resolve. It was a beautiful day. Just at the edge of autumn. I rolled down the window. I did not turn on the radio. I drove very carefully. When I went past the guard station they waved me through. They did not suspect a thing.

Had they stopped the car then, searched the trunk, found the evidence of my thievery, what would I have done? Yielded her? Probably. With regrets? Certainly. But there is always more wood. I would say at this point I felt anticipation. Some fondness, certainly. But not love. I mean she wasn't even real yet. I wasn't sure who she'd be. Most certainly I hadn't guessed at the power she had. I didn't know I would taste her blood, trying to stop the constant flow with a kiss. I didn't know I would come to feel all this. So at that point, had they insisted I give her up, I would have. With regrets but resignation. I probably would have mostly forgotten it, delegated it to an incident only.

But that's not what happened. The guard waved me by with a cheerful salute and I even saluted back with a cheerful wave. I drove down the long curve of mountain, spiraling into the lights dimmed by pollution, until finally I parked in front of my building and carried the wood up to my second-floor apartment where I placed it on the carving block in the middle of the room. I watched it change and move in the shadows. Smoking a cigarette I watched until I knew the shape of her and what she was trying to be and how to begin the release.

When, finally, I went to bed I was already dizzy with the tight breathing of anticipation. I tossed restlessly in the madness of sleep.

The first cut of morning. A sip of green tea. The second sliver. Time passed in shadows and light. I sent out for Chinese. (Delivered by a chatty, fat girl with braids who tried to look around my shoulders to see. Are you an artist? she said. But I did not answer her stupid question and paid her quickly and slammed the door. I was in a wordless place and could not bring myself out of it to discuss titles, to speak to her, when Olivia was beginning to speak to me.)

By Olivia speaking to me I do not mean she actually spoke to me as some have testified. How could she? She did not at this point have a mouth and when finally there were lips (beautiful, full arches-of-butterfly lips), there was no tongue, no orifice for a tongue, no teeth. Wood can do so many things. It can become wings, water, blades of grass. But no wood seemed suited to the soft red palette of fleshy tongue. Nothing I found could reproduce it. Where to get a tongue? What has become of the one I found for her? Murder? I tell them no, creation. But they don't listen because none of them have accepted the violent truth. These are people who want things neat. Creation in a petri dish. "An act so violent, it sickens me," the judge said, and revealed his own narrow vision. As if everything was separate somehow.

I know a doctor (or he says he is a doctor) who tells me that seeing everything connected, "Hyper-connected" is what he called it, is a sign of mental illness. But I hear it all the time, how everything is connected and we are part of the earth, so what's this then, global madness? Or a generation of saints?

Because it is almost holy to really see all the connections, like standing in a beam of light and the colors floating before you in particles of dust, infinitely separate, the tiny particles of everything, and infinitely whole. Even the night in its echoes of blackness and vastness of stars holds that beam. Like wood holds a woman. Like a mouth holds a tongue.

On the fifth day I noticed something peculiar. I was tired by that time, having worked in a frenzy of steady chiseling and revealing, sleeping beside her in the chip and ash of the wood that bound her, living in a daze of smoke and arias, served occasionally by Chinese food too often delivered by the fat one, until I made a horrible mistake and cut just a little too deeply and revealed in that stroke a gash of white, a chip of bone. Olivia.

She was everywhere half-formed, burgeoning from the wood.

Slowly I walked around her. Wide. As if her still half-fused fingers (long and slender and in no way vulgar as the misshapen knuckles of the fat one) would reach out to me and pull me to be trapped in wood too. It was evening. The light dimmed even as I circled her. Warily.

Olivia. I was very careful then. I carved with religion. Olivia. I prayed. I turned off the music and sang only her name. Olivia. Olivia. I caressed, I pressed. I was gentle with the knife.

There was no blood all this time. The first drop came in the curve of vagina and you can understand how at first I thought it was mine. But as I released her from the bind of being joined like a common, sexless statue, as I dug in and carved a vagina measured by my fingers to suit its design, the knife became wetter and redder and I came to realize it was not my blood but hers, so I kissed her there and licked her and I did not think about what it might mean.

(So should I feel guilty for that? The doctor says to me, Do you crave the taste of blood? As if I am some sort of vampire. I tell him blood is everything. I tell him it is the ultimate aspect of creation. He disagrees. He argues for neatness. I argue life.)

She never cried. Not a single tear dropped from her beautiful eyes. She only looked at me in the changing light with the constant expression. I know what she meant. I understood she wanted to speak. Each chip of wood at her lips revealed only more wood and eventually she began to eye the fat girl delivering Chinese who talked incessantly.

I tried to convince her otherwise. I was not sure this was the tongue we wanted. What if it came with the voice? But Olivia insisted and I had no choice. I was a victim. Olivia is a victim and this, what name did they keep saying, this Vicki, had everything. Skin and hair and a vagina not carved of wood. What did she need with a tongue so loose she spoke without meaning?

In here there are no knives or even forks. They keep bringing me mounds of clay. Brown clumps of lifeless sludge. An insult. I am a carver, I say. I need something sharp.

No, because of the blood.

I think of her. The bright red life coating my hands vibrant as a snow plant burgeoning through the earth. The moment of ecstasy when I held the tongue that would sing me awake.

Would you die for your art?

Yes.

Would you die for your love?

Yes.

Would you die for your life?

Yes. Yes. If it takes that.

Release. Me.

Olivia. Here, it is all metal and cold. White sheets so bright I am frozen in a snow of light. No knives. No picks. Ice. I suck each cube in secret joy. With tongue and licks I form a miniature version of the vulva I measured first with hands and knife and later with lips. The evidence of my desire melts and I form it again. I drink you every day. Olivia. You set me free. I am born. Released. Alive.

♦ ♦ ♦

Anyway

"**W**HAT IF YOU COULD SAVE THE WORLD? WHAT if all you had to do was sacrifice your son's life, Tony's for instance, and there would be no more war, would you do it?"

"Robbie's the name of my son," I say. "Remember, Mom? Tony is your son. You remember Tony, don't you?"

I reach into the cabinet where I've stored the photograph album. I page through it until I find the picture I want, Tony and me by his VW just before he left on the Kerouac-inspired road trip from which he never returned. We stand, leaning into each other, his long hair pulled into a ponytail, and mine finally grown out of the pixie cut I'd had throughout my single-digit years. He has on bell-bottom jeans and a tie-dyed T-shirt. I have on cut-offs and a simple cotton short-sleeved button-down blouse and, hard to see but I know they are there, a string of tiny wooden beads, which Tony had, only seconds before, given to me. I am looking up at him with absolute adoration and love.

"See, Mom," I point to Tony's face. She looks at the picture and then at me. She smiles.

"Well, hello," she says, "when did you get here?"

I close the book, slide it into the cabinet, kiss her forehead, pick up my purse, and walk out of the room. I learned some time ago that there is no need for explanation. She sits there in the old recliner we brought from her house, staring vacantly at nothing, as if I have never been there, not today, or ever.

I stop at the nurse's station, hoping to find my favorite nurse, Anna Vinn. I don't even remember the name of the nurse who looks up at me and smiles. I glance at her nametag.

"Charlotte?"

"Yes?"

"My mother asked me the strangest question today."

Charlotte nods.

"Do the patients ever, you know, snap out of it? Have you ever heard of that happening?"

Charlotte rests her face in her hand, two fingers under the rim of her glasses, rubbing her temple. She sighs and appraises me with a kind look. "Sometimes, but you know, they . . ."

"Snap right back again?"

"Would you like to talk to the social worker?"

I shake my head, tap the counter with my fingertips before I wave, breezy, unconcerned.

Once outside I look at my watch. I still have to get the groceries for tomorrow's dinner. It's my father's birthday and he wants, of all things, pot roast. Luckily, my son, Robbie, has agreed to cook it. All I have to do is buy it. I've been a vegetarian for eighteen years and now I have to go buy a pot roast.

What if you could save the world? I remember my mother asking the question, so clearly, as if she were really present—in her skin and in her mind—in a way she hasn't been for years.

"Mom," I say, as I unlock the car door, "I can't even save this cow."

That's when I realize that a man I've seen inside the home, but who I don't know by name, stands between my car and his (I assume). He stares at me for a moment and then, with a polite smile, turns away.

I start to speak, to offer some explanation for what he's overheard, but he is walking away from me, toward the nursing home, his shoulders hunched as if under a weight, or walking against a wind, though it is early autumn and the weather is mild.

On Sunday, my dad and Robbie sit in the kitchen drinking beer while the pot roast cooks, talking about war. I have pleaded with my father for years not to talk to Robbie this way, but he has always dismissed my concerns. "This is men talk," he'd say, elbowing Robbie in the ribs, tousling his hair while Robbie, gap-toothed and freckled and so obviously not a man, grinned up at me. But now

Robbie is nineteen. He drinks a beer and rubs his long fingers over the stubble of his chin. "Don't get me wrong," my dad says, "it's a terrible thing, okay? There's mud and snakes and bugs, and we didn't take a shower for three months." He glances at me and nods. I know that this is meant as a gesture on his part, a sort of offering to me and my peacenik ways.

The smell of pot roast drives me from the kitchen to the back-yard. It's cooler today than yesterday, and the sky has a grayish cast. Most of the leaves have fallen, the yard littered with the muted red, gold, and green. I sit on the back step. "Didn't take a shower for three months," my father says again, loudly. I hear him through the kitchen windows that I had cracked open, trying to alleviate the odor of cooked meat.

I listen to the murmur of Robbie's voice.

"Oh, but it was a beautiful thing," my dad says. "It was the right thing to do. Nobody questioned it back then. We were saving the world."

For dessert we have birthday cake, naturally. My dad's favorite, chocolate with banana filling and chocolate-chip-studded chocolate frosting. I feel quite queasy by this point, the leftover pot roast congealing in the roaster on top of the stove, Robbie's and my father's plates gleaming with a light gray coating—it was all I could do to eat my salad. "Why don't we have our cake in the living room?" I say.

"Aw, no," my father says. "You don't have to get all fancy for me."

But Robbie sees something in my face that causes him to stand up quickly. "Come on, Pops," he says, and, as my father begins to rise, "you and Mom go in the living room and talk. I'll bring out the cake."

I try not to notice the despair that flits over my father's face. I take him by the elbow and steer him into the living room, helping him into the recliner I bought (though he does not know this) for him.

"I saw Mom today," I say.

He nods, scratches the inside of his ear, glances longingly at the kitchen.

I steel myself against the resentment. I'm happy about the relationship he's developed with Robbie. But some small part of me, some little girl who, in spite of my forty-five years, resides in me and will not go away, longs for my father's attention and, yes, even after all these years, approval.

"She asked me the strangest question."

My father grunts. Raises his eyebrows. It is obvious that he thinks there is nothing particularly fascinating about my mother asking a strange question.

"One time," he says, "she asked me where her dogs were. I said, 'Meldy, you know you never had any dogs.' So she starts arguing with me about how of course she's always had dogs, what kind of woman do I think she is? So, later that day I'm getting ice out of the freezer, and what do you think I find in there but her underwear, and I say, 'Meldy, what the hell is your underwear doing in the freezer?' So she grabs them from me and says, 'My dogs!' "

"Ha-a-appy Birrrrrthday to youuuu." Robbie comes in, carrying the cake blazing with candles. I join in the singing. My father sits through it with an odd expression on his face. I wonder if he's enjoying any of this.

Later, when I drive him home while Robbie does the dishes, I say, "Dad, listen, today Mom, for just a few seconds, she was like her old self again. Something you said tonight, to Robbie, reminded me of it. Remember how you said that during the war it was like you were saving the world?" I glance at him. He sits, staring straight ahead, his profile composed of sharp shadows. "Anyway, Mom looked right at me, you know, the way she used to have that look, right, and she said, 'What if you could save the world? What if all you had to do was sacrifice one life and there would be no more war, would you do it?' "

My father shakes his head and mumbles something.

"What is it, Dad?"

"Well, that was the beginning, you know."

"The beginning?"

"Yeah, the beginning of the Alzheimer's. 'Course, I didn't know it then. I thought she was just going a little bit nuts." He shrugs. "It happened. Lots of women used to go crazy back then."

"Dad, what are you talking about?"

"All that business with Tony." His voice cracks on the name. After all these years he still cannot say my brother's name without breaking under the grief.

"Forget it, Dad. Never mind."

"She almost drove me nuts, asking it all the time."

"Okay, let's just forget about it."

"All those fights we had about the draft and Vietnam, and then he went and got killed anyway. You were just a girl then, so you probably don't remember it almost tore us apart."

"We don't have to talk about this, Dad."

I turn into the driveway. My father stares straight ahead. I wait a few seconds and then open my car door; he leans to open his. When I walk beside him to guide him by the elbow, he steps away from me. "I'm not an invalid," he says. He reaches in his pocket and pulls out his keys. Together we walk to the door, which he unlocks with shaking hands. I step inside and flick on the light switch. It is the living room of a lonely old man, the ancient plaid couch and recliner, family photographs gathering dust, fake ivy.

"Satisfied?" he says, turning toward me.

I shake my head, shrug. I'm not sure what he's talking about.

"No boogeymen are here stealing all your inheritance, all right?"

"Dad, I—"

"The jewels are safe."

He laughs at that. I smile weakly. "Happy Birthday, Dad," I say.

But he has already turned and headed into the bedroom. "Wait, let me check on the jewels."

My father, the smart aleck.

"Okay, Dad," I say, loudly, so he can hear me over the sound of drawers being opened and closed. "I get the point. I'm leaving."

"No, no. The jewels."

Suddenly I am struck by my fear, so sharp I gasp. He's got it too, I think, and he's going to come out with his socks or underwear and he's going to call them jewels and—

"Ah, here they are. I honest to God almost thought I lost them."

I sit down on the threadbare couch I have offered to replace a dozen times. He comes into the living room, grinning like an elf, carrying something. I can't bear to look.

"What's the matter with you?" he asks, and thrusts a shoebox onto my lap.

"Oh my God."

"These are yours now."

I take a deep breath. I can handle this, I think. I've handled a lot already; my brother's murder, my husband's abandonment, my mother's Alzheimer's. I lift the lid. The box is filled with stones, green with spots of red on them. I pick one up. "Dad, where did you get these? Is that blood?"

He sits in the recliner. "They were in the bedroom. They're your responsibility now."

"Are these—"

"Bloodstone, it's called. At least that's what your mother said, but you know, like I told you, she was already getting the Alzheimer's back then."

"Bloodstone? Where did she —"

"I already told you." He looks at me, squinty-eyed, and I almost laugh when I realize he is trying to decide if I have Alzheimer's now. "She wouldn't stop. She almost drove me crazy with her nonsense. She kept saying it, all the time, 'Why'd he have to die anyway?' You get that? 'Anyway,' that's what she said, 'Why'd he have to die anyway,' like there was a choice or something. Finally one day I just lost it and I guess I hollered at her real bad and she goes, 'What if you could save the world? What if all you had to do was sacrifice one life, not your own, but, oh, let's say, Tony's, and there would be no more war, would you do it?' I reminded her that our Tony —" His voice cracks. He reaches for the remote control and turns the TV on but leaves the sound off. "She says, 'I know he's dead anyway, but I mean before he died, what would you have done?' "

"And I told her, 'The world can go to hell.' " He looks at me, the colors from the TV screen flickering across his face. "The whole world can just go to hell if I could have him back for even one more day, one more goddamned hour." For a moment I think he might cry, but he moves his mouth as if he's sucking on something sour and continues. "And she says, 'That's what I decided. But then he died anyway.' "

I look at the red spots on the stones. My father makes an odd noise, a sort of rasping gasp. I look up to the shock of his teary eyes.

"So she tells me that these stones were given to her by her mother. You remember Grandma Helen, don't you?"

"No, she died before —"

"Well, she went nuts too. So you see, it runs in the women of the family. You should probably watch out for that. Anyway, your mother tells me that her mother gave her these stones when she got married. There's one for every generation of Mackeys, that was your mother's name before she married me. There's a stone for her mother and her mother's mother, and so on, and so on, since before time began I guess. They weren't all Mackeys, naturally, and anyhow, every daughter gets them."

"But why?"

"Well, see, this is the part that just shows how nuts she was. She tells me, she says, that all the women in her family got to decide. If they send their son to war and, you know, agree to the sacrifice, they are supposed to bury the stones in the garden. Under a full moon or some nonsense like that. Then the boy will die in the war but that would be it, okay? There would never be another war again in the whole world."

"What a fantastic story."

"But if they didn't agree to this sacrifice, the mother just kept the stones, you know, and the son went to war and didn't die there, he was like protected from dying in the war but, you know, the wars just kept happening. Other people's sons would die instead."

"Are you saying that Mom thought she could have saved the world if Tony had died in Vietnam?"

"Yep."

"But Dad, that's just—"

"I know. Alzheimer's. We didn't know it back then, of course. She really believed this nonsense too, let me tell you. She told me if she had just let Tony die in Vietnam at least she could have saved everyone else's sons. There weren't girl soldiers then, like there are now, you know. 'Course he just died anyway."

"Tony didn't want to go to Vietnam."

"Well, she was sure she could have convinced him." He waves his hand as though brushing away a fly. "She was nuts, what can I say? Take those things out of here. Take the box of them. I never want to see them again."

When I get home the kitchen is, well, not gleaming, but devoid of pot roast. Robbie left a note scrawled in black marker on the magnetic board on the refrigerator. *Out. Back later.* I stare at it while I convince myself that he is fine. He will be back, unlike Tony who died or Robbie's father who left me when I was six months' pregnant because, he said, he realized he had to pursue his first love, figure skating.

I light the birch candle to help get rid of the cooked meat smell, which still lingers in the air, sweep the floor, wipe the counters and the table. Then I make myself a cup of decaf tea. While it steeps, I change into my pajamas. Finally, I sit on the couch in front of the TV, the shoebox of stones on the coffee table in front of me. I sip my tea and watch the news, right from the start so I see all the gruesome stuff, the latest suicide bombing, people with grief-ravaged faces carrying bloody bodies, a weeping mother in robes, and then, a special report, an interview with the mother of a suicide bomber clutching the picture of her dead son and saying, "He is saving the world."

I turn off the TV, put the cup of tea down, and pick up the shoebox of stones. They rattle in there, like bones, I think, remembering the box that held Tony's ashes after he was cremated. I tuck the shoebox under my arm, blow out the candle in the kitchen, check that the doors are locked, and go to bed. But it is the oddest thing: the whole time I am doing these tasks, I am thinking about taking one of those stones and putting it into my mouth, sucking it like a lozenge. It makes no sense, a strange impulse, I think, a weird synapse in my brain, a reaction to today's stress. I shove the shoebox under my bed, lick my lips and move my mouth as though sucking on something sour. Then, just as my head hits the pillow, I sit straight up, remembering.

It was after Tony's memorial, after everyone had left our house. There was an odd smell in the air, the scent of strange perfumes and flowers (I remember a bouquet of white flowers already dropping petals in the heat) mingled with the odor of unusual foods, casseroles and cakes, which had begun arriving within hours after we learned of Tony's death. There was also a new silence, a different kind of silence than any I had ever experienced before in my eleven years. It was a heavy silence and, oddly, it had an odor all its own, sweaty and sour. I felt achingly alone as I walked through the rooms, looking for my parents, wondering if they, too, had died. Finally, I found my father sitting on the front porch, weeping. It was too terrible to watch. Following the faint noises I heard coming from there, I next went to the kitchen. And that's when I saw my mother sitting at the table, picking stones out of a shoebox and shoving them into her mouth. My brother was dead. My father was weeping on the porch and my mother was sitting in the kitchen, sucking on stones. I couldn't think of what to do about any of it. Without saying anything, I turned around and went to bed.

It is so strange, what we remember, what we forget. I try to remember everything I can about Tony. It is not very much, and some of it is suspect. For instance, I think I remember us standing next to the Volkswagen while my dad took that photograph, but I'm not even sure that I really remember it because when I picture it in my mind, I see us the way we are in the photograph, as though I am looking at us through a lens, and that is not the way I would have experienced it. Then I try to remember Robbie's father, and I find very little. Scraps of memory, almost like the sensation when you can hear a song in your head but can't get it to the part of your brain where you can actually sing it. I decide it isn't fair to try this with Robbie's father because I had worked so hard to forget everything about him.

I wonder if all my mother has really lost is the ability to fake it anymore. To pretend, the way we all do, to be living a memory-rich life. Then I decide that as a sort of homage to her, I will try to remember her, not as she is now, in the nursing home, curled in her bed into the shape of a comma, but how she used to be. I remember her making me a soft-boiled egg, which I colored with a face before she dropped it into the water, and I remember her sitting at the sewing machine with pins in her mouth, and once, in the park, while Tony and I play in the sandbox, she sits on a bench, wearing her blue coat and her Sunday hat, the one with the feathers, her gloved hands in her lap, talking to some man and laughing, and I remember her sitting at the kitchen table sucking on stones. And that's it. That's all I can remember, over and over again, as though my mind is a flipbook and the pages have gotten stuck. It seems there should be more, but as hard as I look, I can't find any. Finally, I fall asleep.

Two weeks after my father's birthday, Robbie tells me that he has enlisted in the Marines. Basically, I completely freak out, and thus discover that a person can be completely freaked out while appearing only slightly so.

"Don't be upset, Mom," Robbie says after his announcement.

"It doesn't work like that. You can't do this and then tell me not to be upset. I'm upset."

"It's just, I don't know, I've always felt like I wanted to be a soldier, ever since I was a little kid. You know, like when people say they 'got a calling'? I always felt like I had a calling to be a soldier. You know, like Dad with figure skating."

"Hmm."

"Don't just sit there, Mom, say something, okay?"

"When are you leaving?"

He pulls out the contract he signed, and the brochures and the list of supplies he needs to buy. I read everything and nod and ask questions, and I am completely freaked out. That's when I begin to wonder if I have been fooling myself about this for my whole adult life, even longer. Now that I think about it, I think maybe I've been completely freaked out ever since my mother came into my room and said that Tony's body had been found in a dumpster in Berkeley.

I start to get suspicious of everyone: the newscaster, with her wide, placid face reading the reports of the suicide bombings and the number killed since the war began; my friend, Shelly, who's a doctor, smiling as she nurses her baby (the very vulnerability of which she knows so intimately); even strangers in the mall, in the grocery store, not exactly smiling or looking peaceful, generally, but also not freaking out, and I think, oh, but they are. Everybody is freaking out and just pretending that they aren't.

I take up smoking again. Even though I quit twenty years ago, I find it amazingly easy to pick right back up. But it doesn't take away the strange hunger I've developed, and so far resisted, for the bloodstones safely stored in the shoebox under my bed.

When I visit my mother it is with an invigorated sense of dread. Though I grill her several times, I cannot get her to say anything that makes sense. This leaves me with only my dad.

"Now, let me get this right, Mom believed that if she buried the bloodstones—Are you supposed to bury just one, or all of them?— then that meant Tony would die, right, and there would never be another war?"

"He had to die over there, see? In Vietnam. He had to be a soldier. It didn't matter when he died in California; that didn't have anything to do with it, see?"

"But why not?"

"How should I know?" He taps the side of his head with a crooked finger. "She was nuts already way back then. Want my opinion it was his dying that did it to her, like the walnut tree."

"What's a walnut tree have to do with—"

"You remember that tree in front of our house. That was one magnificent tree. But then the blight came, and you know what caused it? Just this little invisible fungus, but it killed that giant. You see what I'm talking about?"

"No, Dad, I really don't."

"It's like what happened with . . . It was bad, all right? But when you look at a whole entire life, day after day and hour after hour, minute after minute, we were having a good life, me and your mom and you kids. Then this one thing happened and, bam, there goes the walnut tree."

That night I dream that my mother is a tree or at least I am talking to a tree in the backyard and calling it Mom. Bombs are exploding all around me. Tony goes by on a bicycle. Robbie walks past, dressed like a soldier but wearing ice skates. I wake up, my heart beating wildly. The first thing I think is, What if it's true? I lean over the side of the bed and pull out the shoebox, which rattles with stones. I lick my lips. What if I could save the world?

I open the lid, reach in, and pick up a stone, turning it in my fingers and thumb, enjoying the sensation of smooth. Then I let it drop back into the box, put the lid on, shove it under the bed, and turn on the bedside lamp. For the first time in my entire life, I smoke in bed, using a water glass as an ashtray. Smoking in bed is extremely unwise, but, I reason, at least it's not nuts. At least I'm not sitting here sucking on stones. That would be nuts.

While I smoke, I consider the options, in theory. Send my son to war and bury the stones? Did my father say under a full moon? I make a mental note to check that and then, after a few more puffs, get out of bed and start rummaging in my purse until I find my checkbook, with the pen tucked inside. I tear off a check and write on the back of it, *Find out if stones have to be buried under full moon or not.* Satisfied, I crawl back into bed, being very careful with my lit cigarette.

There's a knock on my bedroom door. "Mom? Are you all right?"

"Just couldn't sleep."

"Can I come in?"

"Sure, honey."

Robbie opens the door and stands there, his brown curls in a shock of confusion on his forehead, the way they get after he's been wearing a hat. He still has his jacket on and exudes cool air. "Are you smoking?"

I don't find this something necessary to respond to. I take a puff. I mean, obviously I am. I squint at him. "You know, people are dying over there."

"Mom."

"I'm just saying. I want to make sure you know what you're getting into. I mean, it's not like you're home in the evenings watching the news. I just want to make sure you know what's going on."

"I don't think you should smoke in bed. Jesus, Mom, it really stinks in here. I'm not going to die over there, okay?"

"How do you know?"

"I just do."

"Don't be ridiculous. Nobody knows something like that."

"I have to go to bed, Mom. Don't fall asleep with that cigarette, okay?"

"I'm not a child. Robbie?"

"Yeah?"

"Would it be worth it to you?"

"What?"

"Well, your life? I mean, are you willing to give it up for this?"

I bring the cigarette to my lips. I am just about to inhale when I realize I can hear him breathing. I hold my own breath so I can listen to the faint but beautiful sound of my son breathing. He sighs. "Yeah, Mom."

"All right then. Good night, Robbie."

"Good night, Mom." He shuts the door, gently, not like a boy at all, but like a man trying not to disturb the dreams of a child.

The next day's news is particularly grim: six soldiers are killed and a school is bombed. It's a mistake, of course, and everyone is upset about it.

Without even having to look at the note I wrote to myself on the back of the check, I call my father and ask him if the stones are supposed to be buried when there's a full moon. I also make sure he's certain of the correlations, bury stones, son dies but all wars end, don't bury stones and son lives but the wars continue.

My father has a little fit about answering my questions but eventually he tells me, yes, the stones have to be buried under a full moon (and he isn't sure if it's one stone or all of them) and yes, I have the correlations right.

"Is there something about sucking them?"

"What's that?"

"Did Mom ever say anything about sucking the stones?"

"This thing with Robbie has really knocked the squirrel out of your tree, hasn't it?"

I tell him that it is perfectly rational that I be upset about my son going off to fight in a war.

He says, "Well, the nut sure doesn't fall far from the tree."

"The fruit," I say.

"What's that?"

"That expression. It isn't the nut doesn't fall far from the tree, it's the fruit."

The day before Robbie is to leave, I visit my mother at the nursing home. I bring the shoebox of stones with me.

"Listen, Mom," I hiss into the soft shell of her ear. "I really need you to do everything you can to give me some signal. Robbie's joined the Marines. Robbie, my son. He's going to go to war. I need to know what I should do."

She stares straight ahead. Actually, staring isn't quite the right description. The aides tell me that she is not blind, but the expression in her eyes is that of a blind woman. Exasperated, I begin to rearrange the untouched things on her dresser: a little vase with a dried flower in it; some photographs of her and Dad, me and Robbie; a hairbrush. Without giving it much thought, I pick up the shoebox. "Remember these?" I say, lifting the lid. I shake the box under her face. I pick up one of the stones. "Remember?"

I pry open her mouth. She resists, for some reason, but I pry her lips and teeth apart and shove the stone in, banging it against the plate of her false teeth. She stares straight ahead but makes a funny noise. I keep her mouth open and, practically sitting now, almost on the arm of the chair, grab a handful of stones and begin shoving them into her mouth. Her arms flap up, she jerks her head. "Come on," I say, "you remember, don't you?"

Wildly, her eyes roll, until finally they lock on mine, a faint flicker of recognition, and I am tackled from behind, pulled away from her. There's a flurry of white pant cuffs near my face, and one white shoe comes dangerously close to stepping on me.

"Jesus Christ, they're stones. They're stones."

"Well, get them out."

"Those are my stones," I say, pushing against the floor. A hand presses my back, holding me down.

"Just stay there," says a voice I recognize as belonging to my favorite nurse, Anna Vinn.

Later, in her office, Anna says, "We're not going to press charges. But you need to stay away for a while. And you should consider some kind of counseling."

She hands me the shoebox.

"I'm sure I was trying to get the stones out of her mouth."

She shakes her head. "Are you going to be okay? Driving home?"

"Of course," I say, unintentionally shaking the shoebox. "I'm fine."

When I get outside I take a deep breath of the fresh air. It is a cold, gray day, but I am immediately struck by the beauty of it, the beauty of the gray clouds, the beauty of the blackbirds arcing across the sky, the beauty of the air on my face and neck. I think: *I cannot save him.* Then I see a familiar-looking man. "Excuse me?" I say. He continues, head bent, shoulders hunched, toward the nursing home. "Excuse me?"

He stops and turns, slightly distracted, perhaps skeptical, as if worried I might ask for spare change.

"Don't we know each other?"

He glances at the nursing home, longingly, I think, but that can't possibly be correct. Nobody longs to go in there. He shakes his head.

"Are you sure? Anyway, I have a question. Let's say you could

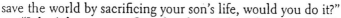

save the world by sacrificing your son's life, would you do it?"

"I don't have a son. Or a daughter. I don't have any children."

"But hypothetically?"

"Is this, are you . . ." He thrusts his hands into his pockets. "Is this some kind of religious thing? 'Cause I'm not looking to convert."

"Are you sure we don't know each other?"

"I've seen you before." He glances over his shoulder. For a moment I'm sure he's going to say something important, but instead he turns away and hurries to the nursing home.

I walk to the car with my box of stones. I have to decide. Robbie leaves in the morning. It's time to stop fooling around.

This, I think, is like a Zen koan. What is the sound of one hand clapping? The secret for these things is not to be too clever. The fact that I am aware of this puts me at risk of being too clever. Okay, focus, I think as I carefully stop at a green light, realize what I've done, and accelerate as the light changes to yellow. It's really very simple. Do I bury the stones? Or not? Glancing at the box, I lick my lips.

When I get home, Robbie is there with several of his friends. They are in his room, laughing and cursing. I knock on his door and ask him if he'll be home for dinner. He opens it and says, "Mom, are you all right?"

"I was just trying to get the stones out of her mouth."

He shakes his head. "What are you talking about?" His eyes are the same color as the stones, without the red spots, of course. "You remember about the party, right?"

"The party?"

"Remember? Len? He's having a party for me? Tonight?"

I remember none of this, but I nod. It's apparently the right thing to do. There's some rustling going on behind him and a sharp bang against the wall, punctuated by masculine giggles. Robbie turns around. "Guys, be quiet for a minute." He turns back to me and smiles, bravely I think. "Hey, I don't have to go."

"It's your party. Go. I want you to."

He's relieved, I can tell. I carry the shoebox of stones into my bedroom, where I crawl into bed and fall asleep. When I wake up, feeling sweaty and stinky, creased by the seams of my clothing, it is like waking from a fever. The full moon sheds a cool glow into the room and throughout the house as I walk through it aimlessly. In the kitchen I see that Robbie amended the note on the magnetic board on the refrigerator. *Gone. Back later. Love.*

I go to the bedroom to get the box of stones. I drop them onto the kitchen table. They make a lovely noise, like playing with marbles or checkers when I was young and Tony was young too, and alive. I pick up a stone, pop it into my mouth, and see, almost like a memory but clearer (and certainly this is not my life), the life of a young man, a Roman, I think. I don't know how long this process takes, because there is a strange, circular feeling to it, as though I have experienced this person's entire life, not in the elongated way we live hours and days and years but rather as something spherical. I see him as a young boy, playing in a stream, and I see him with his parents, eating at some sort of feast, I see him kiss a girl, and I see him go to battle. The battle scenes are very gruesome but I don't spit out the stone because I have to know how it turns out. I see him return home, I see his old mother's tearful face but not his father's, because his father was killed in the war, but then there are many happy scenes, a wedding, children, he lives a good life and dies in a field one day, all alone under a bright sun, clutching wet blades of grass with one hand, his heart with the other. I pick up another stone and see the life of another boy, and another, and another. Each stone carries the whole life of a son. Now, without stopping to spit them out, I shove stones into my mouth, swirling through centuries of births and wars and dying until at last I find Tony's, from the blossomed pains of his birth, through his death in Berkeley, stabbed by a boy not much older than he was, the last thing he saw, this horrified boy saying, "Oh, shit." I shove stones into my mouth, dizzy with the lives and deaths and the ever-repeating endless cycle of war. When my mouth is too full, I spit them out and start again. At last I find Robbie's, watching every moment of his birth and growing years while the cacophony of other lives continues around me, until I see him in a bedroom, the noise of loud music, laughter, and voices coming through the crack under the door. He is naked and in bed with a blonde girl. I spit out the stones. Then, carefully, I pick up the wet stones one at a time until I again find Robbie's and Tony's. These I put next to the little Buddha in the hallway. The rest I put into the box, which I shove under my bed.

The next day I drive Robbie to the bus depot.

"I don't want you worrying about me. I'm going to be fine," he says.

I smile, not falsely. The bus is late, of course. While we wait we meet two other families whose children are making the same trip as Robbie is. Steve, a blue-eyed boy with the good looks of a model, and Sondra, whose skin is smooth and brown, lustrous like stone. I shake their hands and try to say the right things, but I do not look into those young bright faces for long. I cannot bear to. When their parents try to make small talk, I can only murmur my replies. Nobody seems to blame me. It is expected that I act this way, upset and confused. Certainly nobody suspects the truth about me, that I am a murderer, that I have bargained their children's lives for my son's.

When it comes time to say goodbye, I kiss him on the cheek. Oh, the wonderful warmth of his skin! The wonderful certainty that he will survive!

I stand and wave as the bus pulls away. I wave and wave even though I can't see his face, and I have no idea if he can see mine, I wave until somebody, Sondra's dad, I think, tries to get me to stop, then, mumbling, walks away. I stand here waving even after there is no bus on the road. People walk in wide circles around me as if somehow they know that I am the destroyer of the world. They are completely freaked out but act like they're not, because, after all, what can they do about it, anyway?

♦ ♦ ♦

A Very Little Madness Goes a Long Way

SHE IS A YOUNG WOMAN, REALLY, THOUGH coming upon her like this, standing at the window staring out at the bright California sun and palm trees, her hair pulled back in an innocuous ponytail, her shoulders slightly hunched, her arms wrapped around herself in a desultory manner, as if hugging someone who has become tiresome, she gives the impression of being a sad, old woman.

"I thought you'd be happy here," says her husband, who sits at the edge of the bed unlacing his work shoes, his jogging clothes in a heap beside him and his running shoes on the floor by his feet. He isn't rushing exactly, that would be unkind and he is a kind man, but he does have everything ready to go. He wasn't a runner when they lived in Wisconsin. He smiles in spite of her mood, because he isn't much of a runner now either. Who's he kidding? But he likes the heat on his face, neck, and limbs. He likes the vastness of the blue sky, marked irregularly by the palm trees' single thrusts like fingers. Take that, friggin' Wisconsin winters, he thinks when he jogs down Canal and up Avidio Street. He likes the open feeling, so different from their bedroom where she stares out the window like an old woman.

When he's ready, he resists the temptation to bolt from the room. He walks over to her. Places his hand on her shoulder. She sighs. He tries to think of what to say, searching through the ideas as if they were on note cards. I love you. I'm sorry. Everything will be okay. (But he's finally come to understand it might never be.) We could have another child. (He won't make that mistake again.) I love you. I love you. (Does he? Is that what this emotion is? This rooting next to her when he longs to run out of the room and escape into the vast bright world?) "I love you," he says.

She shrugs. It's very slight but he's almost certain that she shrugs. Yet she leans against him, so perhaps he hasn't interpreted that first inflection of muscles right. "Don't you think," she says, "I mean really, I know what you think, but I can't get them out of my head."

"Melinda," he says. Just that. Just her name. But he says it in such a way that she pulls away from him. He lets her. He stands there for a moment and then he shakes his head. If she were paying attention to him, she'd see his reflection in the window, shaking his head. But she doesn't see him standing there and she doesn't see him leave. She doesn't see the palm trees, or the bright blue sky, or the blonde woman across the street bringing groceries into the house, or the man in striped shorts watering his lawn, or the children on bikes in their safety helmets pedaling furiously past as though, on some subconscious level, they know what she has brought with her.

Crows. Their sharp, black beaks. Beady black eyes. Flap of wings, like the sharp crack of pillowcases and sheets snapped open to make a new bed. For someone else's child. She puts her hands over her eyes and sobs. Her husband, in a white blur she doesn't see, blazes past the window. The children on their bicycles shout at each other. She hears them only vaguely through the harsh cawing of the crows. Thousands and thousands of them. Watching her, with those beady black eyes, devoid.

"What you need to do is get involved in something else for a while," her best friend, Stella, says when she calls. "Have you thought of knitting?"

"I'm going to write about them."

"Who?"

"The crows."

Stella moans. Well, it's not exactly a moan, it's a sigh-moan combination, that's what Melinda thinks, and she's been noticing that a lot lately, in the people around her. "You know, I've been thinking," Stella says, "of taking a little vacation. Melinda?"

"I know people think I'm nuts now."

"Nobody thinks you're nuts. It's just, listen, how 'bout I come out there?"

"That crow spoke to me."

There it is again, that combination moan-sigh, perhaps with a small sob or gasp at the end.

"I know you don't believe me. Nobody does. Crows can speak. I just want. . . ." But she doesn't finish the sentence. What she wants is so much. She wants everything. What she's been given is this.

"I'm going to look into some flights, okay? I'll let you know what I find out."

"What? Oh, sure," Melinda says, not really certain what she's agreeing to. All she hears is "flight" and suddenly she is watching them again, thousands and thousands of crows flapping wings and rising only to land swiftly with their cawing sharp cries so loud she can hear them clearly through the closed windows, and all those thousands of miles, and even through time back to that day when she turned from her daughter's bed to stare out the window at those harbingers of death assembled across from the Children's Hospital. No one seemed to notice or understand their significance. Their cold eyes didn't even consider her or the child buried in the clean, white sheets and hospital neat folds of a death they came to carry, the same way they picked through the garbage cans, and the lawn, and on one particularly gruesome day that Melinda still remembers by the strange combination of sweat and cold she felt, as they dove and fought over the corpse of one of their own, a dead crow they pulled apart with their sharp beaks and ate, flying into the trees and screaming at each other, and her daughter moaned or sighed, she made a sound, Melinda turned to her, and knew, by the beautiful light that emanated there, a shiny bright thing in the dark, what would happen soon and who was to blame.

Later, when the crows fell from the sky, plummeting like rocks and landing in yards and playgrounds, and church parking lots, it didn't make her feel better, the way she had thought it would.

Even now, sometimes, she looks to the sky and thinks she sees a black spot hovering above her, destined to spiral down in a swirl of wings and dead weight.

His name is Corvus. His parents, hippies who really did wear flowers in their hair and lived in a bus, had intended to name all their children after birds. He has a sister named Robin and a brother named Jay, but he doesn't see or hear from them much. The one he

hears from is Melinda, born "just at the edge of my change," as his
mother liked to say, during her short second marriage to a carpet
salesman from Iowa who died when Melinda was still a baby of
something like failure to breathe, or some such malarkey of words,
which Corvus can't completely recall. Something stupid like that.
Something bureaucratic to get the paperwork through when all it
really meant was that they didn't know why he died, but he did.

Corvus is the one who flew to the cornfield state to comfort his
mother when no one else would, and even now Melinda, who is a
grown woman with her own life and the sad story of her child's
death, seems to confuse him with her father though he doesn't
think he looks like anyone's dad with his black leather jacket and
his pierced ear and the tattoos of a snake, a naked lady, and on his
back right shoulder, a raven, which he'd done out of deference to
his name (though ravens and blackbirds are not the same) years
before his kid sister went nuts about crows. So when she calls him
from California where they moved to "try to make a fresh start" and
says she is going to write a book about crows, "about the things they
say and do," he rubs his brow and must have made a sound because
she says, "I just wish everyone would quit moaning about me,"
which causes him to pretend he wasn't moaning at all and act
excited and say how he's been thinking of coming out to visit her
and that husband of hers, whose name he can never remember.
What is it again? Not Jack but something normal and ordinary.
Safe.

Is Corvus the only one who realizes the truth about Melinda?
She should have changed her name by now to something extraordinary like Universa. He understands why their mother did what she
did and gave her a pretty but basically normal name. But Melinda
is a grown woman now. Shouldn't she know the truth? Corvus
shakes his head as he begins to sort through piles of black clothes.
What's happening to Melinda, Corvus thinks, can best be described
by a term used for the poor and unloved. Though Melinda is neither, she still suffers from it. "Failure to thrive." She has no idea
how extraordinary she is. She's surrounded herself with bland nor-
malcy. Well, all right, maybe that's not fair, maybe ordinary people
have amazing lives, he wouldn't know, when he sees them, in shopping malls, and coffee shops, or even just driving, they tend to wear
the same expression, which is partly how he identifies them, it isn't
an expression of much, neither satisfaction nor despair, and certainly not harmony. It's like a mask they all wear. And Melinda has
it too. But the thing is, Corvus thinks as he copies Melinda's new

address onto a sheet of paper and tucks it into his wallet, she'll suffocate in that mask, just like her father, like a murder with no witnesses and no blood.

"I can't believe you invited him without talking to me about it first."
"Well, he is my brother."
"He never even remembers my name."
"So, tell him."
"What?"
"It's not like . . . it's not . . . Just tell him."
"I've told him a hundred times."
"So tell him again. Stella is coming out too. What?"
"I thought we moved here to get away from everyone."
"Not me."
"Where are we going to put them?"
"Stella can sleep in my office and Corvus can sleep on the couch. Okay? Okay?"

The thing he hasn't told her about is the crow. It's just one crow, not thousands and thousands of them. It's one crow and he isn't even certain if it's the same one. How's he supposed to know? They all look alike to him. But this crow, well, he knows this is silly, but he thinks it's following him. He first noticed it back in Wisconsin. When the crows started falling from the sky, suddenly paralyzed from the poison. It wasn't unusual to notice a crow then. Circumstances had sort of created a hyper-awareness surrounding them. But this crow always seemed to be looking at him, in that sideways manner of birds. Of course he figured he was imagining it. But then they moved here and he started seeing it again. Just one crow staring at him sideways as he jogged past, watching him when he got into his car in the mornings, standing on the lawn outside the office when he left work. It creeped him out. But he sure wasn't going to tell Melinda, or anyone about it.

Just as he didn't tell anyone about his daughter. People meant well, he knew, but it was nice to not have to deal with sudden kind words and gestures, which, in the end, were woefully inadequate. It was nice to be treated like a regular man and not like someone mortally wounded. That's why he didn't want her brother, or Stella, coming. Well, okay, and he didn't like either of them very much. They were both strange people. He couldn't understand what Melinda got from them that she couldn't get from him.

Corvus isn't surprised to be directed to the side for a security evaluation. They already have his shoes. He takes off his jacket and belt. Raises his arms and turns for the wand. It's silly, really, how they keep trying to change that day in the past by doing the things now they wish they had done then. Corvus is surprised to feel the tear form, and relieved when he's nodded on before it falls, as it does, when he leans over to tie his shoe. How can anyone not have compassion for them? They are so awkward, so earnest, so desperate, and increasingly, so alone. Shut off from the rest of existence, shut off from what would sustain them, by their own fear. He looks at the people waiting in the terminal with him: young families, an old man, some business-suit men and women, a kid playing a little computer game, a baby crying, a young girl. When he takes a deep breath he can smell their human scent, marked as it is by the powerful fear motivator, laced with sweat, indigestion, onion, garlic, perfumes and lotions, and that vague odor of love.

Corvus stands in line and follows them into the plane. He knows there is irony in this, but he made a promise years ago and he intends to keep it. Because he's going to break the other one. He's going to tell Melinda what their mother told him.

He turns sideways to move down the narrow aisle. He senses the seated passengers eyeing him suspiciously. As if evil could be measured by black clothes and long hair. Like children, he thinks, who truly believe they can recognize a bad guy. When he gets to his seat number, he nods at the bald man who looks up at him, and taking in his size, stands in the aisle to let him through. Corvus scrunches into the window seat. He snaps the buckle shut and closes his eyes until the plane takes off. Then he opens them to look at the clouds. How will he tell her? "We are angels."

"What?" the bald man says.

Corvus looks at him, startled. Had he spoken out loud?

"Were you talking to me?"

Corvus shakes his head.

The man frowns and pretends to read his magazine, but Corvus can sense his awareness on him. He readjusts his weight, lowers his seat back, and closes his eyes.

When they land Corvus gets off the plane, just like the rest of them and while most passengers have noticed him, and marked him in their minds, only one passenger has recognized him as someone who knows exactly what he is, only one passenger follows him.

"It wasn't murder," Stella says, rubbing Melinda's back as she weeps, while Joe, who Stella assumes is handling all this the best he can, in his own odd way, runs in circles around the house.

"I mean I was filled with hate. That's the thing," Melinda sobs. "I pretended like it was about reason and logic. But it wasn't. It was just about hate."

"Something had to be done," Stella says, trying to choose her words carefully because the fact is, she'd really been against it all along.

Melinda stops crying. She sits there, staring out the window and biting her fingernail. "Did I tell you one spoke to me?"

"Uh-huh."

"Do you believe me?"

Stella has stood naked in the four directions. She has pledged herself to the earth and the elements. She believes in a lot of things people think are nuts, but even she has trouble believing this.

"What did it say?" she asks.

"You don't believe me, do you?"

"Of course I believe you," Stella says, relieved to find this is true. She doesn't add the explanation: I believe you believe it. She doesn't think she needs to.

"Murderer."

"What?"

"That's what the crow said."

Melinda didn't do anything at all for about two weeks after her daughter died. Slept, mostly. Joe had taken time off too. He slept in late and ate the sympathy food people kept sending over—cheesy casseroles, meatloaf, chocolate cake, banana bread, potato salad, and brownies—in front of the TV where he muttered invectives at talk shows. Then, one day, he got up right in the middle of an episode titled "I'm in love with my mother's husband" or something like that (Melinda could hear it from the bedroom), shut it off, got dressed, and went to work. After that the house was very quiet.

Melinda was surprised to find that sleep was like a drug she could always afford. Sure, sometimes she woke up and stared at the flowered border of her walls, but if she didn't move around too much or open her eyes too wide, she could sink right back into that place where sometimes she found her daughter still alive.

But one day she woke up to the horrible noise of a crow laughing at her. She got out of bed and walked across the room to the window. The ugly bird was on their lawn. Suddenly, it flew up and perched on top of the swing set. If she had a gun she would have shot it. Instead, she ran out into the yard, shouting. That's when it spoke to her. That single evil word, before it raised those great wings and with one last laugh, flew away. Melinda collapsed, just like the bad witch in *The Wizard of Oz*, she sank to her knees in her white nightgown and if she could have melted she would have.

When she got up she went into the house, took a shower, put on sweats and a T-shirt, sat down at the kitchen table, and began writing letters. To the newspapers, the hospital, the PTA, animal control, the local TV news stations. This city was in danger. Didn't what happened to her daughter prove it? It was an invasion. A possible plague. She started a campaign against the crows. Now, after all this time, she sees her motivation. She can only wonder what got into everyone else. Because the plan was absurd, really.

The city council passed the measure with only a vegetarian and a liberal dissenting. They fed the crows bread laced with poison. That's why birds fell out of the sky the way they did. Suddenly paralyzed, they plummeted to the ground. Their corpses littered sidewalks, parking lots, and yards. Once when Melinda was driving to the post office, one plummeted right onto the hood of her car; it's black claws splayed and stiff, its wings spread out like a hard cross.

That night, after Corvus doesn't arrive when he said he would and Stella is asleep on the futon in Melinda's office and Joe is snoring in their bed, Melinda puts on her sneakers and stands in her front yard. They didn't really have a backyard here, just a deck and a strange tree she hasn't identified yet, spindly limbed, a fruit tree of some sort. She stands in the front yard and waits for it to happen. After a while, beneath the white moonglow and the scatter of stars, she begins to rise, she floats up about three or four inches and then, gently, like soft dust, she lands.

She doesn't know what this is all about. She only knows it began happening when things got really bad. She wonders if things are getting really bad again.

Corvus is still alive when the creature removes his jacket, his rings, and the knotted string bracelet Melinda's daughter made for him. He's alive to hear it say, "Clearly a hybrid."

Corvus watches it search through his pockets. When it finds the wallet, it tosses out the money, the credit cards, the driver's license, and the library card. It almost tosses the wallet too, but then the paper with Melinda's address on it slips out. Suddenly its beady eyes focus on his.

"No," Corvus gasps.

The creature smiles.

Corvus looks down and sees a man splayed on the ground, the shape of his limbs at odd angles, but bloodless. Standing beside him is someone wearing Corvus's jacket who turns and looks up at him.

It's like looking at a mirror, only something's not right. The man raises his hand. He is wearing Corvus's rings. He turns and walks away.

Corvus looks down at the body that remains, his eyes ripped out, as though by scavengers. Corvus doesn't have time to mourn. He follows the creature who waves down a taxi and tells the driver Melinda's address.

"Corvus," she says, and she opens her arms to hug the creature but she is glowing with a silver sheen, as if she were the moon; it burns him and he draws upon all his power not to writhe with pain as he walks right past her open arms, pretending he hasn't seen them. He turns at the door to smile at her but everything about her hurts him; even the house contains her glow, even the doorknob.

She stands there in her nightgown and sneakers, her long hair hanging down, so ordinary looking, so easy, a puzzled expression on her face. Clearly, she has no idea.

"It's not me!" Corvus shouts but it comes out faint, having to travel all the distance from death to the living.

"Corvus?" she says.

The creature can't help it. He's terrified of her. Even at this distance, he burns. "I've been sick," he says, suddenly remembering humans and their fear of illness.

Melinda frowns.

The creature smiles. He should have a plan, that's the thing. But he doesn't. He's never needed one before. "Let's go inside," he says, though the house burns him too. Buying time, he thinks, is this what that expression means?

When they go inside a man stands there in boxers and a T-shirt. He puts out his hand. But the creature sees her glow there; he slips his hand into the pocket of the leather jacket.

"He's been sick," Melinda says.

Joe nods. To be polite. But her brother is worse than he remembered. There's even a faint odor coming off of him. Like sauerkraut.

"Do you want popcorn?" Melinda can't help it. Whenever she's around Corvus, she's fourteen again. When he used to visit they'd watch the late movie and eat popcorn.

"I think I'll just go to bed," the creature says, trying to form a plan. But he's finding it increasingly difficult to concentrate and he's worried that he'll lose the disguise if he's not careful, which would not be a problem with the man who looks half-asleep, but he's not sure what would happen with her.

When Melinda brings the creature the sheets and a pillow she looks at his face closely. He looks so different, she thinks, though she can't quite decide why until finally, she sees it. "I never noticed before," she says.

"What?"

"How much you look like a crow."

Behind them, Joe groans.

The creature can't figure out how to get around it, he has to take the pillow and sheets from her or she will just stand there and stare at him, but after he does so he turns away; he is in agony.

"I can help you make it," Melinda says.

"No. I'm going to sit up for a while."

"I'll stay with you. I'll make popcorn."

"I don't like popcorn," the creature says, remembering the strange feel of it in his mouth, once, years ago when he went to a movie with a young woman who was later found raped and murdered. Not by him, of course. He didn't do petty crime. Right away he knows this might be a mistake. He smiles at her again, that baring of teeth. She just looks at him. He raises his hand in a wave.

She doesn't even try to kiss him goodnight. She is surprised to find that she doesn't really want to. Joe falls asleep right away. But Melinda lies there and tries to figure out what's happening. She has trouble concentrating; her mind keeps drifting back to that night, so long ago. When their mother told them she was an angel.

They tried not to laugh but it was impossible not to. Melinda ended up spitting Dr Pepper in a spray while tiny, white flakes of popcorn flew from Corvus's mouth.

"I'm serious," their mother said.

"I'm sorry, Mom. We're sorry," they said.

She stood there in her blaze of red curls and the purple and green kimono and for a minute Melinda thought maybe she was telling the truth, the kimono sleeves sort of looked like wings, and she was the most beautiful mother in the school. Really. Even though she was so old.

Afterward, the three of them sat on the couch eating popcorn and watching a movie about aliens with long, green arms and slits for eyes and the invasion of the world until Melinda fell asleep with her head in her mother's lap, which smelled like dark chocolate.

She had the vague impression that Corvus and their mother spoke then, whispering about angels and demons and wings, but she was never sure if this was something she actually overheard, or something she dreamed.

It's Saturday and Joe likes to sleep late on the weekend so Melinda gets up and tries to be quiet as she walks across the room. She's tired and she can't shake the feeling she's had, since Corvus arrived, of something not being right.

When she walks past the window they begin cawing. She pulls back the drapes. The room blazes with morning sun and the crows' sharp cries. Hundreds of them assembled in her yard, screaming, with their little throats and pointed tongues, the sharp beaks open like her daughter who said, "Mom?"

"Jesus Christ," Joe says, "oh, Jesus Christ." He comes to stand behind her and wrap her in his arms but Melinda doesn't move or soften into his embrace. She stands there, frozen stiff as a corpse while the crows scream. With a sob she pushes past Joe and runs out of the room. She wants Corvus. But he isn't in the living room, or the bedroom either, or the kitchen, or anywhere in the house.

Stella finds Melinda standing in the living room, staring out the window at the crows. It must be the angle of the sun, Stella thinks, because Melinda is glowing, a bright halo of light all around her body, and just like that, with the noise of sheets snapping on a clothesline, the crows rise in flight. Melinda turns and Stella gasps at the odd illusion, the glowing woman surrounded by wings.

"Corvus came," Melinda says, "but he's already gone."

"He'll be back," Stella says, though she really has no way of knowing.

"I don't think so," Melinda says, no longer glowing or surrounded by wings.

Joe comes into the room dressed in his jogging clothes. He says good morning to Stella and gives Melinda a kiss on the cheek. "Corvus is gone," she says.

He suppresses a grin. "Probably just went for a walk." But this is absurd. Corvus is not the kind to go for a walk in the California sun. He is more about shadows and dark rooms. If he is gone, sure, it's weird, but also the sort of thing, Joe thinks, that he's always been capable of. He sighs.

"You can go," Melinda says. "Go. Run."

He thinks of asking her if she is sure but he doesn't want to press his luck.

After he leaves, Stella says, "Are you really worried about Corvus?"

"Something strange is happening," Melinda says. "I feel like I'm in *The Birds.*"

"In them?"

"You know, that movie."

Joe can't help it; every time he leaves the house he feels like he's escaping a great darkness, he feels like he's running away. He loves the hard concrete beneath his feet, the sun shining on his face and limbs. Hell, he even loves the damn birds. When he's running he feels almost whole again. He can feel his muscles and the sweat on his skin. He feels like a man with a body, instead of the husk he's been. God, he misses her. He misses her too, but there's no use trying to talk to Melinda about it because she owns all the sorrow. Well, all right, he thinks as he turns down Avidio Street, that's not fair, but it's been hard enough keeping himself together through all this, and he's not sure how to help her. His feet pound the concrete but he doesn't feel weighted at all, he feels bright, alive, almost winged. He doesn't know what's going to happen to Melinda or to their marriage, but he's already decided, he's going to survive. He's going to learn how to be happy again.

The creature can't believe his luck when her husband runs out of the house like a man making his escape. He watches him and thinks it's just so perfect. He can't destroy her, she's just that powerful, something he understands is both a curse and, he hates to use the word, a blessing, but he can ruin her, oh yes, he can ruin her by ruining everything she loves and believes in.

"Corvus," Joe says, panting and grinning, as if he'd been running to find him. "Melinda was worried about you."

"Come here," the creature says, "I want to show you something."

Joe doesn't know why he's never liked him. That's something the running has helped him with. Afterward, for fifteen, twenty minutes even, once for almost an hour, he feels like he can love again. As though he drank a witch's potion. This time it's landed on Corvus. Joe follows him down a side street and into a narrow California alley lined with concrete walls, roses, and wind chimes.

The creature walks up to Joe who stands there, smiling affably; just for the fun of it, he lets the disguise fall. He watches Joe's face change. Just when he would scream, the creature reaches in, extinguishing the noise, and the light.

*   *   *

"You know what probably happened," Stella says, "they probably ran into each other, went out for coffee together."

Melinda looks at Stella and nods. How can she explain? Evil exists. It stalks her for a reason.

"It's a beautiful day, you should go outside and play."

"I don't wanna."

"Your father and I got you that nice new swing set and you never play on it."

"I hate playing outside."

"Oh, you do not."

"It's buggy. And the grass itches my ankles."

"What are you going to do?"

"I dunno. Sit, I guess."

"I want you to go outside."

"I don't wanna."

"It'll be good for you. You go outside for a while so I can finish my work and then we'll go get ice cream."

"Can't I just stay in the house? I'll be quiet."

"I want you to get some fresh air."

For a while Melinda stood at the window and watched her, lazily swinging and talking to herself. She looked perfectly happy. Safe. But when she came back inside she was probably already dying, though neither of them knew it yet. They went for ice cream. Hers melted so fast she might already have had a fever. "Mom?" she said, and Melinda saved her the way she always had, by licking the dripping scoop until it formed a neat round ball, and by then she might already have been turning into a spirit. Melinda remembers the way she looked, all wide eyes shining with fever and light. Though at the time Melinda thought it was just happiness.

Now, Melinda stares out the window. Stella goes into the kitchen, which is brightly lit by the California sun. She tries not to regret coming here. This is to help her friend, after all. But the depression is palpable. In spite of the blue sky and the light, which pours into this little house, Stella feels like she is walking in a thick fog. It presses her body with unwelcome weight. No wonder Joe has taken up running. Stella glances toward the living room. Melinda is still staring out the window. Furtively, she doesn't know why, Stella walks to the front door. She opens it slowly. It makes a slight popping noise but Melinda doesn't seem to notice. Stella opens the door wide. Just as she takes a step toward it, Melinda speaks.

"What?" Stella says.

"I said, where are you going?"

"I just wanted to step outside for a minute. It's so beautiful out. Wanna come?"

"Do you know what's out there?"

Stella looks out the doorway again. She looks at Melinda. "I'll just be a minute."

Melinda doesn't answer.

Stella steps outside and immediately wants to scream or shout. She shuts the door behind her. God, it feels so good to breathe. She doesn't even think about how she's barefoot and wearing boxers and an old T-shirt but if she had thought about it, she might have concluded that she's been infected by the California spirit. Melinda, staring out the window, might have seen what happened to her, except Melinda isn't staring at what exists, but at what she remembers. It takes her a long time to realize Stella isn't coming back either. It's as if, she thinks, they are being swallowed by the light, the beautiful California day. She stands at the window while the neighbors leave their houses in suits and ties, suits and heels, shorts and sandals, carrying briefcases, school bags, coffee mugs, driving SUVs, Volkswagens, skateboards, and bicycles.

"Be careful," Melinda whispers to the glass. No one hears her and, really, no one would take her seriously if they did. It's obvious she is someone who isn't all there, something not right about her. And that's what the police think too, when they come by later to tell her they found a body, a jacket, rings, a sheet of paper with her address on it. At first she tells them it's her brother but then they mention the jogging clothes, and she says it's her husband and right away they suspect her of murder, maybe a double homicide.

Then things get really strange. The police officers, the detectives, the coroner, the news reporter, everyone who was at the scene of the crime, though they arrive and leave in separate vehicles, have accidents. Every one of them dies.

When a reporter calls to tell her this, Melinda, who has been crying since she had to identify "the body," suddenly dries up. That's it. She's been crying all day and she cried for months before that and now she's done. Because, at a certain point, she thinks, you have to shut down against all the horror of life.

"Do you have any comment?" the reporter asks.

"The body," she says.

There is a long silence. Melinda isn't sure if he's still there or was ever there. Maybe he's just something she imagined. Maybe everyone was.

"Did you say, 'the body'?"

"The body is heavy," Melinda says.

"The body is heavy?"

"We are. . . ."

Again, that silence. Melinda looks out the window and sees the blonde woman arrive home. She gets out of the car and waves to her neighbor, a middle-aged man watering his lawn. He walks over to her and then, in a quick and sudden movement, wraps the garden hose around her neck. She struggles against it, but the man is suddenly amazing in his strength, he pulls the hose tighter, water sprays wildly from the nozzle, the blonde woman kicks but her feet flail in the air, she pulls at the hose, waves her arms in a helpless imitation of its wild gyrations, the stream of water rises and falls, slithering across the blue sky. "My neighbor is strangling my neighbor," Melinda says.

"Right now?"

"Okay. She's dead."

"Did you kill her?"

"No. My neighbor did. Oh, but he's clutching his chest now. A heart attack, I guess."

"Are you saying your neighbors had a fight and killed each other?"

"Uh-oh," Melinda says.

"What now?"

"Children."

"What about the children?"

"Coming down the street. Riding their bicycles."

"Please don't hurt the children."

"What? I would never. Oh, but there they go."

"Where?"

"The car. They're dead."

"Someone hit the children with a car?"

"I suppose. But it didn't look like, wait, here's the driver. She got out of the car. She's covered in blood. She's crying. She's trying to save them. I don't know why. It's obvious, oh, now it's her."

"What?"

Melinda turns away from the window. "Excuse me," she says, "but weren't we talking about something else?"

"The body."

"Oh, that's right. The body is heavy."

"Whose body is heavy? Do you mean your husband's, did you kill him?"

"Kill him?"

"I've done some research. I know about your daughter. Did you kill her as well?"

"It was a mosquito. It bit one of those crows that had it. Then it bit her."

"Yes, well, that's what they said, but now, with all that's happened—"

Melinda moves her thumb and presses the button that shuts his voice off. She watches her neighbors running out of their houses, piling into cars with kids, dogs and cats, ferrets, pet pigs, hamsters, while the adults and children talk on cell phones, wave their arms wildly and scream at each other. She hears a helicopter flying overhead and sirens looming nearer. She opens the front door and is assailed by the violent noise, the screams, the terrible shriek of the helicopter spiraling down, the sirens veering into sick wails, and she smells the blood-metal scent of death. "It's not my fault," she whispers, as she steps outside.

It's just like they say, as if a great weight has been lifted from her shoulders. Melinda begins to rise, but this time she doesn't hover, as she always has in the past; she rises higher and higher until she is as high as the palm trees and even higher still.

The creature, shading his eyes against the bright sun, watches her. With a snort he leaves, going in the opposite direction. The mayhem he brought with him, though it remains, does not continue its relentless course. The wounded do not die, but suffer. Crows swoop down and pick at the shiny parts of the dead: watches, rings, silver hair, and fillings. A wide-eyed EMT, sloshing through the muck of bloody water, turns off the hose. News crews come and set up their mobile units, and food vendors follow. The crows peck at dropped bits of corn dog and discarded fries. The children ride bicycles around the dead, or pick flowers, or go into dark rooms and don't do anything at all. Experts come and say this is recovery. This is the cure.

Melinda soon discovers that she likes to fly so high that she no longer sees anyone, nearer to the sun, unpopulated as it is by human misery. Sometimes she thinks she won't return, but she always does. She understands this is the reason for everything. It took her a whole lifetime to learn how to ascend but it doesn't take her long at all to learn how to dive down again. "We are angels," she whispers to the people. Some of them hear her. Some of them don't.

Waking

What I Saw, When I Looked

*T*HERE ARE OTHERS LIKE YOU, THE BEAST SAYS. "Yes. I know. I'm a human being. There are many of us." *That's not what I'm talking about.*

The beast stands behind me, casting his shadow on the blank paper I stare at, pen poised, waiting for words. Quickly, I turn my head.

The beast stands there on dripping, oily, moldering feet.

Look at me, the creature says.

I look at the disgorged shape of his torso.

No. Look. At. Me.

Slowly, I look up to the festering neck, past the disjointed chin, the bloody caw of its mouth, and then, it is like looking at someone wearing a mask, I gasp, those are my eyes, staring at me from the horrible face.

That's right. The beast nods. *I am you.*

♦ ♦ ♦

The Girl Who Ate Butterflies

I

HER MOTHER CARVED ANGELS IN THE BACK-
yard. The largest was six feet tall and had the face of her
mother's first lover, killed in a car accident when they were still in
their teens. It took eighteen months to sway the purple and blue
webbed stone into wings and skin, to release the wisp of feathers
from the metallic clasp. She carved through the seasons, the easy
spring, the heat of summer. In autumn she moved closer to the
garage and plugged in the space heater, and in winter she wiped
the white ash, that was what she called it, from his broad shoulders
and unformed brow and in fingerless gloves carved him with a heat
that flushed her cheeks and brightened her eyes.

The smallest angel was no larger than Lantanna's pinky and it
was for the memory of an aborted fetus. Lantanna had heard the
woman whisper her request through the closed door on a dark and
moonless night. "I know I made the right decision," she said, "but
still, I feel empty. I want something to mark the absence. A little
angel for the one I sent past. Can you carve it a girl? Can you make
her face at peace?" Lantanna stood shivering in the kitchen doorway, unnoticed by her mother who listened with a passive
expression to the stranger behind the door. "And one last thing?"
whispered the voice. "As you carve will you say a prayer, or whatever, for me. Though I'm sure I made the right choice."

Lantanna turned and walked back to bed. She shivered into her blankets and wrapped them around herself, tight as a cocoon, and fell asleep again without her mother even noticing she had awakened. In her home, as in her life, Lantanna, like a shadow, was rarely noticed.

She was the sort of girl who did not know she was pretty. A pale face with the lightest scattering of freckles on her nose and cheeks. Pale blue eyes the color of dreams. Hair the color of corn.

She wore summer dresses from the 1940s (regardless of the season), thirty years after that time, but unmended and clean as if they had never been worn before. She also wore a slip which was also not the fashion. The dresses were airy as wings, so thin that the slip straps with paper-clip-looking adjusters could be seen through them, as well as the flower at her chest, a squashed tiny pink or white or yellow rose. In the winter she wore little sweaters, the kind with three-quarter-length sleeves and pearl buttons, while the other students at Oakdale High were ripping their jeans and rubbing their new sneakers in dirt. She was pretty but not fashionably so. Hardly anyone noticed. Really, only one.

Quetzl lived in Oakdale in the summer with his father who worked in the city and provided little supervision or restraint. A rare, dark-skinned creature in the town of apple-white, he spent the summers playing his guitar and smoking pot. He watched Lantanna from a distance, first as something vaguely noticed, a blur of color in a vision of black and white, then, with more focus, as she took her daily stroll early each morning past his house, always and mysteriously (in that age when most moved in packs) alone. "She's a space cadet," his friend Emma told him once when she saw him watching Lantanna. But he watched with growing fascination because in the dull, same-paced world of Oakdale, Lantanna was different, and because he was different too, he recognized her as one of his kind.

The day it began Lantanna went to her mother with blood-stained panties. Her mother looked up from the dusty white chiseling to say, "This is the blood of a broken heart all women suffer. It is inevitable. Wounds must bleed." Then, when Lantanna began to cry, scolded, "You should be happy. This is good. You will have a long, pain-filled life."

She showed Lantanna the box of tampons and demonstrated how to use them, watching as she did, tapping her fingers to get back to her work. Lantanna inserted the thin, white cardboard-sheathed cotton with a stab of discomfort and in a tremulous voice asked if she was still a virgin. Yes, yes, her mother nodded. "Though it doesn't matter. Time is relative. After all," she said, "you already have the wound."

Following her mother's instructions, Lantanna washed the blood from her fingers and panties with cold water and yellow soap. By the time she left for her morning walk, her mother was back in the yard absorbed with angel and stone. Lantanna walked past in silence, absorbed in her own study of astral realities. What, she wondered, made true angel wings? Were they gossamer and thinner than glass like butterflies' wings, or were they heavy with flesh and feathers, coursed with veins and blood?

She did not notice Quetzl following her. And he, so absorbed in the swing of her pale pink dress, the arch of her long legs to the drop of short, white slip, did not realize Emma followed him, her eyes glinting with fire.

When Lantanna got to the meadow she walked into the tall grass and lay down. Quetzl stopped at the edge of the meadow and lay down too. At some distance, Emma stood in the shadow of trees that bordered the meadow.

Lantanna lay still. Her arms raised. Her hands like little white stars fallen into the grass. He could only see moments of her face. A small butterfly flitted in the bush nearby, but she did not turn her head or move, only lay there as still and disinterested as a flower. More butterflies flitted nearby. A small orange one lit on her wrist. A tiny blue hovered at her lips but he blinked and in that moment it was gone. Passion rose in him like Jesus' winged heart in the picture over his grandmother's bed.

From her distance it is as if Emma is suddenly sainted, a person who sees spirits and changes in the soul. Seeing nothing that can be described like this, she knows Quetzl has fallen in love with Lantanna. She feels a particular response in her own chest. An expansion of desire, the way flame swells to explode.

Lantanna, in the meadow, knows nothing of those who watch. Lying in the grass, her white arms extended like stems, her hands flower, her little mouth open with one small lilac bloom on her tongue, parched to swallow, dry in the hot sun, her heart beats like the quick wings of the sleepy orange that flits about her and finally lights on her wrist. A small blue hovers at her lips, darts in and out, in a maddening tease before it rests on the lilac bloom. Quickly, she closes her mouth, tastes the fluttering wings. She chews and hears the vaguest crunch of its small body and, treasuring its quick flavor minced with the lilac, swallows. Sighing, she lets her tired arms fall. Eyes closed, she feels the hot sun, the vague itch of meadow grass, hears the insect hum. But the pulse of her heart is the loudest and most vibrant sensation, as if it is filled with all the butterflies she's swallowed since she was a little girl. Wings beating in a blood cocoon. Bursting to be free.

When Lantanna rises from the meadow grass and turns to walk home, Quetzl follows. But Emma does not follow them. She waits until they are out of sight and then walks to the meadow, which is bright at the edge of summer with wild flowers and butterflies, alive with an energy she can describe with only one metaphor. Emma stands at the edge of the meadow, at just about the spot, she estimates, Quetzl lay in. Where the grass looks flattened she bends to touch it, as if it is a holy space, as if by placing her palm where he lay she can touch him. She closes her eyes. Yes, she thinks, she can feel his heat. Then, she lies there too, turns her head to see his vision through the grass, the spear of blades at crosshatch, the flitting of colors, wings, and petals. Here, she knows, he lay and watched Lantanna. Lantanna! Emma rises quickly when she realizes she has been lying in the meadow just like that space cadet. She forgives Quetzl for this. He is bewitched, it is obvious. Everyone knows Lantanna comes from a family of witches.

Emma comes from a family of fire fighters. Her father was a volunteer fireman for the Oakdale Fire Department before he mysteriously disappeared on his way to work two years ago. Almost exactly two years ago, Emma thinks. She remembers the hot tears, the new pain in her mother's eyes. She remembers the first realization of the woman's disappearance that same morning. She wished, for a long time after, that she had paid her more attention. She remembers a vague slash of red lips, dark hair, heavy perfume in church. But she cannot remember more than this. At this point, she can barely remember him.

Emma reaches in her pocket. She pulls out the lighter. She flicks the top with her thumb, expertly. Emma has a secret. She is the girl who loves fire. She used to start fires to make her father come. No matter what time of day or night, how impossible it was for him to be home for supper, how terribly too tired he was for her or her mother, if there was a fire, he was there. Vibrant. Heroic. She used to watch in awe this strange aspect of him, the strength of his stance, the sternness of his face, his power. Now Emma reaches down. With a quick movement she brushes the flame across the grass in front of her. It sizzles, small as a stitch, but she watches it grow in the tangle of grass. She runs quickly to the edge of the woods as the smoke and flame rise behind her, like phantom snakes and devils' tongues.

She runs to the trees at the edge of the meadow and climbs one. The bark scratches her fingers and she tears a pant leg in her rush. But she barely notices such minor pain. Though it has been two years since he left them, it is at moments like these that she feels closest to her father. There is the same rush of excitement, the same heat of anticipation that used to bring him. Now she can relish the feeling. It is almost like having him back again. The meadow burns. A late afternoon breeze pushes it farther. Emma feels the sting of smoke in her eyes. Strains to hear the sound of sirens. Emma climbs higher. She can see the dirt street, the distant houses. Fire snakes through the grass below. Her eyes sting. Her throat tightens. Even the tree is hot. She feels the pores of her skin open and tears weep out. Her hands tighten to hold the limb, her fingers strain like bird claws, the bones pressed against the skin. Smoke fills her lungs with pain. The flames reach for her. She screams. She feels she screams but she hears no sound other than fire.

Suddenly. He is there, in his suspenders and baggy, yellow fire pants. He stands at the edge of the limb. Graceful as a star balanced on its point. He is saying her name over and over again. *Emma, Emma, Emma.* He extends one hand to her; with the other, he parts the sky. She can see just past him a blue and gentle day at the edge of summer. *Emma, Emma,* he says, *Come.* She stands. She stretches her hand to touch his. The limb creaks. *Come,* he says. He parts the smoke and flame with one hand. Reaches for her with the other. She strains to touch him. She hears a sound like a branch breaking and suddenly she is falling. Falling. On fire. Where? In the blur of heat and pain she forms this final thought. Where? Where are you now?

II

It is a long winter. It snows every day and the air is brittle. When the sun shines, it sharpens the points of ice that hang from the eaves like daggered teeth.

Lantanna's mother carves a graveyard angel for the girl who died in the fire. She thinks Emma and Lantanna were friends because of the way Lantanna cried and cried. She wept for days and nights. She would eat nothing but tears.

Lantanna's mother tried to comfort her. "You have to stop crying. You have to make the decision. Death is inevitable," she said. "Joy is not. You have to choose."

Of course there had been other winters. Long months when the meadow was frozen and the butterflies gone. Lantanna suffered through those other winters but only by counting the full moons until summer. Now, she cannot count, for she does not know when the meadow will be alive again.

Quetzl sends her letters. Many, many letters. He writes of beauty, desire, and loss. He wrote, *The lesson of the fire is that we must accept we all burn. I burn for you. I go to sleep with the memory of your eyes. Do they remember me?*

Only vaguely. She had been surprised when, on that last summer day, he had come up from somewhere behind her on the path and introduced himself. He had begun speaking strangely almost immediately. He told her he had been watching her. Then he said he would make her a light lunch of butterfly pasta.

But of course, it wasn't butterflies at all, only bow-shaped pasta sprinkled with parmesan and melted butter, and she did not even taste it, because the fire engines screamed past and she looked down the road in the direction they traveled and saw that the sky was a bright orange of fluttering blues and wings and she knew that the meadow was on fire. Of course, they wouldn't let her near it. She heard them talking about a body, whom she later learned was the girl, Emma. Whenever Lantanna tried to picture Emma, even after she saw her face in the newspaper, she could only hold the image for a fleeting moment. It was true, she was haunted. But not by the death of Emma.

At night she dreamt the fluttering of wings brushed her cheeks and teased her lips.

And it was strange, in the way that strange things happen, that just when she was at her worst, suffering the despair of what was lost from her life forever (some things should be certain, an appetite fed, for instance) that, though she had not answered a single letter, Quetzl came to her, knocking at the door in the midst of another winter storm. He found her wan and pale, shivering in her too-thin dress. She invited him in and brought him to warm by the fire but he could see that she was suffering, and his love sank to the depths of her despair, and he felt it within him, in the place where Emma died, a greater widening of the emptiness. He implored her to eat and removed from his knapsack a bruised peach, a flattened sandwich, a brown-spotted banana, but she wanted none of it. In desperation he moved her closer to the flame where he discovered he could see, not just through the thin fabric of her pale yellow dress to the wisp of shape beneath, but through her skin to the blue course of veins and delicate bones.

He found Lantanna's mother in the garage, huddled near the space heater, carving an angel who looked vaguely familiar. He watched for a long time her intense carving, before he approached, saying, "You give more attention to this statue than you do your own daughter." At which she did not pause but continued to carve, the scrape of metal against stone shrill to his ears. "Did you hear me?" he asked.

"I heard you."

"Well?" he said. "What kind of mother are you? Can't you see what's happening?"

At this the woman laughed. "I see what's happening," she said. "You're happening. And if she can survive you, perhaps she'll live."

"Survive me?" Quetzl sputtered indignantly. "I love her."

"You destroy her."

"I save her," he said, and then turned on his heels, muttering, "Standing here talking to a crazy old witch," he walked out of the garage into the storm.

That night he returned with a car and took Lantanna and a suitcase he directed her to pack and drove through the white snow sifting the sky, soft as petals. "Where are we going?" she asked, suddenly aware that she was confused.

"Mexico," he said.

"But why?"

She slept. When she woke, it was light. He offered her a hamburger and this she refused but she ate some of the lettuce and the tomato so he was pleased. The stars were white-bright, intense. She slept. When she woke again a hot sun followed them. Her cheeks were wet, and she sniffed at her own scent, salty, musty. He drove with a grim resolve, stopping to piss, to kiss her mouth that she was embarrassed tasted of her own bad breath. "Mexico?" she said, and he shrugged his shoulders and nodded as if, yes, it was strange, but somehow inevitable. "Why, we're driving into summer," she said. At night they slept in rest stops where she washed her armpits, and feet, and crotch, and wet a comb through her hair, and still she felt wild somehow and could not wash or neaten the feeling away. She'd squint into the dimpled, mysterious rest-stop mirrors and try to see the change reflected there, the strange strength that grew inside her, and she looked at his face and came to believe she saw it in his profile too. Wild. Free.

When they got to the border there was a wait of traffic and it was the first time she entered another country and she did not know it would be so much like an amusement park. Tijuana was strange, bright with color, and cheap, but he kept driving past chain-link fences with holes cut out of them that marked the border, past cardboard-and-tire shacks with the blue light of a TV inside, past the fish stands, and women with babies, begging. He stopped only to look at the map and she began to think that this was not love, not love at all, but some sort of obsession until just then he said, "We're here. I think." But it was dark and so they slept until morning showed them the edge of the jungle and they followed the strange trail she could not object to because it was inevitable until at last they stood at the top of the hill and he waved his hand across the expanse of valley below. "Here," he said, "I give you this." She had to squint and not really look at all before she saw that the spotted trees quivered with red and black wings, thousands and thousands, so what could she do but walk into them? They lit on her, in her hair, on her hands. They fluttered against her skin. "Monarchs," she said.

"Yes," he said. "For you."

"Monarchs," she said again.

"Because you love them."

Monarchs flitted against her skin and hair. Each touch reminded her of the loss.

"Now you see how I love you," he said. "I left home. I stole the car. I did everything for you. Because I know you miss the butterflies. I would do anything for you. I would die for you."

"But. . . ." She could not continue. She saw the bright light in his eyes and could not cast it out with the venomous truth. He saw the tears in her eyes and mistook them for joy. He broke the distance between them and kissed her with the passion of a thousand wings, of an exile, of an appetite starved.

She returned the kiss with her own pain. Poisonous. All these butterflies, she thought, and not one of them edible. His tongue fluttered in her mouth. She had to concentrate not to bite down. He pressed against her. His hot hands on her thighs, her panties stretched tight as his fingers wiggled inside, eager, one tip, wet, there. She groaned. His other hand pushed the panties down. Yes, why not, she thought. Anything, anything to stop the sound of wings.

"Oh, Lantanna," he said. "I will love you forever."

But this she could not believe. Even as she lay on the jungle ground, monarchs fluttering against her skin and brushing her hands, even as she arched to meet the stab of pleasure, even later in the car where it happened again, and at the rest stops, beneath the desert stars, even as he risked arrest to drive her home because she missed her mother, even though she knew he meant to, she also knew he could not love her forever, for he did not love her now, not really. Not knowing her secret, not understanding her appetite, how could she believe he loved her at all?

III

When they returned to Oakdale, Quetzl was arrested. They talked of arresting Lantanna but Quetzl said she did not know he'd stolen the car. Lantanna did not want to go to prison so she did not argue for truth.

Winter melted. Quetzl wrote to Lantanna every day. Every day she read his mysterious, passionate letters and wept.

Finally, she took the bus and hitchhiked to the county jail.

"How did you get here?" he asked.

"I took the bus and hitchhiked," she said.

"I don't want you hitchhiking. It's dangerous."

"Anyway," she said, to change the subject.

"No. Not anyway. I'll end this visit," he said, "if you don't promise. Promise me you will not hitchhike again."

"Quetzl."

"Promise."

"You're not understanding."

"What am I not understanding? I love you. I want you safe."

"No," Lantanna said. "That's not what I mean. What you don't understand is I won't promise you anything. I am not the one," she said. "You need me. Let's just be clear about this. You need me. And I don't need you. So don't make threats that hurt only yourself."

Quetzl waved for the guard.

Dear Lantanna,

Yes. I need you. Beautiful, beautiful girl. I love you. I need you for your beauty. Your love of beauty. Come visit. Tell me you love me. I live to hear you say it. I would do anything for you. I would die for you. But I don't want you to die for me. I just want you to be safe. Come back to me. I love you. I love you. I love you. Say it.

The second visit.

"How did you get here?" he asks.

"I took the bus and hitchhiked," she says.

"I just want you to be safe."

"How can you love me," she says, "if you don't believe I want the same thing for myself?"

"Lantanna, I love you. Tell me what you want. Tell me what will make you love me."

"Well," she says, "that's a start. Finally, you ask. There are things about me. Things you do not even guess. I have many secrets and there is one that really matters. I've never shared it with anyone. I've never known anyone who would understand."

"Yes. Me. I love you. You can tell me anything."

"This I have to show you."

"Then show me."

"I can't show you here."

"Will you wait for me?"

"How can I answer? How can I know?"

Several nights later she is awakened. "Quetzl?"

"I escaped," he says. "But they'll find me. They'll come here. We have to go."

"What?" she says. "Is this your gift to me? I don't want to go to prison for helping you to escape."

"No, no. Didn't I tell you?" He sits beside her on the bed. He grabs her arm and she feels the pulse and weight of his passion. "You never wrote, you only visited twice, and when you came we fought. I have this all planned. You tell them I kidnapped you. If we're caught you tell them that. See, I have this rope. Let me tie you up."

"You must think I am really stupid."

"Lantanna," he begs. "Trust me. All I've ever done is love you. I am here because I love you. I escaped so you could show me your secret."

"It's not here," Lantanna says. "It's not in this room." She sees now that he is sweating. She sees fear in his eyes.

"Lantanna, please."

It isn't that she really believes he loves her but because she hopes he does, that she agrees. He ties her wrists to the bedposts. She watches his profile as he does. So serious in his work he does not seem to notice her. With the final knot he kisses her. "I won't do this, if you don't want me to," he says as he lifts her thin nightgown.

When he kisses her, she kisses back. It is wonderful, she thinks, to only lie there. He is hungry. It has been a long time and she knows about appetites. He is touching her everywhere. As if his hands had wings. She closes her eyes and tries to feel only these feelings and forget, for a while, the longing, the empty hunger, her own appetite.

Afterward, he takes the silver scissors shaped like a bird from her dresser and saws through the rope. It dangles on the posts and the loops bracelet her wrists. When they stand up together there is a wet spot exposed on the bed. "That's good," he says, "it looks like I raped you."

It is getting light. They sneak down the stairs together as if Lantanna lived in a house with the sort of parent who would interfere.

She takes him down the path, past his father's house, past the burnt trees of last summer's fire, to the meadow, which is stubby as a bad haircut but sprite with flowers.

"I didn't know it would grow back so quickly," he says.

She lies down. She ignores him. He finds this moving, that she has let him in so close now that he can see what she is alone. She picks a bud and puts it in her mouth. He is fascinated. This small gesture he had not seen before. She raises her arms, the knotted rope bracelets her wrists, her hands are like little white stars fallen into the meadow grass. The early morning strengthens with heat. He is restless. But she is still and he has learned patience from her stillness.

Finally, a very small, yellow butterfly begins to flit about. It lands on the rope.

He thinks, This beautiful girl.

It flits around her lips.

Beautiful, beautiful.

It lands on the bud in her mouth.

Beauti—

She snaps her mouth shut. Chews. Swallows. She looks at him. He looks at her.

She covers her face with her hands, like a child, as if by not seeing him she disappears. When she removes them, he is still watching her. She cannot bear what she sees. She closes her eyes.

"Go away," she says.

"I can help you."

"No. Go away."

"But I love you," he says.

She looks at him.

"Really," he says.

"And this?" she gestures toward her mouth.

"I'll help you," he says. "I'll stick by you while you work it out."

"This is not a problem," she says. "This is my appetite."

He bends to kiss her, but just above her mouth, hesitates.

"Don't worry," she says, "they don't fly back out."

She closes her eyes. For a long time the only sound is the scrying of bugs. Then she hears the sound of his feet like a scythe, cutting through the meadow grass.

Now, everything is different. She does what she has never done before. She picks another bud. Places it in her mouth. Today she will eat until she has enough. A small blue flits about. She waits. Waits. Waits. It lands on her tongue. Wings fluttering. She bites. In the distance, she hears sirens. Chews. Yes, everything is different now. Swallows. It even tastes different. It tastes better.

♦ ♦ ♦

Many Voices

*T*HERE ARE MANY KINDS OF PRISONS, AND MINE is not the worst one. I leave it in my sleep anyway, along with that body prison in repose, and travel the starry way to my garden, which even in closed blossom smells so sweet I cannot help but sigh. With ethereal fingers I commence weeding, hence my garden's reputation for being both beautiful and haunted. But I am not a ghost. I return to my body with clang of gate and prison noise, the shouts of women abandoned to this fate by a world of men, mostly men, who cannot accept our witchy ways, we who would direct our own fate, who have saved ourselves the best we can, only to be confined to the cuss and piss of this ugly place. I wake weary from my work. When I open my fist nothing is there. My palm reveals only the tremble of my faith.

"You are delusional," Laura said. "I want you to try to understand that."

"Your whole body is made of space," I said. "You are a solar system."

"Mental illness is nothing to be ashamed of. You, of all people, should know that."

"No."

"It's your best defense."

"Do what you want, it won't change anything."

Laura, with her red-gold hair that will not be tamed, though she tries valiantly, and so has a bubble of curls around her neatly made-up face. I stare at her until she looks away. She is twenty-six and I am her first big case. Huge. She will lose. It isn't really my neck she's worried about. Poor thing in her little blue suit, the beating of her heart in the pulse at her throat, like a sparrow.

"Hey, Rose," Thalia whispers, "I got a friend. She got a problem."

"What sort of problem?"

"Like, is it true? What they say about you?"

"Some. Some not."

"She ass me to ass you if you could help."

"Not if she's afraid of me."

"Oh, it ain't against you personal, you know, it's just the way she is. She thinks you seem real nice though and not at all like the newspapers said you was."

"Thalia, I don't have much tolerance for bullshit."

"What?"

"Just say what you've got to say, all right?"

"It's her babies."

"Okay?"

"She killed them."

"What do you want?"

"She wants them back."

"Well, they already are back."

"What the fuck?"

"They're someone else's babies now."

"Bitch. Crazy white bitch."

" 'Course she's just a bitch," the new girl says, and leans over to spit on me.

"Shut the fuck up," Marlo shouts, "I'm trying to watch this."

"Cunt," the new girl whispers.

A room full of women, a coven of sorts.

"Hey. I don't want you looking at me."

"Will you shut the fuck up?"

"She's throwing a hex."

"She ain't throwing a hex. It's just like they said. She's just crazy."

"Shut up! Shut up! Shut up!"

A storm of fists, and shouting. Guards come into the room and pull us apart. Thalia points at me. "It's all her fault. She put a hex on us."

"Shut the fuck up," says the guard. "Crazy witch."

I knew the jury would find me guilty even before they did. I could see it in the light around their bodies and what happened with it when they sat close together. I closed my eyes and the light around my body mingled with theirs. Laura kept trying to get them to say I am crazy, which tells you how well she understood what was going on. But they weren't buying it. They said I am a sane woman and knew exactly what I was doing, which is my personal victory.

"I refuse to take the blame for this," Laura said through clenched teeth and a sympathetic demeanor, her hand gently rubbing my back as she polled the jury. Each face, each parting mouth, each water soul dissolving said it, "Guilty. Guilty. Guilty . . ."

I couldn't stop smiling.

"Rose, do you understand what is happening?"

The light around her body tells me she is tired and there is a black hole around the area of her throat. I have repeatedly warned her of this problem and she simply ignores me. There is nothing I can do in cases like these except love. I send love light to her through my forehead and heart and it makes a triangle, which closes the black hole but this is, of course, only temporary, and she says, "Rose?"

"They say I'm sane."

"You're going to prison, Rose."

JOAN OF ARC KILLER FOUND GUILTY
"Her angels can go there with her," said Frank Wakind,
husband of the victim.

Dear Rose,

Your father and me are sorry we could not be there for you at the trial. As you know we are having a hard enough time as it is so we couldn't just take off after you out there and leave everything to go to weed. We did talk to that man your lawyer sent down and told him all we could remember about your condition. He agreed with what your father been saying all along about the state of your mind and when he said that your father left the room and got back to plowing which as you know is his way of saying prayers and thanking Jesus for the truth about you which you hated him for but now you see how he was right all along and maybe you can begin forgiving and I can finally have some peace because as you know the truth

shall set you free. Oh I almost forgot to tell you I saw Cather-
ine Shelby at the A and P and she told me to tell you she
prays for you but now you gotta start praying to God and for-
get all this other stuff and remember God loves you and I do
and so does your father and he loves you very much dear.

When I think of you as a little girl I try to point to when it
happened and I remember that tragedy with that boy and
maybe I should of done something better for you but your
father says there is only one place to fix the blame and mostly
I think he is right 'cause you killed that lady. Oh, my little
girl, you need to stop this nonsense about angels because you
are not a saint my dear but a big sinner. I'm checking bus
schedules and will try to see you in October.

> *Love,*
> *Your mother*

The little girl in the apple orchard has red hair and that is why
her parents named her Rose and simply abandoned her given name
of Elinor when they adopted her already almost two years old and
carrying a fancy store-bought baby quilt that neither parent asked
about or saved though Rose memorized each picture that contains
it until she can close her eyes and see the red-haired woman who
bought it. There are only six apple trees. Technically it is not an
orchard but that is what everyone calls it. Rose calls it an orchard
too but she also calls each tree by its name, which she has learned
through careful listening. It is in the spring of her eighth year that
the first angel appears to her, glorious in her body of bright, beautiful in her wings. She appears to Rose in her bedroom, murmuring
things an eight-year-old girl couldn't possibly understand. In later
years angels will appear to Rose anywhere, the kitchen, the bathroom, school, the park, the grocery store, but in those first years
they only appear in the bedroom and the apple orchard.

Sometimes her mother watches from the kitchen window or the
distant field and the angels tell Rose to wave. Her father doesn't
look at her most of the time. The angels try to shield her when he
does, but when it comes right down to it there is little they can do
with their amorphous wings against the awesome fact of his body. At
the supper table he looks at his meatloaf and says, "How old're you
now?"

The day she tells him she's ten, he says, "You'll come with us
tomorrow and pick stones."

She knows better than to argue. She wakes in the dark. Goes to the orchard and tells the trees of her great love. A dozen angels circle her and take turns telling her, her own life story, which makes her weep.

"But we'll always be with you," they say, their voices like bees.

That day Rose picks stones in the fields with her mother and a couple boys from the high school. The stones are rough and sharp. Some are heavy. Some are light. Her fingers hurt and the palm of her hand hurts and then her back hurts and her neck, and the sun is so hot, the straw hat little help, and besides, it itches. In the distance she can see the orchard, lonely without her.

She and her mother leave the men to make lunch. They make cheese sandwiches and ice tea.

"With the extra hands it's all getting done so quick," says her mother.

Rose looks at her hands. They don't belong to her anymore. They look like claws.

"Your father and the boys won't be in for another half-hour."

Rose, who has already begun to see and understand things no one else does, will always be somewhat dense about understanding and seeing herself in the world.

"I wouldn't mind if you was to take a little break."

She loves her mother. She loves her so much she gives her a big hug that fills the room with pink until her mother says, sadly, "Oh Rose," and then she lets go and runs out of the house. The screen door slams shut behind her and the chickens squawk and she runs to the orchard suddenly filled with light. She hugs all her friends. The angels stand at the edge of branches and pretend to fall off, only to swoop up at the last minute like owls diving for field mice, which is an old trick by now but still makes Rose gasp and then laugh which she does until she hears the clang of the bell, and sees the dark silhouettes of her father and the boys in the field coming home. It is then she sees the shadow on the right, the taller one who walks like he's pushing against a heavy wind, fall to the ground, his whole body torn apart as if clawed by a great beast. She covers her eyes. When she takes her hands away she sees him clearly, a freckled young man with close-set eyes.

"It's beginning," the angels say.

Rose walks slowly to the house. The boys are hungry and gobble the sandwiches without saying much. In the silence she tries to choose the best words.

"Frank?" she says.

The boy turns to her, an astonished look on his face, as if he's

only just discovered her presence at the table, or already fears the truth of what she's going to say.

The other boy, Eddie she thinks his name is, laughs as if there is something funny in her voice but no one else seems to hear it, and he swallows the laugh with another bite of his sandwich. She looks at him, and sees how the light around his body is all mixed up, wild colors and a heavy dose of gray that spiral and jag into him. She has seen this before on other teenagers.

She turns back to Frank. He looks at her with those blue eyes, his pale face only slightly pinked by a scattering of freckles like brown sugar. She knows he is not considered a handsome boy but the light around his body is beautiful, like the angels, though not so bright of course, and even as she looks at it, she can see how it is becoming part of the air around him as if he is melting.

"You gotta be careful for the next couple a months," she says.

He raises his eyebrows.

She knows the way it sounded, like a threat and not a warning. Her father glares at her across the table and Eddie starts laughing again but this time he muffles it behind his hand and his shoulders shake.

She thinks maybe she should explain but under the weight of the room she weakens. She looks down at her plate and picks up a small dot of cheese. She can feel her father looking at her and Eddie laughing and her mother taking a deep breath. Only Frank seems unconcerned.

At the end of the summer he falls into the threshing machine. She can hear his screams all the way in the apple orchard. She knows her father and Eddie are with him. Her mother is running to the house. She lies on the grass and looks through the leaves at the small, bitter apples. He doesn't scream for long. In the silence she hears sirens.

"I should of listened to you better, I guess."

She's afraid to look at him. But he looks all right. Not bleeding at all. He squats down beside her. "You ain't like the rest, you know."

"Neither are you," she says.

He laughs and rubs the top of her head. She feels it faintly, as if a gentle breeze moved there. For a moment he looks the way boys do in movies before they kiss the girl, nothing like her dad, but then he stands up real fast. She has to shield her eyes because he stands in front of the sun. He looks toward the field and sighs. "My mom is gonna throw a fit."

"I'm sorry," Rose says.

He shrugs. Puts his hands in his pockets. "I gotta go see if I can find her."

Just like that he is gone. Her mother finds her asleep in the orchard. "Come in now for supper," she says. Rose doesn't mention the specks of blood on her mother's wrist and throat and her mother doesn't mention Rose's warning. Rose thinks maybe it is forgotten until Eddie stops showing up for work and her father can't find anyone to help.

"I just don't understand these boys," she hears her mother say one morning as they walk past her bedroom.

"It's that Eddie Bikwell. If this thing had to happen why couldn't it happen to him?"

"George!"

"He's told everyone she's a witch."

"Well, no one believes in such things no more."

Their voices fade down the stairs. Rose watches the sun rise. When it does, she dresses and goes downstairs to make breakfast. She makes scrambled eggs and bacon and toast. Then she goes to the yard and rings the bell that brings her parents to the house. They come in smelling like hay and manure. Between chores and school she doesn't have time for the orchard anymore. The angels visit her at home. They tell her to be careful but she doesn't really understand. When her father asks her who she's talking to she tells him.

"We got ourselves someone else's problem," she hears him tell her mother one night.

"She's ours, George, sent to us by God."

"Maybe we weren't meant for no children. Maybe this is a curse."

"She loves you like you was her born daddy."

"I'm just sayin' maybe they should of warned us if there was something like this in her family."

"We're her family."

"I'm just sayin'."

Could you just tell me a little about your professional background?

Well, I graduated from Victory High in 1988 and went to the University of Wisconsin, Milwaukee. I graduated there in 1991 with a degree in psychology.

How did you manage that in three years?

I took a full load. I went to summer school. It wasn't so hard. I just stayed focused.

So, why the big hurry to graduate?

It was an economic consideration mostly. I just figured if I could do it in three instead of four, well, that's one less year of student loans.

Is that when you started working at St. Luke's?

I started working there my first year in college and I stayed there.

Doing what?

Oh, at first I was little more than a candy striper. You know, sort of an aid to the doctors and the play-group therapist. I helped get patients to their appointments. Passed out magazines. Changed the TV channel, stuff like that.

Let me back up here a little. What kind of a place is St. Luke's?

A facility for the mentally ill.

A hospital?

Not exactly. The people there are, it's been determined, not in need of hospital care but do need some kind of institutional care.

Sort of like a halfway house?

Well, sort of. Only in a halfway house the expectation is that the people will move on. Become self-sufficient. St. Luke's wasn't like that. Some of the people have been there twenty, thirty years.

By "some of the people" do you mean the patients?

Yes.

So you worked at St. Luke's all the time you were in college?

Yes.

And did your job description change over time?

Well, as I said, I started out doing sort of general stuff and then I got more and more responsibilities.

Such as?

Dispensing medicine. Watching—

Excuse me. You say you didn't even have a bachelor's degree yet but you were given the task of dispensing medicine?

It's not really that complicated.

What else?

I started working night shift and more and more I became the person in charge.

You mean you were in charge of all the other workers at your level?

No. I was in charge of the patients.

Where was the administration, the doctors?

They went home.

How many patients were there?

Thirty-eight.

What was the night duty, when you were in charge, like?

Mostly quiet. I mean once in a while there'd be a wanderer. The people there are heavily drugged. They go to sleep okay, mostly.

So what happened that changed your relationship with the patients?

You mean Mrs. Tate?

Tell us about that.

Mrs. Tate started wandering. She just couldn't get to sleep. She became quite agitated. She came up to me and asked me to help her.

And what did you do?

I helped her.

How?

Well, I could see right away what a mess was around her, in her aura there were these two lost souls. One was okay, just a little baby, but the other was evil, an evil spirit, and it was all attached to her like glue, like she'd walked through it and was all sticky.

How did this happen? In your opinion?

Mrs. Tate's been in and out of institutions for years. I figured somewhere along the way someone died and he or she, you can't tell the sex usually at this stage, attached itself to the first vulnerable one to come along. Mrs. Tate was it.

So, what did you do for Mrs. Tate?

It wasn't really that complicated. The first one was easy. I just reached in and grabbed it and gave it to one of my angels.

Your angels?

Yes.

Please, continue.

Well, as I was saying, that one went fine. She immediately felt somewhat better. I told her about the other one though, that it would take more time.

You told Mrs. Tate her aura was, what would you say, being haunted by an evil spirit?

Well, I'd say invaded, but basically, yes.

What . . . well, how did Mrs. Tate react to this?

She wasn't surprised, if that's what you mean. She said she'd known for years and had just given up on trying to tell anyone 'cause no one believed her when she did.

How did you proceed?

I told her to stop taking the night cocktail.

The night cocktail?

The drugs they . . . I dispensed at night. It wasn't anything she needed. Just sleeping medicine that wasn't working anymore and it was creating all these holes in her aura that this thing had attached itself to.

But don't they usually make patients take their drugs right there, show the under tongue thing?

Yeah, but I was mostly the one doing the dispensing by then.

Right. So are you saying you took her off her medication entirely?

No. She needed some stuff. I'm not anti-medicine, if that's what you think.

So what happened? With Mrs. Tate?

She came every night. Every night I got a little more of the stickiness out.

And how did you do this?

Sort of like a massage. Only I didn't touch her.

Would you call it Reiki, or healing hands?

Well, I wouldn't. It's sort of like that, only messier.

What was the eventual outcome of Mrs. Tate's treatment?

She got better. I mean, she still has some problems but she got so improved that she lives on her own now. She got a job. She's working on getting her GED. She sort of feels bad though. She's the one who told Eva Wakind about me.

Mrs. Tate feels bad about what happened to Eva?

She feels bad about what's happening to me. If Eva hadn't written that note everything would have just kept going the way it was.

To Dr. Rain, Birth hurts like it does and I remember mine and how I didn't want a go out there but I couldn't stop it no way, though I tried to hold back from that light which burned my skin and I would say that the first ever violent thing that happened to me was my birth and it just all got worse from there. Fuck you for trying to make me live because it makes you feel better. I already told you about my daddy and how my mama didn't believe me and then I got pregnant but that baby died when I had the abortion which I had to do by myself since what was I suppose to do borrow money from my mom? Fuck you for saving my life last time I tried. I been seeing someone else and she tells me I am not a victim and she says if I need to die to get a decent start maybe that's what I should do. She understands how it is with me. Finally she says it is time. I

*have to be self aware else I'll come back like in some fucking
mess again, like I'll pick you as a mother or some shit like
that. All you want me to do is cut pictures out of magazines
and glue them on paper and shit and talk about my problems
and she don't know it yet but I pick her. After I die I'm coming
back as her baby.*

Eva

I know right away he is the one. How can such a beautiful thing
come from such a horrible act? My angels tell me I can choose a
different path. I see them before me, like rays of sun, the different
courses of my life. But she is trying to come to me. How can I
refuse? In this cold place of gates and chains, all these angry
women, she comes and the first thing I do for her in this incar-
nation is accept her. How else could it happen here? With love? He
leads me down the hall. He thinks I suspect nothing. We all know.
The angels. Half the women here. He is the one who is ignorant.
He unlocks the door. We walk into the room. He locks it. I hear the
zip, the slap of leather. "Come here, cunt," he says. "Don't try to
fight." I don't. I lie down. When he touches me I feel his sad and
ugly life. My angels stay with me. He feels them too. I know he
does. But he does it anyway. Don't get me wrong. I weep. I grit my
teeth. I want it to be over. When it is, I am pregnant. She is not
my victim. She is me, reborn.

Rose, who did this to you?
    I'm glad you've come. I have something important to say.
    I'm listening.
    I can't get out of here.
    I'm working on the appeal but, Jesus Christ, Rose, who are you
protecting?
    You wanta feel her kicking? She's kicking right now.
    Rose, who?
    Sometimes I go to my garden and pick flower petals but when I
wake up my fist is empty. It's like I wasn't even there.
    Those are dreams, Rose.
    So, I'm running out of time. I mean, if I can't travel with a rose
petal I can't possibly hope to travel out of here with her. It's just
taking longer than I thought.
    Fucking justice.

So here's the thing. I've chosen you.

Well, good, Rose, that's good. But you have to help me, Rose, you have to help me help you.

You don't understand. You're the one.

Rose, what are you talking about?

After she's born she's coming to live with you.

Rose, my God, Rose, that's very kind, really, it's an honor. But I'm gone twelve hours a day. I didn't even think you liked me.

I'm stuck like glue.

Rose, you're not making sense.

Have you taken care of that throat problem?

JOAN OF ARC KILLER HAS BABY

In a shocking twist to the sensational trial of former health care worker Rose Miller, found guilty of murdering Eva Wakind, a patient at St. Luke's Home for the Mentally Ill, under what she said was the instruction of angels' voices, recently gave birth to a baby girl. Prison officials refuse to comment on the pregnancy and birth. Miss Wakind's former attorney, Laura Fagele, has begun the process of becoming the infant's legal guardian. Numerous phone calls to Ms. Fagele's residence were not returned.

Night after night I travel the starry way watching my baby sleep. The room is blue sky and painted clouds, a store-bought quilt of summer flowers. It smells of baby diapers and powder and sweet. She has my red hair, something in the shape of her face comes from the guard, something in the nose or the cheek reminds me of Eva, all these aspects innocent in her, present before ruin.

I am slowly disappearing. No one seems to notice. Laura comes to visit. The hole at her throat is black and huge. It is eating her face. She keeps repeating herself; "Fucking justice," she says. The words break apart in the air and fall to the ground like broken glass.

"The system," I say.

She leans forward, her eyes dark-circled and earnest. She coughs. The angels buzz around us, so loud I can hardly hear myself think. "What about the system?" she says.

"I can't figure how to break out of it."

"You can't break out, Rose." She coughs again. "Do you hear me, Rose? Do you understand anything I'm telling you?"

I learned young how to rise above my bed and escape the body's system of skin and bones, vulnerable and brittle, innocent. What I have not been so successful at is how to escape its sorrow.

I travel to my garden and breathe in the heavy scent of closed blossoms, rub my hands across the flowers, brushing the heavy scent upward, hyacinth, rose, dahlia, the heavy fragrance of dirt. In the distance I hear the voices; girls' voices whispering, shouting, weeping, pleading, accompanied by the angels murmuring like bees.

I wake up to the bright light noise of metal and chains, a laugh, sharp and abrupt. I open my fist; a tiny, red rose petal trembles there. I let it fall. It spirals slowly to the ground and lies against the hard, gray floor. Later, Thalia finds it. She fingers it gently, then, with a furtive glance, stuffs it into her pocket. She sees me watching but I don't say anything about it and neither does she.

♦ ♦ ♦

More Beautiful Than You

I DON'T EVEN FUCKING USUALLY READ THE PAPER but I'm home for Thanksgiving and it's the same old shit, my mom and the aunts getting wasted in the kitchen, nobody paying no attention to the turkey. The stuffing sits in the box on the counter, next to the cans of cranberries. They're cackling away in there like they do every year and every year it's mostly the same except Uncle Freddie ain't here 'cause he died last spring of a busted vein in his brain and my cousin Eddie ain't here and nobody knows where he is, but my aunt says she ain't worried. I wonder if he's dead. Could I of done more to keep him off the streets? Maybe I should of told him, yeah, this is one fucked up family, and the turkey is always dry and shit but it's your family and that means something. But I never did try to say nothing like that. Who knows? Maybe he ain't dead or living under some city bridge. Maybe he's sitting down right now, turning on the tube, watching the game in a house that smells good like Thanksgiving should and maybe he's even happy. But I doubt it. He's probably in some crack house somewhere and don't even know what day it is.

I'm just sitting there listening to my mom and the aunts while the light gets dark and I think how it's good to be home for Thanksgiving. Fucked up as it is. So I get to start looking through the Fullbrook paper, reading the articles like how the Maynards' cows got loose and how Cindy Falloway got a blue ribbon in spelling. I guess she's in fourth grade and it's hard to believe that Becky Falloway who got knocked up senior year and was the best piece of ass at Fullbrook High is now the mother of a champion speller. I look at the kid's picture and she is grinning a big, stupid ten-year-old grin and it's way too early to tell if she'll be anything like her mother, but thinking like that starts to feel kind of twisted so I turn the page and that's when I see Ronnie Webster's name and it takes me a few seconds before I realize it's his fucking obituary. Ronnie Webster is dead. I don't go in and open the cans of cranberries or turn on the light or any of the shit I traditionally do to get my mom and the aunts moving, a tradition Ronnie Webster had something to do with starting, actually. I just sit there and it gets darker and darker. The turkey is going to be drier than usual this year but I don't give a fuck.

So this weird thing happens in Omaha. I'm in the second round going at this Tae Kwon Do teacher from Michigan and all a sudden I have a minute, while this guy is getting his head pressed into the rope, to sort of scan the crowd, you know, take a breath, and it's like I'm hallucinating or something because all a sudden there's Ronnie Webster's face and I swear this is freakin' weird but I swear he's sitting there in the stands and then he sees me looking and waves. I have to get my concentration back so I pound this guy until he signals submission, and I raise my hands clenched over my head 'cause it's a victory. When I try to see Ronnie I can't find him nowhere in the crowd. Course, 'cause he's fucking dead.

He was ugly. Take out the Fullbrook High yearbook, class of '82, and see for yourself. That's me on the same page. I'm about two-fifty there. Not so many high schoolers go my size. But the difference ain't just the weight. I've met some badass skinny dudes but not Ronnie Webster.

There he is. Bet you thought I was just being mean. But I can tell you agree. You want not to agree. But you see what I mean. Fish eyes. Crooked nose. It was straight before it got broke. I'll take the blame for that even if it ain't only me. And those teeth. Actually we improved them. Five got knocked out and replaced. That's how come they look pretty good in the picture. What you can't see is the way he used to dress. Weird. I mean it's like he just tried to make himself ugly. His parents were loaded. They lived in one of those houses on Fox Ridge. He could of dressed any way he wanted. He was their only kid. Somebody said he was adopted but I don't know nothing about that and I don't give a shit. I saw his parents that time I followed him home and they just looked like regular parents. He was a freak. We beat him up and put him in the hospital. This was a long time ago and we didn't kill him. So why the fuck is he haunting me now?

Raine says I think too much. She says thinking is overrated. "What did thinking ever do for anyone?" she says. "You just sit there and stare into space and nothing happens. That's what I liked about you. I thought you was an action man." She pulls off her little white underpants and throws them at my face. "Ronnie Webster," she snickers as I unzip my pants, "is long gone. Forget about him."

But what Raine don't know is everything. It's not just a little detail, it's the whole bang. She's moaning and I'm grunting and if she was the thinking kind at all she'd be thinking it was only us; the ultimate fighter and his girl. She don't know.

Ronnie Webster is watching us. He's sitting in the corner in the rocking chair, and he's grinning. Like I don't know how he looked by the time he died but here he looks like he did in high school, like a girl, except he's got his dick in his hands. I look at it and then I look at him and he just grins. White teeth. Pink cheeks. "Oh, Action," Raine says. I close my eyes. When I open them he's gone.

We got him on the Wednesday night before Thanksgiving. I guess you could say we was in a bad mood. Not Ronnie. But me and the guys. None of us wanting to go home or be anywhere. We used to say we fuckin' hated school but when it was closed we just stood around different street corners and smoked. We didn't talk about it but we all fuckin' hated being home even worse.

So it's Wednesday night and we're hanging out by Myer's Grocery store, the dark side of the building. It's the night before Thanksgiving so it's been kind of busy for a while. A new Price Chopper just opened up on Highway 10 and we don't know it, but it's the last Thanksgiving for Myer's store. It ain't that late but the street is pretty quiet. I don't remember what we're talking about. Then along comes Ronnie Webster in those weird red sneakers and those straight-leg jeans and this hat, this flat pancake hat with the little tip of material at the top and he's whistling and one of us, and I can never remember if it was me or who, but somebody goes, "Get him." We pulled him in and wailed on him. He made these little whimpering sounds. Then he got quiet and all you could hear was fist and flesh. Breathing. And all a sudden, without any signal or word, we stopped. Ran in different directions. Left him there like roadkill.

You didn't think this story would be pretty, did you?

It happens again in Cleveland. During the first round, when I am actually restraining myself from completely smashing this stupid kid into pieces because you gotta give the crowd at least a little show. I am putting on a sparring act and he's doing all his Ninja Turtles moves on me and I'm thinking how pitiful it is because I know, and the crowd knows, and he seems to be the only one who don't know, he's doing his last good breathing for the next few days. I look into the crowd for just a minute like, 'cause I'm sort of bored, and there's Ronnie Webster selling hot dogs for Christ sake, and I guess he sees me 'cause he waves and then the kid lands a sidekick to my face that's got the whole crowd roaring and I'm busy for a while. This lasts maybe forty seconds. But when I look up again to raise my arms in victory, the whole crowd chanting, "Action, Action" (they call me Action), I can't see him nowhere. Maybe he's ashamed. Who would of guessed it? Ronnie Webster. A hot dog vendor ghost.

He was the artist type in high school, getting poems in the school paper and shit. I never read none of them so I can't say much about that but during the time when I was following him I watched him paint once. It was after school. Chorus was singing some Jesus joy song about Christmas and the janitors was down in their office in the basement getting stoned. Mrs. Smythe was in her room correcting papers and Mr. Lyman was sort of wandering around the way he did. I didn't know it then but after we graduated Mrs. Lyman hung herself with the afghan she'd been basically knitting and ripping apart for the past ten years. It turns out she was a real nut case all along, and Mr. Lyman stayed at school sometimes 'cause he didn't wanna go home. Which is funny in a way 'cause that's not so different from me and my friends that he was always busting on. It was getting close to Christmas vacation, you know the chorus singing "Joy, joy, joy" and those construction-paper snowflakes and candy canes and all that shit, and Ronnie Webster all alone in the art room. I'm just standing in the hall. He's gotta know I'm there. I ain't hiding or nothing.

I have to squint at first 'cause the art room's got all these big windows and because of the snow it's all this bright white. Ronnie's got on these queer, knee-high boots with fuckin' fringe on them and these striped pants and this fem yellow sweater. Then he stops whistling and he starts waving his arms over the canvas and it changes into a slash of red, black, purple. He's gotta know I'm watching, and then, all a sudden, he stops and I think, okay, it's gonna happen now. I can hear my own breathing and the fuckin' Christmas carols. And I ain't thinking nothing except, okay, it's gonna happen. He just stands there, hanging his head like he's praying or something and then, real careful like, he puts down his paintbrush and pulls the sweater off. He's got on just a wife-beater but he ain't got no muscle, his shape is the shape of bones. For the first time I see all the bruises we give him and where it's not bruised he is white as soap. He just stands there. Then he looks up, right at me with those eyes laced with lashes like a girl. But I don't say nothing. We just look at each other. Then I hear Mr. Lyman coming down the hall and I leave.

When we left him like that, a heap of flesh and blood, we didn't know if he was dead or alive. Not that I was worried about him. All I thought about was how I just screwed up my whole life.

Thanksgiving day is my mom and the aunts sitting around the kitchen table getting drunk on Budweiser and forgetting to do anything with the turkey once it's in the oven. Me and my cousins and my uncle watch the games and eat crackers and salami and crack open a few beers, but I don't let the little kids drink and they start whining and I holler at them to go outside and act like normal kids. My little cousin Eddie tells me to fuck off and I just ignore him 'cause I fucked up so bad already. I just stare at the TV set but I ain't watching it and after a while nobody bothers me. I guess you can tell I'm in a mood or something and I am 'cause I'm just expecting any minute the cops to come knocking on the door. But it just keeps getting later and later and finally it starts getting dark and I go around turning on the lights. When I turn the big light on in the kitchen my mom and the aunts look up at me all a sudden all quiet and I say, "Shouldn't you be mashing potatoes or something?" When I walk away I hear them laughing but the chairs scrape back and my mom starts swearing at the turkey.

Then the phone rings and it's B. T. and he tells me Ronnie Webster is at Fullbrook Hospital and he won't tell no one who got him 'cause he wants to take care of it himself. So we have a good laugh over that. "What's he gonna do, write mean poems about us?"

The turkey's dry like it's always dry. The mash potatoes and gravy is lumpy. The only thing really good is the cranberries 'cause you can't mess them up right out of the can. My mom and aunts all have pink faces and when I look at them I think how they really are sort of pretty. Even my mom. The TV is on 'cause my Uncle Frankie and his son, Eddie, are football freaks and they holler from the other room where they are eating, and there's little kids running all over the place and I gotta tell you, for like one minute, two even, I just sit there grinning. And I ain't even stoned.

In Tulsa I see Ronnie sitting next to Raine. This is before the fight. The crowd is screaming, "Action! Action! Action!" I'm waving my arms in my pre-victory stance and there's Ronnie Webster sitting next to Raine. I give a sort of salute wave and they both wave back. Ronnie, just raising his hand, and Raine, jumping up and down like a fuckin' cheerleader. I am so distracted by the thought of Ronnie Webster sitting next to Raine and what he might say to her that I fuckin' almost lose the fight.

Afterward I ask Raine about him. "He was sitting right next to you," I say. "A skinny guy."

"I didn't notice him," she says, addressing my wounds. "Jesus, you let that guy tear you up."

"He don't tear me up," I say, "he's just some kid I use to know from high school."

"I don't mean stupid Ronnie Webster," she says. "I mean the guy you was fighting."

When he comes back to school he is ugly in a different way. His face is just a fuckin' wound. He got stitches hanging all over the place. He got stitches in his mouth for Christ's sake. But he acts like the same. Walking down the hall in those red shoes. Suddenly he's like the most popular kid in school. But he's not into it, you can just see he's still ol' Ronnie Webster and as far as he's concerned nothing's changed. Then he sees me. He looks right at me, and it's the weirdest thing, he's gotta know. But he just looks at me like I don't matter one way or the other and he just keeps walking. That's the first time I really think about what I did. Jesus, I nearly killed that kid. All a sudden I realize people are watching. When I look at them, they turn away.

That's when I start following him. I follow him to all his classes so I'm late or I skip mine. I don't give a shit about school. I follow him home to that big house with all those windows on Fox Ridge. I keep a good distance but he's gotta know. The way you know when you're being watched. You can just feel it in your skin, even if they turn away when you look at them. It's like how I can feel him now, watching me.

Back then it's like I'm the ghost following Ronnie. I watch him in the john. I watch him paint. I watch him shovel his driveway on Saturday morning. I watch him and his parents leave for church on

Sunday. Finally, the day before Christmas vacation, we're in the cafeteria. He sits slurping his food for Christ's sake and reading some book about leaves and grass. People say things to him and he smiles or laughs even though with his mouth open you can see the stitches hanging there. I don't even know I'm gonna do this. I go sit across from him. You can just feel the whole cafeteria go silent. Like everybody's watching now. Ronnie puts down his book and looks at me. I can feel my muscles tighten. I can feel the muscles in the room tighten. But Ronnie just looks at me.

"I'm one of them," I say, soft like, so only he can hear.

"I know," he says.

We sit there like that for a few seconds. Then he just picks up his book and keeps slurping and reading and after a while I get up and walk away.

I ain't scared, if that's what you're thinking. When he's in the stands waving at me while I turn some guy's face into blue-ribbon chili, or when he's in the room watching me and Raine and she says, "It don't matter, honey, it happens to everyone. Did I tell you I'm going to be busy for the next few weeks?" and he just sits there, laughing, or even when it's just me alone with him, I ain't scared. Even as a ghost Ronnie Webster is mostly just annoying. Like right now. He's standing in the mirror and he's fucking laughing. I know why, okay? I mean my face is right there to prove it. I'm a ugly fuck. Okay? You satisfied, you fucking ghost? "I'm a ugly fuck! I'm a ugly fuck!"

I don't even realize I'm shouting until the downstairs neighbor starts pounding on the ceiling. "Shut the fuck up, you ugly fuck," he screams.

"Fuck you!" I holler.

"Fuck you, you fucker!"

He pounds on the ceiling again and I stamp on the floor. He turns his music up. Loud. Fucking Aerosmith. And I sit down on the edge of the bed.

Fuck, I feel like shit. Ronnie comes and sits beside me. Right on the bed. I say, "Fuck, Ronnie? What the fuck you want?"

He turns and looks at me and, fuck, how could I be wrong about this for so long? I look at him and he looks at me, and then, like we are fucking *Twilight Zone* people, we both open our mouths but I'm the only one who actually talks.

I say, "Beautiful."

And then, just like that, he's gone and I'm fucking sitting there on the edge of my bed. Alone.

♦ ♦ ♦

Peace on Suburbia

THE CHILDREN COME HOME FROM SCHOOL, spinning off the bus, screaming nonsense, waving at glowering strangers in their warm cars, then running into the house, shedding coats, dropping book bags with heavy thuds, and racing up the stairs to open the refrigerator and stare at its cheesy, milky, brown lettuce contents and moan about hunger and homework. You say, "Close the refrigerator. Choose something healthy. How about an apple?" and your son looks up at you with those blue eyes that have recently become hooded by eleven-year-old lids that do not reveal the clear, wide beauty you remember and says, "I think I'm going to be one of those kids who die young."

"What?"

He shrugs. Turns away. "So it doesn't matter what I eat."

You don't know what to say. He wanders out of the room and you stand there, your mouth hanging open, and wonder if he is right, which sends a shiver down your spine that causes you to lose your mind, evidenced by your daughter standing there talking and you have no idea what she's saying. She spins away, like a nutcracker snowflake or a Sufi dervish.

You are worn out from the weekend spent with your parents. Your mother will not admit that your father is dying, though the hospice workers said, well, not that word, but that they were there to "help with the final stages of life," and your father, his eyes closed, his breath heavy, but sitting in his favorite chair and only a minute before talking to you, must have heard them, though he gave no sign and your mother nodded as though she understood but later, after he had gone to bed and you had called home to make sure everything was fine, she sighed and said, "Don't change your plans for Christmas. This could go on for years."

"I want the ones I circled most and the ones with stars I want a lot and the ones with stars and circles I also want." Your daughter hands you the Target insert from Sunday's newspaper. You flip through the pages and see that almost everything is starred or circled, or starred and circled. She even starred a box of tampons, which, actually, are on sale at a very good price. You stare at it until you feel like crying and then you set it on the kitchen counter, carefully, as though you will peruse it closely later to discern out of all those circles or stars, or circles-and-stars, what is the right combination to give your daughter a perfect Christmas.

The thing is, you might not need a box of tampons that large. Things are changing, you notice, your emotions especially seem so strange lately, as though they weren't yours at all, the way they used to feel like they came from you, but rather, they seem to be happening to you, like a train wreck. Mostly the emotion that keeps happening to you is the feeling that there isn't enough. Enough what, you couldn't say.

"Hey, Mom, come look at this," your son calls from his bedroom where you find him lying on the floor. "I can shoot darts laying down." He does. The plastic dart with the dull tip sails through the air in a perfect arc and hits the dartboard with a small thwack. "Pretty cool, huh? I don't even gotta stand up."

"Is your homework done?"

"We had a substitute."

"Again? Was Mr. Festler out again?"

"She yelled at us because we were doing stuff RIGHT!"

"What are you talking about?"

"Mr. Festler says he wants us to share our work and help each other but Mrs. Buttface yelled at us and said we were cheaters."

"What's her real name?"

"Butta, Battaf. I don't know."

"Do your homework."

"What's the point?"

"I want you to stop talking that way right now, do you hear me?"

He looks at you as if he fully knows he is going to grow up and write a bestselling book about his recovery from your abuse, which will make him a very rich man who no one will begrudge because look what you put him through, and says, "Well, why should I do it when she ain't even gonna be there tomorrow and we'll have some other teacher who won't even look at it?"

You turn and walk out of the room. You finally learned not to answer these questions that unwind only more questions and put off the inevitable task the questions seek to avoid. You wonder what he is muttering but you just keep walking to the kitchen where your daughter sits at the table bent with serious expression over her homework. She looks up at you and smiles.

"That's quite a lot of stuff you circled and starred," you say.

She shrugs. "I just thought I could show Santa everything I want, but I don't expect all of it."

You nod, slowly. It's a hard game, this. What does she know? What does she believe? Doesn't it seem strange to circle things in the Target catalog for Santa Claus to bring? After all, she's eight years old. Certainly she can't be so gullible? Certainly she knows the truth?

The phone rings. You answer it.

"Did you hear?"

You hate it when he calls from the cell phone. His voice crackles like a fire or an old man's voice and he isn't old. Or burning.

"Mr. Festler was out again. Don't you think this is getting a little strange?"

"They declared war. Turn on CNN."

You don't even get to say goodbye. You stand there saying his name over and over again but you've lost the connection and it's only a coincidence that it's happened at this time, which makes it seem so apocalyptic. You hang up the phone. It has begun to snow. You stare at the falling snow.

"It's snowing!" your daughter shouts. Your son comes out of his room, a pencil tucked behind his ear. He blinks rapidly, and his eyes widen, he grins at you and says maybe tomorrow will be a snow day.

You ruin it by saying, no, the weather report says it'll be just an inch, and then you hug him which he allows for a full thirty seconds before he pulls away and walks into his room as though things are vastly safer in there.

The snow swirls big, beautiful flakes that fall and fall without a sound.

You go downstairs into the cold family room of your split-level ranch. You like this room in the summer and hate it in the winter. You lift cushions and blankets and pillows and shoes until, in exasperation, you stand in the middle of the room and feel your chest expand, your breath fill with anger, and then you see it in the damnedest of places, right where it belongs, on top of the television. You pick up the remote control and aim it at the TV. You walk to the couch and sit at the edge of it as you press through the channels, which almost all feature someone beautiful in an open collar revealing a young throat, you press through to CNN and then sit and look at the blue screen dotted by spots of light that blink bright and dim while someone's voice says things you only vaguely hear like "explosions" and "missiles" and "Mom?"

You point and press the power button.

She stands before you with her hair pulled back in an undone braid, her eyes clear and bright, she looks at you as if she knows something so immense you could never understand it and you wonder where she got that expression from.

"Oprah," you say.

She nods but smirks as she does, so you think she knows you weren't watching Oprah at all. How long had she been standing there?

"They wanta talk to you."

"Who?"

"The men. At the door."

You open your mouth and close it. Haven't you told her a million times not to answer the door without you? You walk up the stairs and find three men standing politely on the front porch, in the snow, the door wide open. You look at your daughter. She looks at the bearded strangers, only curious, with no idea that she just risked all your lives. How to make her understand danger? You turn to the men who all smile and actually sort of bow. "We've come for your son," the tallest one says.

"What?"

The tall man steps forward slightly. "We have gifts."

You notice that all three men carry packages wrapped in brown paper tied with string.

"There seems to be some mistake," you say, beginning to inch the door shut.

You hear him coming down the hall, the pad of his feet against the carpet. You press the door shut faster but not fast enough and for a moment their eyes meet; your son, and the strangers whose eyes widen when they see him. You push the door shut and lock it.

"Who were they?"

"Salesmen." You turn to your daughter. "Didn't I tell you never to open the door to strangers?"

"I think they're still out there."

You make sure the door is locked and then you tell your children, in a calm voice, to get back to their homework. They ignore you but don't follow as you go through the house making sure all the doors are locked.

"They're going!" your son calls. "Hey, they left us presents!"

"Don't touch that door."

"But they left us presents."

"Go do your homework."

He mutters. Again you do not ask him what he's saying. Your daughter stands there, watching you. "Homework," you order.

"Why?"

"Why what?"

She shrugs and walks away slowly, as if weary and old.

You look out the window. The packages, simply wrapped, sit in the snow. What if it's anthrax? Smallpox? A bomb? Oh Jesus, what if they are bombs? You run to the telephone, dial 9-1-1. All in a rush you tell the operator about the three strangers, the packages, the possibilities you've imagined.

"Well, did you try shaking them?"

"What? Are you kidding?"

"Maybe it's just chocolate or something."

"Who are you? What are you doing answering this phone? Don't you know they've declared war? Don't you know we're in real danger here?"

"You don't have to be so hysterical. I'll send someone over. The fire department, how's that? But you should know you're not in any danger."

"How would you know that? Hello? Hello?"

You try calling your husband but you only get a recording saying that the cell phone customer is out of reach at this time. The fire engine comes wailing down the street and pulls into your driveway. Your children come running into the living room to look out the large picture window that overlooks the porch and driveway. The fire engine has a green wreath attached to the front with a paper menorah in the center. The firemen jump out of the truck and then they just stand there talking to the one with the fanciest hat. Your children narrate everything that's happening in excited voices. "They're standing around talking. The light is still going.

Oh, look, now he's coming on the porch." They both squeal away from the window heading toward the stairs until you command them back. They groan but run back to the window, giggling. "He's shaking them! Now he's smelling them! He's ringing—"

The doorbell rings. The children scream.

"Calm down!" you yell. "Stay right there." They stare at you like wounded animals, perfectly still. You walk down the stairs. Open the door. You hear the children behind you, at the top of the stairs.

The fireman has a face like chiseled rock, and kind eyes. He holds, in his big hands, the presents wrapped in simple brown paper with string for bows. "I don't think you got anything to worry about here."

"Please. Just take them away."

He looks over your shoulder and smiles. "How you doing?" he says.

"Good." Your son answers as if they know each other.

"I just think, well, you know, under the circumstances, just some admirers probably left these."

"Admirers?"

Behind him the other firemen are all creeping closer to the porch, pointing and whispering.

"Just take them away," you say again.

"Sure." The fireman smiles but he is not smiling at you. You turn to follow the direction of his gaze. Your son smiles down at him. You move to block the exchange.

"Well, all right then," the fireman says. He turns. You close the door.

"What was that all about?"

Your son shrugs.

"Do you know him?"

He shrugs again.

The phone rings. You walk upstairs to answer it. The children stand at the window waving as the fire engine backs out of your driveway. Several firemen wave back. You don't see faces, just hands, waving through the falling snow.

Your mother is on the phone. She is crying. At first you think it is about the war but then your realize it is about your father. Oh, yes, she's saying, he's gone completely nuts now. He says he sees angels. She cries and you try to comfort her. "We'll come up," you say, "we'll leave after dinner." "What are you talking about?" she says. "Aren't the kids still in school?" "But he's dying," you say. For a moment there is only silence and then she says, "Not yet he

ain't. He's sitting right here eating goulash. You wanta talk to him?"
You hear her saying, "Your daughter thinks you're dying," and then
his voice, the one you remember from before he got sick, "How's
my girl? How's my girl?"

You feel like crying for that old voice. "Dad?" you say, and your
own voice cracks as if he is already a ghost.

"Don't you go burying me yet, little girl. I'm feeling great. Just
great."

You can hear your mother in the background, your father's muffled reply. "Dad?"

"Your mother says to tell you about the angels."

"Angels?"

"Yeah. But I don't think she believes me. You do, don't you?"

"So you're seeing angels?"

"If I only knowed, you know?" he says all earnest. "I tried to be a
good father."

"You were, Dad."

"So the angels tell me our grandson's going to be some kind a
hero."

"He is?"

"Don't that make you proud? What's that? Your mother says to
tell you how the angels look, you wanta hear?"

"Yeah, sure, but what's this about him being a hero?"

"First they is real small like fairies, you know?"

"Fairies?"

"Yeah, tiny like snowflakes. Hell, first time they came I thought
it was snowing right in my bed. Jesus Christ, I thought I was losing
my mind."

"But you weren't?"

"Heh, heh. Good one. But then they sort of grow and it's just
what you expect, a lot of light, wings, you know, angels." He lowers
his voice. "Listen, I wanta talk to you about your mother. I think
maybe she's got the oldzheimers, she's—" Suddenly his voice
booms through the receiver, "So? Is that right?"

"Dad, what do you mean a hero?"

"Well, you know," he says, and then your mother is back on the
phone.

"Fairies," she says. "Snowflakes that turn into angels."

"It's snowing here," you say.

"Not you too?"

"No. Snow. You know, flakes. Outside. Mom? What's he talking
about?"

"Who knows? Nothing makes sense."

"Have you talked to his doctor? Called the hospice?"

"The doctor's too busy to talk to me. The hospice workers all wanta come and take over the house but they don't know nothing. You know what one of them says to me?"

"What?"

"She says, well, maybe he really does see angels."

"What did you say?"

"I said nothing. I got one person to talk nonsense with all day. I don't need another."

"Mom? Did you hear the news? About the war?"

"War? That ain't news. War happens every day. Did I tell you about Hilda Mealene's daughter? You remember Tanya, don't you? She went to school with you?"

"Listen, Mom. I gotta go. Can I call you later? Tonight?"

She says goodbye and you stand there listening to the dial tone. That's how things have always been with your mother. You hurt her feelings all the time though you don't mean to, not since you were a teenager. You hang up the phone. Walk down the hall. Your son lies on his bed doing his homework.

"Honey, do you ever see, you know, angels?"

As soon as you say it you know you are doomed. He will remember this question, this absurd question and it will rend him from you forever. He will enter his teen years remembering that you asked him such a thing and he will describe you and know you always by this single mistake. It will define you and your relationship and it's happened and you can't take it back. You turn away.

"Sometimes," he says. "Just the usual."

You stop and consider this fantastic reply. You can't think of anything to say. You walk down the hall and find your daughter standing at the window, watching the snow fall. Sometimes you catch her like this, in a dreamy state, she turns and looks at you with a beatific smile.

"Honey, do you see angels?"

She walks over to you and lays one small, warm hand with purple painted fingernails on your thigh. She looks up at you but suddenly you feel small. She doesn't answer your question, she just stands there smiling and touching you as if she is sainted. As if you are forgiven.

You watch the snow fall. Your daughter wanders out of the room. Across the street, the Smythe's Christmas lights glow primary colors against the white, and down the road several more houses are lit with color and white, a deer made out of light, and a moose.

Suddenly one of those feelings comes to you, the way that's been happening lately. Standing there, in the dim December living room, you see flakes of falling light and for just a moment you are part of this light and its silence. This is temporary, but it is enough.

Across the street shepherds gather and point at your house. No, they must be school children, carolers, a large family from a foreign country. In the distance you hear the voices of your own children. You don't know what they're saying but by the pitch you can tell they're fighting. You walk to the window and press your fingers against the cold glass. The shepherds kneel in the snow. You watch them for a moment, then you pull the drapes shut.

Rising

Flight

I AM SITTING AT MY WRITING TABLE, STARING out the window, when the big, gray bird lands in the clearing. She has the stick-thin legs, large body, and long curved neck of the crane family, but with the thick, red stripe around her head she more closely resembles a strange bird-girl wearing a scarf. She arches back that long neck, opens her wings, and dances, spinning in circles and swirls as the dust rises around her.

In the Dreamtime, Brolga was the most wonderful dancer anyone had ever seen. Back then, she was not a bird, but a young woman. Brolga danced the stories of her people. She danced the stories of the stars. She danced the stories of the sun and the moon. She danced the wind. People came from all over to watch Brolga dance. The elders worried that Brolga would become vain. But Brolga didn't dance for attention. She danced for joy.

One day, as Brolga danced the wind and the stars and the sun, an evil spirit descended from the Milky Way. He saw Brolga dancing, and like everyone else, he was entranced. It was not enough for him to watch Brolga. Instead, he made himself into a big wind and took her. He carried her back up with him, to the black hole in the Milky Way.

The people cried for Brolga. They cried and threw stones at the sky. There was nothing else they could do. They gathered by the coolibah tree to weep for her.

Then, from behind the coolibah tree, came a beautiful gray bird they had never seen before. The bird slowly stretched its wings and began to dance, hopping and soaring with the same grace Brolga had possessed. The people cried out, "It's Brolga! It's Brolga!"

The bird seemed to understand. She walked toward the people and with one last, graceful bound flew above them.

The bird outside my window stops her dance and walks slowly toward me, for a moment we look at each other, though I cannot be certain that she sees me through the glass, then, with a graceful bound, she flies away. I lean out of my chair and crane my neck to watch her.

Later, I tell Herrick, "Today a Brolga danced for me."

He says, "Oh, no, that's just a silly legend. Brolgas don't dance, they are clumsy and awkward like this." He squats, juts his chin, and flaps his arms. Daisy laughs and claps her hands.

"No. She danced. Like this."

I close my eyes and open my arms. I dance the stars and the sun and the wind. My fingers turn into feathers. My arms turn into wings.

"Why didn't you tell me?" Herrick says.

"I did," I laugh, thinking he has tricked me into performing this dance.

"No." He shakes his head. "You never told me that you are a Brolga." He wraps his arms around me. I close my eyes. I am in his arms, firmly on the ground, and I am rising over us, my great wings extended to the stars, a part of now, and forever.

◆ ◆ ◆

Moorina of the Seals

*H*ER NAME IS MOORINA. KEEPER OF SONG.
Children, old ones, everyone loves to be near Moorina.
When she opens her mouth, there is song. "If the sun had a voice,"
they say, "it would be this voice." The Old One, in the maddening
way she has, both agrees and disagrees. "It is true," she says, "though
this is not that voice." Moorina has an even heart, loves equally and
favors none until her fourteenth year, when she develops a special
fondness for the seals that gather on the rocks at sundown. There,
she sings her golden songs and the seals sing with her. This was a
long time ago, when seals still had beautiful voices. They come
from many miles to join the chorus and crowd on the rocks around
Moorina. The island trembles with their song. It becomes known
as Seal Island.

White hunters hear about this island, far out in the sea, where
seals number thousands, and even the white sands are made dark by
them. It is possible someone mentions the beautiful songs but years
of hunting have destroyed their hearing. As their boat steers toward
Seal Island the hunters only hear a sound like waterfalls, the rush of
lifeblood they seek to silence.

The General lost his name years ago in the storm of clubs and
blood he commanded. It is said he can kill a man or boy as easily as
a seal, and has. A young boy sneaks aboard the great ship. He wants

to be a hunter like the General. When he is found, the General says he is more like a seal and clubs him, laughing as he does. The General has a deft hand for death and the blow is placed, without thought, perfectly between the boy's eyes. They throw his body overboard. When they reach their next port, three of the men sneak away in the night. They tell this story and others. Ever after, wherever his name is spoken, the General is feared.

But the people of Seal Island never hear these stories. When the ship approaches, a dark scathe on the horizon, they watch it with awe and reverence. Moorina and the seals sing the ship in. It sets anchor. Twelve small boats row toward the shore carrying the General and his men.

As they approach they see that the stories about the island were not exaggerated. It is a beach of seals. The General raises his binoculars and tries to count. There are more seals than numbers he knows. He gives up counting and scans the view. He passes her twice before he realizes she is not a seal. Moorina, with her dark hair and dark body. He sees her mouth open and close, though all he can hear is the intense sound of waterfalls, a deafening rush of liquid in his ears. With this limited observation, he believes he understands.

The island people have heard of the White Ones. They have seen the white bones dug up by forest animals. The Dead. How have these Dead gotten lost on their journey to the sky? They prepare a ceremony of dance and song. Welcome the lost Dead and help them on their journey home. The Dead sit stiffly, already foreigners on this fertile ground. Speaking a strange tongue. Pointing to the seals and grinning.

The General is the whitest of all. He has yellow hair and teeth, and blue eyes so pale they are almost white. He sits at the feast as still as a rock and does not dance. Some of the men try, but death has made their bones stiff and they have forgotten the movements.

"We have come for the seals," says the General, pointing to the shore.

"We welcome and honor your presence," says the Old One, pointing to the stars. "We sing you to your new home."

Each speaks in separate tongues.

The General shrugs his shoulders and picks up his gun. "Now," he says to his men, who pick up their guns.

Everybody stands still. The White Ones only move their eyes. Looking first where the guns point, then to the General, then back to where the guns point. The island people watch this strange eye dance. "These pogies don't know what hit them," one of the Dead says. The Old One takes half a step forward. She points to the stars. There is a blast. A spurt of red. The Old One falls to the ground. Smoke steams from the General. He grins his yellow teeth and points the gun with a motion that makes them all understand they are to stay back.

The worst that can be done is done. The island women watch the old ones fall, the children, the men. Even babies are not spared. Ropes are used. Fire. Of course, the guns. Until only the women are left. Then the hunters use their bodies as weapons too. The air stinks of blood. The earth grows a song of grief and bones.

By sundown, it is fair to say even the women are mostly gone. Like shells that hold the sound of water, they hold the breath of life, but are given, at least partly, to death. The Dead Ones herd them, pointing guns and grunting, down to the shore, where they are made to understand that they are to sit on the rocks. By opening his great, yellow mouth, the General communicates that he intends them all to sing, the way Moorina used to. When they open their mouths there is no song, only a terrible braying sound, a wounded bellow. Even Moorina's voice does not survive. The women sit on the rocks and look at each other with stone eyes, opening their mouths to sing the sorrow. The hunters do not seem to notice but wait behind the rocks with clubs at their sides. The seals do not notice either. They seem to think it is some sort of game and bray the horrible noise in reply. Their beautiful black bodies surround the women, their black eyes trusting, until the clubs come raining down. You think there could be no more weeping. But the women weep. The seals fall dead by the hundreds. Some, in terror, look to Moorina.

The first night is followed by others. The women are kept in tents at the edge of the hunters' camp. Each evening they are herded to the rocks and made to bray the seals to shore. The hunters, who cannot count, soon come to realize that there are enough, already more than they can possibly carry in the boats but, still, the General commands. More. More.

The women are ordered to skin the seals. The pelts hang in the sun and stack up around them like towers of doom. Those who do not cooperate are shot, or clubbed, or set on fire. Depending on the General's mood.

When Moorina feels the new life grow inside her, she wants to tear it out and thrash it against the rocks. Moorina thinks this. The one who used to sing the sun. She hears herself think this and knows something has to be done.

That night, in the tent, Moorina combs her hair with bones and plaits it with shells. The other women watch. She paints her skin with dirt and red clay she digs from the earth.

"Look at this one," says Phyloma. "She thinks she is still the sun. Just the way the Old One said you would be." Phyloma turns to Moorina. "She always said that you would forget us."

Moorina draws the knife from the leaf rope at her waist and holds it up in the dark tent. "Do you think this will only cut seals?" she asks.

The women smile, small smiles that disappear quickly. Moorina draws back the tent flap and the gun points at her. "I am prepared to see your General," she says, trusting the Ancestors to help this evil one understand her tongue. "I bring him the gift of my body."

The hunter sets down the gun. "Oh, boy," he says, "get a load of this."

The men, sitting around the campfire, turn to see Moorina standing in the tent entrance, a wild woman if they had ever seen one, dressed in dirt and bones. They hoot and cheer.

The women in the tent watch Moorina's back tremble.

"Let her come," calls the General, "we can use some entertainment."

The tent flaps shut. The women creep closer together. Without Moorina, they feel cold.

Moorina walks to the circle of men and fire. Her shells and bones clink with each step. This is marriage attire. She holds up her chin.

"God, she's a ugly fuck," says the General. The men laugh.

Moorina begins to dance. "O Ancestors," she calls, raising her arms to the stars, "drum for me tonight."

The men around the fire applaud and cheer. Raise their cups to the sky and bring them to their lips, leaning so far back some of them fall over.

"She's so ugly I wouldn't touch her with a stick," says the hunter whose child she carries.

Moorina stamps her feet and circles. Closes her eyes. Begins singing the wordless chant she has heard sung all those times before when she was still wondering who she would choose.

"I think she's putting a hex on us," says one of the hunters.

She can hear drums. The Old Ones drumming and the women singing by her side. "O sisters," she calls, "sing me to a new life."

The women sing, the chant so close, Moorina opens her eyes and sees that they have joined her, each with a leaf rope tied at her waist. They are a small tribe now. There are many more hunters. The women know how this will end.

"I say we fuck 'em all and get 'em to shut up," says one of the hunters.

They form a circle around the men. "O Ancestors," Moorina sings, "we come to you tonight. We bring the lost."

She stands behind the General. He turns to the hunter who had spoken. "I think you're right," he says.

"Now," Moorina cries.

Each hand at roped waist raises up with a sealskin knife. Moorina thrusts the knife into the General's neck and tears it across his throat. Skin thinner than a seal's. The last breath seeped in red. The stench of blood. She lets him fall to the dirt. She hears the sharp blasts and feels pain tear through her. Dying with the General she sentences herself to a marriage in the deathrealm with him. But there will be no others. It is only her life and the life of her sisters, already gone since the arrival of the Dead. No babies grown in this blood of hate. She closes her eyes. "O Ancestors," she whispers, "I am coming." She feels herself rise without body. The evil General, at her side, twists into her like a knotted rope.

Pain. Nothing before has felt like this. Even her breath hurts. She opens her eyes into the General's dead ones, the slit of red and red down his shirt. She raises up like a baby on trembling arms. The fire cinders ash. Phyloma lies beside it, her legs and arms at odd angles, her black hair streamed in blood. Was it really not so long ago that they walked arm in arm and giggled secrets about village boys? Not far from her lies a hunter. For every one of them, there is a hunter. "O sisters," says Moorina, "joined in eternity to these lost Dead, you have done a great service to your people." There is no sign of the other hunters. The tents stand open and empty. Seal pelts are scattered among the corpses. She turns her head, groaning, and sees the stacks of seal towers are much smaller. She rolls over onto her back. Looks down at her body. Through the blood, both his and hers, she finds the source of her pain, a hole at her side dried to a scab of dark red. A blood flower that blossomed there and died. So cold. She reaches for a sealskin and pulls it across the dirt. She wraps herself in it and sleeps.

The Old One who had named her appears at her side. "It is so good to see you," says Moorina. "I want to stay with you." But the

Old One shakes her head. "No. You are not one of us. Go." She pushes Moorina in the side, where the pain is.

Moorina wakes, groggy and bleary-eyed, in the field of death and flies. So, this is how it is, she thinks, I am alone. She wraps the sealskin tighter and stands on shaking legs. "I can't stay here. There is too much sad song."

The beach is empty. She scans the horizon. There are no boats. The hunters are gone. Is she to live like this, alone on this dead land? She walks to the water's edge, the seal pelt wrapped tight around her. "O family," she says, "it was not my hands that harmed you. It was not my voice." She bows her head. "I am more you than I was ever them," she says. She walks into the water. "The Dead will not take me. Will you?" She dives into the wave and is pulled down by the weight of skin. The salt burns her wound. She opens her mouth. In pain she swallows water.

Moorina feels her body change, stretch, and expand to fill the seal's pelt. She kicks and it is a seal's flipper she kicks. The water no longer chokes her. She looks down and sees, not wounded skin, but a beautiful black seal stomach. She rises through the water, first her nose and then her face breaks through the wave and the sun shines down on her in a blue sky so clear she can see Seal Island, once her home, and now the place from which she is happy to have escaped. She opens her mouth and sings but the song is shortened by her own disgust. Moorina has found a new life but lost her old voice forever.

She dives into the water. I have given up everything, she thinks. Family. Friends. Home. My body, even. But this, this is just too much. I cannot live with such horrible song. She swims deeper and deeper, as if the ocean holds the levels of her despair. When she gets to the bottom, she stops there and considers the option of wedging herself beneath a large rock. But even as she considers it, she swims away from this place to a destination that pulls at her from something deep inside. She swims and swims, until she can no longer see the island. Even this does not satisfy the urge. She dives into this strange new world of sea creatures and dangers she cannot define, still not certain if she cares to live or die. She knows she will not sing again. Fish swim by, and once she thinks she sees, at some distance, another seal, but she remains friendless. Days and nights pass, yet after all these changes she is not changed by them. She remains locked with indecision. Should she just let herself sink to the bottom? Instead of hiding behind the rock when the hungry shark swims past, should she swim to it? Life? Death? Neither, she thinks in despair, neither wants me.

She sees more and more seals, all swimming in the same direction as her. When one approaches, she rises through the water, now almost black with seals, and sees before her another island filled with them. No, she thinks, I cannot. But even as she decides to turn away, her body moves toward the crowded beach. For the first time she understands what a completely different creature she has become, pulled by tides, decided by body.

She presses through the crowd of seals. She does not want to know any of them. She lies in the sand, exhausted, falls asleep in spite of all their horrible noise.

She wakes to a new sensation, a strange pulling, pain, blood. Well, she thinks, so the hunters have returned after all. The pain is sharp but quick. She is ready to close her eyes when it stops, and she feels the pulling at her teat. She looks down to see the baby seal sucking. Her mind reels in confusion. Is this the hunter's child? She wants nothing to do with it. She pulls away. It cries, that horrible, new seal song. Moorina moves away from it. She will go back to the water. She will direct her body with her own urges. Slowly Moorina moves down the crowded beach.

Another pup, untended by its mother, cries. See, thinks Moorina, I am not the only one. She stops to look at the abandoned pup just in time to see the great bull, clumsy and huge, crawl over it, leaving it bloody and silent.

Moorina looks quickly for her child. She hears its cry. The great bull, who does not even know the damage he has done, continues across the beach, heading right toward it. The pup cries and cries. Moorina opens her mouth and sings. The pup turns toward her voice. She sings again and the pup moves toward her. It is hardly any distance at all but it is enough. The bull lumbers past.

Moorina drags her new, tired body through the mass of seals until she reaches her pup, who both cries and sings to her. She nuzzles the pup and it sucks from her greedily. It is a pleasant sensation, as is the wind on her face, the smell of salty sea, the sound of crashing waves. It isn't that she forgets, it's just that she lets herself be. Here. Who she is now. Seal. Keeper of song.

♦ ♦ ♦

The Harrowing

I HAD BEEN TRAVELING ACROSS THE COUNTRY
for some time, trying to find myself in America, in the lonely
streets of small towns with no streetlights, and names like Hender-
sonville (where everyone was a Henderson) or Mitchelton (largely
inhabited by the Mitchels). I explored the dirty streets and shop
windows of Chicago and New York, and stared in wonder at the
odd palm trees and strange antiseptic streets of L.A.; I tasted grits
and hush puppies in Atlanta, fresh cashews in Florida, blueberries
in Maine, and also, the dull flavor of hunger, the sour flavor of
bread crusts found in garbage cans, and the taste of copper from
kissed pennies found on cracked sidewalks and in wet gutters. I had
stood at the edge of the ocean and watched seagulls struggle against
the wind's arc, and listened to their cries at a pitch that always created, or found, in me a longing, for what I never knew—that's at
least part of what my journey was about.

At last I found myself sitting on a bench outside the train station
in Fullerton, California, an actual purchased ticket tucked in my
backpack, checked and rechecked in my fear that it would somehow disappear, become lost amongst the smelly socks, underwear,
and T-shirts, as certainly it should be, my recent readings (by the
light of city lights; in the small town parks with children's noises; in
the empty lifeguard station on a California beach, early morning,

only the seagulls, and, in the distance, dolphins to keep me company) of Herman Hesse and Allen Ginsberg, these wild minds that told me (even as I sat there, staring glumly at the empty train tracks, nervously fingering the clasp and buckle of my backpack) that I wouldn't get away with it. Karma, you know.

I tried to call home every so many weeks and had I not been so absorbed in trying to make my adventures sound glamorous and exciting rather than the more accurate truth of my bouts of loneliness and the rapid depletion of my savings, I might have been quicker to notice a change in the tone of my parents' voices. But I never did. It was my mother who finally told me, whispering so that Dad wouldn't hear, that they were going to lose the farm. "I'll come back," I said.

"It won't matter," she said, meaning the words kindly.

"I'm coming home," I insisted, surprised to hear the catch in my voice, thinking, before it's not there anymore.

By the time my father got on the line, I made it sound like it had been the reason I called. "You need some money?" he asked. But what could I do? Picturing him in his overalls, his face lined by sun and work, the fields of corn unfurled behind him, I didn't dare tell him the truth, he, who had worked, literally, all his life, while I, his son and heir, had rejected everything he believed in, including that Midwestern German-American work ethic, so that I could find myself, or something, that unnamed thing I could not describe, something that would fill the emptiness.

I had a coach ticket, which meant I'd be sleeping sitting up (and I pitied the poor bastard who'd be sitting next to me, it had been that long since I showered) but there was enough money left over so that I could eat. This thought once again sent my hand nervously fingering through the flapped fold of my backpack's pocket, for the rustle of paper that held my tickets, and the crumbled bills, my purloined guilt.

Just then a man joined me on the bench. It was a long bench, and there was a reasonable amount of space between us, but there was something so compelling in his presence that I immediately became acutely aware of him. He stared straight ahead, though I glanced at him several times, inviting the cursory nod between strangers sharing space, as we were, but he remained unaware, or uninterested, in my meager attempt at polite exchange. I began to wonder if he was a cop. My eyes, almost beyond my control, slid sideways to check this notion against his appearance. He struck me as being too slender, but what did I know, I had only recently become a criminal, and besides, there was power held by that slender physique. I could sense it even at a distance. Not like the man I robbed, his eyes wide and terrified as he reached for his wallet, not knowing that I would never do it, I would never have cut him with that knife, he had been safe with me all along. Hadn't he?

"Waiting for the train?" I said, surprising myself but evidently not the stranger. He turned his head slowly, a bemused smirk on his face. "Suppose you are," I said, nervously. "I mean what else would you be here for?"

At that he smiled, revealing thick, yellowed teeth and a cold glint in his blue eyes. I couldn't help it, I shuddered. "Someone just walked on your grave," he said, in a slow drawl, reminiscent of Saturday morning westerns.

"Excuse me?"

"It's a saying, for when you get the chill up your spine like that." I nodded, and once again glanced down the empty tracks. "You might just as well quit worrying about it," he said. I could have sworn he eyed my backpack. "You're going to be here awhile."

He looked deep into my eyes, and saw my karmic debt. I nodded, now certain I was not speaking to an ordinary man. Maybe he was one of those psychics I'd heard about.

"Four-oh-nine," he said, "it's always late."

And here I did a ridiculous thing. When I think back over that meeting I always think how strange it was that I scooted over on the bench, to be nearer to him, even though I feared him. It was almost because I feared him that I did it. That strange smile of his, which had nothing to do with happiness, intensified.

"Josh Walton," I said, introducing myself with the fake name I'd been using since the beginning of my travels, as if I knew I would one day be a man in need of a pseudonym.

He nodded, rubbing his thick tongue along the inside of his cheek, as though trying to stop from laughing. My nervous fingers rubbed against the pocket of the backpack as I tried to think how to extricate myself from this odd encounter. Just when I made up my mind to simply stand up and walk away, using an excuse of stretching my legs, he spoke, once more in that slow drawl, staring straight ahead, not like a man at all, but like an animal that sees best sideways. "You may as well just sit awhile."

Right then I knew. I was defeated. This was only a game he was playing. I really had no choice in this. He had me like a puppet on a string, and I would not be released until he decided. Confirming this thought was the way he turned to me, still grinning that evil grin. "Where you headed?"

"Home." My voice sounded small and scared, like a lost child.

I glanced around. We were alone. Even the small terminal looked empty.

"Oh, it gets kind of quiet around here this time of day," he said. "Almost everyone knows about the Four-oh-nine."

"Yeah," I said, "they'll be waiting for me."

"What's that?"

"My parents. They're waiting for me."

He laughed, but it did not disprove my earlier assumptions, it was a sharp sound. He even leaned over as though to tap my knee but at the last second he seemed to catch himself and instead just tapped the air above it. I was certain I felt a searing heat emanating from his palm. "Good thing I'm not a priest, boy."

"What do you mean?" I asked, feeling more and more that I was a boy of six or seven when I believed in such notions as good and evil, and never guessed that I would point a knife at an old man in a dark street and tell him to pull out his wallet.

"Not much of a liar, that's for sure."

"No, really," I said, sounding false by the absurdly high register of my reply, "they're expecting me."

"Why don't you call them? Let them know you'll be late?" He jutted his chin at the payphone inside the deserted terminal.

This was my opportunity for an escape, but there was something about the way he did it, something so obvious in it, as if he wanted me to go into that dark space, which caused me to hesitate, consider, and resist. "Already did," I lied.

He nodded, rubbed his hand along his jaw as though checking for stubble (though there was none). I noticed his fingernails were unusually long and sharp but clean.

"What if I was to say I know your folks?" I only had time to swallow before he continued. "Your father's a worker, ain't he? The kind of man who worked for everything he owns and your mother, well, there are still folks who say she's beautiful, though it's been what, five, six years since anyone told her? Sometimes, when nobody is home she stands in front of the mirror and sometimes she takes her clothes off—"

"Hey!" The blade of the knife, still in my backpack, flamed like hot metal in my mind.

He tilted his head, raised his gray eyebrows, and smirked. I didn't even realize I was once again nervously rubbing the backpack, searching, unconsciously, for the bladed shape until he glanced at my fidgeting hand, but then he looked down the tracks, first left, then right, so maybe it didn't mean anything at all.

"You expecting someone?" I said.

He shook his head and spit on the ground. "Just like the view, I guess."

I looked at the cold tracks, the bare horizon.

"What do you do?" he asked, sounding almost innocuous, innocent, like an old man. For a moment his wallet flashed through my mind. Did he carry one? How much was in it? I caught myself falling into this evil reverie with a start.

"I'm going to be a writer," I said.

We sat for the longest time, not speaking at all. Why was he, of all people, the first to hear about my secret dream? But as the quality of light changed, and still, we just sat there, in the ordinary way of sitting anywhere, I realized my guilt had imbued him with unreasonable power. He was just an old man with nothing better to do than stare at the train tracks and make dull conversation with strangers while I was already living the adventurous life I would write about. Maybe, even, one day I would write about my criminal act and in that way atone for it, at least somewhat.

At this point my legs really did feel cramped and I stood up to stretch them. I was reaching for my backpack when he spoke.

"You ever heard of the Harrowing?"

My fingers were just touching the buckle on the strap and I urged myself to tell him that I'd return in a minute; that I had to stretch my legs, or take a piss.

He tapped the bench with those long, sharp fingernails of his. He didn't look up at me, but stared straight ahead.

"I—"

"Sit," he said. And I did.

When I was a young man, around your age, I believe, I decided to become a priest. I reckon you are surprised by that but fact is, I was a good boy, or so I thought, devout at least.

So I packed my bag and left my home where I had growed up, and with my parents' blessings, took the train to Duty, to join the seminary there. I took to it like a pig to mud. I was a farm boy, see. It was easy for me to get up early for the morning chant and mass. Easier by far than getting up in the ice of winter to pull cow teats, that's for sure.

Father George is the one who told us about the Harrowing. He didn't necessarily follow the church line, so to speak. He had his own way of doing things.

Anyway, Father George was fond of quoting from the Letter of James, the part that goes, "You believe in one God. Well and good. So do the devils, and they shudder." He liked to confuse us with crap like that. He said we had the narrow view of children when it came to notions of good and evil. And he was right.

Most of the seminarians didn't give him much credit. They're the ones who started saying he was crazy. They came to class. They took the notes. They even passed the tests. But most of them didn't give it no more attention than that.

There was just six of us: me, Theodore, Frank O'Nan, Stephen (the red-haired one), Paul, and Michael who took some interest in Father George's way of looking at things. We formed a society of sorts. It wasn't formal at first. You know, just us boys getting together and talking, discussing his ideas, that sort of thing. We didn't have that much free time and, besides, this sort of breaking off into groups was frowned upon. So by necessity we became a secret organization. Though the whole thing was over before Christmas, with Stephen dead along with Father George.

At first we just ended up in one of our rooms, talking. But the more our conversations veered east of traditional Catholic beliefs, the further we moved out of that physical space. We said things like, "It sure is stuffy in here. Let's go for a walk." We didn't say we was trying to deceive anyone. We deceived ourselves that way.

Father Joe began to notice the six of us always together whenever we could be, and he took each of us aside, separately, and encouraged a widening of our social circle. "It isn't good," he said, "to search for truth in the souls of only a few."

What he said made sense. But we couldn't help it. We were bound in some way. We was still boys, really, fond of secrets and mysteries. Heck, at least half of us, that's what drawed us to the church. Not the light of God necessarily but the shadow of His mystery.

So we met at one A.M., in the bell tower, which, Stephen had discovered, had a door that had been sealed shut for so long it at first seemed impenetrable. Stephen took his crucifix and jabbed at the sides and corners, scraping away some of the years of dirt and loose cement and the like, and we pulled and after a while the door opened.

We walked up the dark stairs, single file, turning with the spiral of the narrow passage and brushing against cobwebs and stone. I don't know which one of us started it but someone, maybe it was Stephen 'cause he was first in line and, I think, out of all of us, the most taken with our inquiry, began to murmur the sacred syllables Father George had taught us. By the time we reached the bell room we were all saying them. Whispering, of course.

This became our Thursday night ritual. I think each of us had occasion to lie to our roommates about it, saying we was going to chapel if someone woke to hear us dressing in the dark. No one seemed to question it very seriously. Well, you know, they naturally assumed we was honest.

We got to the point where we had candles up there. Someone brought some of the wine from the chapel. Not consecrated, of course. We just drank out of the bottle, which seemed particularly bold. Like I said, we was good boys. And really, this was just good old youthful fun. You know, meeting in secret, talking about the teachings of Father George. What, for instance, did he mean by "ecstatic understanding" when he said, "the soul can only escape from its bondage to material existence through the attainment of true ecstatic understanding"?

We debated the meaning of "ecstatic" and "understanding" between sips of red wine, huddling against the cold, exposed like we was by the tall, open windows on four sides surrounding the bell that never rung.

Sometimes, warmed by the wine and the excitement of own young minds, we'd lay back and watch shooting stars.

We were good boys, see. That's important. What we was doing, breaking the rules of sleep, though really such a small transgression, was bold enough for all of us. We found it exciting and empowering both. But it ain't like we was up there talking dirty or nothing like that. I would say each of us, in his own way, was trying to penetrate the illusions, not just of the physical world, which, I gotta say, being teenagers and arrogant like that, we about all figured we'd done, but we was also trying, under Father George's teachings, to spear the illusion of the spiritual worlds. You get what I'm saying? 'Cause just 'cause you get there don't mean you're really there, right?

Eventually we noticed that Stephen seemed, perhaps, a bit too fond of the wine. For every gulp each of us had he took three or four. It wasn't like it is these days. There wasn't all sorts of talk about alcoholism and the like. We didn't know nothing about that. We just knew that sometimes he got too loud and we had to force him to be quiet; once we even had to wrestle him to the ground and I covered his mouth with my hand because he didn't seem to appreciate the gravity of the situation when Father George came outside and stood beneath the bell tower. It was the first snow of the season. The next morning in his class Father George said, "Did any of you see the snowfall? Were any of you up last night to see it?" I felt, when he said it, that he looked at each of us, particularly, but then, you know how it is, guilt infects your thoughts.

The following Thursday, the bell tower door, which had a habit of sticking, and which needed to be pried open from week to week, popped open easily which I think did give us pause. But then we went ahead up that dark and narrow way, murmuring the sacred syllables. When we got to the top, well, you probably see this coming all right, Father George was there. It was the first and only time I heard Stephen swear. But, you know how it goes, each small transgression sets the way for those that follow.

Father George, who had this great head of wavy white hair that stood up like he'd just been electrocuted or something, stood in the center of the bell room, nodding at us as we each entered it. Last of all was Stephen, who stumbled into me when he saw him and said, "Oh shit."

He, Father George that is, looked at each of us in turn, the way someone in authority does when they are about to give a lecture. "Seems you boys have formed yourselves a society of sorts," Father George said, not whispering exactly, but keeping his voice low.

We glanced at each other and nodded. What else could we do? It was true.

"You boys do understand about this sort of thing?" he said.

Again we glanced at each other, confused.

"Well, the Magi for instance. The Magi were initiates in the Mysteries. The Mysteries are bound to a community of souls. One person cannot get there alone, right? It takes a lot of strength."

We nodded. I think mostly to just be polite. I know I was wondering what the punishment would be and would I get kicked out of the seminary for this. That's when he said, "Which one of you handles the candles?"

Paul stepped forward like he was in military school or something. He goes, "I do, Father."

So, Father George just looks at him and nods and says, "All right then."

Paul glanced at the rest of us, the candles in a pile in the center of the room, and then at Father George who said, "Aren't you going to light them?"

Was this a trick question? But Father George closed his eyes, bowed his head, and began murmuring the sacred syllables. We formed a circle with him while Paul made a larger circle of candles around us.

After that Father George was sometimes there and sometimes not. He never stayed the entire time, which meant we always had a little space in which to talk about him after he left. We had entered into this secret with him, see. Sitting in the classroom, while he lectured on the Christian source of Tarot cards, most of the students rolled their eyes as they took notes but we each held the little secret card of our relationship with him. Feeling that way, at that age, it felt like there was electricity shared between us. I guess you might even say, to our young, misguided spiritual minds, it felt divine. I mean, he was a priest, see? He was a priest who taught us that the ancient Mysteries existed for everyone, not just the priests. And because he believed it we did too. Do you see what I'm getting at here? He said we was already holy. That even though we weren't ordained we was already equal to him. Of course, it wasn't really true. Because if he had told us the exact opposite, that the Mysteries were for the priests and that we had to remain loyal to them and him, well, we would have believed that too. Sort of like when the torturer stops, and the prisoner with the knife holes and the burns and what have you is grateful, right? When, really, gratitude ain't got no place in the exchange. It was kind of like that with us. He couldn't really be the one to tell us we were worthy. That's something a man has to find in himself.

So. The Harrowing. One night Father George tells us about it. What the Harrowing is, see, is that after Jesus died and before he was resurrected, well, he went to Hell and he released all the souls that had been trapped there. That's how come it's called the Harrowing. The Harrowing of Hell. He released these souls, see, these evil souls, and he set them free upon the earth.

They walk it still, to this day. Oh, sure, they take on different bodies and the like because bodies don't last, but they exist, okay?

Father George watched us while we talked about this, all excited like the boys we were. Finally, he raises his hand, palm out to us like he was giving us a blessing or something, and he goes, "Boys, boys, I'm afraid you're not looking at this the right way. What you should be fearing is not that you will meet one, but that you are one."

That gave us something to think about for sure. We all got quiet after that.

I can trace it to that day when things began to change between all of us. We started fighting more. We didn't trust each other. Maybe the fellow we thought was a friend was really one of the Harrowed, see? I don't think it occurred to any of us to look at Father George that way.

Around this time Father George took a special interest in Stephen. Anyone could see it. It was just obvious. Even in class, he always seemed to show a special fondness toward him. We didn't think much of it. It ain't uncommon for a teacher to have a pet. Certainly we never thought of nothing, well, you know, evil. Even though Father George tried to open our minds to it, we still thought of good and evil as being obvious, when it ain't always so, right?

Father George started having these secret meetings with Stephen. Come to find out. On Tuesday nights. Just the two of them, see. I don't even remember how the rest of us found out exactly. I remember it as being a suspicion at first and then a source for speculation between the five of us, until finally it was something we needed to investigate. Which is what we did.

I snuck into the bell tower that afternoon and oiled the door hinges so they wouldn't make no noise and, since we figured the two of them might be particularly prone to listening for any suspicious sound coming from the direction of our usual passage, we made an elaborate plan, later executed, in which we snuck out of the far west door, instead of the east one, circled around the monastery, and snuck into the bell tower from the north side, at intervals of five minutes. Once assembled there, we had no need to speak. Our plan had been formed and discussed. We took off our shoes. Left them there, outside the door.

Me, well, I'm the one who opened the oiled door, and though I had to tug at it a bit to get it unstuck, when it finally opened, it gave a little pop but it didn't squeak. We walked, in our socks, up that narrow staircase. I went first, see. I rounded that bend and stood in the doorway first.

Maybe you've already guessed what I saw up there, the two of them naked, though it was so cold that night and there was a breeze and I remember there was even snow on the floor and snow falling through those open windows around the bell. They was surrounded by candles of course, the very ones we used for our ceremonies of fire, with its trinity of flame, light, and smoke; a bridge, Father George had said, between the physical and spiritual world, now reduced to mood light. The four other boys came up right behind me and as you can imagine there was a lot of gasping and horrified looks and shame, and Father George said, "Now boys," and Stephen was crawling across the floor to his pile of clothes next to Father George's clothes with his crucifix and rosary neatly set on top. The whole place smelled sickly sweet like there had been wine spilled. Anyway, that's when I turned and stumbled out the room. I don't know if one of us knocked over a candle or if something even more sinister occurred. We all crashed together at the bottom of that stairway while I pushed on that door and it wouldn't open and we was like little girls, crying and blubbering because, you got to understand, nothing like that had ever occurred to us. I mean, we knew about homosexuality but we didn't know nothing about priests doing that with seminarians. The five of us are pushing at that door and blubbering and we was all as frightened as if we'd just seen a ghost, and just when I heard Father George, standing there at the top of them stairs, saying, "Now boys," it finally popped open and we ran out and I shut the door. Hard. Like he would come out after us, naked like he was. Stupid. I was just a stupid boy then, like you. Anyway, we run through the yard, not even trying to be quiet, and none of us said nothing about it but just kept running up to our rooms.

I was under my covers and shivering from the cold and the horror when I heard the bell tower ring. It rang slow at first, like maybe somebody was just giving it a try, and then it rang faster and faster and it woke everyone up and that's when I realize the room is glowing and the bell just rings faster and faster until it's almost a deafening noise but by the time we all was out there on the snowy lawn looking up at it, the tower was just one huge flame and pretty soon the ringing stopped.

Father George once told us that the world was made with smoke, that if you looked close you could see the elemental spirits there. I saw them that night. Small, about the size of your thumb maybe, naked little boys with vicious teeth coming toward me and I ran into the chapel, just as the sirens approached, and kneeled down to pray but you know how chapels are, all lit with candles and in their blue smoke I saw those vicious little creatures gnashing their teeth and making that sound of sizzling flames and it took me awhile to realize, since I was so distracted by my fear and their evil countenances, that each of those little creatures had Stephen's face, twisted, sure, but it was him all right. I pushed the door shut when we all got to the bottom, and I pushed it shut extra tight. I wanted to keep them up there. Not burned, see, I didn't know nothing about the fire at the time, but still, if it hadn't been for me they'd still be alive. That's when I figured it out. I was one of them. The Harrowed. I'd already been given salvation once and this is what I'd done with it.

Like you, son, I had a dream of myself once. I thought I would be someone who would put good into the world. What you are too young and stupid to realize is that when you hold a dream you hold the whole thing, see? Every dream has got its opposite, okay? All that time I thought I was finding Heaven, I was walking right back into Hell.

I got news for you, son, you ain't ever going to be no writer. You ain't never going to be nothing but an old man who sits and stares at empty train tracks.

I opened my mouth to protest but he reached for my knee and slapped it, hard. "Now that's a story, heh?"

He placed both his hands onto his own thighs, bent over at the waist, and stood. "Here comes your train now," he said, jutting his chin toward the distant engine.

"I am going to be a writer," I said weakly, sounding like a little boy again.

He turned, as though he'd just discovered me sitting there, and then, with only that quizzical look for a response, he walked away.

It took three days to travel cross-country from California to Wisconsin on the Four-oh-nine. I sat next to a pretty girl who was moving back home, just as I was, but she had clear, honest eyes and I felt that if I spoke to her she would soon see what the stranger had seen in me, my evil nature, the sinful fact of my undeserved position on the train, and my undeserved position in the world.

On the second night I went to the dining car for dinner. The porter seated me with a couple who had two young kids. They tried to be polite and make small talk but I had developed a fear of that sort of exchange. Besides, they really were too busy attending to the needs of their two young children to pay attention to me. I ordered the steak but found I couldn't stomach it; no matter how small the pieces were cut, I found it difficult to swallow. I excused myself from Rob, Lisa, and the two snot-drippers and returned to my seat where my seatmate had already fallen asleep, her blonde hair smashed against the window, creating a golden halo around her pretty face. Had circumstances been different, I thought (and sometimes still believe), this girl might have become my wife.

I switched trains in Chicago. With a queasy stomach and a vague sense of anticipation, I boarded the small commuter to Milwaukee. Though I was not returning home under ideal circumstances, I was returning, and that felt good after having traveled, for so long, to places I had never been before. By the time I reached the terminal there, I was actually quite excited. I stopped in the bathroom and went into a stall where I unlaced my backpack and found the knife, which I wrapped heavily in toilet paper and tossed into the garbage can, making sure to press down through the accumulation of wet paper towels, less someone innocently be hurt by it. Yes, it had been wrong what I had done, far less innocent than the stranger's actions for instance, if any part of that story was, in fact, true, but that one mistake, that one bad choice didn't mean I was evil, right?

I hitchhiked from Milwaukee all the way to the foot of our long driveway without incident. It was midafternoon and my father was likely in the fields. My mother would either be out there with him or hanging clothes in the backyard, baking bread, getting dinner ready. At least that's what their routine had been like. Before.

As I walked up the driveway I started marking the way I felt. The way the area of my chest around my heart was filled with that longing again, the same feeling I had when listening to the seagull's cry, and how the tempo of my walk changed from the scuff-footed pace I had adopted beneath the backpack's weight to light-footed and fast. I noticed the blackbirds' sheen against the peeled white clapboards of the home I'd grown up in, and the smell, the rich, moist scent of dirt and the heavy odor of manure, and the delicate but distinct scent of my mother's herb garden, minty and sweet. I was determined to prove the stranger wrong. I would be a writer. And that meant that I could no longer simply dream of it but I had to start doing it, first by noticing the details that composed my life. When I opened the front door, the knob felt unfamiliar in my palm. I had never before entered the house this way. I shrugged out of my backpack and set it down. It was almost too much. The familiar smell of laundry and soap and something vaguely lemon, and boxes stacked up all around marked with my mother's neat printing: *Kitchen* and *Living Room* and *Canning Jars*.

"Mom?" I called. "Ma?"

She came from the kitchen, her hair tied up in a scarf knotted at the front, her eyes blue-gray and wide, but caverned by worry and age. Her hand, in a bright yellow plastic glove, flew to her mouth, as she gave a little scream of delight and I knew then that the stranger had been right about one thing, at least. A person can just speak nonsense and still get one or two things right. "Ma, you're beautiful," I said, walking through the labyrinth of boxes to hug her and be hugged by her. For one last time to stand in that house I had been so eager to leave, and to hold onto her, and everything, tight.

Every October, I pick one night to go to the train tracks outside of town. I sit in my car and stare at the ugly flat of land there and I think of that old man, appearing, as he did, at a time in my life when I was choosing direction and had made some bad choices and one evil one. I think how, for the longest time, he was the devil to me, one of those set free between death and resurrection. Then I pour a glass of Merlot, raise it to the sky, and toast the stranger, wherever he may be.

Because, you see, I am a writer. My first book, *Karma Rides the Rails*, was published a few years after these events and I've been writing and getting published ever since. Not rich, or anything like it, but generally, I'm a happy man, one of the lucky ones. Living a dream come true.

Now that I am, if not old, approaching it, I think how maybe I've been wrong all this time. What he said about good and evil not always being as clear as we might like to believe, maybe that was a hint of his true purpose. Who knows what would have happened had I not been confronted with my deepest fears of what kind of man I was becoming and what kind of man I could never be. Though I am not a religious man, I am a man who believes in directing gratitude where it's due, and that's why now, I sometimes think, maybe he wasn't the devil at all, but something else entirely, sent by Heaven to set me free.

The Super Hero Saves the World

*W*HEN MARCADO WAS THREE A PYTHON SWAL-
lowed her alive. Her mother was dead but when they cut
Marcado out, she was sucking her thumb, peacefully asleep. The
rescuers crossed themselves, then spit on the red ground. Her father
stared at her in the split belly of the beast, the odd stamen of its
brutal flower, until the cook, who was used to dealing with the
bloody facts of appetite, pushed past the men and lifted her out.
She tried to hand the bloody child to her grieving father but he
would not touch her, shocked, the veterinarian said, by the double
miracle of the mother's death and child's recovery.

It was the cook who strung together tiny bells and tied them
around Marcado's ankles to warn away any other attacks. You'd
think such a noisy child would know no secrets. But she did. Like a
house with a belled cat, the family soon became accustomed to the
constant ringing. Marcado knew that the cook mixed poor flour in
with good and sent a sack of it off each week with her cousin (a
small dark man with a moustache that curled beyond his cheeks)
and in this way fed two families on the budget for one. Marcado
knew that her sister, Elsine, had a crush on the veterinarian who
was married and did disgusting things to the farm animals when he
thought no one was looking. Marcado also knew what her father
did and did not do when the python swallowed her mother, though

this memory was from the time before the bells and was becoming a ghost.

Her father had been strange ever since that day. Marcado knew there were rumors about him, but she was too short to hear what they were. He had taken to standing beneath the pepper tree, weeping and eating the hot fruit until his mouth became red with blisters or the cook pulled him back into the house, whichever came first. He gave Marcado peppermints, rubber balls, and dolls with eyelashes, his dark, sad eyes searching her face in a way she was too young to evaluate, while Elsine colored black hearts and sucked on stones.

Then, one day, while Marcado pirouetted through the house, and Elsine tore the petals off the orchids in the vase on the dining room table, their father announced that they were moving to Los Angeles, or "Ellay" as he said in the flat-sounding, new language.

Elsine cried for her veterinarian and in a desperate attempt left several paper hearts and polished stones in strategic locations where he was meant not only to find them, but to discern their meaning. He did find the strange gifts that led him to believe, correctly, that he was being followed, and, incorrectly, that he was being warned. He shredded the paper hearts, threw the stones in the river, and became fevered in his prayers of apology, then angry at a God who had abandoned him to such immoral desires that he could neither comprehend nor ignore, and finally, upon the occasion of finding a whole basket of stones outside the Rineros' barn, fell to his knees, babbling and weeping until Elsine, whom he called his "angel," led him home to his wife who took him into the kitchen and set him to peeling onions.

The cook wept too, as she packed the linen tablecloths and lace curtains, lavender sachets tucked into the corner of each box. But Marcado just danced. She knew the tears belonged more to the stolen flour, the cakes and bread and tortillas, than to her.

Even Marcado's father, though he smiled and waved his arms expansively when he spoke about Ellay, was discovered many an early morning standing next to the pepper tree as if rooted there himself, whispering to no one.

Only Marcado was happy. She was happy to leave the ghost of her mother who followed her around with useless information about washing her hair with rosemary, and who had temper tantrums, throwing herself across Marcado's bed and screaming as if she was the little girl and Marcado the mother.

Marcado was so excited her bells rang through the night. Her father and sister lost all their dreams in the shiver of excitement she could not contain even in sleep. They stared at the ceiling as if even it had become something to be missed while Marcado dreamt of a great city of glass-spired buildings, golden castles trellised with roses, angels everywhere, winged in clouds, and on sidewalks white as pearls. Los Angeles, City of Angels, here we come.

Now, at fifteen, Marcado's life before L.A. is a distant sort of dream. A family legend. Pomegranates remind her. In the split of red she sometimes sees her mother, but that ghost was left behind, and maybe that was a dream too. That business about being swallowed by the python, alive and whole, doesn't make sense, it can't be true. Though Elsine insists. "Oh, yeah. And when they cut you out you were wrapped in Mama's skin."

"I don't think so."

"Papa and her were both trying to save you. It's your fault she's dead. Lucky you didn't kill him too, or we'd be orphans."

After she finishes her homework Marcado changes into purple tights, a red leotard, a little black skirt. She takes the dirty, knotted string of bells, ties it around her ankle, and dances through the house.

"Your mother used to dance like that."

She nods but doesn't speak. Around her father she remains, after all this time, mostly silent.

He is a lonely man. He thought America with its grinning ways and endless fruit could save him. But he is equally unhappy amongst the palm trees, white concrete, and stucco as he'd been amongst the pepper tree, the velvet house, her grave. His skin is yellow-tinged, his moustache ragged. At night his youngest daughter dances in her room, those bells ringing darkly.

He drinks *cerveza* on the front steps and watches the white light of police helicopters searching. He wonders how it has happened that his oldest daughter has become so successfully Anglo while Marcado isn't really anything, not Latino, or Anglo, only strange. All that business with the python, he thinks. How much does she remember?

The school counselor brings Marcado into her office to discuss her amazing test scores.

"You could do anything if you make the right choices, Marcado. What are your plans for the future?"

"I want to be a super hero."

The counselor speaks to Marcado's teachers who all report her

as a quiet, good student. Mrs. Fiddlestein adds, "Her poetry is, well
. . . read this."

> The super hero
> folds her cape,
> tucks it in her drawer,
> in the back in the dark.
> She takes up eating eggs instead,
> wowing crowds by swallowing them whole,
> in their shells, cracked first to prove
> the point.
>
> Sometimes a reporter asks,
> But why did you stop saving lives?
> She answers by eating twelve raw eggs.
>
> What can an ex-super hero say?
> There were always more.
> She was never enough.
> The world is like an egg,
> such potential, such possibility!
>
> At night, in her brightly painted
> circus trailer, she checks eggs
> by the light of a candle,
> revealed fetuses set aside
> to be swallowed in the dark.
>
> She dreams the world on fire,
> rises weary to dress for the act.
>
> In the tent the people cheer
> for the elephants, the lion tamer,
> the trapeze artist,
> but when she stands in the center,
> swallowing eggs, they boo,
> and throw cotton-candy cones,
> popcorn cartons, and empty cups.
>
> Nobody likes a super hero
> who gives up her act.
>
> She paints her face with wide eyes,
> like a clown,
> and wears dresses of silk, reds

and purples that reveal her strong arms
going slack.

One night they throw stones.
She has to be hurried off the floor,
and hidden in the fat lady's trailer,
while the angry mob tries to find her,
carrying guns and rope.

Oh how they love to hate her!
"Ladies and gentlemen, the legendary, ex-
super hero who could save the world,
will now eat eggs instead."

The roar of hate is what she lives for.

Sometimes, she pulls out the cape,
touches the red silk and remembers
the cheers of thousands, the clasp
of grateful hand, the thrill
of catching a falling body,
now she catches hate instead.

Each night she vomits
outside her trailer.
The other performers insist
to not be near her.
In the starry dark she retches
all she's swallowed,
then buries it in the hole
she digs each morning.

It's the sound of a funeral shovel.
We are the dead, she tells them.
"Why don't you go back where you came from?"
She smiles,
they boo and throw things.
She lifts one white orb,
they jeer,
she puts it in her mouth
they stamp their feet on the bleachers,
she inhales
they cheer, as she struggles for breath.
She bends over to swallow.
They clap. They scream for more.

The counselor calls Marcado's father to school. He sits nervously and listens as she tries to explain.

"She's special. I mean in a good way. She might be a poet." She hands him the poem to read.

He massages his forehead with thick fingers, swallows before he speaks. "Why have you called me away from work to read the ramblings of an adolescent girl?"

"I thought—"

He stands, tosses the paper on the desk. For a moment the counselor is frightened and maybe a little turned on. But he just turns and walks out. She catches her breath. Picks up the paper. Reads it again. Shrugs. Tucks it into a manila folder. She stares at the wall of posters promising different futures and thinks maybe she made the wrong choice. Maybe she should have become a lawyer, or a dentist, or the woman who works at the coffee shop, obviously years too old for such work.

Marcado receives a letter. In the mail! She opens the envelope carefully, in her bedroom after school. Outside her open window, cars hum and honk past, but when the letter is pulled out she hears the sound of birds. She unfolds the vellum, faintly lined like skin. In the center, in neat square letters, is printed the single word:

MURDERER

Marcado looks at the envelope. No return address, the postmark, local. She slips the word back into the torn envelope, tucks it in her drawer with her panties and bras. She puts on her tights and her leotard, the little black skirt. She ties the knotted string of bells to her ankle. She puts Carmina Burana into the CD player. She opens all the doors in all the rooms and dances through the house.

Her father hears the noise halfway down the block. He thinks he sees dark birds circling his roof but then realizes they are seagulls, lost and looking for the ocean, perhaps made crazy by his daughter's wild dancing. Then, just like that, he thinks of boiled eggs, peeling the cracked shells from the gelatinous orbs, and he smells their gaseous odor. He hurries to his house.

She leaps away from him into the open mouth of her bedroom. Closes the door. Turns the music off. In the silence she can hear her own breathing. She stares at the closed door.

She makes sugar cookies shaped like jack o' lanterns. With black and white icing she turns the grinning faces into skulls. "Don't you have anything of mama's?" she asks.

He shakes his head and pats his moustache with one thick finger. "We haven't celebrated this for years."

Elsine stops by with her new boyfriend. He is tall and blond. His blue eyes widen at Marcado's cookies. Elsine pulls him into the living room where Marcado has put the TV in the closet and turned its table into an altar of red and lace, construction paper crosses, and plastic skeletons. Elsine rolls her eyes and turns David so his back is to the altar and he faces her father instead. "We just stopped by on the way to the movie. I forgot something." She goes into her bedroom. They listen to drawers open and close while they appraise each other silently. When she comes out, she is still grinning and now, he smiles too. She takes his hand and leads him through the kitchen. She grabs four warm skulls and hands one to him. They leave a trail of crumbs, flour footprints, and a strange feeling in the air that doesn't belong in the house without them.

Marcado lights the candles and turns off all the lamps. "It's not the same," her father says. "Besides, I didn't know. I had these plans for a while."

Marcado is glad to be alone. She places cookies on the altar. She sits at the kitchen table and pours two glasses of wine.

But though she waits a long time, and the candles shorten, and she empties and fills her wineglass many times, the other remains full, the cookies, unbroken.

She rises unsteady from the chair. She blows out candles. Question mark spirals of smoke linger in the air. She falls asleep with all her clothes on. She doesn't hear her father return.

He watches the girl sleeping in the crook of a python. He stands like a fear statue, an ordinary man who cannot escape the terrible truth of himself. He propels forward, feet last, as though pushed. She sleeps peacefully in shadows and blankets that take on the shape of his demon. Where does she get her courage? Not from him, that is certain.

She is twenty feet tall. She can keep buildings standing with her palms. She can catch lightning and spear the bad guys with it. She can fly and also disappear. Nobody dies on her watch. Her kryptonite? Sleep. When Marcado sleeps, evil things happen.

She wakes with a start. "Papa?"

"Go to sleep, *mi hija*."

She listens to his footsteps receding.

*   *   *

Elsine is getting married! Marcado can't quite believe that Elsine has found someone who loves her. She knows this is an unkind thought. Elsine starts doing weird things like kissing Marcado on the cheek, or buying her little presents, perfume, earrings, things she has no idea what to do with. Maybe this is the real Elsine. Maybe the mean one was just a twenty-year stage.

"How about paper like this? For the invitations?" Elsine pulls a vellum sheet from a stack in her dresser drawer. The paper is faintly lined like skin, and in the center the word *murderer* is written in cursive, crossed out, then printed in the straight square letters Marcado remembers. She traces the word with her finger. Elsine looks over her shoulder. "Oh Marcado, can you forgive me?"

"You?" Marcado says.

"I hated you." Elsine's face strains with the emotion as though it still exists.

"Don't worry about it," Marcado says. Elsine gives her a hug. Their father, who is eavesdropping behind the door, bows his head into his hands and weeps. When the sisters hear this they hug him and shower him with kisses. They think his tears are about the wedding.

"Don't worry," Elsine says, "you will always be my papa."

For a treat they make hot chocolate with cinnamon and nutmeg, swirled to a froth. They are sitting around the kitchen table when she finds them. She stands in the doorway, watching. Oh, how they have aged! She looks at her husband and shakes her head. What trouble he's put her through. How many miles, how many wrong houses, how many years has it taken to get here! Nobody understands this about the dead. They think nothing can hurt them. As if pain is only a body thing.

The hair on the back of Marcado's neck stands up. Her father is laughing; Elsine waving her arms and speaking loudly, but Marcado has lost trace of the story. She smells something funny.

Her mother waves frantically from the doorway but it is useless. The girl has lost her vision. The mother shakes her head. All she wants to do is get on with her death. Why does everything have to be so difficult?

She wanders through the little house. She looks into her husband's room. She can smell peppermint, dust, and his scent like good dirt. She sighs, and he, in the kitchen, in the middle of laughter, stops and thinks of her, the way she was on their last morning together. How unlimited their love! How limited his courage! He wipes a tear from his eye that both daughters think was put there by laughter.

She finds the bride's room littered with magazines of white girls in six-thousand-dollar dresses, books titled *How To Plan a Perfect Wedding* and *It's Your Day To Be a Princess!* Elsine. She didn't come with them that day and so has been spared and slighted.

The last room is Marcado's. She walks in and sits at the edge of the unmade bed. She wants to throw herself across it and cry, the way she used to, but she just sits there and tries not to lose control until the girl comes into the room and gets undressed, revealing a beautiful, healthy body, before it is sheathed by a cotton nightgown. She seems slightly disoriented. She opens wrong drawers and turns in circles. "Just go to sleep," whispers her mother. And she does.

The steam of boiled eggs fills the kitchen with pungent odor. Her mother laughs and her father spins her in his arms. He nuzzles her neck and she lets him. Together they pack the basket with mangoes, tortillas, cold chicken, chocolate, wine, the boiled eggs.

They try to leave without her but Marcado stamps her feet and cries. They laugh and shower her with kisses. The three of them go together, leaving Elsine, who is busy coloring hearts, with the cook.

They sing songs as they drive. They pull over and spread out the flowered tablecloth. They kiss each other and they kiss her. They eat and drink. Marcado is full. Sleepily, she crawls to the edge of the blanket to watch the clouds until her eyes hurt. She rolls on her side and watches them through the lace of her lashes. Her father lies on top of her mother who is surrounded by eggshell and mango peel. He caresses her body and moves his hips in a strange, lying-down dance. They both look over at her but her eyes are so heavy she cannot do anything but close them.

She wakes to the sunlight falling around her in rainbow circles and a strange noise. Her father stands with his back to her, by the river, his legs spread apart. His gold urine flows in an arc. The strange sucking noise is closer. Her mother screams. Marcado turns and sees the great, dark slither. A beast is eating Mama! Marcado screams. She looks at her father. He turns and stands there, his pants still unzipped, his thing shrinking in his hands. Papa! Papa! He stands there with his mouth open, his eyes wide. Marcado screams again. Papa! He is a tree. A rock. Useless. She stands. He does nothing to stop her. "Mama!" The great mouth opens.

Sun streams all around her. She does not shake the dream from her sleep, nor does it slip away the way they usually do, when she remembers it.

There, the ghost says, now you remember.

*   *   *

Marcado is a bridesmaid and has to suffer her sister's style, a shiny green dress with little straps that slip down her shoulders, and green shoes, dyed to match, that hurt. The flower crown keeps sliding and only her black tangle of hair stops it from falling off. She watches her sister dancing the first dance with David. They smile and stare into each other's eyes. They do not seem to care that today of all days, L.A. is experiencing a thunderstorm. The guests are all a little soggy. The reception hall's lights flicker but Elsine and David just dance and smile at each other. Apparently they think love is enough. When the dance ends he leans over and kisses her. The crowd cheers and the drummer bangs his drum.

The father's dance is announced. He comes to the spotlight. A handsome man in his tuxedo. He smiles at Elsine and takes her hand. The crowd claps. The lights flicker. Marcado watches the dance and thinks this is the first woman he's danced with since her mother. Maybe. What does she know? Everyone has their secrets.

Other couples join them. Somebody cuts in, a bald man Marcado thinks is David's uncle. Her father just stands there. Alone in the middle of the dancers. Searching faces in the crowd. The silver ball spins spots of colored light between them. He rubs his moustache. In another second he will turn away. She steps forward. Limping slightly in the stupid green shoes. She walks through the spinning spots of light. He takes her hand.

"You look beautiful," he says.

"I look green."

He laughs. When did his teeth turn this un-white shade? When did his skin loosen around the jaw? Was he always so afraid?

"Papa?"

"Yes?"

She shrugs and smiles. He cocks his head, then tries to do something fancy with spinning her and they laugh in the tangle he creates.

The lights flicker then shut off. Marcado thinks they have all been swallowed by the beast; the bride, the groom, the guests in soggy shoes, strangers on the beach, families in TV rooms, the homeless on the street, the dead, the brave, the weak, the forgiven and unforgiven. They continue dancing and, in only a few steps the light returns. The crowd claps and hoots as if this simple act is something extraordinary, heroic even. They don't know about the beast. Only Marcado knows. What does she do with such powerful information? She dances. In this way, she begins to save the world.

The Chambered Fruit

STONES. ROOTS. CHIPS LIKE BONES. THE MOLD-
ering scent of dry leaves and dirt, the odd aroma of mint.
What grew here before it fell to neglect and misuse? I remember
this past spring's tulips and daffodils, sprouted amongst the weeds,
picked and discarded without discrimination. I was so distracted by
my dead daughter that I rarely noticed the living. I take a deep
breath. Mint thyme. It should have survived the neglect, perhaps
did, but now has fallen victim to my passionate weeding, as so
much of more significance has fallen victim before it. I pick up a
small, brown bulb and set it, point up, in the hole, cover it with dirt.
Geese fly overhead. I shade my eyes to watch them pass, and then
cannot avoid surveying the property.

Near the old barn are piles of wood and brick meant to further
its renovation. Leaves and broken branches litter the stacks. The
wood looks slightly warped, weathered by the seasons it's gone
untended. The yard is bristly with dried weeds and leaves. The
house has suffered the worst. Surely, instead of planting bulbs I
should be calling a contractor. It can't be good, the way it looks like
it's begun to sink into the earth or how the roof litters shingles
that spear into the ground around it. But who should I call? How
far do I have to search to find someone who doesn't know our story?

I think of it like the nursery rhyme. Inside the old farmhouse with the sagging porch, through the large, sunny kitchen, past the living room with the wood-burning stove, up the creaking stairs and down the hall lined with braided rugs, past the bathroom with the round window and claw-footed tub, past the yellow and white bedroom we called the guest room, past her room (where the door is shut) to our bedroom—my bedroom now—there is, on the bedside table, a picture of the three of us. It's from her last birthday. Twelve candles on the cake. She is bent to blow them out, her face in pretty profile. Her dark hair brushes against the smooth skin of her puffed cheek; her eye, bright with happiness, dark-lashed beneath its perfectly arched brow. Jack and I stand behind her. Both of us are blurry, the result of Jack having set up the camera for automatic timer, his running to be in the shot, me moving to make room for him. He looks like her, only handsome, and I look like, well, someone passing by who got in the picture by mistake, a blur of long, untidy hair, an oversized shirt, baggy slacks. The camera captures and holds their smiles forever, locked in innocence and joy, and my smile, strained, my focus somewhere past the borders of the picture, as if I see, in the shadows, what is coming.

When I think of everything that happened, from the beginning, I look for clues. In a way, there are so many it baffles strangers that we couldn't see them. But to understand this, and really, I'm beyond expecting anyone else to understand this, but for my own understanding, I have to remember that to be human is a dangerous state. That said, Jack's nature is not profoundly careless, and I am not, really, in spite of everything you might have read or concluded, criminally naïve. Though of course I accept, even as I rebel against its horrible truth, that a great deal of the fault was ours. Sometimes I think more ours than his. When I look for clues to the dangerous parents we'd become I have to accept the combustible combination that occurred, just once, when Jack was careless and I was naïve and that's all it took. We lost her.

You may be familiar with my old work. Folk scenes, sort of like Grandma Moses except, frankly, hers are better. Maybe the difference is that hers were created from real memories and mine were made from longing. No one I know has ever ridden in a horse-drawn sleigh, with or without bells. We did not hang Christmas wreaths on all the doors and from the street lamps lit with candles. We did not send the children to skate at the neighborhood pond (which didn't exist, the closest thing being the town dump) or burn leaves and grow pumpkins (well, the Hadley's grew pumpkins but their farmhouse was an old trailer so it didn't really fit the picture). We did garden, but our gardens did not all blossom into perfect flower at the same moment on the same day, the women standing in aprons, talking over the fence. The sun shone but it didn't shine the way I painted it, a great ball of light with spears of brightness around it.

These are the paintings I made. Little folk scenes that were actually quite popular, not in town, of course, but in other places where people imagined the world I painted existed. I made a decent living at it. Even now, when all I paint are dark and frightening scenes of abduction and despair that I show no one (who would come anyway, even old friends keep their distance now), I live off the royalties. My paintings are on calendars, Christmas cards, coasters, T-shirts. In the first days of horror, when the news coverage was so heavy, I thought someone would certainly point out that I (the neglectful mother of the dead girl) was also the painter, C. R. Rite, but as far as I know the connection was never made and my income has not suffered for my neglect.

Jack still represents my work, which also makes it strange that no one ever made the connection. Maybe people assumed we were actually farmers, though the locals certainly knew that wasn't true. Maybe the media was just too busy telling the grisly details of our story to focus any attention on the boring issue of our finances. Certainly that matter isn't very titillating. What people seemed to want to hear was how our daughter died, an endless nightmare from which I can't ever wake, that strangers actually watch and read as some form of entertainment.

I accept my fault in this, and I know it's huge. I live every day with the Greek proportions of our story. In the classic nature I had a fault, a small area, like Achilles's heel, that left me vulnerable.

But not evil. As Jack likes to point out, we didn't do that to her and we would have stopped it from happening if we knew how.

The unforgivable thing, everyone agrees, is that we didn't see it. How evil do you have to be? We did not keep our daughter safe and she's dead because of that. Isn't that evil enough?

When we moved here, Steff was eight. She didn't know that we were really country people, having lived her whole life in the city. At first she spent all her time in her room with her books and her dolls but eventually, during that giddy, first hot summer when I walked about in my slip (when the construction crew wasn't working on the barn) eating raspberries off the bushes and planting sunflower seeds, and hollyhocks (though it was too late and they wouldn't bloom), she joined me, staying close, afraid of all the space, the strangeness of sky. Eventually, she came to love it too and brought blankets into the yard for picnics, both real and imagined, and paper to color, which, in true Buddha-child fashion she left to blow about the yard when she was finished. When one of these pictures blew across my path, a scene of a girl picking flowers, a shimmering angel behind her, I memorized it and then let it blow away, thinking it would be a gift for somebody unlucky enough not to have a child who drew pictures of that other world which children are so close to.

In the city, Steffie had attended a small private school with a philosophy that sheltered children from the things in our world that make them grow up so fast. The influence of media was discouraged and, contrary to national trend, computer use was considered neither necessary nor particularly beneficial to children. At eight, Steffie still played with dolls, and believed in, if not magic, at least a magicalness to the world; a condition that caused strangers to look at her askance and try to measure her IQ but for which I took great pride. In her school they learned the mythic stories, needlework, and dance. Friends of mine with children in public or other private schools talked of the homework stress and the busyness of their lives, transporting kids from practice to practice. When I visited these friends their children did not play the piano, or happily kick soccer balls in the yard. In spite of all those lessons, or, I suspected, because of them, these children sat listless and bleary-eyed in front of the television or wandered about the house, restless and bored, often resorting to eating, while Steffie played with dolls or spoons, whatever was available. I feel that our society has forgotten the importance of play, the simple beginnings of a creative mind. The value of that. Not that anyone is interested in parental guidance from me now.

At any rate, Steffie got off the bus, that first day, in tears. Several of the children would not sit with her because, they said, we were a bunch of hippies who ran around the yard in our underthings. When Steffie told me this I cried right along with her. I'd made a life out of forgetting the world. I found its reminders sharp and disturbing.

Eventually, she adjusted and I did too. I wore clothes in the yard, though I was baffled how anyone knew I'd ever done differently. Steff put away her dolls and proudly carried her heavy backpack filled with books and maps and serious questions about the real world, completely neglecting anything about the spiritual. Incredibly (to me) she liked it. A lot. She loved the candy they were rewarded with, the movies they watched. "I like it because it's normal," she said, and I realized that she knew we were not.

The years passed. I had the barn converted to an art studio and planned to further the renovation so that I could turn it into a sort of community art center for teenagers. I imagined Saturday mornings teaching painting, others teaching things like weaving, or, when Steffie began to take an interest in it, even dance. I think part of the motivation for this plan was the idea of filling the place with teenagers and helping Steffie's social life, which still seemed, though she never complained, strangely quiet for a child her age.

So, when Jack bought the computer, I thought it was a good idea. He said he needed it for the business and Steffie had been complaining for some time that she "needed" one too. He brought home the computer and I didn't argue. After all, he and Steff were the ones dealing with the notorious "real" world and I was the one who got to spend all morning painting happy pictures and the rest of the day gardening, or baking cookies, or reading a good book. Who in the world lived a life like mine?

When the computer was set up and ready to use in his office, Jack called me to come look. I looked into the brightly colored screen and felt numbed by it. Steff, however, was thrilled. Soon the two of them were talking a strange language I didn't understand. I drifted off into private thoughts, mentally working on paintings, scenes from a time before the world was enchanted by screens.

About three months before (oh, God, I still cannot write these words without trembling) her last birthday, Jack began campaigning that we get Steff her own computer. I didn't like the idea but I couldn't say why, though I held my ground until one Saturday when I drove into town to the post office and saw a group of girls who looked to be Steffie's age, and who I thought I recognized from classroom functions, sitting at the picnic table outside the ice cream place. A few of the girls caught me staring, and they began whispering behind open hands. I turned away. Had I done this to her? Was it my strangeness that made her unpopular? I went home and told Jack to go ahead and buy the thing. We gave it to her for her twelfth birthday, that's when we took the picture, the one I still have on the bedside table.

Steff was thrilled. She hugged us both and gave us kisses and thanked us so much that I began to believe we had done the right thing. I was baffled how this silent box was going to make her life better but after seeing those girls together, I was ready to try anything.

They set up the computer in her room. At night, after dinner, they each went off for hours, clicking and staring at their separate screens. I lit candles and sat, with the cat in my lap, reading. I guess I had some vague ideas about homework, and I'd heard that there were ways to view great paintings from distant museums on the computer. I assumed she was doing things like that. I thought she should be doing more interacting with the world. I thought this as I sat reading, with the cat on my lap, and tried to believe that one solitude is the same as any other.

As though she'd been given the magic elixir for a social life, she began talking about various friends. Eventually one name came up more and more frequently. Celia read the same books Steffie did and liked to draw and dance. When Celia asked Steff to sleep over I was thrilled until I found out Stephanie had never actually met the girl but only "talked" to her on the computer.

Of course, I said this would not happen. She could be anyone; why, Celia might not even be a girl, I said. No, she could not sleep over at this stranger's house, who, coincidentally lived only twenty-four miles away.

Steff burst into tears at the dinner table, threw her napkin on the plate. "You don't want me to be normal," she said, "you want me to be just like you and I'm not!" Then she ran out of the kitchen, up the stairs to her bedroom where she actually slammed the door, all of this perhaps not unusual behavior for an almost teenager but completely new for Steff.

Jack looked at me accusingly.

"You can't expect me to let her go off to some stranger's house. We don't even know the family."

"Whose family do we know?"

I understood his point. I had sheltered us, all of us, with my sheltered ways.

"When it comes down to it, if she went anywhere in town, we wouldn't know those people either."

"It's not the same thing. People have reputations." As soon as I saw the look on Jack's face, I realized that our reputation was probably more extensive than I knew. If not for me, they would be having a normal life. I was the odd one. It was all my fault.

"What if I speak to the girl's parents, would that make you more comfortable?"

For a moment, I considered that we invite the girl's family over, we could have a barbecue, but the thought of having to spend a whole evening entertaining anyone horrified me. When it comes right down to it, my daughter died because of my reluctance to entertain. How ridiculous and horrifying. Instead, I agreed that she could go if Jack talked to Celia's parents first.

We went up to her room together. We knocked and entered. I expected to find her lying across the bed, my posture of teenage despair, but instead, she was sitting at the desk, staring into the computer.

"We've decided you can go, but we want to speak to her parents first."

She turned and grinned, bathed in computer glow, all the color gone from her pretty face and replaced with green.

"Is that Celia now?" Jack asked.

She nodded.

"Ask her for her number."

She began typing. I turned and walked away. What was I so creeped out about? This was the new world. My daughter and my husband were a part of it, as was I, even if with reluctance.

Jack spoke to Celia's father that night. It turned out they had a lot in common too. He was an insurance salesman. His wife, however, was very different from me, a lawyer out of town until Friday night. Jack covered the mouthpiece. "He wants to pick Steff up around 4:30 on Friday. He's going to be passing through town. They'll pick Celia up at her dance class, and Sarah will get home from D.C. about 5:30. He's spoken to her and she's happy to have Stephanie over. What do you think?"

"How does he sound?"

"He sounds a lot like me."

Steff was standing in the kitchen doorway watching. I wasn't used to her squinty-eyed appraisal, as if suddenly there was something suspicious about me.

"Okay," I said.

Steff grinned. Jack took his hands off the mouthpiece. "That'll work out fine," he said in a boisterous voice. They really both looked so thrilled. Had I done this to them? Kept them so sheltered that Stephanie's sleepover at a friend's house on a Friday night, an absolutely normal occurrence for any girl her age, was such an enormous event?

Was this all my fault?

He was right on time. It was a beautiful spring day, unseasonably
warm. I found him immediately affable, friendly, grinning dimples.
I thought he looked younger than Jack or me, though in reality he
was a year older. I guess people without consciences don't wrinkle
like the rest of us. I opened the door and we shook hands. He had a
firm handshake, a bit sweaty, but it was a warm day. Jack came out
and the two of them got to talking immediately. I slipped away to
get Steff. I went to her bedroom. Her backpack was packed, the
sleeping bag rolled next to it, but she was not in the room. I walked
over to the window and saw her in the garden, picking flowers. I
opened the window. She looked up and waved, the flowers in her
hand arcing the sky. I waved, pointed to his car. She nodded and
ran toward the house. I brought the ridiculously heavy backpack
and sleeping bag downstairs. When I got to the kitchen, she was
standing there, her cheeks flushed, holding the bouquet of daffodils
and tulips while Jack and Celia's father talked. I helped her wrap
the stems in a wet paper towel and aluminum foil. "This is a very
nice idea," I whispered to her at the sink.

She smiled and shrugged. "Celia said her mom likes flowers
too."

What was it about that that set off a little warning buzzer in my
head? All these coincidences. I shook it back; after all, isn't that how
friendships are made, by common interests? We turned and the
fathers stopped talking. Celia's father grinned at Steff. Once more
the alarm sounded but he bent down, picked up the pack, and said
something like, What do kids put in these things, Celia's is always
so heavy too. They walked to the door. I wanted to hug Stephanie
but it seemed silly and probably would be embarrassing to her, and,
after all, hadn't I already embarrassed her enough? The screen door
banged shut. I stood in the kitchen and listened to the cheerful
voices, the car doors slam, the engine, the sound of the gravel as
they drove away. Too late, I ran out to wave goodbye. I have no idea
if Steffie saw me or not.

Jack wrapped his arms around my waist, nuzzled my neck. "The
garden? Kitchen? Name your place, baby."

"I should have told her to call when she gets there."

"Honey, she'll be back tomorrow."

"Let's call her, just to make sure she's comfortable."

"Chloe—"

"After we call her, the garden."

*   *   *

There was a sudden change in the weather. The temperature dropped thirty degrees. We closed windows and doors and put on sweaters and jeans. It began to rain about 5:30 and it just kept raining. We called at six, seven, eight. No one answered. It began to hail.

"Something's wrong," I said.

"They probably just went to a movie."

We called at nine. It rang and rang.

"I'm going there."

"What? Are you kidding? Do you have any idea how embarrassing that would be for her?"

"Well, where are they Jack?"

"They went to a movie, or the mall, or out for pizza. Not everyone lives like us."

Ten. Still no answer.

I put on my coat.

"Where are you going?"

"Give me the directions."

"You can't be serious."

"Where are the directions?"

"Nothing's wrong."

"Jack!"

"I don't have any directions."

"What do you mean? How are we supposed to pick her up?"

"Turns out he's coming back this way tomorrow. He's going to drop her off."

Lightning split the sky and thunder shook the house. "Do you even have an address?"

"I'm sure everything's all right," he said, but he said it softly and I could hear the fear in his voice.

We called at 10:20, 10:30, 10:41, 10:50, 10:54. At last, at 10:59, a man's voice.

"Hello, this is Steffie's mother, is this—" I don't even know his name "—is this Celia's father?"

"I just picked up the phone, lady, ain't no one here."

"What do you mean? Who are you? Where is everyone?"

"This is just a phone booth, okay?"

I drop the phone. I run to the bathroom. In the distance I hear Jack's voice, he says the number and then he says, "Oh my God," and I don't hear the rest, over the sound of my retching.

Police sirens blood red. Blue uniforms and serious faces. Lights blaze. Pencils scratch across white pads. Jack wipes his hand

through his hair, over and over again. Dry taste in my mouth. The
smell of vomit. The questions. The descriptions. Fingerprint powder. I take them to her bedroom. Strange hands paw her things. Her
diary. Someone turns her computer on. "Do you know her password?"
I shake my head. "Well," says the man reading her diary, "it
appears she really believed there was a Celia." What? Of course she
did, can I see that? "Sorry, ma'am, it's evidence." Downstairs. More
uniforms and raincoats. Police banter about the weather. Blazing
lights. The telephone rings. Sudden silence. I run to answer it.
"Hello." It's Mrs. Bialo, my neighbor; she says, is everything all
right? No, it's not. I hang up the phone. The activity resumes. Suddenly I see a light like the tiny flicker of a hundred fireflies
hovering close to me and I hear her voice, Mom? I fall to my knees
sobbing. Jack rushes over and holds me like I'm breakable. There is
a temporary and slight change in the activity around us but then it
continues as before and goes on like this for hours. In early morning
there is a freak snowfall. We start getting calls from newspapers and
magazines. A TV truck parks at the end of our drive. My neighbor,
Mrs. Bialo, shows up with banana bread and starts making coffee. I
stand on the porch and watch the snow salting down. The red tulips
droop wounded against the icy white. The daffodils bow their silent
bells. I listen to the sound of falling snow. I haven't told anyone
what I know. What would be the point? Who would believe me?
But I know. She's dead. She's dead. She's gone.

Let's go quickly over the details. The body. Oh, her body. Found.
The tests confirm. Raped and strangled. My little darling.

Then, incredibly, he is found too. Trying to do the same thing again
but this time to a more savvy family. He even used the name Celia.
The sergeant tells me this with glee. "They always think they're so
clever, but they're not. They make mistakes." How excited everybody is. They found him. He can't do it again. This is good. But I
don't feel happiness, which disappoints everyone.

Jack agrees to go on a talk show. They convince him he will be
helping other families and other little girls but really he's there so
everyone can feel superior. One lady stands up. She is wearing a
sensible dress and shoes. She is a sensible mother, anyone can see
that, and she says, "I just don't understand, in this day and age, how
you could let your daughter go off with a stranger like that?" She
says it like she really cares, but she beams when the audience claps
because really, she just wants to make her point.

Jack tries to say the stuff about how really everyone takes chances when they send their children off to other homes. I mean, we're all really strangers, he says. But they aren't buying it, this clever audience. The sensible lady stands up again and says, "I'm really sorry about what happened to your daughter but you gotta accept that it's at least partly your fault." There is scattered applause. The host tries to take it back. "I'm sure no one here means to imply this is your fault," he says, "we only want to learn from your mistakes." The audience applauds at that as well. Everyone gets applause except Jack.

After the taping he calls me in tears. I'm not much help as I am also feeling superior since I would never be so stupid as to fall for the "You're helping others" line the talk show people keep trying. He says it was terrible but on the day it airs, he insists we watch. It is terrible.

We move through the house and our lives. I think I will never eat again and then, one day, I do. I think I will never make love again and then, one night, something like that happens but it is so different, there is such a cold desperation to it, that I think it will never happen again, and it doesn't.

Six months later there is a trial. We are both witnesses for the prosecution so we can't attend. The defense attorney does a mean job on us but the prosecutor says, "He's just trying to distract the jury. It's not going to work. In fact, it'll probably backfire, generating more sympathy."

Fuck their sympathy, I say.

Jack looks as if I've just confirmed the worst rumors he's heard about me. The attorney maintains his placid expression, but his tone of voice is mildly scolding when he says, "The jury is your best hope now."

I think of her picking flowers in the garden that afternoon, the way she waved them in an arc across the sky.

When the verdict is read I stare at the back of his head. I think how, surely, if I had really studied him that day, instead of being so distracted by self-doubt, I never would have let him take her. The shape of his ears at the wrong height, the tilt of his head, something about his shoulders, all of it adds up. It's so obvious now.

"Guilty," the foreman says.

The courtroom is strangely quiet. Somehow, it is not enough.

When Jack and I get home he goes into his office. I wander about, until finally I settle on a plan. I take the fireside poker and walk up the stairs to her room where I smash the computer. When I'm done Jack is standing there, watching. "That's a very expensive machine," he says.

"Fuck you," I say.

It doesn't get any better. At the end of the month, he moves out.

Fat, white flakes fall all day. The pine trees are supplicant with snow. I sit in my rocking chair like an old woman, the blue throw across my lap. I thought about starting a fire with the well-seasoned wood left over from last winter but when I opened the stove and saw those ashes I didn't have the energy to clean them out. I rock and watch the snow fall. The house creaks with emptiness. The phone rings. I don't answer it. I fall asleep in the chair and when I wake it's dark. I walk to the kitchen, turn on the outside light. It's still snowing. I turn off the light and go to bed, not bothering to change out of my sweats and turtleneck. The phone rings and I grumble into the blankets but I don't answer it. I sleep what has become my usual restless sleep. In the morning it's still snowing.

Day after day it snows. Finally, the power goes out. The phone lines are down. I don't mind this at all. Oddly, I am invigorated by it. I shovel the wood-burning stove's ashes into an old paint can, find the wood carrier, and bring in stacks of wood and kindling. I build a fire and once I'm sure it's really started good, go upstairs and get my book, some blankets and pillows. I find the flashlights in the kitchen, both with working batteries, search through the linen closet and then the kitchen cupboards until I remember and find the portable radio on the top shelf in the basement. I stoke the fire, wrap myself in a blanket. How efficient we were, how well organized, how prepared for this sort of emergency, how completely useless, even culpable, when she needed us most. I turn on the radio. It will snow and snow, they say. We are having a blizzard. There are widespread reports of power outages. The Red Cross is setting up in the high school, which, actually, is also currently out of power so residents are advised to stay home for now. I click off the radio.

The phone is ringing.

"Hello?"

"Mom, where are you?"

"Steff? Steff?"

But there is no response. I stand there, holding the phone while the kitchen shadows lengthen around me. Still I stand there. I say her name over and over again. I don't know how long I stand there before I hang up but when I do, I'm a changed woman. If I can't keep her alive, and it's been all too obvious that I can't, I'll take her dead. Yes, I want this ghost.

The person you most love has died and is now trying to contact you. You are happy.

You do whatever you can to help. You go out in the middle of the worst blizzard on record since there has been a record and drive to town. A trip that usually takes ten minutes today takes an hour and a half and you are happy. You go to the local drugstore and walk right past the aisles stripped of batteries and Sterno cans and candles to the toy section where you select a Ouija board and tarot cards and you don't care when the clerk looks at you funny because you already have a strange reputation and who even cares about reputation when your dead daughter is trying to talk to you. You are not scared. You are excited. You know you probably should change your expression and look bored or disinterested as the clerk tallies up your purchases on a notepad because the cash register doesn't work due to the power outage and you probably should say something about buying this for your teenage niece but instead you stand there grinning with excitement. You sense the clerk, who looks to be a teenager herself, only a few years older than your dead daughter, watching you leave the store and walk through the storm to your truck, the only vehicle in the parking lot.

It takes even longer to get home and by the time you do the fire has gone out and the house is cold. You are too excited to stop everything to build another fire. Instead you set up the Ouija board on the kitchen table. The cat comes over to smell it. You light a candle. The cat rubs against your leg. You sit at the table. You rest your fingers lightly on the pointer. You remember this from when you were young. "Steff," you say, and the sound of it is both silly and wonderful in the silent house. As if, maybe, she's just in another room or something. "Steff, are you here?" You wait for the pointer to move. It does not. "Steff?" Suddenly the house is wild with light and sound. The kitchen blazes brightly, the refrigerator hums, the heater turns on. The phone rings. You push back the chair, stand, and bang your thigh against the table. The phone rings and rings. "Hello?"

"Mom?"

"Steff, Steff, is that you?"

The dial tone buzzes.

You slam the phone down. The cat races out of the room with her tail puffed up.

You turn to the Ouija board. The pointer rests over the word. Yes. You try to remember if you left it there but you don't think you did or maybe it got knocked there when you hit your leg but why are you trying to explain it when there is only one explanation for your dead daughter's voice on the phone? Slowly you turn and look at the silent phone. You pick up the receiver and listen to the dial tone.

You don't know whether to laugh or cry and suddenly your body is convulsing in some new emotion that seems to be a combination of both. You sink to the kitchen floor. The cat comes back into the room and lies down beside you. The dead can't make phone calls but the living can lose their minds. You decide you won't do that. You get up.

You try to believe it didn't happen.

But just in case, every time the phone rings, I answer it. I speak to an endless assortment of telemarketers wanting to sell me newspapers, a different phone service, offering me exciting opportunities to win trips to Florida, or the Bahamas. Jack calls about once a week and we generally have the same conversation. (I'm fine. He can't come back. I haven't forgiven him. I haven't forgiven myself. I don't expect to. Ever.) Once there is a call where no one speaks at all and I'm terrified to hang up the phone so I stand there saying hello, hello, and finally I say, Steff? and there's a click and then the dial tone. Once, an old friend of mine from the city calls and I tell her all lies. How I've begun painting scenes of idyllic life again, how I've begun the healing process. I tell her the things people want me to say and by the end of the conversation she's happy she called and for a few minutes I feel happy too, as though everything I said was true.

I start receiving Christmas cards in the mail, strange greetings of Peace on Earth with scrawled condolences or blessings about this first Christmas without her. Jack calls in tears and tells me how much he misses her and us. I know, I know, I say gently, but you still can't come back. There is a long silence, then he hangs up.

I go into town only for groceries. I lose track of the days so completely that I end up in the supermarket on Christmas Eve. Happy shoppers load carts with turkeys and gift wrap and bottles of wine, bags of shrimp, crackers and cheese. I pick through the limp lettuce, the winter tomatoes. While I'm choosing apples I feel someone watching me and turn to see a teenage girl of maybe sixteen or seventeen standing by the bananas. There is something strange about the girl's penetrating stare beneath her homemade knit cap though it is not unusual to catch people staring at me; after all, I'm the mother of a dead girl. I grab a bag of apples. I wonder if she knew Steff. I turn to look over by the bananas but she's not there.

"I don't know if you remember me or not."

The girl stands at my elbow. The brown knit cap is pulled low over her brow with wisps of brown hair sticking out. She has dark brown eyes, lashed with black. She might be pretty.

"I waited on you during the first storm at Walker's drugstore."

I nod, at a loss at what to say to this strange, staring girl.

She leans close to me. I smell bubblegum, peppermint, and something faintly sour. "I can help," she whispers.

"Excuse me?"

She looks around, in a dramatic way, as if we are sharing state secrets, licks her chapped lips and leans close again. "I know how to talk to dead people. You know, like in that movie. I'm like that kid." She leans back and looks at me with those dark, sad eyes and then scans the room as if frightened of the living. "My name is Maggie Dwinder. I'm in the book." She nods abruptly and walks away. I watch her in her old wool coat, a brown knit scarf trailing down her back like a snake.

"Oh, how are you doing, dear?"

This face sends me back to that day. Snow on tulips. My daughter's death. "Mrs. Bialo, I never thanked you for coming over that morning."

She pats my arm. One of her fingernails is black, the others are lined with dirt. "Don't mention it, dear. I should of made a effort long before. I wouldn't bother you now, except I noticed you was talking to the Dwinder girl."

I nod.

"There's something wrong with that child, her parents are all so upset about it, her father being a reverend and all. Anyhow, I hope she didn't upset you none."

"Oh no," I lie, "we were just talking about apple pie."

My neighbor studies me closely and I can imagine her reporting her findings to the ladies at the checkout, how I am so strange. I'm glad I lied to the old snoop, and feel unreasonably proud that in this small way I may have protected the girl. It doesn't take a Jungian analyst to figure it out. It felt good to protect the girl.

It's the coldest, snowiest winter on record and Christmas morning is no different. The windchill factor is ten below and it's snowing.

I stack wood into the carrier, the icy snow stinging my face. My wood supply is rapidly dwindling but I dread trying to buy more wood now, during the coldest winter anyone can remember. I can just imagine the bantering, "Lady, you want wood? Seasoned wood?" Or the pity, "Is this, are you, I'm so sorry, we're out of wood to sell but wait, we'll bring you ours." Or the insult, "What? You want me to bring it where? Not after what you did to that girl, they should have put you in jail for child neglect, letting her leave like that with a stranger." Head bent against the bitter chill, both real and imagined, I carry the wood inside.

There is nothing like that feeling of coming into a warm house from the cold. I turn on the classical music station, make a fire, fill the teakettle, and put it on the kitchen stove. The radio is playing Handel's *Messiah*, the teakettle rattles softly on the burner, the cat curls up on the braided rug. I wrap my arms around myself and watch the snow swirl outside the window. Inexplicably, it stops as suddenly as if turned off by a switch. The sun comes out, the yard sparkles, and I realize I'm happy. The teakettle whistles. I turn to take it off the burner, search through the cupboard for the box of green tea. I wrap the teabag string around the teapot handle, pour the hot water. If we never got that stupid computer, if we never (stupidly) let her go with him, how different this morning would be, scented by pine and punctuated with laughter, the tear of wrapping paper and litter of ribbons and bows. I turn, teapot in hand, to the kitchen table and see that the storm has returned to its full vigor, the crystallized scene obliterated. As it should be. In my grief this stormy winter has been perfect.

I find my strange Christmas perfect too. I make a vegetable soup and leave it to simmer on the stove. The radio station plays beautiful music. All day the weather volleys between winter wonderland and wild storm. I bring out the old photo albums and page through the imperfect memories, her smile but not her laughter, her face but not her breath, her skin but not her touch. I rock and weep. Outside, the storm rages. This is how I spend the first Christmas without her, crying, napping, in fits of peace and rage.

I go to bed early and for the first time since she died, sleep through the night. In the morning, a bright winter sun is reflected a thousand times in the thick ice that coats the branches outside my bedroom window and hangs from the eaves like daggers. The phone rings.

"Hello?"

"Mom?"

"Steff, talk to me, what do you want?"

"Maggie Dwinder."

"What?"

But there is no answer, only a dial tone.

I tear up half the house looking for the local phone book, searching through drawers and cupboards, until at last I find it in Jack's old office on the middle of the otherwise empty desk. Jack used to sit here in a chaos of papers and folders, a pencil tucked behind his ear, the computer screen undulating with a swirl of colored tubes that broke apart and reassembled over and over again. I bring the phone book to the kitchen where I page through to the Ds and find, Dwinder, Reverend John, and Nancy. My hand is shaking when I dial.

"Hello," a cheerful voice answers on the first ring.

"Hello, is Maggie there?"

"Speaking."

"Maggie, I spoke to you on Christmas Eve, at the grocery store."

"Uh-huh?"

"You said you could help me."

"I'm not sure I, oh." The voice drops to a serious tone. "I've been expecting you to call. She really has something important to tell you." While I absorb this, she adds, "I'm really sorry about what happened." Her voice changes to a cheerful tone, "Really? All of it? That's great!"

"I'm sorry I—"

"No way! Everything?"

"Maggie, are you afraid of being overheard?"

"That's the truth."

"Maybe you should come over here."

"Okay, when?"

"Can you come now?"

"Yeah, I have to do the dishes and then I can come over."

"Do you know where I live?"

"Doesn't everybody?"

"Can you get here or should I . . ."

"No. I'll be over as soon as I can."

She took so long to arrive that I started watching for her at the window. In the midst of more bad weather, I saw the dark figure walking up the road. At first, even though I knew she was coming, I had the ridiculous notion that it was Steffie's ghost, but as she got closer, I recognized the old wool coat, the brown knit hat and scarf crusted with snow. She walked carefully, her head bent with the wind, her hands thrust in her pockets, her narrow shoulders hunched against the chill, her snow-crusted jeans tucked into old boots, the kind with buckles. I asked myself how this rag doll was going to help me, then opened the door for her. For a moment she stood there, as if considering turning back, then she nodded and stepped inside.

"You must be freezing. Please, take off your coat."

She whipped off the knit hat and revealed straight, brown hair that fell to her shoulders as she unwrapped the long, wet scarf, unbuttoned her coat (still wearing her gloves, one blue, the other black). I took her things. She sat to unbuckle her boots, while I hung her things in the hall closet. When I returned, she sat at the kitchen table, hunched over in a white sweatshirt. It occurred to me that she might fit into one of Steffie's baggier sweaters but I offered her one of mine instead. She shook her head and said (as she shivered), "No thanks, I'm warm enough."

"Do you want some tea?" She shrugged, then shook her head. "Hot chocolate?"

She looked up and smiled. "Yes, please." I opened the refrigerator, took out the milk. "I like your house. It's not at all like I heard."

I pour the milk into the pan. "What did you hear?"

"Oh, different stuff."

I set the pan on the burner and start opening cupboards, looking for the chocolate bars from last winter.

"Some people say you're a witch."

This is a new one and I'm so startled by it that I bang my head on the shelf. I touch the sore spot and turn to look at her.

"Of course I don't believe it," she says. "I think of you more as a Mother Nature type."

I find the chocolate and drop two bars in with the milk.

"I never saw anyone make it like this before. We always just add water."

"We used to make real whipped cream for it too."

"Of course I wouldn't care if you was, 'cause, you know, I sort of am."

"Excuse me?"

"Well, you know, like, I told you, dead people talk to me."

I stir the milk to just below a boil then pour two mugs full. There is a temporary break in the weather. Sun streams across the kitchen table. I hand the little witch her mug. She holds it with both hands, sniffs it, and smiles.

"You don't look like a witch."

She shrugs. "Well, who knows?"

I sit across from her with my own mug of hot chocolate. Yes. Who knows? All I know is that Steffie told me she wanted Maggie Dwinder. So here she is, sipping hot chocolate in my kitchen, and I'm not sure what I'm supposed to do with her.

As if sensing my inquiry, she stops sipping and looks at me over the rim of the cup. "She wants to come back."

"Come back?"

"She misses you, and she misses it here." She slowly lowers the cup, sets it on the table. "But there's a problem. A couple problems, actually. She can't stay, of course. She can only be here for a little while and then she has to go back."

"No she doesn't."

"She's been gone a long time."

"You don't have to tell me that."

She bites her chapped lips.

"I'm sorry. This isn't easy for me."

"Yeah. Anyway, she can't stay. I'm sorry too, but that's the way it is. Those are the rules and, also . . ."

"Yes?"

"I don't think you're going to like this part."

"Please tell me."

She looks up at me and then down at the table. "The thing is, she doesn't want to stay here anyway, she sort of likes it where she is."

"Being dead?"

Maggie shrugs and attempts a feeble smile. "Well, you could say that's her life now."

I push back from the table, my chair scraping across the floor. "Is that supposed to be funny?" Maggie shrinks at my voice. "Why?"

"I don't know," she says, softly. "Maybe she figures she sort of belongs there now."

"When?"

"What?"

"When does she want to come?"

"That's why she talked to me. 'Cause she said you've been really upset and all but she wonders if you can wait until spring?"

"Spring?"

"Yeah. She wants to come in the spring. If it's okay with you." Maggie watches me closely as I consider this imperfect offer, my daughter returned but only borrowed from the dead. What rational response can there be? Life is composed of large faiths, in the series of beliefs that sustain us, we little humans whose very existence is a borrowing from the dead. I look into Maggie's brown eyes, I fall into them and feel as if I'm being pulled into the earth. All this, as we sit at the kitchen table, a world done and undone, a life given and taken. "Yes," I say. "Tell her spring will be fine."

We are like one of my paintings. Small, in a vast landscape. The snow glistens outside. We are not cold, or hungry, or anything but this, two figures through a lit window, waiting.

Maggie and I became friends of sorts. She liked to sit in the kitchen and chat over hot chocolate about her school day. (Most of her classmates, and all her teachers were "boring.") The cat liked to sit in her lap.

There were no more phone calls from Stephanie. "Don't worry about that," Maggie reassured me, "she'll be here soon enough and you can really talk."

It was the worst winter on record. Maggie said that the students were really "pissed" because they would have to make up days in June.

I grew to look forward to her visits. Eventually we got to talking about painting and she showed me some of her sketches, the ones assigned by the art teacher: boxes, shoes, books, and the ones she drew from her imagination: vampires and shadowed, winged figures, pictures that might have warned me were I not spending my days painting girls picking flowers, with dark figures descending on them. I thought Maggie was wise. She understood and accepted the way the world is, full of death and sorrow. This did not seem to affect her happiness. On the contrary, she seemed to be blossoming, losing the tired, haggard look she had when I first met her. I mentioned this to her one day over hot chocolate and she opened her mouth, then bit her lip and nodded.

"What were you going to say?"

"I don't know if I should."

"No, go ahead."

"It was your daughter."

"What was my daughter?"

"She was wearing me out. I know she wasn't meaning to but it's like she was haunting me ever since she, I mean, she wouldn't leave me alone."

"That doesn't sound like Steffie."

"Yeah, well, I guess people change when they're, you know, dead."

I nod.

"Anyway, it stopped once I talked to you. I guess she just wanted to make sure you got the message."

I remember that time as being almost joyful. What a relief it was to think of our separation as temporary, that she would return to me as she had been before she left, carrying flowers, her cheeks flushed, her eyes bright with happiness.

I got the phone call on a Tuesday afternoon. I remember this so clearly because I marked it with a big, black X on the calendar, and also, that day, though it was already April, there was another storm, so sudden that six motorists were killed in a four-car pileup, one of them a teenage boy. But that was later, after Maggie's parents left.

Maggie's mother calls in the morning, introduces herself, and says that she and her husband want to talk to me, could they stop by for a visit.

How can I refuse them? They are Maggie's parents and I'm sure concerned and curious about this adult she is spending so much time with. Nancy, Maggie's mother, sounds nice enough on the phone. When they arrive an hour later, I think I could like her and, to my surprise, the reverend too.

She has a wide, pleasant face, lightly freckled, red hair the color of certain autumn leaves, and hazel eyes that measure me with a cool but kind mother-to-mother look. She wears a long, dark wool skirt, boots, and a red sweater.

Her husband has a firm handshake and kind, brown eyes. His hair is dark and curly, a little long about the ears. He has a neatly trimmed beard and mustache. I am immediately disturbed and surprised to find myself somewhat attracted to him. He wears blue jeans, and a green sweater that looks homemade and often worn.

They sit side by side on the couch. I sit in the rocker. A pot of tea cools on the table between us, three cups and saucers on the tray beside it. "Would you like some tea?"

Nancy glances at her husband and he nods. "Thank you," he says, "allow me." He reaches over and pours tea for the three of us. I find this simple gesture comforting. How long it has been since anyone has done anything for me.

"I have to thank you," I say, "you've been so kind about allowing Maggie to visit and her company has been much appreciated."

They nod in unison. Then both begin to speak. With a nod from his wife, the reverend continues.

"I feel I owe you an apology. I should have visited you much sooner and then, perhaps, none of this would have happened." He laughs one of those rueful laughs I was always reading about. "What I mean to say is, I should have offered you my services when you were suffering but I thought that you probably had more spiritual assistance than you knew what to do with." He looks at me hopefully.

But I cannot offer him that redemption. Oddly, there had been no one. Oh, many letters offering prayers, and accusations, and a couple Bibles mailed to the house, but no one stood and held my hand, so to speak, spiritually. There was something distasteful about my involvement in Steffie's horrible death; no one wanted any part of it.

He looks into his teacup and sighs.

"We're sorry," Nancy says in a clear, steady voice. "We've been involved with our own problems and because of that it seems we haven't always made the right choices. It's affected our judgement."

"Please, don't worry about it. You're kind to come now."

The reverend sets his cup on the table. "We're here about Maggie."

"She's a lovely girl."

Nancy sets her cup and saucer on the table, licks her lips. I smile at the gesture, so reminiscent of her daughter. "We thought, well, we want you to understand, we hope you understand, that we thought you, being an artist, and Maggie, being so creative. . . ."

The reverend continues. "We prayed and pondered, and thought maybe you two would be good for each other."

"We made the choice to let her be with you for both your sakes."

"Certainly we had no idea."

"Oh, no idea at all."

Suddenly I feel so cold. I sit in the rocking chair and look at the two of them with their earnest faces. I want them to leave. I don't understand yet what they've come to say, but I know I don't want to hear it.

The reverend looks at me with those beautiful eyes and shakes his head. "We're sorry."

Nancy leans forward and reaches as though to pat me on the knee but the reach is short and she brushes air instead. "It's not her fault. It's just the way she is. We only hope you can find it in your heart to forgive her."

The reverend nods. "We know what we're asking here, a woman like you, who has so much to forgive already."

My hands are shaking when I set my teacup down. "I don't know what you're talking about."

The reverend just looks at me with sorrowful eyes. Nancy nods, bites her lower lip, and says, "We know what she's been telling you," she says. "We found her diary."

I open my mouth. She raises her hand. "I know, I would have thought the same thing. It's horrible to read your child's diary, but I did, and I don't regret it." She glances at her husband who does not return the look. "How else can a mother know? They're so secretive at this age. And I was right. After all, look what she's been doing."

I look from her to the reverend. "We know, we can guess how tempting it's been for you to believe her," he says.

"She's ill, really ill."

"We knew this even before—"

"I read her diary."

"But we never thought she—"

"How could we? We hope you understand, she's mentally ill. She didn't mean to cause you pain."

The cold moves through me. Why are they here with their petty family squabbles? So she read her daughter's diary, while I, imperfect mother, never even looked for Steffie's, or had any idea what her e-mail address was. Why are they here apologizing for their living daughter? Why do I care? "I'm not sure I—"

"There's also a scrapbook. If I would have known, if we would have known—"

"A scrapbook?"

The reverend clears his throat. "She was obsessed with your daughter's death. I try to understand it, but God help me, I don't. She saved every article—"

"Every picture."

I imagine Maggie cutting up newspapers, gluing the stories into a red scrapbook, the kind I had as a girl. "It's all right," I say, though I'm not sure that it is. "A lot of people were fascinated by it." I imagine myself on an iceberg, drifting into the deep, cold blue.

The reverend opens his mouth but Nancy speaks, like a shout from the unwanted shore. "You don't understand. We know what she's been telling you, about your daughter coming back, and of course, we hope you realize it's all made up."

There. The words spoken. I close my eyes. The ice in my blood crashes like glass. The reverend's voice whispers from the distance. "We're sorry. It must have been tempting to believe her—"

"She called me. I spoke to her."

He shakes his head. "It was Maggie."

"A mother knows her daughter's voice."

"But you were so upset, right? And she never said much, did she? And in your state—"

"Nancy," the reverend says gently.

The room is filled with sad silence. I can't look at either of them. How stupid I have been, how unbearably stupid. I see the reverend's legs, and then his wife's, unbending.

The world is ending, I think, all darkness and ice, like the poem.

"We should leave," says the reverend.

I watch the legs cross the room. Listen to the closet door, the rattle of hangers. Whispering. "We're sorry," says Nancy. Footsteps in the kitchen. Door opened. "Snow!" Closed.

All darkness and despair. The greatest loneliness. A shattering. Ice. Who knows how long until at last I throw the cups across the room, the teapot, still full. Brown tea bleeds down the wall. I scream and weep into darkness. Now I know what waits at world's end. Rage is what fills the emptiness. Rage, and it is cold.

How we suffer, we humans. Pain and joy but always pain again. How do we do this? Why? Some small part of me still waits for spring. Just to be sure. I know it is absurd, but the rational knowing does not change the irrational hope.

I figured Maggie's parents had told her that they talked to me. I couldn't imagine she would want to face my wrath, though she couldn't know that I didn't even have the energy for anger anymore. Instead I felt a tired sorrow, a weariness with life. She did come, in the midst of a downpour, knocking on my door after school, wearing a yellow slicker. I finally opened the door just a crack and peered out at her, drenched like a stray dog, her hair hanging dark in her face, her lashes beaded with water.

"Go home, Maggie."

"Please. You have to talk to me."

She is crying and snot drips from her nose toward her mouth. She wipes it with the back of her hand, sniffing loudly.

I simply do not know what to say. I close the door.

"You were the only one who ever believed me!" she shouts.

Later, when I look out the window, she is gone, as if I imagined her, made her up out of all my pain.

I decide to sell the house though I don't do anything about it. I sleep day and night. One day I realize I haven't seen the cat for a long while. I walk around whistling and calling her name but she doesn't appear. I sit at the kitchen table and stare out the window until gradually I realize I'm looking at spring. Green grass, leaves, tulip and daffodil blooms thrust through the wreck of the garden. Spring. I open windows and doors. Birds twitter in branches. Squirrels scurry across the lawn. Almost a year since we lost her. Gone. My little darling.

Then I see someone, is it, no, in the garden, picking daffodils, her long, dark hair tied with a weedy-looking thing, wearing the dress she had on last year, tattered and torn, my daughter, my ghost.

"Stephanie!" I call.

She turns and looks at me. Yes. It is her face but changed, with a sharpness to it I had not foreseen. She smiles, raises her arm and sweeps the sky with flowers and I am running down the steps and she is running through the garden calling, "Mom, Mom, Mom!" I think when I touch her she will disappear but she doesn't, though she flinches and squirms from the hug. "You can't hold me so close anymore," she says.

So I hold her gently, like the fragile thing she is, and I'm weeping and she's laughing and somehow, with nimble fingers she braids the bouquet into a crown which she sets on my head. She covers my face with kisses, so soft I'm sure I'm imagining all of it but I don't care anyway. I never want to wake up or snap out of it. I want to be with her always. "Steffie, Steffie, Steffie, I've missed you so much."

She has bags under her eyes and her skin is pale and cold. She stares at me, unsmiling, then reaches up, takes the crown from my head and places it on her own. "You've changed a lot." She turns and looks at the yard. "Everything has."

"It's been a hard year," I say to her narrow back and bony elbows. She looks like such a little orphan, so motherless standing there in that dirty dress. I'll make her something new, something pretty. She turns and looks at me with an expression like none I'd ever seen on her in her lifetime, a hate-filled face, angry and sharp. "Steff, honey, what is it?"

"Don't. Tell. Me. How hard. This year. Has been."

"Oh sweetie," I reach for her but she pulls back.

"I told you. Don't touch me."

"At all?"

"I'm the queen," she says. "Don't touch me unless I touch you first."

I don't argue or disagree. The queen, my daughter, even in

death maintains that imagination I so highly prize. When I ask her if she is hungry she says, "I only ate one thing the whole time I was gone." I feel this surge of anger. What kind of place is this death? She doesn't want to come inside while I make the sandwiches and I'm afraid she'll be gone when I come out with the tray, but she isn't. We have a picnic under the apple tree which is in white bloom and buzzing with flies, then she falls asleep on the blanket beside me and, to my surprise, I fall asleep too.

I wake, cold and shivering, already mourning the passing dream. I reach to wrap the picnic blanket around me and my hand touches her. Real. Here. My daughter, sleeping.

"I told you not to touch me."

"I'm sorry. Honey, are you cold?"

She rolls over and looks up at me. "You do realize I'm dead?"

"Yes."

She sets the wilted crown back on her head and surveys the yard. "You really let everything go to shit around here, didn't you?"

"Stephanie!"

"What?"

Really, what? How to be the mother of a dead girl? We sit on the blanket and stare at each other. What she is thinking, I don't know. I'm surprised, in the midst of this momentous happiness, to feel a sadness, a certain grief for the girl I knew who, I guess, was lost somewhere at the border of death. Then she sighs, a great old sigh.

"Mom?" she says, in her little girl voice.

"Yes, honey?"

"It's good to be back."

"It's good to have you here."

"But I can't stay."

"How long?"

She shrugs.

"Is it horrible there?"

She looks at me, her face going through some imperceptible change that brings more harshness to it. "Don't ask the dead."

"What?"

"Don't ask questions you don't want the answer to."

"Just stay. Don't go back."

She stands up. "It doesn't work like that."

"We could—"

"No, don't act like you know anything about it. You don't."

I roll up the blanket, pick up the tray. We walk to the house together beneath the purple-tinged sky. When we get to the door she hesitates. "What's wrong?" She looks at me with wide, frightened eyes. "Steff, what is it?" Wordlessly, she steps inside. I flick on the kitchen light. "Are you hungry?"

She nods.

The refrigerator is nearly empty so I rummage through cupboards and find some spaghetti and a jar of sauce. I fill a pan with water and set it on the stove.

"Is Dad coming back?"

"Would you like to see him?"

She shakes her head vigorously, no.

"Steff, don't be mad at him, he didn't know—"

"Well, he really fucked up."

I bite my lip, check the water. Where is my little girl? I turn and look at her. She is walking around the kitchen, lightly brushing her hand against the wall, a strange, unlovely creature, her hair still knotted with a weed, crowned with wilted daffodils.

"Do you want to talk about it, what happened to you?"

She stops, the tips of her fingers light against the wall, then continues walking around the room, humming softly.

I take this to be a no. I make spaghetti for six and she eats all of it, my ravenous ghost child. What is this feeling? Here is my dead daughter, cold and unkind and difficult and so different from the girl she used to be that only now do I finally accept that Stephanie is gone forever, even as she sits before me, slurping spaghetti, the red sauce blooding her lips.

The dead move in secrets, more wingless than the living, bound by some weight; the memory of life, the impossible things? Dead bones grow and hair and fingernails too. Everything grows but it grows with death. The dead laugh and cry and plant flowers that they pick too soon. The dead do not care about keeping gardens in blossom.

Dead daughters don't wear socks or shoes and they won't go into old bedrooms unless you beg and coax and then you see immediately how they were right all along. Dead daughters have little in common with the living ones. They are more like sisters than the same girl and you realize, just as you miss the daughter you've lost, so does the dead girl miss, really miss, the one she was.

The dead pick up paint brushes and suddenly their hands move like rag dolls and they splatter paint, not like Jackson Pollack, or even a kindergartner. All the paint turns brown on the paintbrush and drips across the canvas or floor or wall, until they, helpless, throw it to the ground.

All the dead can do is wander. You walk for hours with your dead daughter pacing the yard she will not (cannot?) leave. She picks all the flowers and drops them in her step. She sleeps suddenly for hours, and then does not sleep for days. She exhausts you. The days and nights whirl. The last time you felt like this was when she was an infant.

One day, as you sit at the kitchen table, watching her tearing flowers from the garden in the new dress you made that already hangs raglike and dirty around her, you think of Maggie Dwinder and you realize you miss her. You put your face in your hands. What have you done?

"What's wrong with you?"

You would like to believe that she asks because she cares but you don't think that's true. Something vital in her was lost forever. Was this what happened at death or was it because of how she died? You accept you'll never know. She refuses to talk about it, and really, what would be the point? You look at her, weedy, dirty, wearing that brittle crown. "Maggie Dwinder," you say.

"As good as dead."

"What?"

She rolls her eyes.

"Don't you roll your eyes at me, young lady."

"Mother, you don't know anything about it."

"She's your friend, and mine. She told me you would come. She suffered for it."

"Oh, big deal, mommy and daddy watch her very closely. She has to go see the psychiatrist. She doesn't have any friends. Big fucking deal. What a hard life!"

"Steff."

"Don't tell me about suffering. I know about suffering."

"Steff, honey—"

"Everyone said it was a mistake for me to come back here. They said you wouldn't like me anymore."

"Honey, that's not true. I love you."

"You love who I used to be, not who I am now."

"Well, you're dead."

"Like it's my fault."

The dead are jealous, jealous, jealous and they will do anything to keep you from the living, the lucky living. They will argue with you, and distract you, and if that doesn't work, they will even let you hug them, and dance for you, and kiss you, and laugh, anything to keep you. The dead are selfish. Jealous. Lonely. Desperate. Hungry.

It isn't until she brings you a flower, dead for weeks, and hands it to you with that poor smile, that you again remember the living. "I have to call Maggie."

"Forget about her."

"No, I have to tell her."

"Look at me, Mommy."

"Sweetheart."

"Look what you did."

"It wasn't me."

She walks away.

"It wasn't."

She keeps walking.

You follow. Of course, you follow.

The phone rings. Such a startling noise. I roll into my blankets. Simultaneously I realize the night was cool enough for blankets and that the phone didn't ring all summer. I reach for it, fumbling across the bedside table, and knock off the photograph from Steff's last birthday.

"Hello?"

"See you next spring."

"Steff? Where are you?"

There is only a dial tone. I hang up the phone. Throw off the covers. "Steff!" I call. "Steff!" I look in her bedroom but she's not there. I run down the stairs and through the house, calling her name. The blue throw is bunched up on the couch, as if she'd sat there for a while, wrapped up in it, but she's not there now. I run outside, the grass cold against my feet. "Steff! Steff!" She is not in the garden, or the studio. She is not in the yard. A bird cries and I look up through the apple tree branches. One misshapen apple drops while I stand there, shivering in my nightgown. Everything is tinged with brown, except the leaves of the old oak which are a brilliant red.

A squirrel scurries past. There is a gentle breeze and one red leaf falls. I wrap my arms around myself and walk into the house, fill the teakettle, set it on the burner to boil. I sit at the kitchen table and stare at the garden. I should plant some bulbs. Order firewood. Arrange to have the driveway plowed when it snows. The teakettle whistles. I walk across the cool floor, pour the water into the pot. I leave it to steep and go to the living room where she left the blue throw all balled up. I pick it up and wrap it around myself. It smells like her, musty, sour.

It smells like Maggie too, last Christmas Eve when she spoke to me in the supermarket. What a risk that was for her. Who knows, I might have been like Mrs. Bialo, or her parents; I might have laughed at her. Instead, I became her friend and then cast her aside at the first sign of trouble.

How many chances do we get? With love? How many times do we wreck it before it's gone?

I don't even drink the tea but dress in a rush. All my clothes are too big on me and I see in the mirror how tired I look, how much new gray is in my hair. Yet, there's something else, a sort of glow, a happiness. I miss her, the one who died, and her ghost is my responsibility, a relationship based on who we lost, while Maggie is a friend, a relationship based on what we found.

All summer I only left for groceries. Stephanie would stand at the top of the driveway, watching me with those cold, narrow eyes as if suspicious I wouldn't come back. Out of habit I look in the rearview mirror, but all I see is a patch of brown grass, the edge of the house.

It's easy to find the Dwinder residence. They live right next to the church in a brick house with red geraniums dropping teardrop-shaped petals onto the porch. I ring the bell. Nancy answers, in a pink terry cloth robe.

"I'm sorry, I forgot how early it is."

She brushes a hand through her red hair. "That's all right. We were getting ready for church."

"There's something I have to tell Maggie. Is she home?"

"I don't know if that's such a good idea."

"Honey, who is it?" The reverend comes to the door in plaid flannel pants and a T-shirt, his dark hair tousled, his face wrinkled with sleep. "Oh. Chloe, how are you?"

"I'm sorry to disturb you, it's just—"

"She wants to talk to Maggie."

"I'll tell her you're here." The reverend turns back into the house.

Nancy continues to stare at me, then, just as I hear Maggie saying, What does she want? she blurts, "She's been better since she's stopped seeing you." I'm not sure if this is meant as an accusation or an apology and before I can find out, Maggie comes to the door dressed in torn jeans and a violet T-shirt, her hair in braids. She meets my gaze with those dark eyes.

"Coffee's ready!" the reverend calls and Nancy turns away, her pink-robed figure receding slowly down the hall.

"Yeah?"

"I was hoping, if you can forgive me, I was hoping we could be friends again."

"I can't be her replacement, you know."

"I know."

"You hurt me a lot."

"I know. I'm sorry. Can you ever forgive me?"

She frowns, squints, then tilts her head slightly, and looks up at me. "I guess."

"Please. Stop by. Any time. Like you used to."

She nods and shuts the door gently in my face.

On a sunny but cold day, as the last crimson leaves flutter to earth, and apples turn to cider on the ground, I shovel last winter's ash onto the garden. A flock of geese flies overhead. I shade my eyes to watch them pass and when I look down again, she is standing there in baggy jeans and an old blue pea coat, unbuttoned in the sun.

It's as though I've been living in one of those glass domes and it's been shaking for a long time, but in this moment, has stopped, and after all that flurry and unsettling, there is a kind of peace. "Maggie."

For a moment we only look at each other, then she puts her hand on her hip, rolls her eyes, and says, "You wouldn't believe what they're making us do in gym, square dancing!"

All life is death. You don't fool yourself about this anymore. You slash at the perfect canvas with strokes of paint and replace the perfect picture of your imagination with the reality of what you are capable of. From death, and sorrow, and compromise, you create. This is what it means, you finally realize, to be alive.

You try to explain this to Maggie. You hear yourself talking about bitter seeds, and sweet fruit. She nods and doesn't interrupt but you know you have not successfully communicated it. This is all right. The grief is so large you're not sure you want her, or anyone, to understand it, though you wish you could describe this other emotion.

You stand in the ash of your garden. All this time you didn't realize what you'd been deciding. Now you are crying, because with the realization of the question comes the answer. It is snowing and white flakes fall onto the garden, sticking to the brown stems and broken flowers, melting into the ash. You look up to the sunless white sky. Cold snow tips your face and neck. You close your eyes, and think, yes. Oh, life. Yes.

Afterword

*U*NLESS YOU LIKE TO READ AFTERWORDS FIRST
(in which case, what's wrong with ya?), there's little point in
my rhapsodizing here about M. Rickert's writing. You've seen it for
yourself: the eye for detail, the easy hand with character, the turns
of phrase as graceful as the best ballet, the pyrotechnical psycholog-
ical insights. Consider yourself lucky that you've been spared my
long-winded praise of her short fiction, because I can go on and on
about the similarities in her work with Joyce Carol Oates's fiction,
with Gabriel García Márquez's, with Jonathan Carroll's, and with
James Tiptree, Jr.'s. I can marvel at the way she manages stories
within stories as well as the best of 'em (and, in the case of "Cold
Fires," better than the best of 'em). I can point to "Map of Dreams"
and "Moorina" to show how wonderfully a love of the natural world
imbues the fiction. In fact, I can give some ambitious English
major the start of a fine paper by waxing on about how the juxtapo-
sition of contemporary life in the Electronic Age with an appre-
ciation of a life in balance with nature (what some would call a
"simple life") gives stories like "The Chambered Fruit" their
potency. And of course there's the love of myth and story running
through the fiction like power lines, charging everything. If I really
wanted to bore you, I could go on about how wonderful it is that
these stories *matter*, that fiction is about saving or losing the world

. . . but you've read "The Super Hero Saves the World" and "Anyway" so you already know what I mean. And then there's the sensitivity shown in how themes of abuse and mental illness are treated—I could tell you how these themes echo with my own life and experience, but wouldn't I just be repeating what you already know? Because obviously you've seen for yourself how these stories reach into your heart like there's no protective rib cage around it, you've already discovered how the lives of her characters echo with your own life and experience. You already know what I mean. You know.

So okay, if I can't talk about the stories, how do I ice this lovely layer cake of a book?

How does a little behind-the-scenes tour sound?

Unless you're like me and you read the copyright acknowledgments page of a collection closely (in which case, what's wrong with ya?), you probably don't know that I'm the editor who had the good fortune to publish most of the stories in this collection first. So I've got some ends and odds in my files that might interest even the most devoted M. Rickert aficionado.

For example, here's a handwritten note from May or June of 1998:

> Dr. Mr. Van Gelder,
>
> A few years ago I discovered the annual anthology "The Best of Fantasy and Science Fiction 19—" The stories were a revelation to me. Here were stories that embraced imagination and entertained me in a way most of the homogeneous fiction in mainstream magazines did not.
>
> Enclosed is my story, "The Girl Who Ate Butterflies". I am not really certain how to classify this story but I think it might be fantasy. At any rate, thanks for publishing courageous fiction.
>
> Sincerely, M. Rickert

Back in those days, I still read cover letters before sampling the fiction itself, and I remember this one because (1) it was handwritten and (2) it sounded like someone who was drawn to the fantasy genre by the writing itself. (As opposed to the people who are drawn to it by the movies or by social concerns, that is.)

I also remember starting "The Girl Who Ate Butterflies" in my office, but quickly realized that it called for my full attention—and thus it went into the bag for reading at home. And I remember reading the story itself and being wowed by the sensuality and the imagery of it.

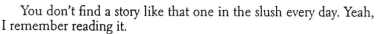

You don't find a story like that one in the slush every day. Yeah, I remember reading it.

The next letter in my file is dated August 5, 1998:

> Dear Mr. Van Gelder,
>
> I am so happy you are publishing my story "The Girl Who Ate Butterflies". I've had poetry published in the small press but this is my first published fiction. (!) I'm sorry that I don't have it on computer disk. Thanks for being flexible about this.

This second letter was signed *Mary Rickert,* and that's when I grew certain of the author's gender. (Well, there was a slight bit of wonder if the signed "Mary" was "Marv," but it seemed unlikely, especially since the letter also mentioned past jobs as a nanny and as a hotel maid.)

Almost a full year passed before the story appeared in print. When it ran, I went overboard in the story notes, editorializing on how most stories billed as "North American magical realist" felt like kids dressing up in mismatched clothes, but here, here was the real deal, an American who *obviously* was influenced by García Márquez. (See, I told you I can go on and on.)

I regretted the introduction immediately and I apologized to Mary, which brings me to another choice letter from the file, this one from 1999:

> Dear Gordon,
>
> Your last letter arrived just as I was thinking of how to compose a thank you letter to you. Really, the whole experience of having my story accepted and published by The Magazine of Fantasy & Science Fiction has been so pleasant. You needn't apologize for the story notes. I think it's commendable that you do them. I have read Gabriel Garcia Marquez's work, and though I hadn't noticed it before you referred to it, I do see his influence in "The Girl Who . . ." This inspired me to finally read One Hundred Years of Solitude. How can I describe what an experience that was? I am sure you, a fellow reader, understand. Years ago I was surprised by a Van Gogh at the Chicago Art Museum. Until then I thought I knew his work, but I had never seen an original. It moved me in every way. That's what One Hundred Years of Solitude was like for me. I am grateful that you helped me realize Marquez as one of my teachers.
>
> I am pleased that William Sanders and Marc Laidlaw had nice comments about my story. I am so happy it is being

read. For years I've heard that actual publication is sort of anticlimactic, but that hasn't been true for me at all. The best way I can describe it is that it's like my definition of a perfect party, I'm connecting with all these amazing people but I don't have to be there!

This has all been so wonderful, I look forward to working with you again. (Soon)

"Soon" was accurate, as "Moorina" followed in September and then "Angel Face" arrived in December. "Angel Face" stands out in my memory because I remember sending it to the magazine's publisher, Ed Ferman, with a note to the effect of, *I think M. Rickert now officially qualifies as a "find."* As Nelson Bond told that newcomer Isaac Asimov back in the '30s, anyone can sell one story, but when you sell two, you're on your way. And when your editor is grumpy and not in a good mood at all and *still* gets knocked out by story #3, yeah, you're a find.

The stories have been coming at a steady pace since then and I certainly won't bore you with details of each one, but at last I've located the letter I was looking for. I'd thought it was the first letter, but here it is, from late in 1999:

As far as header notes, if you could mention Moorina being an excerpt from a novel in progress that would be nice. (It's a story in the novel) I'm mostly working on that novel right now. I think I can finish it within the next few months which fills me with joy and fear. Certainly the whole experience has been more pleasant than the quit-my-job-and-work-on-it-for-five-years-then-put-it-in-three-boxes-novel. I finally figured out what the problem with that was. There were all these elements of magic or fantasy that kept trying to happen and I wouldn't let them.

This is all by way of saying that I will always be grateful to MF&SF and especially, you for helping me find my voice.

That was, for me, the defining moment in understanding M. Rickert's fiction. These were not stories that chose to be fantasy. They were stories that *had* to be fantasy.

Kate Wilhelm says that her first book editor told her she'd be a bestseller if she would stick to one genre. "And he was probably right," she says, "but I couldn't do it." I sometimes think that writing fiction is like sculpting: you start with a big block of raw material and you pare and prune and chisel until you find the underlying shapes and forms. My favorite storytellers are the ones who can feel what's lying in that marble and be true to it, regardless of market considerations. If the grain of the marble shapes the sculpture one way, you go that way. If a story takes you into the fantastic, you go with it.

Mary Rickert's stories usually veer into the fantastic. Me, I'll follow them wherever they go.

Gordon Van Gelder
Hoboken, New Jersey
October 2005

CHRISTOPHER BARZAK's stories have appeared in a variety of magazines and anthologies such as *Lady Churchill's Rosebud Wristlet*, *Nerve*, *Strange Horizons*, *Trampoline*, and *The Year's Best Fantasy and Horror*, among many others. He's written one novel, *One for Sorrow*, and is currently at work on a second, set in Japan, from which he has recently returned after living in a suburb of Tokyo for a year and a half where he taught English. You can read more about him in his online journal, *Meditations in an Emergency*, at http://zakbar.blogspot.com.

GORDON VAN GELDER published his first short story while in high school and says his writing career went downhill from there. He worked as an editor for St. Martin's Press for more than twelve years, during which time he helped publish such writers as George P. Pelecanos, Kate Wilhelm, Christopher Priest, and William Browning Spencer. In 1996 he became the eighth person to edit *The Magazine of Fantasy & Science Fiction* over its fifty-plus year history. In 2000 he left St. Martin's Press in order to become the magazine's publisher. He lives in New Jersey, with his wife, Barbara.

Two thousand copies of this book have been printed by the Maple-Vail Book Manufacturing Group, Binghamton, NY, for Golden Gryphon Press, Urbana, IL. The typeset is Electra with Palette display, printed on 55# Sebago. Typesetting by The Composing Room, Inc., Kimberly, WI.